PRAISE FOR JEREMY BURNS' FIRST NOVEL, FROM THE ASHES:

"With *From the Ashes*, Jeremy Burns establishes himself among the best authors of taut, historical thrillers. In this gripping debut, Burns lays bare a fascinating conspiracy of deceit, full of action and twists. You'll find yourself rooting for his heroes, repulsed by his villains, and rethinking what you think you know about one of history's darkest times. Truly, a must-read for fans of suspense, action, and history."
– Robert Liparulo, bestselling author of *The 13th Tribe, Comes a Horseman,* and *The Dreamhouse Kings*

"*From the Ashes* is a thrilling race against time to expose a diabolical conspiracy that would shatter everything we think we know about the 20th century. With clever puzzles, enigmatic clues, and hidden secrets, Jeremy Burns re-imagines New York's landmarks so vividly that you will want to explore them all over again."
– Boyd Morrison, bestselling author of *The Ark* and *The Vault*

"*From the Ashes* is an ingenious, thought-provoking, and emotionally engaging thriller. This novel will resonate with you for a long time."
– Lou Aronica, *New York Times* bestselling author

"*National Treasure* meets *The Bourne Identity* in this riveting debut. Blending history, suspense, and adventure, Burns takes readers on a nonstop thrill ride through some of the country's most famous sites – and infamous periods of history – ensuring that you'll never look at New York City, the 1930s, or the name 'Rockefeller' the same again. Not to miss!"
– Jeremy Robinson, bestselling author of *Threshhold* and *Secondworld*

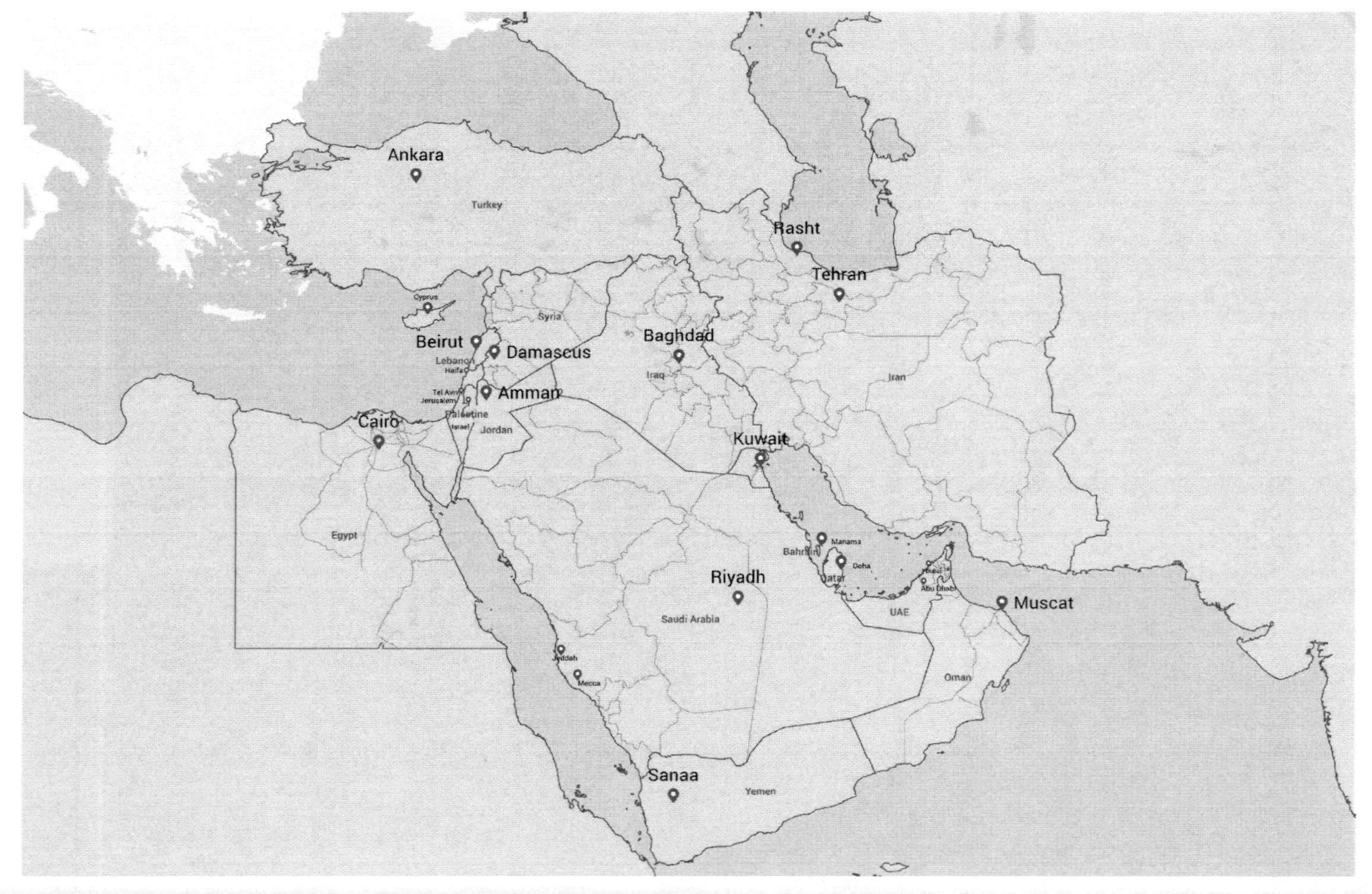
Ankara
Turkey
Rasht
Tehran
Cyprus
Syria
Beirut
Damascus
Baghdad
Lebanon
Haifa
Iraq
Iran
Tel Aviv
Jerusalem
Amman
Palestine
Israel
Jordan
Cairo
Kuwait
Egypt
Manama
Bahrain
Doha
Qatar
Abu Dhabi
Riyadh
Muscat
Saudi Arabia
UAE
Jeddah
Mecca
Oman
Sanaa
Yemen

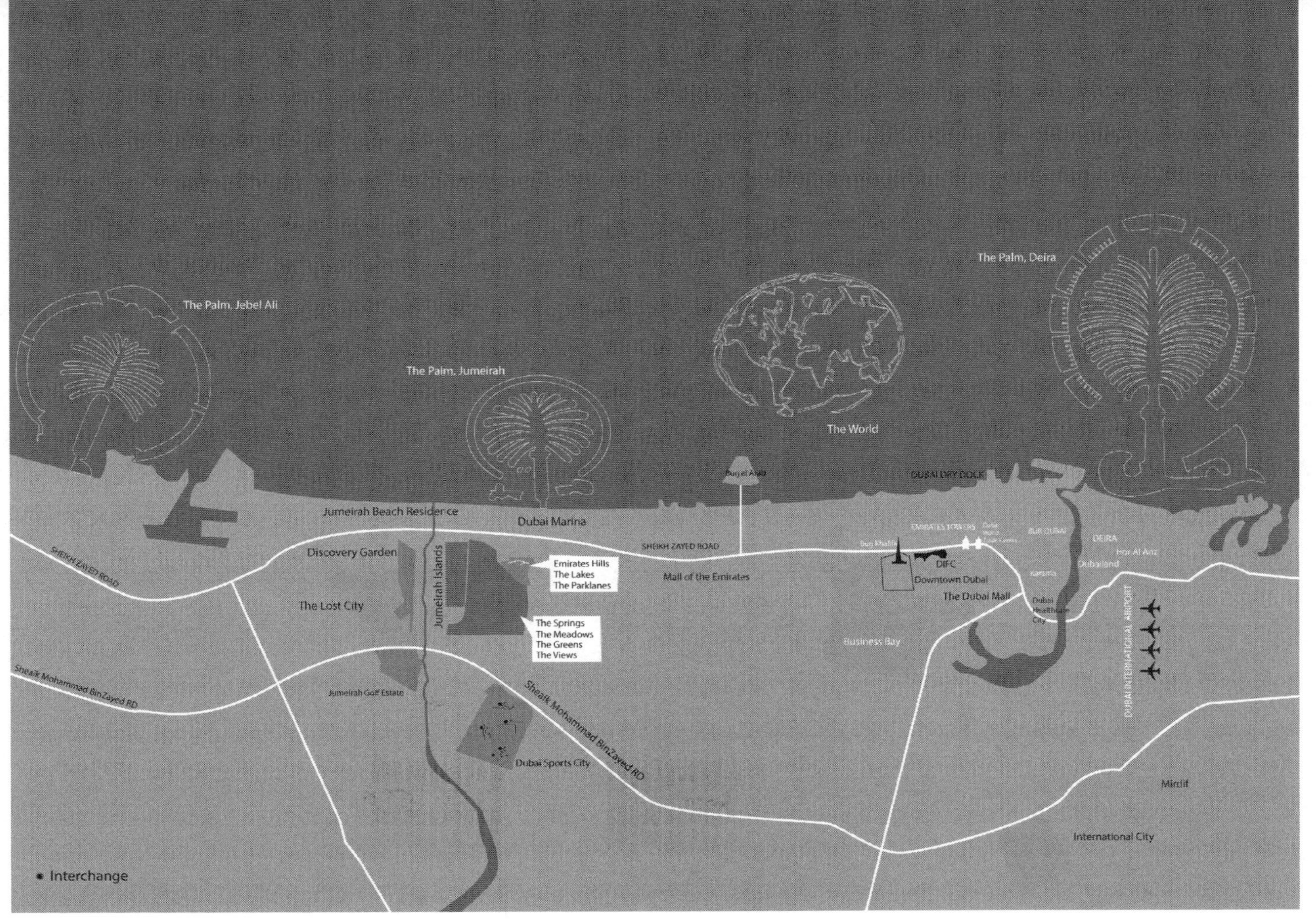

The Palm, Jebel Ali
The Palm, Jumeirah
The World
The Palm, Deira
Burj al Arab
DUBAI DRY DOCK
Jumeirah Beach Residence
Dubai Marina
Discovery Garden
SHEIKH ZAYED ROAD
Jumeirah Islands
Emirates Hills
The Lakes
The Parklanes
The Lost City
The Springs
The Meadows
The Greens
The Views
Mall of the Emirates
EMIRATES TOWERS
BUR DUBAI
DEIRA
Hor Al Anz
Dubailand
DIFC
Downtown Dubai
The Dubai Mall
Karama
Dubai
Healthcare
City
Business Bay
DUBAI INTERNATIONAL AIRPORT
Sheaik Mohammad BinZayed RD
Jumeirah Golf Estate
Dubai Sports City
Mirdif
International City
Interchange

THE DUBAI BETRAYAL

JEREMY BURNS

This is a work of fiction. Names, characters, places, and incidents are either products of the author's imagination or are used fictitiously. Any resemblance to actual events, locales, organizations, or persons living or dead, is entirely coincidental and beyond the intent of either the author or the publisher.

Studio Digital CT, LLC
P.O. Box 4331
Stamford, CT 06907

Cover design by Aaron Brown

Story Plant Paperback ISBN: 978-1-61188-229-2
Fiction Studio Books E-book ISBN: 978-1-943486-89-2

Visit our website at www.TheStoryPlant.com

First Story Plant Printing: May 2016

Printed in the United States of America
0 9 8 7 6 5 4 3 2 1

For my parents, John and Anita
for teaching me the power of hard work
and of chasing your dreams

PROLOGUE

Final Preparations

> *"If Iran becomes a nuclear weapon state, it is the end of non-proliferation as we know it. If Iran gets a nuclear weapon, you are likely to see Saudi Arabia, Egypt, and other countries follow suit. We will bequeath to the next generation a nuclear arms race in the world's most unstable region."*
> *– Liam Fox*

> *"I can tell you one thing: Iran is closer to developing nuclear weapons today than it was a week ago, or a month ago or a year ago. It's just moving on with its efforts."*
> *– Benjamin Netanyahu*

RASHT, IRAN
SUNDAY

Dr. Omid Khosh had roughly six minutes before he would be reduced to a quivering mass of irradiated flesh and vomit, on a one-way trip to death's door. He had to make every second count.

As a nuclear scientist working on an extremely secretive project, he had seen firsthand the effects of radiation poisoning on a human being. His team had studied dozens of prisoners who had been subjected to varying doses of radiation, watched as their hair had fallen out, their fingernails sloughed off, their haunted eyes sink deeper into their toxic skulls. Depending on the strength and duration of the exposure, the process took anywhere from a few minutes to several months, but the result was always the same: painful, dehumanizing death.

Khosh had been hit with an extremely high dose, though not as high as those of his colleagues, whose irradiated bodies now littered the floor of the lab. By his calculations, he had ten minutes post-exposure before he lost control of his faculties and would be forced to watch the painful march of his own death as a heap on the concrete floor. Four of those minutes were now gone, and his body's most basic motor functions were already starting to fail. Such a strong dosage meant his death would be relatively swift compared to the prolonged agony he had observed in many of the prisoners. The downside was that he only had minutes to pass on the vital secret he carried. A secret that would soon shake the world in every sense of the word.

Once he had realized what had happened in the lab, he knew there was nothing he could do to save himself. He was a dead man walking. Accepting his death though unwilling to just lie down while the same fate was delivered to millions more, he attempted to call someone, anyone, on the outside, but the receiver offered not even a dial tone. Of course they would have cut the phone lines before revealing their betrayal. Hoping against hope, he tried to access his email via a nearby terminal, but the router was dead, disconnected from the rest of the world. He was completely cut off in his irradiated tomb, sole caretaker of a world-changing secret and no one else to share it with.

In a last-ditch effort, he went to the safe in his office and retrieved what he needed: a backup plan to the backup plan. A hastily scrawled note went into the envelope, along with the evidence the world had to see, evidence he prayed hadn't been contaminated by the radiation burst that would soon claim his own life. He forced his fingers to write the letters and numbers of the recipient's address, gripping the pen with both hands and using deliberate, painful strokes to finish his task. He added a false return address, since anything coming from this facility would immediately set off alarms with the security detail that surrounded his addressee.

Three minutes.

The lab flashed red with the emergency lighting, coating the lab in the ominous hue of blood. The containment-breach siren blared throughout the facility, letting everyone who worked within know that their worst nightmares had come true. The source of the contamination had been shut off, but for those present when the breach occurred, the damage was done. Hopefully, the remaining radiation would be low enough to not only avoid damaging the evidence he had sealed in the envelope, but also to allow the package to reach the well-guarded hands of its intended recipient.

He cursed his greed, his lust for importance in this world. He had long justified taking this job by how much better he would be able to provide for his family, compared to the out-of-work university professor who had voiced the wrong sort of political sentiment in earshot of the wrong sort of people. He used the same justification when he lied to his wife and son about what sort of work he was now doing that allowed them to indulge in some of the finer things of life. But the lies he told himself were harder to swallow. He wasn't doing this out of honor or nationalistic duty. He was doing it for himself. He was doing it to matter again—to his family, to his field. He was doing it for his own beleaguered self-image. It was the first time in years he had felt that his life was worth something.

Only now, he had discovered it was all a lie.

His legs gave out and he crumpled to the floor. The alarm continued to blare, but it seemed to be growing quieter. His vision began to dull around the edges. His time was almost up. Khosh crawled across the lead-lined concrete floor of the lab, dodging shards of bullet-shattered glass and the freshly dead corpses of his friends and colleagues. Reaching the wall, he forced himself up on one arm, and then used the other to open the mail slot.

Sealed shut. Of course.

His betrayer had considered every contingency. The entire facility was a tomb. An irradiated time-bomb that would soon plunge the world into nuclear flame.

All the pieces were coming together now, but it was too late for him. The subtle machinations, the secret plots, the nuclear facility hidden away from the world.

He had put in place another contingency, of course. Once he'd begun to realize what was really going on here, the millions of lives set to be purged from the earth in blinding light, Khosh had made arrangements. Everything he knew, everything he suspected, with all the proof he could muster, entrusted with his solicitor. He had intended to use it as insurance in the event that his employer should attempt to stab him and his fellow scientists in the back, but when the betrayal came, it was too quick and too ferocious for him to use it to save his life.

But perhaps it wouldn't be too late to stop the apocalypse that now loomed on the horizon. He wasn't coming home anymore, and when he didn't contact his solicitor in the next twelve hours, the back-up plan would be put into action. Whether that worked or not would be up to Allah.

One minute.

He slumped against the wall, fighting for every breath now, only now fully realizing that the darkness overtaking him would be permanent. He couldn't see how anyone could truly greet death with complete peace of mind and spirit. But then, unlike him, most people didn't die knowing that their life's work would be used to upend the world, knowing that the very people who betrayed them would use that work to kill untold millions. There were many people who wanted his work to fail. There were many more who wanted his work for themselves.

The not knowing was the hardest part. The powers aligned against his evidence reaching its intended target were potent. The chance of its getting through, and of its recipient being able to use it to avert the coming crisis, was a long shot indeed. But he had to have faith. Right now, that was all he had.

Suddenly, a spark of horror-tinged realization jolted through his ebbing consciousness. The letter. The address. He had another contingency, but in his attempt to send the evidence himself moments ago, he may well have ruined everything. He had to destroy the card, the envelope, every shred that connected the intended recipient to his attempt to expose the conspiracy that was about to claim his life. If his betrayer discovered who he had tried to spill his secrets to . . .

The siren, the flash of red and black, the cold concrete of the wall and floor all slipped away into nothingness for Omid Khosh. With a failed attempt at a heavenward glance, he commended his spirit—and the world he left behind—unto the care of Allah, and died, leaving behind a deadly secret, a shocking betrayal, and knowledge of a terrible conspiracy.

A conspiracy that would consign untold millions to an equally painful death at the hands of the nuclear genie. A conspiracy that would shake the world to its very core.

PART ONE

The Fateful Ascent

"Those who insist on having hostilities with us kill and destroy the option of friendship with us in the future, which is unfortunate because it is clear the future belongs to Iran, and enmities will be fruitless."
– Former Iranian President Mahmoud Ahmadinejad

"The world should be very clear about making sure that Iran does not get nuclear weapons. Period."
– Israeli Prime Minister Benjamin Netanyahu

CHAPTER 1

CAIRO, EGYPT
TUESDAY

Rick Weiland floored the accelerator as the looming hulk of the tractor-trailer bore down on the diplomatic car. Ben Rosen, the other personal-protection agent, rode shotgun. In the back seat, Christine Needham, special ambassador for Middle Eastern affairs, had been mulling over the gravity of going against the president's orders, when the impromptu car chase derailed her thoughts. Dan Krumholtz, her assistant, continued to format notes from the morning's meeting on his MacBook from the seat beside her.

Traffic in Cairo was a nightmare, and Christine couldn't wait to get back stateside, if only for a week or so. Just a few days before, she had been in Tel Aviv, and though the infrastructure had been much better there, attacks on the city had caused enough chaos to fracture that orderly façade. Hamas had fired a series of rockets into the outskirts of the Israeli capital from the Gaza Strip hundreds of miles to the south, one of which had slipped through the nation's famed Iron Dome missile defense system and hit a primary school, killing twelve. Long-range rockets, the sort that Hamas didn't usually have access to, which meant another regional power, perhaps Iran or Egypt, was supplying them.

Egyptian President Faraj al-Qassim had denied any involvement in Hamas's newfound armaments, both publicly and to Ambassador Needham's face, but then, of course he would, whether he was involved or not. Politics in the region was full of duplicitous moves and countermoves, with a thousand sub-alliances shifting and shaking on a daily basis. Public perception, power, and what you could get away with often held more sway than integrity, the truth, or the public good.

Kind of like Washington, Christine mused.

Despite the difficult nature of negotiating with many of the leaders in the Middle East, she had been sent here for a purpose, and she wasn't going to let a few egotistical, compulsive liars get in the way. And though she was a woman in a part of the world where testosterone reigned supreme, she had the chops and experience to succeed where her male counterparts had failed. Or so she hoped.

Israeli Prime Minister Elijah Shihmanter was livid at the attacks on his capital city and was proposing the building of more housing developments in Gaza Strip to more fully colonize the occupied territory. The violence was escalating daily, and international opinion was steadily turning in the Palestinians' favor, despite the recent aggression against Israeli civilian targets.

Beyond the Palestinian question lay a pair of even more far-reaching issues: regional terrorism and a nascent nuclear arms race. From Syria to ISIS to Iran to Yemen, the Middle East was a powder keg threatening to consume the lives of millions and—considering the resources that came from the region and the global nature of the modern-day economy—the livelihoods of billions more.

This was her area of expertise. After spending the bulk of the so-called War on Terror helming a Washington-based think tank that the previous two administrations had used for insights into the fractious and turbulent world of the Middle East, she had been tapped as a special envoy by the current president, giving her the position of special ambassador for Middle Eastern affairs. Fending off critics decrying the appointment as vaguely nepotistic, owing to the close relationship he and her father had shared during their long senatorial career, President James Talquin had created the position to deal with the increasingly important—and increasingly volatile—region with fresh insight and understanding.

Having lived in the region, as a military kid whose family was stationed throughout the region during the seventies and eighties, and as a Peace Corps worker during the early nineties, she had grown to love the region and its people. For much of the Clinton era, she had served as a business consultant for several corporations looking to expand into the region, while also serving as a consultant for the Senate Committee on Foreign Relations, over which her late father had presided.

Then the towers fell, and the world changed. The region that had long been near and dear to her heart, from Israel to Iraq to Iran and back again, was suddenly thrust into the spotlight again. Not since Desert Storm a decade earlier had the general populace cared a lick about what happened in the Middle East, except to the point where it affected their oil prices. Now the region was on everybody's radar, but for all the wrong reasons.

She founded the Lawrence Institute for Middle Eastern Studies, named after British diplomat and archeologist T. E. Lawrence, popularly known as Lawrence of Arabia. Though the parallel only held up so far, she appreciated Lawrence's ability to befriend and live among the Arabs, even while he ultimately sought his own nation's best interests. Through the Lawrence Institute, Christine sought to bring some of that much-needed understanding to policymakers in Washington who were now laser-focused on the Middle East, many for the first time in their lives. Though not all of her recommendations were heeded—the Lawrence Institute, after all, was hardly the only think tank offering advice on the subject—there were quite a few key strategic victories in both the War on Terror and on rebuilding foreign relations in the region that stemmed from her advice.

President Talquin, having campaigned against the warmongering proclivities and the apologetic weakness of previous administrations, had brought Christine on board to help steer a new path in the Middle East. Though he had plenty of real-world experience and was a decade her senior, Christine still felt he was a bit starry-eyed and overly optimistic when it came to achieving a lasting peace in the region. People had been splitting into groups and killing each other for the reason *du jour* since Adam and Eve were kicked out of the Garden, and she didn't foresee any outsider-initiated agreement changing that. In fact, considering how polarized and fractious many of the religious, ethnic, and political groups had become, she doubted even the ability of a native Arab or Muslim to make that change from within. And yet, some peace was better than full-scale terror and anarchy, so she was determined to do her best for the administration.

That was why she was making this unauthorized visit to Dubai. Her direct supervisor, Secretary of State Lyle Molina, had been working behind the scenes with state leaders across the Middle East to reach some sort of lasting peace agreement on Israel. A comprehensive, long-lasting peace that not only answered the decades-old Palestinian question, but also provided for a universal recognition of Israel's right to exist. Needless to say, it wasn't an easy task and had met heavy resistance from camps in the Middle East, Israel, and even at home in the US.

One party that wanted nothing to do with the prospective peace deal currently being floated was Sheikh Abdelrahman bin Rashid al-Futaim, president of the oil-rich United Arab Emirates. The country, like most in the region, currently did not officially recognize Israel, but rather saw the Jewish nation as an illegal occupier of Palestinian lands. The West-friendly UAE hadn't called for the complete eradication of Israel or held Holocaust denial conferences as had their Persian neighbors to the north, but its policies and viewpoints were decidedly hostile to Israel nonetheless.

With Needham's strategic insight, Molina had succeeded in bringing several previously anti-Israel nations on board with the administration's plan, most notably the new regime in Iraq and a hesitant but influential Saudi Arabia. Pundits had speculated that it had been the anti-terrorism and the anti-nuclear elements of the three-pronged approach to the talks that had appealed to most of the parties, as the twin specters of ISIS and a nuclear-armed Iran posed more of a real threat to their homelands than the existence of Israel. Many key holdouts still persisted, though, including Iran, Syria, Lebanon, and the United Arab Emirates.

Iran had obvious objections to both the Israel and nuclear element, and, as they were key supporters of myriad paramilitary groups throughout the region that the US considered terrorists, they were unlikely to see eye to eye on any of the three components in the near future. Talquin, Molina, and Needham hoped that, by bringing most of the rest of the region in on the talks, Iran would be forced to choose between considering the offer or risking even further isolation from its neighbors.

Syria was entrenched in its own endless civil war, while Lebanon counted anti-Israel Hezbollah members among its parliament and would be hesitant to make a move hostile to a small but powerful minority within their community. Plus, neither nation had forgotten decades of war and hostility with their Jewish neighbors. But while there wasn't much Needham could do about resistance from Iran, Syria, or Lebanon, she might be able to exert some influence in the United Arab Emirates.

She was a woman, with Jewish ancestry on her mother's side. This normally would have presented two strikes against her abilities as a front-line negotiator in most of the Middle East, which was a key reason for taking a mostly advisory role during her brief but important tenure under Talquin's administration. But her bargaining chip in Dubai was something that only she could bring to the table: her late father.

George Needham had been heavily invested in Middle Eastern oil from the sixties through the nineties, and he had maintained relationships with some of the key figures in the Arabian Peninsula until his death in 2010. One of the men he had been particularly close to was Sheikh Khalid bin Rashid al-Futaim, head of the emirate of Dubai and second in command to Sheikh Abdelrahman himself. It also didn't hurt—the United Arab Emirates being an absolute monarchy— that Khalid was Abdelrahman's brother. If she could convince Khalid of the benefits of greater, region-wide stability stemming from a comprehensive peace deal, then maybe he could convince Abdelrahman. And if Abdelrahman was on board, the rest of the Emirati sheikhs would likely follow. Getting another Islamic nation on board could be just the momentum shift the peace accords needed.

Molina had rebuffed her plan, as had President James Talquin when Needham ignored her boss's admonition and asked the commander in chief directly. If word got out of her subterfuge, they argued, and, even worse, if Sheikh Khalid didn't want to play along, it could not only destroy any hopes for reaching a region-wide peace deal, but it could also hurt American relations and interests throughout the Middle East, they argued. Tensions were already high between the US and the UAE owing to the deaths of two Emirati citizens at the hands of a CIA agent covertly operating in Dubai the month before. The UAE was one of the few stalwart allies America had left in the region, and neither Molina nor Talquin would sign off on any plan that might undermine whatever trust remained between the two nations.

But neither of them was on the ground every day, seeing the growing tension and increasingly bold attacks against the isolated Jewish nation, feeling the aftershocks of the countless brewing conflicts between Sunni and Shia, between frustrated extremists of all stripes. She was daily confronted with stark evidence that the status quo could not hold for much longer. So, for the first time in her professional life, she was disobeying a direct order from her superiors. She was flying to Dubai to talk with Sheikh Khalid, face to face.

She didn't pretend that this would be an easy endeavor. The Middle East was a man's world and, despite Western nations' attempts to be more progressive by pushing female appointees to ambassadorial roles, the truth was that many opportunities were closed to her simply because she was a woman. It could be hard to negotiate with foreign diplomats whose culture for centuries had taught that women were second-class citizens, mentally and morally inferior to their male counterparts. And while Israel was among the more forward-thinking countries in the region when it came to gender-equality, the nations and communities with which Israel held its tenuous armistice generally were not.

Moreover, she didn't even have an appointment to speak with the sheikh. Advance notice of such an unorthodox request would give Khalid time to contact Talquin or Molina about her visit, and that could prove a death knell for her mission. Better to ask forgiveness than permission, she rationalized.

The tractor-trailer switched lanes and went around their black Audi, but the rest of the motorists that afternoon wanted to get to their destination just as badly. Rick had been driving her since her appointment to the post three years ago, and he had proven more than adept at maneuvering through the often unpredictable streams of traffic in cities from Beirut to Baghdad. Even now, in rush-hour traffic, he was making good time while still maintaining his cool. Allowing for traffic, they would be at the airport inside an hour, and then she'd have another host of travel issues to inwardly complain about.

A sheaf of documents sat on the seat beside Christine. She picked up the folder, paused in thought, and put it down again. She had gone over her notes from the most recent meeting with Prime Minister Shihmanter a dozen times already, as well as the casualty and damage reports, the latest briefings on the Palestinian situations in Gaza, the West Bank, and Golan Heights, and developing sentiments about the crisis from both the Israeli government and the Israeli public. She would likely be studying the reports during her upcoming flight as well, looking for an edge in her negotiations with Sheikh Khalid, demonstrating how peace in Israel and Palestine benefitted everyone. For now, her last few minutes on the ground for the next several hours, she simply looked out the window, enjoying the scenery, even if most of it at present was bumper-to-bumper traffic.

She glanced at the drivers and passengers of the cars next to hers. Cairo was a massive city, a metropolitan area home to more than 80 million people. Millennia of history, from the Pharaohs to Alexander the Great to the heyday of Coptic Christianity to the rule of the Calilphs, the colonization of the British, and the rapidly changing span of the twentieth century. Her own ancestry had once found refuge from famine here, then had to rely on Yahweh's wrath and mercy to extricate themselves from slavery. The infant Christ had been hidden here from Herod's massacre of the innocents. And yet, as her mind did now, her ancestors had always returned to Israel.

Still staring out the window at the glut of Egyptian traffic, she found herself reflecting on her ancestral homeland, where a similar commute to the airport had taken place less than 48 hours ago. As Rick had navigated the evening traffic through the Tel Aviv streets, she had studied the faces of Israeli citizens driving home from work, from the store, to their families and their lives. Tel Aviv was a modern city, yet it continually lived under the shadow of fear. It was perhaps unique in the world today, excepting isolationist rogue states like North Korea, in that all its neighbors either barely tolerated its presence or called for its outright destruction. And the Palestinian question was one of the major catalysts for anti-Israeli campaigns throughout the Middle East. Most Israelis simply wanted to live out their lives in their ancestral homeland. So did the Palestinians. The fact that that land was one and the same presented a no-win situation for two sides which refused to budge, particularly when Israel's Muslim neighbors throughout the region continued to spew vitriolic rhetoric, calling for the young nation to be wiped from the map. Hackles were raised on both sides, as Holocaust denials and an absolute refusal to recognize Israel's existence—even in textbooks or newspapers—by Islamic nations was met with Israeli muscle flexing as they bulldozed another Palestinian community or shelled another Hamas or Hezbollah leader's neighborhood. It was a chest-beating, geopolitical shouting match that neither side could win. And so an ever-shifting stalemate had taken over, with occasional armed conflicts boiling over the borders into Lebanon, Jordan, Syria, and Egypt. Thus far, Israel had been successful in staving off attacks from without, but their policies toward Palestinian territories under their control had done little in recent years to endear them to the international community.

The United States' relationship with Israel had always been close, owing as much to America's role in helping end the Holocaust as with its own Judeo-Christian origins and heritage. No matter what party controlled Washington and no matter what international sentiments were currently in vogue regarding the embattled nation, Israel had long been able to count on the support of the world's number-one superpower. Part of Christine's job as special ambassador to the region was not only to maintain this relationship, but also to ensure that American interests were represented properly. Right now, she felt that the relationship was going the other way.

The sun was low in the sky, continuing its descent westward, Osiris' daily death ritual, only to be resurrected at sunrise the next morning. The day after tomorrow she would be watching the sun rise over the Chesepeake, a glimmering spectacle of light and water that reminded her of everything she admired about the United States. Despite all the trouble the nation had endured over the past few years, from the War on Terror to the financial collapse to an increasingly divided populace, she firmly believed there was something special about America. She loved her country and what it stood for, and she loved its people, even when they had trouble standing for much of anything. But in her time in the region, her admiration for the Israeli people had also grown. Like Americans, they were resilient in the face of adversity. For better or worse, each modern nation had been built on the backs—and corpses—of those who had lived there before. And each nation's citizenry was often held hostage to the overbearing policies and rhetoric of its government. The only problem was that here, those policies might well get the citizens killed.

She turned from the window to face forward, just in time to see a passenger bus three cars ahead explode into a ball of flame. A split second later, the shockwave hit their car, jolting the vehicle and finally jarring Rick's cool demeanor.

"Off ramp," Ben said, pointing to the beginnings of a clover leaf interchange to the right.

Rick spun the wheel to the right and began swerving through traffic, receiving a barrage of horns from angry drivers. "You all right back there, Madam Ambassador?"

"Fine, Rick, thank you," she responded with a slight tremor in her voice. No matter how much violence she had seen during her time in the region, it still affected her. She supposed that was good, all things considered. It meant she wasn't becoming desensitized and losing another part of her humanity. She watched the flames lick skywards from the shattered windows as the bus's momentum carried it through a rolling crawl. She could swear she saw a face in a window, the skin half-melted, its expression twisted in agony. But then it was gone, replaced by billows of black smoke, carrying the stench of melted vinyl, nitrate fuel, and burnt human flesh.

She shuddered and faced forward again as the off ramp took them out of view of the burning bus, flashing back again to a few days ago in Tel Aviv. The Israeli and Palestinian people were the real victims in a new cold war that was raging throughout the streets and villages of the Levant. Despite its rich history and natural beauty, the region had been stricken by war and conflict since its earliest historical accounts, from the armies of Joshua overtaking Jericho to the Israelites defeating the Philistines under King David; from the invasions of Israel by Assyria and Babylon to the final Jewish revolt against Rome in the first century AD. The conquests of Islam and the Crusades left the area in conflict for the better part of a millennium, and the dissolution of the Ottoman Empire after World War I and the area's postwar British mandate forged the way for a modern-day Jewish state in the land that was once their forefathers'. But three full-scale wars and innumerable armed conflicts in its nearly seven decades of existence had shown modern Israel's short history to be even more contentious and conflict-ridden than that of its forebears. Many of her more religious countrymen would find something prophetic in the conflicts affecting the region today, but while Christine believed that religion was a huge element in the equation—the land, and Jerusalem in particular, were sacred to the three great monotheistic religions, each believing it was "promised" to their tradition and must be kept pure in the hands of the faithful—she recognized the very human element to what was going on: power, territory, safeguarding your homeland. The problem was that those policies ran over other people who had very similar desires: the Palestinians.

There were no easy solutions, she had long ago realized. If an elusive peace deal was ever reached, neither side would be completely satisfied with the results. For the better part of a century, Israelis had built homes, families and lives in this land. Before that, so had Palestinians. Uprooting either would only serve to further the injustices served upon these two peoples. And both sides wanted the whole pie. Though Israel was a nation friendly to the US, Christine had often been haunted by the probability that, one day, their unflinching support of the Jewish state would rope them into a massive and unwinnable war across the Middle East—possibly even spiraling into a third world war.

Her religious countrymen would have seen something prophetic in that too. Armageddon itself was named for a battlefield in Israel—Har Megiddo—that was to be the site of the final battle between good and evil. However, as ambassador—and as a human being—her goal was to avoid a world-ending war whenever possible.

When Rick finally pulled the car up to the VIP wing of Cairo International Airport, the sky had turned deep orange, with the setting sun's power magnified by its reflection across the desert dunes to the west. Christine grabbed her folder, tucked it into her briefcase, and then exited the car. Ben retrieved her wheeled suitcase from the trunk, as well as his and Rick's bags, and they made their way through the concourse and onto the tarmac, where the chartered flight awaited them. The Gulfstream was idling on the pavement with its runway stairs lowered for entry. Beside the stairs, an anxious-looking young man in a blue shirt and red tie was hopping from one foot to the other, as though he was trying to stave off an impending trip to the restroom. When Christine drew closer, she recognized the man as Dennis Moore, a courier employed at the American embassy.

"Madam Ambassador, a package came for you. Marked urgent. I was instructed to get it to you before you left the country." Moore handed her a padded manila envelope with the embassy's address written in poorly scrawled English.

"This has been screened already?" asked Ben, always the more brash and outspoken of her bodyguards, as he plucked the envelope from her hand and held it at arm's length away from her.

"Yes, sir, it has," Moore nodded hastily. He seemed to be breathing a little more slowly now that he had managed to make his delivery on time.

"Thank you, Dennis," Christine said with a smile. Even at forty-four she could still turn heads and she recognized the gleam in the courier's eye as one she had seen in the eyes of countless men before him. "Now, if there's nothing else, we need to get going. The president awaits." A small lie, as she was sure she would be flying back to Washington to meet with Talquin as soon as Sheikh Abdelrahman voiced his support for the peace deal—and hopefully not before.

The mention of the president seemed to jerk Moore back to reality. Perhaps he was a little starstruck, too. Not many people, after all, were able to get a private audience with the most powerful man in the world.

"No, ma'am, nothing else." He stepped back and gave her a little salute, but then screwed up his face and turned away, kicking himself inwardly since hers was not a position to which one salutes. Still, the kid was cute. She gave him another smile as she began to climb the stairs. He got an A for effort.

Two minutes later, she had settled into her seat, their bags stored in a closet at the front of the plane. Rick was adjusting his headphones as he prepared to watch *The Bourne Ultimatum* for the millionth time on his portable DVD player. Ben, who had been chatting with the pilots up front, returned to his seat as the plane's engines whirred to life. He would likely be burying himself in Brad Thor's latest thriller for the duration of the flight to Dubai. Dan, meanwhile, stared at his hands while biting his lower lip. He didn't like flying—or the take-off and landing parts, at least—and he had voiced his concerns about going behind the president's back on this mission, which she had noted. It was his job on the line too, after all, but Christine believed what they were doing—what *needed* to be done—was bigger than any of them. Hopefully, Dan would look back on this and realize that the risk was well worth the return.

Christine took a deep breath and sighed to herself. She was on the way at last, heading for what could be one of the greatest strategic coups of her career.

She picked up the envelope next to her and opened it, dumping the contents into her hand. Out spilled an unmarked Micro SD card and a single, typewritten page. She recognized the name of the law firm on the letterhead, an Amman-based group she had consulted on multiple occasions during her work with the Lawrence Institute. As she read the message, her chest tightened as a nightmare scenario began to take shape in her mind. Once she was done, she read it again, just to make sure she hadn't misread something. She hadn't. With a now-shaking hand, she picked up the Micro SD card between thumb and forefinger and looked at it in terrified awe. It had to be a hoax. That was her mind's only recourse to sanity. Because if it wasn't . . .

The plane accelerated down the runway, and she felt the wheels leave the tarmac as they ascended into the sky. She shook her head in disbelief. She knew she had to verify whatever information was on the memory card, but her hands quivered with fear at what sort of terror-laden rabbit hole she had stumbled upon. These allegations, if voiced without the requisite evidence to back them up, could destroy everything she and the administration had worked so hard for, perhaps preventing the chance for a comprehensive peace agreement for decades to come. But if the allegations were true, the consequences could be infinitely worse.

Christine normally hated hyperbole, but she realized that it was no stretch to say that the she quite literally held the future of the world in her hands.

CHAPTER 2

San Ignacio de Velasco, Bolivia

Wayne Wilkins fought the urge to swat at the microswarm of gnats flitting around his eyes. Despite the darkness and his all-black outfit, any sudden movements could call attention to himself. And that was something that he, hidden in the jungle just outside the high-walled compound, could not afford. Ramon Esperanza, owner of the estate and the palatial mansion within, had more money than any one man should ever need, and he spent a sizable portion of it ensuring that his little slice of paradise was safe from anyone who would endeavor to take it away. Someone like Wayne.

The agent watched the second guard pass by, walking the perimeter wall in the opposite direction to his counterpart. He had timed it out: the guards made a complete rotation every two-and-a-half minutes, give or take. Every seventy-five seconds they would cross paths—once in the middle of the front fence, and then, seventy-five seconds later, again in the back. The real window Wayne had to play with was, in fact, much smaller.

Surveillance cameras, pressure plates, and tripwires lined the wall and the interior of the compound, but the informant within Esperanza's cartel who had given the DEA the information had pinpointed a spot on the near wall where coverage was lax. But the DEA was about border security, seizing drug shipments, and shutting down operations. They would have loved a high profile arrest like Esperanza, but he hadn't been seen in public for years, and the Bolivian government wasn't about to take on a kingpin of his caliber just to satisfy the desires of another Washington bureaucracy. So the agency passed it off to the CIA, who in turn passed it off to their own black-ops, wet-work division. Which was where Wayne came in.

Esperanza had made his fortune in cocaine as a young man, climbing the ranks in the eighties narcotics boom that had led Reagan to declare a War on Drugs, a "war" America had been losing since its inception. As he built his illicit empire, he consolidated power one rival territory at a time, a hostile buyout here, a key assassination there, until he controlled nearly forty percent of all the cocaine, heroin, and marijuana coming out of Bolivia. He was worth billions, and every peso was soaked in blood. His magnificently appointed hacienda—the largest of seven he owned throughout the country—was a testament to the vastness of his wealth. The highly trained ex-soldiers who guarded the complex from outsiders served as a warning of how far he would go to keep it.

Wayne had studied the terrain between his position at the jungle's edge and the fence he'd need to scale to access the complex. Every rock, every contour, every branch and twig that he would need to cross to get to his destination he committed to memory. There would be no room for error today. In Wayne's line of work, there rarely was.

He did one last check of the environment. The few villagers who lived nearby rarely dared to draw too close the tyrannical kingpin's estate, and the hour was too late for anyone to be out of their homes without purpose. Wayne had purpose.

Satisfied that there were no extra witnesses or potential problems save for those he'd already assessed, he shrugged off the ghillie blanket he'd used to conceal his position in the brush. He counted down silently as the guard walked the center point of the wall directly in front of him.

Three.

Two.

One.

Wayne slid from the cover of jungle as silently as he could, speed-walking his way toward the outer wall, softening his footfalls as he advanced and conscious of every sound he made. Normally he would just kill the guards and be done with it, but that wasn't an option this time around. Were he to kill the guards, the cameras, regular check-ins with the estate's central security office, and other failsafe protocols would betray the presence of an intruder and set off the alarms. He was alone on this mission, and though he was confident he could successfully infiltrate the estate and eliminate his target through cunning and stealth, he had little doubt that he would lose the all-out firefight that would erupt should the alarm be raised. Silent but deadly was the name of the game.

He reached the wall just as the guard turned the corner and stepped out of sight. After counting to three once more, allowing the sentinel to move a few meters further from a potential line of sight on his position, he pointed two rubber-gripped cylindrical devices at the top of the wall and squeezed the embedded triggers. Twin carbon-fiber cables shot from the devices and pulled taut once their claw-grip ends had latched onto the other side of the wall. Wayne squeezed the triggers again, and the cables began to retract into the devices, slowly pulling him upwards. He placed his feet against the stucco and started walking up the wall. A voice sounded from where the guards should have been passing each other in a few seconds. Angry. Suspicious. The beam of a flashlight danced just past the corner to his left. The guard was coming back. Wayne was running out of time.

He squeezed the triggers twice more, and the devices quickened their extraction. He had to move fast, but he didn't want to make any more noise than he already had. Raising the guard's suspicions was one thing. But giving him confirmation that an intruder was on the premises was a great way to fail a mission in hurry. And to get killed in the process.

More voices, closer. Two distinct flashlight beams now, and their motion was even more erratic than before. The guards were running. Towards him. Three feet from the top, Wayne kicked up on the wall and pulled his arms toward his sides. The upward boost gave him momentum and he swung his right leg over the fence. He pushed a button on the back of each claw holding the cables to the wall, and they released their purchase, allowing him to pocket the grappling devices so he could use his hands without fearing that the devices would clatter against the stone.

He glanced toward the corner as he swung his other leg over the wall. One guard, then the other, dashed into sight. He slowly lowered himself so his body hung against the warm, rough stucco of the interior wall. He forced himself to slow and silence his breathing, even though the balaclava wrapped around his face made it difficult. The guards were on the other side now, and if he allowed himself to drop to the ground six feet below, the sound of his boots hitting the ground would likely be enough to confirm his presence, effectively shooting his mission in the foot. He thought that a large jacaranda tree in full bloom behind him was likely obscuring his position from cameras and sentry positions within the grounds, but he wasn't sure. All he could do now was hold on, breathe softly, and pray.

An interminable moment passed, and then a voice from beyond the wall said, "Es nada." *It's nothing.*

Wayne sighed as he heard the men move away and resume their rounds. He lowered himself to the ground and crouched to get a feel for the compound. It was one thing to see it from an aerial view via satellite imagery. Being on the ground with your life on the line was a whole different ball game.

He began to move through the underbrush toward the hacienda, using the elephant leaves and palmetto fronds to disguise his approach.

This was who he was now. The Rangers had wanted a killer. The CIA needed an assassin. And for better or worse, they had made him into both.

It was time for Esperanza to pay for his crimes.

CHAPTER 3

DUBAI, UNITED ARAB EMIRATES

Seconds after her chartered flight touched down at Dubai International Airport, Christine Needham dashed to the door, anxious for the pilot to give the all clear and to lower the air stairs. She had Dan contact the US Consulate in Dubai while en route, and they would be sending an SUV to pick her up on the tarmac and take her straight to the consulate. She wanted to tell them what she had discovered, but she couldn't trust a revelation of this magnitude over an unsecured line. They had secure lines at the consulate, and it was there that she would place the call to the president.

The most important phone call of her career.

As ambassador to the most beleaguered and controversial region in the world, Christine was no stranger to feeling the pressure of the world on her shoulders. But this was something else altogether. Even lobbying Sheikh Khalid for his support on the peace summit on the issue of Israel and Palestine didn't come close. What she had discovered on the memory card was even worse than the accompanying note had portended. This was instantly and irrevocably world-changing.

The most devastating conflict the world had seen in generations was looming. And only she had the key to stopping it.

She had been in high-pressure situations before, when economies hung in the balance, and had come out on top. Still, without her surging adrenaline, she might have had a panic attack. If she were completely honest, she'd have to admit she was terrified for her nation and for her diplomatic charge.

Despite her role as arbiter for the United States across the region, she couldn't deny that she harbored a particular affinity for Israel. Her maternal grandmother had immigrated to the United States from Nazi-controlled Germany before the borders were closed to Jews, so she felt a passion for the tiny nation that always seemed to be in the world's crosshairs. At the same time, she was a pragmatist and realized that within a decade, and without some sort of course correction, there might not be an Israel anymore. America's influence in the region was waning, and sentiments at home and across the Western world were shifting toward the Palestinians' cause. The recent refusal of the West to stand up to ISIS or the Iranian nuclear program in any meaningful way had emboldened Hamas and Hezbollah, and conflict in the region seemed to be moving to a point where Israel's own potent military capabilities might not be sufficient to stave off a massive multi-nation attack on its own. The possibility of losing the homeland her forefathers had been denied for nearly nineteen centuries was unthinkable.

The package she had received in Cairo changed all of that. It changed everything. Peace—in Israel, in the Middle East, and even across the globe—might never again be attainable if she couldn't get this information to the president before it was too late.

As soon as she reached the stairs, she could see something was terribly wrong. Not one SUV waited outside, but three. And the men getting out of the vehicles were not diplomatic staffers holding agendas and sat phones.

They were jihadists. Guns drawn, well organized, no official uniforms, and very much where they shouldn't have been. They had come for her.

Christine froze atop the first step and tumbled back into the cabin, rolling away from the open door. She heard shouts from outside, some in Arabic, others in English.

Rick looked at Christine on the ground, and then at the men outside, and also dove out of the doorway. Ben rushed to her side while Dan conferred with the pilots, trying to figure a way out of this mess.

The evidence! Christine thought. That had to be why the gunmen were here. She opened her briefcase and withdrew the Micro SD memory card that had been delivered to her just hours earlier. Back when the world was only marginally screwed up and Christine wasn't aware of a deadly conspiracy, nor of being actively threatened by terrorists. None of that mattered now. She had to protect the evidence at all costs.

The briefcase was not an option. Far too obvious. But she couldn't leave it either. Surely they'd either scour the plane for anything they could use to their advantage or, more likely, they'd torch it when they were done. Either way, the revelations on the card would be lost. *Then where?*

The answer came to her like an inspiration from heaven. She knew all too well that men like these perverted the teachings of Islam to suit their political needs, but she had to hope that they were at least observant enough of their faith's basic tenets. The fact that she was one-quarter Jewish—and thus, decidedly unclean in these fanatics' eyes—should work in her favor as well.

As if that would matter if they did manage to get their hands on her.

She took the Micro SD card between thumb and forefinger and, being careful to ensure the tiny memory stick would remain secure, placed it underneath her left breast inside her bra.

They may be terrorists, she prayed silently, *but don't let them be savages.*

Dan and one of the pilots left the cockpit armed with two 9 mm handguns.

"Are you serious?" Ben asked. "You're going to try to shoot your way out?"

"You got a better idea?" Dan asked, clearly frustrated by their lack of options.

"I think we should get the heck out of here." He looked at the pilot, who shook his head.

"No can do," the captain said, a faint tremor breaking through his usually in-control tone. "They've put chocks under the wheels. Unless we can remove those, this plane isn't going anywhere."

"You think this is about the package?" Dan asked.

Standing from her crouched position, Christine cocked her head. "I hope not. Fingers crossed that they're just not fans of the peace summit."

Rick poked his head around the corner of the doorway for a quick glance outside. "Yeah, they don't look like the types to sit down and talk out plans for peace. More like shoot it out and whoever is left standing wins."

"I'm not taking my odds with those peashooters," Ben said, nodding at the handguns Dan had brought from the cabin. "Look, if we delay them long enough . . ."

"Ambassador Needham, please exit the plane now, and we will let your friends live," an Arabic-tinged British voice called from outside. "This is your only opportunity to avoid bloodshed. You have fifteen seconds to comply."

"You can't," Dan said.

Surely the terrorists' presence hadn't gone unnoticed by airport security. Even if there had been clear breaches that allowed the men outside to surround and attack her plane, the authorities were surely on their way. The terrorists would know this. Their window of opportunity was quickly closing. She would be a tremendous prize for any jihadist group, so once she was in their hands, they may well turn and run with her in tow before they found their escape no longer possible. Even if the terrorists did their worst to her, it still would be preferable to knowing that she had the capability of stopping the planned horrors described on the memory card, yet failed to do so.

She was but one life. Millions hung in the balance.

"The evidence is all that matters," Christine said, starting to reach under her shirt to retrieve the memory card. If she handed it off to her team, they could see that the president received the information. It was their best shot.

"They'll kill you," Dan said, putting his hand on her arm. "They'll kill all of us. I'm not letting you go out there like a lamb to the slaughter."

The co-pilot leaned out from the cockpit. "Can't get anyone on the radio. They must be jamming our ability to transmit."

"Are you kidding me?" Rick said. He kicked a nearby seat in impotent frustration. "So now what? We just going to sit here and wait for airport security to show up? If they were doing their job, those guys wouldn't be out there waiting to gun us down in the first place."

"Your fifteen seconds are up, Ambassador Needham," sounded the voice from outside.

"Let me go talk to them," Ben said, flicking the safety off his semi-auto pistol as he headed for the open door.

"Ben, don't!" Christine shouted. A split second later, Ben's body convulsed as he was perforated with bullet holes, scarlet spraying the wall and ceiling behind him like a hellish Jackson Pollack. A scream escaped her lips before she managed to stifle it. Tears began to well, but she fought them away. She could not afford time for mourning right now.

"Ambassador Needham, you try my patience. Three seconds to reveal yourself. Two."

"I've got to go try to stop this," she said to Rick and Dan.

"One."

"I'll go," Rick said, brandishing his pistol and turning toward the door.

The men outside began to shout in a surge of sound that resembled a roar. Seconds later, they were on the stairs and through the door. They stepped on and over Ben's body. Rick fired his pistol at one of the men, winging him, before a fusillade of bullets knocked him to the ground in a pool of blood.

Christine stood in shock, wanting to get away but realizing there was no escape. Two of her closest friends had just been gunned down, and before she could turn to see if any of the bullets still flying had killed Dan, a pair of men grabbed her arms while another pulled a strange-smelling burlap bag over her head. Within moments, she felt strangely dizzy. They'd drugged her. She felt consciousness slipping away as they cinched her hands tightly behind her back and hoisted her into the air like a rolled Persian carpet.

They were kidnapping the most influential US diplomat in the Middle East. And they were getting away with it.

CHAPTER 4

San Ignacio de Velasco, Bolivia

Wayne held his breath, watching the sentry standing by the side entrance to the hacienda. The Bolivian was young and strong, but also seemed impetuous. Young men often were, and waiting around with little to stimulate his mind or muscles could be an unbearably tedious affair. The guard shuffled his feet and stared off into the distance, seemingly bored out of his mind.

This one would be easy.

Wayne picked up a stone from the underbrush and tossed it past the other side of the entrance. It hit a wooden pole—one topped by a security camera that Wayne was keeping tabs on—and sounded a thud that carried back through the air. The bored sentry started, looking over at the pole, and then scanning the area. Cautiously, he left the well-lit safety of the doorway and headed toward the source of the sound.

Sucker, Wayne thought, glancing at the camera once more and committing the sweeping path of its lens to memory. He crept toward a point of intercept, positioning himself behind the guard. In one fluid motion, he stood up, grabbed the Bolivian by the throat, and pulled him tightly against his body. The guard struggled for a few seconds as Wayne starved the man's lungs of oxygen, but then the struggles ceased. Wayne lowered the man to the ground and checked his body for keys. He found a ring of metal house keys and a white plastic keycard, which he pocketed. He then took the guard's radio—an old-fashioned walkie-talkie that seemed a bit below Esperanza's income level—and removed the battery pack, which he slipped into another pocket.

As quietly as possible, he used some dirt and leaves to obscure the fallen guard's form. Satisfied that the man's presence was hidden from easy view, Wayne eyed the camera above for an opening, and then sneaked up the concrete path to the entrance alcove. He checked the doorknob. No keyhole. Then he noticed the flat, plastic box on the wall next to the door. It was painted the same beige as the stucco exterior, but he recognized it for what it was. Careful not to jingle the guard's metal key ring, he pulled the white keycard from his pocket and swiped it over the box.

Beep.

He was in.

Wayne eased open the door and slid inside the entryway. Domingo Santana, the DEA's source within Esperanza's organization, was off tonight. Just in case things got messy.

Holding his breath as he stood in the shadows of the hallway, Wayne listened for any signs his entry had been noticed. No cameras guarded this hall, and he took the opportunity to survey his surroundings, matching them up to the blueprints he'd seen in his briefing.

This side entrance led through a kitchen and into the main foyer. Wayne would take the stairs there to the second floor, left to the east wing of the house, right down another hallway, and at the end of that hallway, facing a courtyard fountain below, was the corner bedroom of Esperanza himself. According to Domingo, Esperanza always watched his favorite game show—a Bolivian original called *¡Puedes Ganar Todo!*—in his bedroom at this hour. A distracted target in a designated place, a place the mark felt safe, was always a plus in Wayne's book.

He crept down the hallway and entered a white-tiled kitchen. Original. The marble-topped counter wrapped around Wayne's position in an L shape, with the opening to his left. An island in the center was topped with a well-scoured cutting board and a block of Ginsu knives. *Apparently they have those commercials down here, too,* Wayne mused as he sized up the real issue at hand. A guard was standing at the countertop facing away from Wayne, making himself a late-night snack.

Pobrecito, Wayne thought with a wry sense of humor. The guard would have to be dealt with, but thankfully he was occupied with his food preparation. Wayne slid into the room and slowly made his way around the island, preparing to choke the man out as he had the guard outside.

He was almost within grabbing distance when the guard turned around, halfway through his first bite of empanada. His eyes went wide as Wayne took advantage of the man's surprise, shoving the man's snack deeper into his throat. The guard choked, but pushed forward against Wayne, shoving him against the island. Spitting out the empanada, the Bolivian pressed his hips against the CIA assassin, pinning him in place while he went for his gun. Wayne's left arm was pinned behind his back and his right was unable to reach the gun at his hip or the knife in his ankle sheath. He had to end this before things got out of control. Nonlethal options were no longer available. The guard had just nominated himself for collateral damage.

Wayne reached behind him and found the block of knives. He knocked it over and fumbled at the handles until he found a nice big one. Yanking it from the block, he pivoted his wrist and stabbed it into the guard's upper back. The man's eyes widened once more, staring into Wayne's, before he slumped to the ground with a thud, his heart pierced from behind.

Cuts through a rib cage just like a tomato, Wayne mused as he slid the knife back into the block. His black leather gloves eliminated any concerns about fingerprints—not that Wayne's would show up on any databases Esperanza's men could ever search. He stepped over the body and continued on his mission. With one missing guard outside and a bloody carcass in the kitchen, it was only a matter of time before his presence was discovered. It was time to kick it into high gear.

Wayne left the kitchen and passed through a large dining room that could easily seat twenty at its dark oak table. The chandelier that hung over the table was not illuminated at present, but ambient light from neighboring rooms created a dancing menagerie of light and shadow across the walls as he advanced.

Through another doorway was the main foyer, with twin staircases curving up the sides of the room. The chandelier here made the one in the dining room look like a mobile over a crib. An intricately woven carpet ran from the main entrance through the hall, widening at the base of the stairs to split into three. Wayne took the left staircase, toward the east wing which held his quarry. The soft carpet absorbed his footfalls as he strained his ears for any sound that his presence—or, at the very least, his handiwork—had been discovered. He heard nothing.

The upstairs hallway was covered in the same burgundy carpet as the downstairs foyer. The walls and ceilings were paneled in dark wood, and the electric lights in faux candelabras set into the wall were dimmed. Immediately before the T-intersection that would lead directly to Esperanza's room, Wayne saw a bar of light escaping beneath a door to his left. He froze, and then continued to pad down the carpeted walkway, holding his breath, praying that no one would hear . . .

A shadow blotted out part of the light. Someone had moved toward the door. Wayne pushed himself against the wall and crouched to retrieve his KA-BAR knife from its sheath. A click as the doorknob was turned from the inside, and then the fragile form of a young woman appeared, her hair tousled from the pillow, looking at Wayne questioningly, and then with accusation in her gaze.

"*Silencio*," Wayne said. "*Vaya a tu cuarto y no diga nada*." Adding a threat to have the rival Santiago cartel slaughter her entire family if she tried to alert anyone, he asked her, "*¿Entiendes?*"

There was a fighting spirit behind the woman's eyes, but she realized she didn't want to have Santiago coming after her personally. Even with the protection of Esperanza and his guards, Santiago's men could be merciless in pursuing and exacting justice from anyone who had wronged the family. That wasn't a risk she was willing to take. She said nothing, but nodded with resignation, realizing that, on this night, she was allowing another man to take her place at the gates of Hades by remaining silent.

Once she had closed the door behind her, Wayne realized he had been holding his breath. That had been too close. He didn't like threatening the young woman—a woman who had likely just gotten snared by the all-consuming power of the Esperanza cartel—but the alternative had been killing her. Had she put up a fight, he would have been forced to go with Plan B, but, thankfully for her, she had acquiesced.

He turned the corner and was grateful to see that no other doorways along the final stretch had lights on behind them. The door at the end of the hall, however, did.

Esperanza's room.

Wayne put his hand on the door handle and took a deep breath. He could hear the raucous cheering of the game show spilling from the TV inside. As Domingo had described the room, Esperanza should be seated on a couch, facing away from the door. Wayne prayed that information was correct, or else things were about to get a lot more difficult.

He waited for the TV audience's cheering to swell, and then opened the door and slipped inside. Esperanza sat on the couch as promised, his back to Wayne. The contestant on the screen was scurrying along an obstacle course, narrowly avoiding hazards before finally being blindsided in the back by a foam pillar and falling to the ball pit below. Esperanza laughed a mucous-laced guffaw that gave way to a coughing fit. Wayne crept up behind him, his knife at the ready in his right hand, his left prepared to clamp around the kingpin's mouth to stifle his dying screams.

Perhaps it was a preternatural sense of danger, for Wayne was certain his approach had been silent, but Esperanza turned around, fear flashing in his eyes before giving way to fiery determination.

"You dare trespass into my home?" the man said in English as he stood and moved toward the corner desk, the drawers of which likely held at least one gun. Wayne cursed his luck. Not only was his target no longer unsuspecting, but he had pegged his assassin as an American.

Time to end this.

Wayne lunged at the fat drug lord, stepping on the back of the couch to launch himself toward his quarry. Esperanza was reaching into a desk drawer when Wayne hit him, knocking the kingpin backward. The assassin maintained contact with his target, slashing at Esperanza's hand as it brought a Beretta from the drawer. Esperanza flinched and dropped the gun onto the floor, shoving back against his assailant. Wayne was surprised at the fat man's strength as he stumbled back toward the couch.

"¡Guardias, ayudame!" Esperanza began to shout. Wayne flung his knife at the drug lord's throat, cutting him off mid-syllable. Esperanza's eyelids fluttered, and his face convulsed in pain and fearful recognition of what had just occurred. A fountain of crimson began to bubble over his lips as he slumped against the desk, and then slid to the floor, dead eyes staring at nothing for all eternity.

Wayne shook his head and pulled the knife from where it had lodged in the man's neck.

"Getting blood all over my favorite knife and everything," he chastised the corpse. Black humor was a crucial component to many in professions that dealt with death on a regular basis. Surgeons, undertakers, cops, soldiers, and whatever the heck his job title was officially supposed to be. Assassin was the closest he could figure. The people he killed—at least, the ones he set out to kill and weren't spur of the moment, self-defense killings like the guard in the kitchen—tended to deserve a quick and painful death, but that didn't make the killing easy for him. On the outside, he was a master assassin, the best the CIA had. On the inside, though, he still struggled with the taking of life. The downside of being a killer with a conscience, Wayne supposed, but he recognized the good that his work did, even if it wrought havoc on his own subconscious at times.

A shout sounded from downstairs, followed by a female voice screaming down the hall. So much for putting the fear of the Santiago clan into the woman. More shouts, nearer now. The guards were coming—too late—to the defense of their boss. Of course, now that also meant Wayne's only route of egress was blocked by gun-toting hooligans. He did not fancy getting into a prolonged gunfight with them. In total, Esperanza's forces were thousands strong, and though Wayne was a crack shot and master strategist, he only had so many bullets.

He turned and looked over the desk and into the black of night. Out the window it was, then. He flashed back to the blueprints he'd studied and thought he remembered a terra cotta awning below one of these windows, but he wasn't sure. He picked up a chair from in front of the desk and smashed one of the legs against the window. The glass shattered and showered deadly shards upon the ground below. Wayne wiped his knife on the carpet so as not to leave a blood trail, secured the blade in its sheath, and then leapt out the window. After a free fall of a few feet, he landed on the terra cotta ledge and slid to the edge, rolling off and landing on the ground below.

As soon as his feet hit the ground, he took off toward the fence, mentally adjusting his escape route to compensate for his new exit point from the house. Shouts sounded from behind as he ducked into the foliage at the perimeter of the property. Reaching the stucco wall bordering the hacienda, he leapt up and grabbed hold of the ledge, hoisting himself up and over. He landed hard on the other side just as bullets tore over the fence and through the space he had just occupied.

One of the two guards on patrol outside the wall ran around the corner and opened fire on Wayne. The American ran toward the dark tangle of rainforest a dozen yards away, ducking and weaving so as not to present an easy target. Wayne heard the hesitation in the man's shots as he tried to draw a bead on his unpredictable mark.

Moments later, Wayne entered the cover of the jungle. Though the guards—the first had been joined by two more now—were still yelling and firing at him, the CIA assassin had the upper hand. He would head toward a known Santiago stronghold several miles through the undergrowth before breaking away toward his exfiltration point. It was dark and they didn't know where he was going. Within a hundred yards—particularly after Esperanza's corpse was discovered and the woman repeated Wayne's threats on behalf of the Santiago cartel—they would assume they *did* know where he was going, which was exactly the kind of diversion he had sought to create.

After five minutes of hot pursuit through the increasingly dense forest, Wayne broke left, realizing he had already lost his pursuers. Of course, once they had decided that Santiago was responsible for the murder of their leader, they would return to the compound and drive to their rival's stronghold, rather than hoofing it through the jungle, but Wayne wanted to make sure the trail was fully set.

Twenty minutes later, he arrived at a clearing where a helicopter was waiting for him.

"About time," said Jordan Finney, the pilot who was sitting up front, door open. "Mission accomplished, I assume?"

"I think I may have just started a cartel war, but yeah, mission accomplished."

Finney shrugged. "Good enough for me. I say let 'em kill each other off for a while. Bolivia's too freakin' hot for my tastes."

Wayne climbed in the back while Finney started the engine and brought the rotors up to speed. Once they were airborne, Wayne watching the black canopy of jungle give way to the endless expanse of night sky, Finney turned to the side and shouted back at his passenger.

"This came for you while you were on mission," he said, handing him a printout from the encrypted onboard fax machine.

RETURN TO MAIN HQ. EMRGNCY MTG AT BIG HOUSE AX RIVER. YOUR SKILLS REQD.

Wayne read the note twice, then flicked his lighter and watched the note burn into black oblivion. The phrasing was off, perhaps an attempt at CIA shorthand by someone outside the agency, but it was the content of the message that gave him pause. While there were plenty of field offices and safe houses in Bolivia and other nations across the globe, "main HQ" would be Langley. Across the Potomac was Washington and the "big house" in D.C. had to be the White House.

So what would the president of the United States need with a CIA assassin? As much as the question intrigued Wayne, he was afraid he wouldn't like the answer.

CHAPTER 5

WASHINGTON, D.C., U.S.A.
WEDNESDAY

Wayne Wilkins had been to the White House three times before. The first time was in eighth grade, a social studies field trip to the nation's capital. He had gotten the quintessential schoolkid tour—the Natural History Museum, Lincoln Memorial, Washington Monument, Capitol Building, and, middle-school Wayne's favorite, the White House. That such power could be wielded from one building, by one man, no less, was fascinating for his developing mind. Unlike some of his classmates, Wayne never aspired to be president. He desired neither the power nor the responsibility of running the most powerful country in the world. But he did aspire to work with that power, to be an arm of it, a force for good in the universe. Those were happier days. Naïve days.

Then, one sunny Tuesday morning in September 2001, nineteen jihadists hijacked some airplanes and went on a kamikaze death spree that claimed the lives of both of Wayne's parents. For good or for ill, this was the catalyst that had driven Wayne to join the military in the wake of the attacks and the buildup to war in Afghanistan. More than a decade of unorthodox service with the Army Rangers and, later, the CIA, had made him an underground legend in covert ops, assassinations, counterterrorism, and other black-budget missions buried so deep that no Freedom of Information Act requests could ever touch them.

His second trip to the White House was shortly after he'd left the Rangers and joined a controversial secret segment of the CIA that targeted American citizens deemed to be a threat to national security. This time he hadn't been invited inside, nor did he particularly feel like darkening the presidential mansion's doorway. He'd just stood outside the gates, staring at the semicircular, second-story balcony for nearly an hour, wondering when his country had gotten so far off course. When that project went belly up—a turn of events Wayne's own actions had a hand in—he was again brought to the White House and excoriated by the vice president and the secretary of state for refusal to obey orders and threatening national security. The president, however, saw promise in Wayne and gave him a position with the National Clandestine Service, the main black ops division of the CIA.

Today, fresh off a chartered flight from La Paz to Reagan National, he had been summoned by the president again. It was the first he'd heard from the White House since joining the National Clandestine Service, and he couldn't fathom why he was being called in. Esperanza was dead, and Wayne had gotten away clean. Mission accomplished; no loose ends. But if it wasn't about the mission, then what?

He grudgingly went through the requisite surrendering of his weapon at the side entrance to the White House. An ID check and metal-detector scan cleared him for entry, and the Secret Service man waved him through.

Inside, another Secret Service agent speed-walked down the hall to meet Wayne. "You're the last to arrive. Please, come this way."

"The last to arrive?" Wayne asked. "Who else is here?"

The agent's only reply was silence as he led the way down the richly appointed corridors of the most famous—and, in many circles, infamous—home in the world. Wayne had expected to be brought to the Oval Office, but instead the agent pushed a camouflaged button that blended into the wood grain of the wall. Two wooden panels slid open, revealing a secret elevator.

"Cool," Wayne said, his confusion and frustration at being called out of the field mitigated by the architectural intrigue hidden in the White House's very walls, mirroring the political smoke and mirrors with which the office housed within was so intimately associated. He loved his country and was proud to serve it in the best ways he knew how. It was the people who ran it that, often, he just couldn't stand.

Wayne stepped into the elevator after the Secret Service man, and they descended six floors into a subbasement that clearly doubled as some sort of emergency bunker. The elevator opened into a narrow hallway. Paintings of former presidents hung from gray, concrete walls. Celebrating the office's history, even in this stark, subterranean corridor. Wayne wasn't sure whether it was reverential or pretentious, but he didn't have long to contemplate the issue.

The agent turned right at a T-intersection and came to a wide door of solid steel. He placed his palm against a silver, biometric pad, and then put his eye to a retinal scanner. The devices reminded Wayne of a darker time more than a year before, when his distrust of those in power truly ripened. His time with the CIA since closing that chapter in his life had renewed his patriotism and his zeal for doing the unspeakable to keep his country safer. But the wounds still stung. You could never put something like that completely behind you, Wayne had concluded. It would always be lurking beneath the surface, tainting perceptions and eroding trust.

Burn me once . . .

The steel door hissed and slid to the left, revealing the room beyond. The agent motioned Wayne inside, and then closed the door behind him, leaving the CIA assassin in the room with four men and one woman—three of the men and the woman he didn't recognize, but one man he most certainly did: President of the United States James Talquin.

"Agent Wilkins, so good of you to join us," said President Talquin. He motioned to an empty seat at the conference table in front of him, between two of the three men seated across from the president's chair. "Please, take a seat."

Wayne obliged, casting sidelong glances at his unknown companions and receiving curious glances in return.

"I know you're all wondering why I've called you out of the field and into this concrete dungeon. Well, first, let's get introductions out of the way. I'll start. My name is James Talquin, and I'm president of the United States of America."

Wayne and the others let out a suppressed chuckle. He *knew* there was a reason he had voted for the man, even if it felt like the lesser of two evils at the time.

The serious-looking man on Talquin's left went next. "Logan Pierce, deputy director of the CIA, National Clandestine Service." Wayne's boss's boss's boss. He'd never met the man, but he'd heard his name bandied about in Langley plenty enough. Despite being well into his forties, Pierce had a full head of thick, black hair, swept back into a ponytail. The strong set of his jaw and reputation for ruthless efficiency was undercut somewhat by a glimmer of something friendly behind the deputy secretary's hard eyes, as though, under different circumstances, he'd be great to go Friday-night bar-hopping with. Whatever circumstances had summoned Wayne and the others to this subterranean chamber had drained the merriment from the room. Though Wayne knew at least part of the source of his pain.

A fifth-generation marine, Pierce had been part of the first wave of soldiers that swept across Hussein's Iraq in Desert Storm. Though the attack was quick, decisive, and overwhelming, resulting in a relatively quick withdrawal of Iraqi forces from Kuwait, it was not without bloodshed. An artillery shell blew off Pierce's left leg and shredded his right. He received a Purple Heart and an honorable discharge, along with the physical therapy to get used to using his prosthetic leg; but that wasn't enough. Four generations of Pierces before him had defended the homeland in the marines. But through a horrible twist of fate, that door was now forever closed to him. His decorated military family, including uncles, cousins, brothers, and his own father, continued to serve with distinction, but he would never join them in that pantheon of military heroes. And that loss was infinitely worse than his missing leg.

He had joined the CIA as an analyst, offering his natural instinct for battlefield tactics on a macro level. Over the next two decades, he had proven himself an effective agent and, later, administrator, rising eventually to his current position as director of NCS. Despite the power and internal prestige that came with his title, it hadn't stopped him from developing a reputation of a different sort. The white whale of destiny had stolen his leg from him, and, like Captain Ahab, he couldn't quite let it go.

"Wayne Wilkins, National Clandestine Service," Wayne said, leading the charge for his side of the table. What he did for the NCS classified far beyond the CIA's official public mandate, so he chose not to elaborate further. Men like him were often used to create plausible deniability between the controversial nature of necessary wet work and the public faces of the government. Which made his presence here, with the most public face of all, even more puzzling.

"Mahmoud Nasef, Intel, MENA," said an Arab-looking man in his late twenties to Pierce's left. MENA was the CIA's designation for divisions focused on the Middle East and North Africa. Which, in the years since 9/11, had required a lot of manpower. Black-framed glasses perched on Nasef's nose above a neatly trimmed goatee. He seemed nervous, as though he was out of his element here in the president's secret meeting. But then, Wayne reflected, weren't they all.

"Robert Suarez, NCS," said a dusky-complexioned Hispanic man with the tiniest trace of a Latin accent. Wayne hadn't worked with Suarez before, though he had heard his name mentioned once or twice before at Langley. He was supposedly a whiz with technological gadgets and computer systems, a tremendous boon for a field agent with combat experience.

"Janan Ibrahim, Office of Terrorism Analytics," said the only woman in the room. Wayne pegged her to be around his age, mid-thirties. She wore a royal-blue scarf around her head, hiding her hair from view. The presence of Ibrahim and Nasef gave Wayne an idea of where the upcoming op would be. But Pierce and Talquin being here intimated this would be far beyond the scope of any mission he'd undertaken before.

"Quick and to the point," Talquin said, wearing a pleased look that wasn't quite a smile. "Very good. Precision and focus is exactly what we need from you. What your country needs from you."

The president rose from his chair. Wayne started to rise out of respect, but Talquin waved him down. "Unless you'd prefer to join me in presenting, Agent Wilkins, I'd prefer it if you all remained seated for the time being."

"Yes, Mr. President," Wayne said, returning to his chair, his face growing warm from the stares that were surely upon him now.

Talquin picked up a small, black remote from the desk and clicked a series of buttons. The lights dimmed, and the screen behind him illuminated. A photo of Christine Needham, the administration's special ambassador to the Middle East, speaking before the UN General Assembly last year, appeared on the screen.

"I'm sure you're all familiar with Ambassador Needham. She's been helping the secretary of state and me in our effort to get the nations and factions of the Middle East to sit down for another peace summit, the biggest and most comprehensive one of the modern era. Some people in the region aren't happy about that prospect. And they just made their voices heard."

He clicked the remote again. An image captured from a surveillance camera replaced the picture of Needham. Three black SUVs were parked on the tarmac next to a Gulfstream. Muzzle flashes created sparks of light on the image, and smoke was billowing from one of the vehicles.

"This was taken twelve hours ago at Dubai International Airport. Just moments after the ambassador's plane landed, three airport security SUVs surrounded the aircraft. Armed men climbed out of the vehicles and stormed her plane as soon as it was on the ground. The plane's crew is dead. Of her team of three staff members traveling with her, one is dead, one is in critical condition in a Dubai hospital, and one is missing. The ambassador herself is also missing.

"Needless to say, these men were not airport security personnel. The SUVs were rigged to explode shortly after this all went down, and the ensuing fireballs sent the Dubai authorities chasing their tails."

Wayne couldn't help but reflect on the surrealism of being briefed for a mission by the president himself. This was about as closed-circle as you could get, even in the secret-laden world of Washington powerbrokers.

Talquin clicked to another slide. This showed an aerial shot of the Dubai airport, with some sort of architectural schematics superimposed on the image.

"There are service tunnels that run underneath the airport. We think that's how they got away. Unfortunately, the explosions created enough of a diversion to cover their tracks until they could disappear. Sheikh Khalid bin Rashid al-Futaim, ruler of Dubai and prime minister of the United Arab Emirates, has promised to track track down the culprits and recover the ambassador safely, but I'm afraid Ambassador Needham and what her work represents to our national security interests is too important to entrust solely to a foreign power, ally or not."

"And that's where we come in," Wayne surmised.

"Yes, but unfortunately, it's not that simple. The Dubai police are extremely averse to foreign agents operating on their territory after last month's incident with Agent Akers."

Shawn Akers had been an undercover CIA agent investigating a Dubai-based holding company that had ties to several jihadist organizations. When he was discovered inside the holding company's offices after hours, Akers got into a shootout with security personnel. Two Emiratis had died in the firefight, Akers' cover was blown, and the United Arab Emirates had withdrawn its support for the peace summit in retaliation for the United States' violation of its sovereignty.

"And that was hardly the first such incident in the city. Mossad agents assassinated Hamas leader Mahoud al-Mabhouh in a Dubai hotel back in 2010. And I don't need to tell you that, despite the UAE's alliance with us, they are no friend to Israel."

The Jewish state didn't have many friends these days, and virtually none in the region, though the UAE was somewhat less vocal in its animosity toward the nation than some other regional powers. The United States had long been one of Israel's staunchest supporters, but the federal pocketbook was not as full as it once was. Political tides were shifting both at home and with long-standing Israeli allies in Europe, and without some sort of peace deal, there was no guarantee that America would be able to support the beleaguered nation through the next crisis. In the Middle East, it seemed, there was always at least one new crisis brewing. And at least half of them seemed to be directed at Israel.

"Dubai is very concerned with controlling its image, so any outside intrusion into this admittedly embarrassing situation for the emirate would be met with force. I've already requested that American agents be allowed to help locate the ambassador, but Sheikh Khalid has steadfastly refused. Obviously, considering our naval presence there and the ever-present possibility of war with Iran, we don't want to press our luck with the Emirati royal family, but we can't just sit back and see if the Dubai police can drudge up a corpse for us in a few months. We need Ambassador Needham back alive, and we need her now."

"Sir, if I may," Suarez interjected. "What was the ambassador doing in Dubai?"

"Good question, Suarez, and, to be honest, we don't know. She had just finished up meetings with Prime Minister Shihmanter in Tel Aviv and with President Qassim in Cairo. The next item on her official agenda was a meeting with me in the Oval Office, slated for tomorrow morning. In theory, she was supposed to be arriving in D.C. early this morning and using today to recover from jet lag and prepare for our meeting. Instead, she chartered a private plane on her own dime for the flight to Dubai, likely to remain under the radar from official channels. I suspect she was going to be lobbying Sheikh Khalid for his support on Molina's peace summit, which makes the whole thing all the more complicated. Molina and I both denied her previous requests to speak with the sheikh, as I believe that kind of surreptitious dealing could easily blow up in our faces, shattering an already tenuous relationship with the UAE. We don't need this to explode into another scandal, particularly now that we stand at the brink of the greatest chance for a lasting peace in the Middle East since before World War II."

Perhaps Talquin was in politician mode, trying to bolster the group's hopes and reinforce the importance of the mission, or perhaps he truly was that optimistic, but Wayne had his doubts about peace in the Middle East happening anytime soon, peace summit or not. The cradle of civilization had been fraught with conflicts between its myriad shifting factions over religious, ethnic, and social differences since long before the dawn of Islam, Christianity, or even Judaism. Peace summit or not, he saw no reason why an outside power, long viewed with suspicion as an imperialist exploiter, would be able to assuage 5,000 years of tumultuous conflict. Still, hope springs eternal, and even if Wayne believed that nothing short of the Second Coming of Christ would truly bring peace to the region, Needham's work would at least help temper some of the conflicts for the short-term. Of course, her death, assuming they were not already too late, could also have the opposite effect on the region, fanning the flames of fanaticism as a powerful unifying force for respectful dialogue was wiped out. So Wayne kept listening.

"The ambassador's recovery is crucial to the success of the proposed peace summit. If she dies, so too may this opportunity to bring the Middle East back from the brink. Mass terrorism, genocide, skyrocketing energy prices . . . and, of course, this may be our last chance to get the Arab nations to accept Israel as a permanent fixture in the region."

Another prospect Wayne doubted. The persecution of the fledgling Jewish nation had been foretold centuries before its citizens' ancestors had been cast out from the Hebrews' ancestral homeland in the first century AD. Though he didn't agree with some of the tactics Israel used to reinforce its position in the region, he understood their motivations. Being attacked by your neighbors just days after your country was formed, and then on a regular basis in the decades that followed, tended to instill a sense of distrust and self-reliance in a nation's mentality. But though Israel had been besieged by its neighbors since its inception, Wayne had been surprised to find a growing trend among its traditional Western allies in Europe and North America to vilify Israel, while unquestioningly siding with the Palestinians, despite clear terrorist activities on the part of Hamas, Hezbollah, and the PLO. In truth, there were no easy answers to any of the issues between Israel and Palestine. Both peoples had occupied the land for generations, and both sides had dug in their heels. Of course, as Israel had learned over the years, it was rather difficult to negotiate with someone whose primary talking point was advocating the destruction of your homeland

and your people. The Jews had dealt with that line far too many times throughout their history. Perhaps, Wayne thought, the summit would be able to help address those seemingly impossible questions. But without the ambassador, all that could be thrown into jeopardy.

The president paused as he dabbed his forehead with a handkerchief. "And beyond all that, Ambassador Needham is a great friend. Her father and mine were colleagues in the Senate together years back, and she has done great work for this country. This cannot be how it ends for her or for her passion to finally bring peace to the Middle East.

"Deputy Director Pierce will be overseeing this mission personally." Talquin gestured to his left. "Agent Ibrahim here will be your primary contact in Washington during the mission. She will have full access to the CIA's and the NSA's computer servers, satellites, databases, scanners, and all the fun tools both agencies have gotten in trouble for over the past few years, including several more that thankfully haven't leaked yet. She's also fluent in Urdu, Farsi, Hebrew, and five dialects of Arabic, so she should be able to help you out on that front. Agent Nasef is fluent in Arabic and knows some Farsi; and Agent Wilkins, I understand you speak and understand some Arabic."

"*Na'am*," Wayne said, the Arabic word for *yes*.

"Good. Considering your breadth of experience in the region and undercover in civilian population centers, you'll be taking point on this one."

Wayne blinked. "Yes, sir." He was surprised, but what else could he say?

"Agent Suarez, you'll be our resident tech guru in the field. Agent Ibrahim will fit you all out with some pretty interesting gear that the Office of Science and Technology has been working on, but if you run across anything you can't analyze in the field, send it back to her and she'll take care of it. Obviously, I've got a schedule to keep, but report regularly to Ibrahim, and Pierce will keep me in the loop."

Talquin looked at each of the three field members in turn. When he reached Wayne, the agent felt the passion and intensity of the man behind the stare. This wasn't just any mission.

He wasn't just offing Bolivian drug lords or Afghani terrorists anymore. This was bigger than anything he had done for the CIA or for the army before that.

"I'm sure I don't need to impress upon you the importance of this mission, both for the future of the Middle East and for our own national security." Talquin put his palms on the table and leaned forward slightly. "Go get her back, men."

Wayne nodded. "Hooah."

CHAPTER 6

Dubai, United Arab Emirates
Thursday

The Gulfstream V shook as another burst of turbulence buffeted the fuselage on the final descent toward DXB. Wayne and his new teammates were comfortably seated in first-class-style chairs toward the front of the otherwise-unoccupied plane. They had tried to sleep as much as possible during the flight, each man knowing from experience that, once the operation was in play, there was no knowing when the next opportunity for rest would come. Now that the sands of the expansive Arabian Desert below were giving way to spots of civilization, they began to stir, their minds switching to mission mode.

Wayne was ready for action. Though he appreciated the chance to rest en route, he realized that the fourteen-hour flight had cost them precious mission time. He understood President Talquin's desire for this mission to be under the radar. Unfortunately, more than twenty-four hours had passed since the ambassador's abduction, and the trail her kidnappers left wasn't getting any warmer. The one part that brought some semblance of solace was the fact that they had taken Needham prisoner instead of killing her outright. They would have had a reason for doing so, and chances were that she was still alive. For now, at least.

This wasn't the first time Wayne had worked for the federal government off the official record. Many of his missions with both the Rangers and the CIA had been clandestine, offering the powers-that-be plausible deniability should something go horribly wrong. He had also been briefly involved with a secret subset of the CIA known only as the Division, a covert containment unit left over from the Cold War that still left a bad taste in his mouth. Since joining the CIA, he was cautiously hopeful that this time around would be different.

Even this mission was different from most of his post-Division work. The primary mission objective was ensuring the safe return of a United States ambassador, rather than the elimination of one or more targets someone above his pay grade had decided would better serve America's interests dead than alive. But Wayne had seen photos of the carnage leveled at the ambassador's plane, and he knew full well the sort of fanatical violence that could breed in the Middle East. He had no illusions that this mission wouldn't involve a body count by its conclusion.

Further, several of his missions over the years had involved infiltrating enemy organizations through deception and, when the situation warranted, brute force. And as the president had said, he had a wealth of professional experience in the region as well as operating in major metropolitan centers.

Unlike his time with the Division and much of his time in the CIA and with the Rangers, however, Wayne was working directly with a team. Leading it, no less. Directly after their meeting with the president, Pierce had briefed the agents on their roles for the mission. Suarez was a technical wunderkind, with an uncanny knack for jury-rigging electronic devices. Nasef, meanwhile, was a demolitions expert, with experience setting and detonating strategic charges as well as deactivating IEDs and traditional bombs. His knowledge of the region's cultures and conflicts—his father was Saudi, his mother Bahraini—would also be useful, as would the language skills that dwarfed Wayne's own moderate proficiency. And, of course, all three were well versed in firefights with sidearms as well as semi-auto and automatic weapons.

Wayne would serve as the team's leader, bringing his lateral thinking abilities, vast array of undercover experience, and infiltration techniques for the battlefield and for civilian areas to bear as master strategist for the mission. It had been a while since he had planned and executed missions that included more than one main player, so planning for a team of three primary actors instead of just a solo op would be an interesting and challenging change of pace.

Ibrahim, Wayne learned, was a second-generation American citizen of Iranian heritage. She held a doctorate in computer science from MIT and another in international relations from Cambridge. Highly adept in all things digital and well versed in the history and complexity of the region's peoples and conflicts, Ibrahim also brought to bear another invaluable trait: she was fluent in nine languages, including Urdu, Farsi, Hebrew, and five dialects of Arabic.

She had given the team an array of gadgets, including disassembled pistols disguised as fully functioning laptops, scrambled sat phones, secure uplink hookups, and several other devices Wayne hoped not to have to use. Though she would be staying stateside, Ibrahim would be accessible at all times during the op, and would be the primary link between the team and the president.

Wayne had practiced assembling and disassembling the laptop/pistol three times already during the flight, scoured maps and schematics of the Dubai airport and the city itself, and read the Lonely Planet guide to the desert metropolis cover to cover twice. Now he found himself at once bored and antsy.

"So what drew you to the CIA, Suarez?" Wayne asked.

"Me?" He looked a little put out by the question, and then gave a quick, nervous chuckle. "I'm not proud of my story, but it's what brought me to who I am today. My father's the pastor at a pretty big church outside El Paso. Great man of God; but having that many congregants demanding your time can chip away at your family time. I'm the youngest of three boys, and I guess I lived up to the stereotype of a pastor's kid. I rebelled. My mama, God rest her soul, died from cancer when I was twelve, so my dad had to raise two teenagers and one almost-teenager by himself, along with helping out hundreds of other hurting souls. After years of acting out in school, messing around with girls, and drinking on the sly, I finally went too far."

Nasef had looked up from the field report he was studying, also apparently eager to get to know his teammates before they landed.

"I was seventeen, a year behind the wheel and four behind the bottle," Suarez continued. "There was a big party over at

Eddie Gonzalez's house. You know the kind: lots of liquor, vomiting in the bushes, illicit liaisons in the bedrooms upstairs. Well, I was mad at my dad for one thing or another, so I decided to go all out that night. I must've had five or six beers in me when Eddie challenged me to a race. He had this hot little Mustang he'd redone, and all I had was my Civic. But machismo, alcohol, and teenage stupidity mixing all together does not make for level-headed decision making. So Eddie gets in his Mustang and me in my Civic, and we take off, two laps around the block, first one to hit the driveway the second time around wins."

Suarez smirked sadly as his gaze found the floor, focused on a life-changing scene many years before. "We took off, him leading as we rounded the first corner. By the end of the first lap, he had a full car length on me. Well, safety be damned, I couldn't lose face in front of all our friends, so I put the pedal to the metal that second lap. I made the first two turns, barely. The third one, I clipped Eddie's bumper, causing us both to spiral out of control. Eddie's Mustang slammed into a light pole, flinging him through the windshield and onto the pavement, where my Civic ran him over. Where *I* ran him over."

A single tear began to trickle down Suarez's cheek. He didn't wipe it away. "I spent the night in jail, while the cops sorted out the charges. DUI, vehicular manslaughter, underage drinking, reckless driving. If they charged me as an adult, which they wanted to, I was looking at ten to fifteen years, minimum. But the judge was a member of my papa's church, and he offered me a deal: I could avoid prison time and a felony on my record if I enlisted in a branch of the armed forces and kept my nose clean for at least five years. I accepted, and they sealed my record. I picked the marines. They whipped me into shape, in every sense of the word, but it wasn't fear of jail that kept me going. It was remorse for taking my friend's life. It's been ten years since I first enlisted, four since I was tapped by the DIA, and two since I moved over to the CIA, but I'm incredibly grateful every day for the discipline and sense of honor that the marines instilled in me. I just wish it hadn't taken such a drastic wake-up call to get me there."

"Dang, man," Wayne said. "That's rough."

"For better or worse, it's made me who I am today. Who we are is the sum of our experiences and how we choose to react to them, my *abuela* used to say. In Spanish, of course, though it was true regardless of the language."

Wise words, Wayne thought.

"My own experiences and reactions certainly shaped me," Nasef said. "After 9/11, as I'm sure you both know, Arabs and Muslims weren't exactly the most welcome faces in many places in the country. I was a teenager when it happened. My junior year of high school. And though my observance of the five pillars of the faith might have made me seem different or even a little weird before, after the towers fell, I learned what it meant to be hated and feared. Everywhere I went, I was met with suspicion. Maybe not overtly, but it was clear as day in their eyes. Was I going to blow them up? Was I wearing a jacket because it was cold out, or because I was concealing a suicide bomb underneath? I had gone from being a quirky part of our American melting pot to a potential enemy terrorist. And it didn't feel good.

"I was determined to change that. I dual-majored in international relations and Middle Eastern history, graduated top of my class in each, and applied to the CIA. Seemingly against all odds, I got in on my first try. As it turned out, the nationwide fear that had propelled me to do something for Arabs' image in our country had also created an opportunity for me. Intelligence agencies, just like the military, had downsized a lot of Arabs and other Muslims in the wake of the attacks and the buildups to the wars in Afghanistan and Iraq. My language skills and cultural knowledge of the nations we were trying to stabilize and the terrorists we were fighting made me a prime candidate, so they gave me a shot. And, thank Allah, the CIA seems to be pleased with the choice they made in me."

"Hmm," Suarez grunted under his breath.

"You got a problem serving with a Muslim, Suarez? If you do, now's the time to say it."

"No, it's just weird is all. No offense or anything, but I've spent most of my career being shot at by people who look like you."

"Well, no offense, *ese*, but I've spent most of my life hiring people who look like you outside of Home Depot to work on my yard."

"Why you racist son of a—"

"Hey, knock it off you two," Wayne interjected. "Whitey says chill out."

His self-deprecating comment served to break the tension, eliciting chuckles from Nasef and Suarez alike.

"Sorry, man," Suarez said. "Nothing personal. It's just something I've got to get used to is all. It won't be a problem. I'm looking forward to serving with you."

"Don't worry about it, Mexican," Nasef said with a wink. "I'm sorry, too."

"Thanks Mr. A-rab," Suarez retorted with a grin, emphasizing the first syllable *à la* the first President Bush.

"Thank God," Wayne said. "I was afraid I'd have to leave you knuckleheads here on the plane and go save the ambassador by myself."

"See, that's just like white guys, trying to steal all the glory for themselves," Suarez said, giving Wayne a playful punch on the shoulder.

"All right, Mr. Melanin-Deficient, what's your story?" Nasef said.

Wayne chuckled uncomfortably. He didn't like talking about himself, but then, these guys were going to be closer than a brother for the duration of the mission at least. They'd shared their stories with him. It was only fair that he return the favor.

"I was a college kid when 9/11 hit. Just a semester or two away from graduation, but I turned in my degree for a gun. My mom worked in Tower One. My dad was a first responder. I became an orphan that day. The terrorists hadn't just declared jihad on my country. They declared it on my family. And so I was more than happy to attack them back. I was a war machine of singular focus, drawing the attention of the higher-ups who drafted me into a series of increasingly questionable black-ops missions. Somewhere along the way, I regained my humanity, realizing that the 9/11 hijackers only represented a small segment of the Middle Eastern population, and I was finally able to mourn my parents properly. Eventually, I got selected for a secret branch of the CIA doing some . . . unorthodox work on the home front. After that gig ended, I transferred to NCS, and now I'm here leading you guys."

"You led anything like this before?" Suarez asked.

Wayne smiled. "Come on, Suarez, you know the line. Every op is unique and has to be treated as such. There are no replays, no second laps. Plus, the mission zone is a highly populated civilian area within an allied nation that has expressly forbidden the United States from doing what we're going in there to do. Intel is minimal, the political and national security implications for failure or for having our cover blown are high, and, no offense to any of you, but we're the newest unit in the entire federal government payroll. So to answer your question, I've got plenty of experience with most of the techniques likely to come into play on this mission, but have I done anything exactly like this before? No. No one has.'

An electronic tone sounded, followed by the captain's voice on the PA system. "We're on our final approach. We should be on the ground in five."

Wayne grimaced to himself. Five minutes. And then the real fun began.

CHAPTER 7

DUBAI, UNITED ARAB EMIRATES

Wayne looked out the window at the shimmering spectacle of Dubai rising out of the endless desert sands. The sunlight glinted off glass and steel skyscrapers, framed on one side by the waters of the Gulf. The name of the Gulf—separating the Arabian Peninsula from Iran and Central Asia—had long been a contentious issue between Arabs and Iranians. Iran and much of the western world referred to it as the Persian Gulf, recognizing the long history of the region as the seat of the once-great Persian Empire and its descendants who still inhabited the land. The Arab world—ethnically, culturally, and often religiously distinct from the Persians—insisted that the proper name was the Arabian Gulf. Many reporters in the region, in an effort to not offend any of their readers or viewership, referred to it simply as "the Gulf." Everyone knew what they were talking about even without the descriptor. It was the only gulf that really mattered around here, and by far the most politically, economically, and strategically important gulf in the world.

Wayne and his team braced themselves in their seats as the plane descended to the runway, hovered as it leveled its wheels, and then made contact with the tarmac. Two minutes later, they had taxied to their gate—a private one reserved for visiting dignitaries and corporate elites who didn't wish to spend their time waiting in lines or rubbing elbows with the hoi polloi.

Their cover was that they were American businessmen trying to get a feel for the city and meeting with potential investors for a hotel construction project. Obviously, none of these meetings would ever play out, and the company they represented was a dead-end shell corporation created by the CIA specifically for this purpose. The cover did, however, allow them to smuggle the weapons and equipment they'd need into the country. In Dubai and the United Arab Emirates, private ownership of firearms was strictly prohibited.

As if that stopped the terrorists from gunning down the ambassador's staff, Wayne mused as the flight attendant lowered the stairs to the private hangar. They would have to be very careful not to run afoul of the local authorities. The cards were stacked against them enough already, and Wayne didn't want to make things harder for themselves.

The desert heat hit Wayne like a blast in the face as he led the team down the stairs. *But it's a dry heat* was hardly a comfort when the temperature was in excess of 110 degrees. Ten seconds off the plane and he was already sweating.

An air-conditioned airport shuttle met the team at the bottom of the air-stairs and transported them to the ostentatiously designed terminal. In many ways, Dubai International Airport was indicative of the spirit of the metropolis itself: luxurious, its quasi-futuristic design an homage to its Arabic heritage, and, above all else, superlatively large. The baggage handling system was the largest and deepest in the world, and it was host to the largest airplane hangars in the world. The largest of the three terminals, Terminal 3, was the largest airport terminal in the world and the largest building in the world by floor space. A major Middle Eastern hub that hosted direct flights to every continent save Antarctica, the airport was the busiest in the world for international passenger traffic. A generation before, the city's main airport had been a small, backwater landing strip in the middle of a relatively minor port on the Arabian Gulf. Now, much like the city it served, Dubai International Airport was a paradoxical beacon of progress and decadence, at war with its own heritage and culture in its pursuit of growth, and surrounded by the untamed desert.

Wayne had heard rumors that the Dubai government regularly paid off al-Qaeda to keep the terrorists at bay. The city was chock full of prime targets, right in the terrorist network's backyard, and, whether those rumors held any truth or not, it was a wonder that none of them had sought to wipe out what could be construed as a Western-influence blot on the "holy" Arabic Peninsula. Of course, there was always the chance that the attack at the airport was merely a sign of things to come. It took a great deal of planning, intelligence, and brazenness to pull off the kidnapping of an American ambassador on friendly soil, particularly when even her superiors didn't realize she was coming to Dubai. Wayne's intuition told him that this was only the beginning of a much larger endgame.

"Man, check this place out," Suarez said, eyes on the ceiling.

Wayne looked up. From gilded columns easily a hundred feet high flew a series of thin sails hardened into wind-filled shapes, reflecting the city's maritime past and its commitment to forward momentum. Painted windows along the arabesque ceiling revealed a stylized nighttime sky Scheherazade would have been proud of. Kiosks selling perfumes, incense, silk scarves, and kitschy souvenirs dotted the concourse, trying to squeeze a few more dirhams out of departing travelers, and giving those arriving a taste of the shopping culture that had become a new national pastime for the city.

Wayne led the team through a long, white pavilion at the end of which an array of customs agents manned their stations. Though the terminal itself was crowded with people festooned with a wide variety of cultural attire—both from within the Middle East and from outside the region—here, the employees were locals. Government jobs, held by Emirati citizens, a demographic whose representation in the Emirate had dwindled to a mere seventeen percent. Here in the city itself, the glittering metropolis built to attract investors, businesspeople, and rich tourists from the world over, that percentage was even lower, as the desert towns and villages further from the coast had not drawn expatriates in the same way.

The team split up, Wayne and Suarez getting in line for one agent, Nasef for another. They were here together, and their cover provided enough clout for them not to be hassled about their bags in a random search. There were weapons in there, and all the tools Ibrahim had provided them with, but none of it could be identified as such in its current form. Another ingenious trick of the trade, breaking down guns and other occupational necessities into innocuous-looking but easily assembled components and disguising those as razors, shaving cream cans, and other standard traveling fare.

Next was customs—here on business, nothing to declare, getting their fake but not-too-fresh-looking passports stamped with a ninety-day tourist visa. Once officially in the country, the team headed to the rental-car desk, where Wayne used his shell-company credit card to rent two black Land Rovers, a model as ubiquitous in Dubai as Civics or Accords were in the US.

"Suarez and I will go to the hospital and see if we can get anything out of the survivor," Wayne said once the three of them were alone by their cars, keys in hand. "Nasef, I want you to recon the entrance to the tunnels where the terrorists likely made their escape. Entrances, exits, security, nearby foot and vehicular traffic: anything that could help or hurt our successful search of and escape from the area. We shouldn't need more than an hour at the hospital—provided Mr. Weiland hasn't slipped back into a coma. Once we're done, we'll join you for infiltration, hopefully with some new intel in hand. If there's someone suspicious on site, follow them and we'll stay in contact over the radios."

He tapped his right ear, into which he had already inserted the tiny, clear micro-transmitter that, when activated, would keep the team connected to each other at distances of up to ten miles. Any further than that, and they'd have to use the special satellite phones Ibrahim had given each of them. Externally, each looked like a Samsung Galaxy Note—big screen, built-in stylus, the works. Inside, however, was a different matter. The tech wizards at the CIA had filled each of the devices with thousands of dollars' worth of proprietary technology, from secure fingerprint scanners and real-time infrared mapping technology to scrambled satellite connections and crypto-analysis software. Though the odds for this mission were not naturally in their favor, Talquin's men had done what they could to give the team a fighting chance.

"And if I see the ambassador? Or somebody starts shooting at me?" Nasef asked.

"You can engage, but low-contact only. If they've left a sentry behind or, for some reason, decided to set up camp there, which I find highly unlikely, simply observe from afar unless actively engaged by the enemy. If by some stroke of luck the ambassador is on site and you get a visual, contact us immediately, but observe and assess only. Unless, of course, her life is in imminent danger. Then move, but carefully. If we find her only to accidentally kill her in the crossfire . . ." He didn't have to finish the thought. Everyone present had already realized the steep consequences of failure, but to fail because of a poor decision on their part would be far worse.

They climbed into their respective vehicles—Wayne and Suarez in one, Nasef in the other—and drove out of the parking garage, Wayne bearing southwest down the coast toward the hospital, Nasef heading east to loop around for the external entrance to the maintenance tunnels.

"You think Weiland will be able to tell us anything?" Suarez asked once they were clear of the snarl of cloverleafs and flyovers that constituted the airport area's exit.

Wayne shrugged. "*If* he's able to speak, and *if* he actually saw something of value, then yeah, maybe. Let's just say I've got my fingers crossed, but I'm not counting my chickens just yet."

The hospital was several miles away, but the drive would give Wayne a chance to acquaint himself with the city. He had studied maps and guide books on the plane ride in, and he'd caught a few *60 Minutes* specials about the revolutionary desert metropolis, but nothing compared to being on the ground.

The Dubai skyline almost looked as though it had been designed to be seen as a skyline. Most of the iconic skyscrapers were set along Sheikh Zayed Road—the main thoroughfare through the city that ran parallel to the Gulf coast a few kilometers away. Like the Egyptian cities of old or the Australian metropolises of today, most desert settlements tended to hug the sources of water. The United Arab Emirates was in a section of the Arabian Peninsula called Rub al-Khali, or the Empty Quarter, so named for its inhospitable conditions and the relative lack of permanent settlements in the area. Along the coastal areas, including Gulf nations such as Bahrain, Qatar, Oman, and the UAE, the locals had bucked this trend with a building boom that allowed city planners carte blanche to shape a metropolis from scratch.

Dubai had been a relatively small Arab town since its founding in the third or fourth century AD. Its claim to fame for centuries had been its pearl-diving industry, but the advent of Japanese synthetic pearl growing in the 1930s had caused a precipitous drop in Dubai's market share. The discovery of oil in its neighboring sister emirate of Abu Dhabi, followed by Dubai's own discovery in 1966, had brought another reversal of fortune for the emirate. And in the 1980s, a forward-thinking sheikh began to chart a path that would turn the modest city of Dubai into a global metropolis.

Sheikh Rashid bin Saeed al-Maktoum realized that the emirate's oil reserves would not last forever, and so he decided to invest back into the city, creating the blueprint for a unique project that would draw investment from all over the world. Harkening back to its historical significance as a trade city, owing to its proximity to Persia, Dubai was to be a world banking hub on par with London and Hong Kong. It was to be *the* place for the world's elite and wealthy to do business, vacation, shop, hold conventions, and invest. It was to be Vegas without the vice, New York without the crime, Disneyland for the rich and famous—and the rich and unknown.

The UAE being an absolute monarchy, the royal family of Dubai owned a controlling stake in many key real-estate development firms that would take the lead in shaping the audacious project. This internal investment fueled external investment, a snowballing cycle that brought—at its building peak—one-third of the world's high-rise cranes to the growing skyline of Dubai. Many large tracts of land were designated as zones for superlatives. Dubai Healthcare City, the most innovative and high-quality, health-centered complex in the world. Dubai Mall, the largest and most glamorous mall in the world. The world's tallest building, the sleekest metro system, the world's first underwater hotel, the world's first in-mall skiing slope, the world's first seven-star hotel. Private islands dredged from the bottom of the Gulf, reachable only by private yacht. The world's largest theme park complex—a 109-square-mile goliath more than twice the size of Walt Disney World. The prevailing wisdom seemed to be that if something was worth building in Dubai, it was worth building bigger and better than anyone ever had before.

And then the global economic crisis hit. As external investors retreated to safer bets in their home countries, much of the funding for half-finished projects in Dubai dried up. The price of oil plummeted, hindering the investment ability of both the Dubai government and of other Arab investors. Dubai had struggled back into the growth phase, but it had been a long and painful process. Momentum was lost, and several key projects had fallen into disrepair or otherwise regressed in the intervening years, prompting their investors to write them off. It was a chimerical city of contrasts: futuristic buildings in an otherwise hostile desert wasteland; all the semblances of Western modernity built in a Muslim dictatorship.

Wayne crossed the Dubai Creek, a wide waterway running in from the Gulf that split the town in two. In truth, the name was a misnomer, as the "creek" was merely an inlet from the Gulf that had been dredged to allow more and more water traffic further into the city. Despite its lack of water flow, it did provide a convenient boundary line and reference point for dividing the city. To the northeast lay the older parts of the city—Deira, Al Mamzar, Hor Al Anz, Abu Hail, and, just a few miles further, the border with the neighboring emirate of Sharjah. To the southwest, Sheikh Zayed Road and nearly all the iconic buildings and superlative projects that Dubai had become known for. There were some exceptions, as parts of the old city—such as the market district of Karama or the residential district of Jumeirah—were on the "new" side of the creek, while Dubai Festival City—a new project encompassing a sizable mall and convention center, hotels, schools, and thousands of freshly built homes—was on the "old" side, but for the most part, the creek was the dividing line, much as "the tracks" often were in American cities.

Traffic was awful, with roadwork forcing cars into bottlenecks or detours. Horns were laid on in traditional Middle Eastern fashion, a sonorous cacophony somewhere on the scale of a South African World Cup match, though there was no patriotic exuberance behind these noisemakers.

Wayne noticed how many luxury cars were on the road around them. In fact, almost all the cars were European imports, with nary a Kia or Chrysler in sight. In the strange world of Dubai, driving a car that would stick out like a gold-plated thumb almost anywhere else was the best way to blend in.

A series of loud, electronic chirps sounded behind them. Wayne glanced in the rear-view mirror to see the very thing he'd wished to avoid, especially this early in the mission: a cop car. The driver signaled for Wayne to pull over, which he did, reluctantly. Two police officers got out of the vehicle, service pistols drawn, and walked toward the car in firing stances.

"Oh good," Wayne said. "A welcoming committee."

CHAPTER 8

DUBAI, UNITED ARAB EMIRATES

Christine Needham awoke to a smelly, swarthy man shouting in her face. She blinked to clear the fog from her mind as the bearded man, dressed in a dirty, white tank top and cargo shorts, smiled to see her arouse from her restless slumber. Her hands were tied behind her back with nylon zip-ties, and her face rubbed in the cool grit of the sand-strewn, concrete floor as she lay on her side. A piece of cloth that tasted vaguely of oil and dirt was wrapped tightly around her head and forced through her open mouth. She struggled to focus as the room seemed to tilt on edge.

Where am I?

The sonorous tones of the adhan—the Muslim call to prayer—floated above the distant drones of traffic, but mosques were ubiquitous in Islamic countries. Not too far from civilization, at least, but her current circumstances didn't offer much hope of joining the bustle of humanity that was surely no more than a mile away.

Her prison was a small, stark room with cinderblock walls and plaster ceiling, all painted white. A film of fine, desert sand coated the walls and had congregated in swirling patterns across the floor. Light filtered through a small, grated window high up on the far wall, and a shadeless table lamp sat on a stool in the corner. Her hirsute, hygiene-averse alarm clock was beating on a steel door beneath the window. The door opened, and the man disappeared through it, closing the exit behind him.

She tried to sit up, shuffling her legs across the floor as the sand scoured her shins. Her clothes, though filthy with smoke, dirt, and blood, were intact.

How had she gotten here, wherever *here* was? She fought against her dazed state to recall the final events before she lost consciousness. The plane landing at DXB. The air-stairs descending. Black SUVs. Angry men with angrier rifles. Shouting. Ear-splitting percussion of gunfire. Ben falling down the stairs face first, his shirt blossoming in crimson stains. Burlap in her nostrils. And the scent of something else, until everything faded to a chemical black.

Then nothing until the bearded man's shouts awoke her just a few minutes ago. How long had she been out? Who had taken her? Where was she? Where was her staff?

The image of Ben falling to the ground invaded her thoughts again. Tears welled in her eyes, both at the death of her loyal assistant and at her plight. Voices from the other side of the door. She blinked away the tears and tried to focus her thinking. Even though she felt absolutely broken inside and out, she knew she couldn't show weakness to whoever came through that door.

What Christine assumed to be a deadbolt screeched, and the heavy door swung inward. Through it stepped another Middle Eastern man, this one well kempt and—dare she say it—somewhat attractive. At least, to someone not currently bound and kidnapped in this cinder-block dungeon. His beard was trimmed shorter than that of his hirsute colleague who had initially woken her, and his long-sleeved, white shirt and fresh-starched khakis looked as though they had been cleaned and pressed at some point in the last twenty-four hours.

"Ambassador Needham," he said in a calm, somewhat British-accented voice, pausing by the open door. "So kind of you to join us at this momentous point in history. I do apologize for your accommodation, but rest assured, you won't be staying here long."

Her breath caught in her throat as she grasped the implicit threat in his statement.

"You have caused us quite the headache," he said as he began pacing in slow, measured steps, occasionally turning to look at his bound captive on the ground. "You may have won over the UN with your platitudes and promises, but even if the weak-willed leaders of some parts of the Arab world bought into your pack of lies, rest assured that your unholy crusade is now at its end."

He crouched a few feet away from her, as though to engender familiarity with her. She knew enough about the Arab world and men like this to know that he was toying with her. For a man like this, no woman would ever be remotely on the same level with him.

"Some of my friends out there think I'm wasting my time keeping you alive like this, but you and me, we think bigger than the here and now, don't we, Ambassador? Killing you now would be fun, to be sure, but not when there are greater things that could be accomplished through a little patience and creativity."

She thought he looked vaguely familiar, but considering the number of Arabs she'd encountered throughout her career, she'd likely met several men with similar facial characteristics. Her grogginess probably didn't help with the differentiation, of course, and she was sure she'd remember if she'd encountered her interlocutor before. She would remember the chill his calm yet creepy tone gave her for the rest of her life.

"What do you want?" she tried to say through the gag, her voice raspy through parched lips. "Where are Dan and Rick?"

He stood and nodded to himself, smiling. "Just as a little tip: I know you're used to nicer places while you're traveling, but it's all in how you organize your space. For example, you'll want to do your sleeping and eating as far away as possible from where you take care of your unmentionables. I'd recommend picking opposite corners of the room." He gave her a smug grin, clearly relishing the thought of his once-high-powered American captive being reduced to urinating and defecating in the corner of a concrete prison cell.

"I'll see you soon, Ambassador." Then he slipped through the door and was gone, the steel barrier to freedom closing behind him. As she heard the screech of the deadbolt being driven home, Christine felt a rush of bile surge up her throat. She turned to the nearest corner and vomited what little liquid remained in her otherwise empty stomach.

As she leaned back on her heels, trying not to fall face-first into the oblong green puddle of bile, she thought to herself wryly, *I guess the other corner's my sleeping one*. Although she didn't see herself sleeping too much anytime soon. Sleep could wait. Getting out of here couldn't.

CHAPTER 9

Dubai, United Arab Emirates

Wayne had learned a few things about Dubai from Brian Gilbert, a college friend who had taught at an international school in the city a few years back. One thing Wayne remembered was that the city automated almost all their traffic ticketing, using a Big-Brotheresque network of cameras along most major roads and intersections to catch speeders and red-light runners. If you got pulled over here, it usually meant something more than a lead foot or a broken taillight. Which made the cops approaching the car, and the guns they brandished, seem all the more menacing.

"There's no way our cover's blown," Suarez said, already looking agitated. "Right? I mean, what the heck, man?"

"Just stay calm," Wayne said. "Trust the cover. It's a role, not just a name. You're not a soldier or an agent. You're a businessman. No matter what they say or what they do."

This was why Pierce had put him in charge of the team, Wayne now realized. All three of the men had extensive experience with covert and overt operations across the world, but even though the others had more years of experience with the agency, he had one thing they didn't: experience running his own op. They were soldiers—and brilliant ones at that—but his insight into shifting the direction of a mission on the fly as the situation warranted was what put him ahead of his teammates. And now, his abilities in that regard—and his ability to lead his teammates in this new level of spycraft—were about to be tested by fire.

The policemen flanked the car, one on each side. The man by Wayne's door was dressed in a fancier uniform, golden epaulettes bespeaking a position above the surrounding rank and file. He was clearly the one in charge.

The captain, as Wayne preferred to think of the commanding officer outside, rapped on the window. Wayne glanced at Suarez in the seat beside him and rolled down the window.

"Is there a problem, Officer?" Wayne said, wincing even as he said the American cliché. But then, there really wasn't anything better to say that wouldn't end with him face down in the dirt and on the way to an Emirati jail. Dubai, for all its Western-style glitz and glamour, was also known for a seedy undercurrent of corruption and double standards that could quickly blindside the foolhardy and unprepared.

The captain, a tall Arab man with a bushy mustache that culminated at two bulging cheeks, smiled mirthlessly. "What is the purpose of your visit?" he asked in accented but flawless English.

"We just told your buddies back there at the airport," Suarez said, adding "sir" as an afterthought. "Business. Investment in your fine city."

Wayne took a deep breath. Not the most tactful of answers, but then, perhaps this was his way of stepping into his role.

"We're representatives from Orion, a US-based investment firm, Officer. We do have a meeting with Nakheel Properties tomorrow morning we need to prepare for . . ." Wayne left the unspoken ending hang in the air. *If there's anything you need, let's hurry it up.*

"Sure, sure," the captain said. "Your passports, please."

Wayne and Suarez reluctantly handed over their government-issue, fake passports, hoping to God that they stood up under intense scrutiny.

The captain spoke in rapid Arabic to his fellow officer, who opened a flip phone and dialed a number. "This will just take a moment," he said, a threatening edge to his voice, while his subordinate spoke with someone on the other line. The cop hung up the phone and said something to the captain, prompting a heated exchange that Wayne had trouble catching even parts of.

When the captain returned his attention to Wayne, the man looked shaken. "My apologies, Mr. Jensen, Mr. Gomez. There must have been some mistake with our information. I do apologize, and allow me to welcome you to Dubai." He smiled and handed Wayne the passports through the window. "Can I offer you a police escort to your hotel? Clear traffic out of the way for you?

"That won't be necessary," Wayne said, trying to hold an expression between indignation and relief. In his cover identity and his real one alike, he had very real reasons to be upset, although with different people. Causing too much of a stink, though, would draw more attention. Better to remain hurried, aloof; bigger and better things on his horizon than dealing with this distraction longer than necessary. "We are free to go, I assume."

"Yes, of course. Have a pleasant stay in Dubai. May your business investments go well, *inshallah*."

"Wait, that's it?" Suarez asked. "Why did you stop us in the first place?"

The captain leaned down so he could see Suarez better. "Why did I stop you? We received reports that illegal foreign agents might be attempting to infiltrate our fine city, and the airport would be the logical place for them to enter from. As you know, Dubai is the jewel of the Arab world, and many would like to see our success falter. They will fail, of course, but we remain vigilant."

The captain spun on his heel and motioned to his subordinate, who followed him to the waiting police car behind.

"That wasn't a routine inspection," Suarez said. "Something feels very wrong here."

Wayne, keeping an eye on the rear view mirror, had to agree.

«»

Deputy Chief of Police Saeed Dahhan watched the car pull out of sight. He frowned as he dialed a preprogrammed number in his phone.

"Yes?"

"They were not American agents after all. Businessmen, looking to invest in a Nakheel project."

"And you believed them."

"Of course, I didn't just take their word for it. I called Nakheel and verified. It all checks out."

"American agents wouldn't come here without a fleshed-out cover, you fool. Foreign spies are now operating on Emirati soil. And you just let them slip through your fingers."

Dahhan gritted his teeth. He could feel his million-dollar payday slipping away.

"I'll keep an eye on them. They won't be a problem."

"They're already here. That's a problem. You now need to keep them from causing more. Otherwise, losing your bonus check will be the least of your worries."

CHAPTER 10

DUBAI, UNITED ARAB EMIRATES

Walid Abushakra was about to be a very rich man. He sat in his makeshift office in the compound he had rented for this mission, while they waited for the other team to complete their mission. Unlike his followers, he realized the truth of what they were doing here. The ambassador was merely a pawn in a bigger game. Technically, so was he, but when this was over and done, he would be worth millions, while the woman would be quite dead.

He very much preferred his own circumstances. In the meantime, he would have some fun with this American woman. He had seen enough Western cinema and television while attending the University of London to know all the tropes of traditional American villains. For some reason, they seemed to have British accents more often than not, which gave him an edge in his little game with the ambassador. Perhaps it had something to do with the American Revolution, but as none of those filmmakers had ever met anyone involved in that conflict, Walid didn't buy it. He likened it to a concept he'd deemed "the other." Like us, but not. Different enough in thinking and ultimate goals to be foreign to the Western notions of goodness and justice. The Russians had played that trope during the Cold War. Crazed, Balkan dictators and Venezuelan drug lords largely filled that void in the nineties. And since the attacks of September 11 in 2001, Islamic fundamentalists had been the villain du jour.

If America only knew how much they had underestimated the strength, cunning, and resolve of that enemy.

One element that many in the Western world failed to understand was how inextricably integrated religion, politics, history, identity, and culture were in the Middle East. The cradle of civilization had invented writing thousands of years before the Greeks began anything resembling high culture in Europe. And there was plenty of history that had transpired even before that momentous invention by the Sumerians. For America, history began in 1776. So shortsighted were they, so concerned about the next fashion craze, the next iPhone iteration, the next election. Their boorish lack of vision was about to send them stumbling headlong into a conflict from which they would never recover.

For centuries, the Western powers had utilized contractual labor in its security forces. From ancient Rome to the Hessian riders to the French Foreign Legion and beyond, the West had used soldiers-for-hire to do the dirty work that the nation's regular forces couldn't or wouldn't do on their own.

Mercenaries. It had become a dirty word in recent years, as Blackwater and other private security contractors had made a killing—literally and figuratively—from their part in the wars in Iraq and Afghanistan. Mercenaries could make five times what they had been paid when serving in their country's armed forces, and the private nature of the companies sliced through a lot of the bureaucratic bull that plagued the governmental militaries. After all, there was none of the "Captain America" patriotic pretense in private military groups. They were all there for one thing: to use their unique skill-set to collect a hefty paycheck.

In many ways, the Western militaries themselves fueled the rise of Blackwater and the rest. Many of the mercenaries in these organizations were trained to be hardened killers, smart, strategic, merciless in the face of the enemy. When their tours were up, there wasn't a lot of demand for those skill-sets in the life of a nine-to-five civilian. And, as Walid knew firsthand, once these mindsets were ingrained in you, it was hard to let them go.

Western efforts at re-integrating combat veterans back into society were laughable at best. The one thing they were trained to do was the one thing they were expressly forbidden from doing as a private citizen. Was it any wonder that so many of yesterday's soldiers became today's homeless? Thus, private security contractors stepped in to give former soldiers a chance to continue using their skills in a much more lucrative fashion. And despite the far higher price tag, Uncle Sam continued to foot the bill.

In the Middle East, however, there tended to be two types of soldiers: those working on behalf of a government, and those working for a movement. Al-Qaeda, Hezbollah, ISIS, Hamas, and their ilk had seen recruiting soar in recent years. Of course, the lines between the two often became blurred as governments funded and farmed out their dirty work to true believers in strategic parts of the region and world.

One key problem with the jihad movement, Walid saw, was that there were essentially two kinds of men involved: the planners and the grunts. The planners—bin Laden, Zubadayah, and their ilk—usually orchestrated events from afar. The grunts were given basic training, a Soviet-era machine gun, and sent off on a suicide mission. The vast majority of jihadist attacks were decreed successful solely according to how much damage was dealt to the other side, regardless of how many of their own grunts had to blow themselves up or get shot in the process. After all, millions of impoverished young men across the region were ready to step up and fill the roster for the next suicide mission.

But what if you wanted to do something that required a little more finesse? A sleeper cell filled with men who not only got the job done, but lived to fight another day. A black-ops Blackwater for purposes of jihad only. Walid had identified the void and filled it. Most of his men were contracted on a case-by-case basis, but there was very little turnover. After all, the money was good, but the not-dying at the end of the mission was even better. Seventy-two virgins were great and all, but if you could delay that heavenly journey to kill more of the infidels—and spend one's newfound wealth in the process—surely Allah smiled upon such an enterprise more than blindly making a one-way trip into a firefight.

Uhmar Haidar, Arabic for "Red Lion," was the most beautiful invention since the suicide bomber, and though it flew under most intelligence agencies' radars, their effectiveness had filled plenty of headlines—and morgues—across the globe. But what

Walid's organization had most recently been contracted to do was as much a game changer for jihad as the group itself. While *Uhmar Haidar* had added a powerful new piece to the board, what they were about to do would completely rewrite the rules of the game.

Permanently.

This mission's plan was perfect. Though some of his new hires pretended to bemoan the fact that they were unable to be on the delivery team a thousand miles to the northwest, he was quite glad to be safely here in Dubai. He was no martyr. Though he performed the five pillars of Islam more often than not, he had his own vices and desires that he had no plans to forsake. Especially since his own fortunes were soon to turn so nicely.

Neither was he a fanatic. He was a pragmatist. But long ago at the madrassah in London he had seen the value in commanding fanatics. The imam had so skillfully woven his tapestry of words—painting the villains, stirring the hatred, tapping into the warrior spirit that men were often forced to repress in this over-civilized world—that Walid, while unfazed by the call to arms the leader had issued, realized the power of those words on the young men around him. The power of words to command an army. Hitler was no Christian. Stalin believed in Marx's communist ideals only as a platform to power. And though martyrdom and seventy-two virgins were the last thing on Walid's mind, he saw the militant fundamentalist movements that were sweeping through the Muslim world as a means to a much more important end.

Walid had grown up in Dubai, had seen the city transform itself from a modest Gulf city to a glitzy, artificial monument to vice and the Western idea of progress. The city's leaders had sucked the soul from the city and replaced it with all the worst aspects of American conspicuous consumption. While his paymaster had set his sights on an even larger goal, Walid's main target was America. Not because it was the Great White Satan. Not because he wanted a global caliphate. Not even because he commanded jihadists. No, he hated America because its main export was debauched morality and shiny, hollow spectacle. America's values had robbed him of his homeland. Now, he would help return the favor.

His second in command, a Syrian named Omar Sawaf, entered the room. Sawaf was shorter than Walid, with a wrestler's build. Omar was a true believer, and Walid was careful to maintain his fanatical façade around him as well as the rest of the men. There were few things in this world more dangerous than a true believer. The trick was to ensure that you aligned your cause with theirs so that you could use that fearsome power for your benefit. They were deadly weapons, to be sure, but now they were *his* deadly weapons.

"Dahhan let the American agents slip through his fingers," Sawaf said, sweat dripping a trail in the dirt that glazed his forehead. "Just arrived. Plausible covers, but then, they would have those in place."

"Yes, they would." Walid sat back in his chair. The Americans were here quicker than he had expected. But regardless of their haste, Walid was more than prepared.

"I assume Dahhan is fixing his mistake," he said.

"Of course. However, I wonder if it might be prudent to prepare a move to one of the alternate sites. Just in case."

Walid nodded. The American agents could quickly become a thorn in his side, but not the only one. There was still the matter of the missing package sent by the Jordanian lawyer. Walid's associates had learned, through a persuasive interrogation of the man, that the intended recipient had been Ambassador Needham, a logical choice for the one with whom Iranian nuclear scientist Omid Khosh would attempt to share his role in the plot. Apparently the lawyer didn't know the exact contents of the package, as it had come to him sealed from his client a week ago, along with delivery instructions. Worst case scenario: Khosh theoretically could have known enough—and gathered enough positive intel—to derail the entire operation.

At the moment, that was purely speculation, and Walid prayed that the scientist's understanding of the larger plot was negligible. But he couldn't leave that up to prayer and chance. It was his job to eliminate any threat to the mission. Unfortunately, his men's attempt to scour the airplane for the package and its contents had been fruitless, cut short by the sound of approaching sirens. And now, the plane was surely locked away in a well-guarded hangar somewhere, preventing a second look. Of course, even if evidence had been delivered to the ambassador, locking it away within a hangar until it was too late would suit his purposes as well. There was at least one contingency he had to cover, however.

"Tell the men. Prepare the ambassador to move at a moment's notice, should I decide it is Allah's will that we do so."

"Of course," Omar said. "Tomorrow will be a great day for jihad and the people of Allah. We shall strike a great blow at the heart of the infidels."

"*Inshallah*," Walid said.

Omar bowed his head in agreement. "*Inshallah*."

CHAPTER 11

DUBAI, UNITED ARAB EMIRATES

Minutes later, Wayne and his team were back on Sheikh Zayed Road, heading toward Dubai Healthcare City. Since modern Dubai was a planned city, the new metropolis's architects in the government, alongside major real-estate developers, had parceled up chunks of land for dedicated purposes. Some, like Dubai Festival City, aimed to be all-in-one mini cities: residential, business, shopping, and schools, all in one inclusive enclave. Others, like Business Bay and Dubai Media City, were more focused in their aim. Dubai Healthcare City fell into the latter category.

"Anubis, check in," Wayne said into his headset, using the call sign Nasef had chosen for the op. Their signals were supposedly scrambled with proprietary encryption, but then, their entry into the country should not have raised any red flags with overzealous police officers. Something was certainly amiss, and already Wayne felt that old, familiar feeling of not knowing who to trust.

"What the heck, man?" Nasef's voice was taut, distressed. "I just got pulled over and given the third degree by some local cops. I thought our covers were airtight."

Wayne winced at Nasef betraying the fact that their given identities were, in fact, covers. Clearly the use of his call sign hadn't clued him in that Wayne was trying to continue the ruse even over their secured radio line. But the cat was out of the bag now.

"Did you get away clean or not?" Wayne asked.

"As far as I can tell. Haven't spotted a tail yet, but with this traffic, who could tell?"

"Stick with the plan. I'm going to call base and see what happened. Watch your back, though. Somebody screwed up, and I don't want any of the fallout to jeopardize the mission or our lives."

"Copy that. Keep me posted. Anubis out."

Keeping his eyes on the road, Wayne instructed Suarez to dial Ibrahim on her direct, secure line back at Langley, patching the call through to Wayne's earpiece..

"Yes?"

"We just got accosted by cops not two miles from the airport. And they don't like to do that here without cause. What gives?"

A moment of silence from the other end of the line, and then Ibrahim said, "I don't know. You got away, I assume?"

"Yeah, they let us go. Apparently Support set up the meeting with Nakheel properly, but somebody either has a big mouth or dropped the ball somewhere else."

"Maybe it's because they're expecting a covert, American intervention after the sheikh rebuffed the president's request to spearhead the investigation. They're kind of paranoid after the Akers affair."

"There must have been dozens of young American men at the airport; probably hundreds, if not thousands, filtering through there on a daily basis. I guarantee you they're not pulling over all of them and putting guns to their heads. Very bad for business and PR."

"Good point. But the circle that knows about this operation is very small, and all of them have a long history of faithful service, and have obviously been thoroughly vetted."

Wayne knew trust only went so far, particularly when power and bureaucracy were concerned, but then he lit upon another idea.

"The plane. Who did you charter it from?"

"Let me see here . . ." The sound of keys tapping. "It looks like . . . nobody. It's government property."

"What's the government doing with its own Gulfstream?"

Ibrahim seemed to be reading from a computer screen as she answered Wayne. "Confiscated in Miami two years back in a major DEA bust. Looks like the powers-that-be decided it would help to have its own luxury business jet to establish covers in covert ops like the one you're on now."

"And how many ops has it been on since then?"

"Um . . . four. Details are classified, but I can see it hasn't been used in the Middle East. Thailand, Colombia, Chechnya, and Venezuela."

Wayne felt like punching something. "And you don't think, in this day and age, America's enemies might talk to each other on occasion? Venezuela and Russia have both been involved in backdoor deals with Iran, for crying out loud. If one of the targets in the other ops got wise to what was going on, the plane immediately became a liability for any mission it was used in. This one included."

Ibrahim muttered something under her breath that Wayne couldn't make out. "You might be right," she said. "That's . . . wow. I don't know how that slipped through. I'm really sorry if that's the case."

"Are there any other slipups I might need to know about? I've got three men's lives, plus the ambassador, two of her entourage, and the fate of the Middle East depending on the setup you guys provided us with. If there are any other holes in the plan you've given us, I'd love to know about it beforehand."

"No, there aren't." There was an edge to Ibrahim's voice. "Look, I'm sorry somebody screwed up here, but don't start souring on the whole operation. I've read your file and know you've been screwed over on black-ops missions before. This isn't like that. The ambassador's life, and possibly the stability of the region—not to mention the continued flow of oil from the region—still depend on you and your team."

"And our ability to do our job depends on you guys safe at home not screwing up simple things like this."

"You're right, Wilkins. Next time, I'll remember to ask the terrorists for advance notice before they kill our staff and kidnap our ambassador on foreign soil. That way we can make sure we've got all our ducks in a row for a nice, pretty rescue operation. That sound better?"

Wayne took a deep breath. Ibrahim was right. This op was hastily drawn together by necessity. If they'd known the attack was going to happen, it wouldn't have happened in the first place. As it was, they were all fighting the clock, and corner-cutting oversights like their plane's operational history were understandable, if not entirely forgivable. Even so, someone had dropped the ball, and he couldn't abide having his team's efforts undermined by negligence from Washington.

"I'm sorry for jumping at you. Please keep a closer eye on all of this. We've already got the chips stacked against us over here, and time is even less on our side now that the local authorities are suspicious. Once we don't show up for our meeting with Nakheel tomorrow, they'll be gunning for us hard. It should go without saying, but I'll say it anyway: we can't abide any more mistakes. We may not be able to abide the last one, but we can't do anything about that now. The ambassador's life and all the rest that you said depends on my team, but it also depends on you and the support Washington can offer. No more mistakes, please."

"No more mistakes. I'll apprise Pierce and the president of the development and get back to you if there are any further foreseen ramifications of the incident on our end."

"Copy that. We'll let you know what, if anything, we discover at the hospital shortly. Wilkins out."

Wayne disconnected the call and dropped the phone into his lap.

"Ibrahim screw up?" Suarez asked.

"Somebody did. Our Gulfstream was CIA property. Undercover, of course, but as we all know, covers get blown. Like ours just did."

"Or almost did."

Wayne grunted. "Either way, I'm not counting on it to get us through another scrape. We *have* to stay under the radar from here on out. Any attention is unwanted attention."

"Of course."

Wayne took the turnoff for the hospital. "I'm tired of getting jerked around. It's time to get some answers."

CHAPTER 12

TEHRAN, IRAN

Paiman Parmaei could hear his heart beating over the padding of his feet as he ran down the thick-carpeted corridor in Sa'adabad Palace. As deputy minister for External Affairs, he was one of three men responsible for overseeing the Iranian government's investments in sister organizations that helped to advance the cause of the Islamic republic and of the greater Shia Islamic cause. Through back channels that he had kept alive despite tensions between the two Gulf powers, Parmaei had learned some very interesting news from his contacts in the United Arab Emirates. Christine Needham, the infidel part-Jew American special ambassador to the region, who was trying to drum up support for the Zionist puppet regime in Palestine, had been abducted in Dubai.

Normally, this would have been cause for celebration. The woman had caused significant problems for the Iranian regime. Her speech before the UN General Assembly the previous year had been instrumental in securing further sanctions against Iran as they pressed on toward their Allah-given right to becoming a nuclear-armed world power. The economic strains caused by previous sanctions had helped a more moderate president, Arsalan Hosseini, to win victory after years of fiery rhetoric. But Hosseini was no less committed to gaining nuclear weapons in order to wipe out the blot on Allah's kingdom that was the impostor state of Israel. He was just smarter about not bringing the world's powers down upon him while his nation worked toward that end.

Under the auspices of establishing a peaceful nuclear program to provide power for its eighty-one million people, Iran had brokered and signed an agreement with the United States, Great Britain, France, Germany, Russia, and China allowing inspectors access to all their declared nuclear facilities. Of course, Iran's military facilities were out of bounds, a concession Hosseini had argued no sovereign nation could be expected to give up, especially to her enemies.

The six world powers were so proud of the foreign policy win, despite the stringent objections of their allies in the Middle East, that they had ignored all the warning signs. Even when a Czech intelligence team intercepted a container of Russian-made parts for creating nuclear warheads, the news was quickly dismissed as the ramblings of conspiracy theorists. But, though new-found ally Russia had been an asset in continuing their military buildup and secret nuclear weapons programs, Iran had made plenty of progress on her own. And while nuclear-armed Israel cried foul and regional foe Saudi Arabia endeavored to acquire an atomic arsenal of its own, Hosseini's Iran continued worked unabated on its own projects, smiling in secret defiance at the world powers they would soon destroy.

The true power of the Iranian state rested not with any popularly elected official, but with the Supreme Leader, Ayatollah Khomani Mahoud Naghinejad. Being the most powerful cleric and political leader in the republic, he determined the direction of the nation and its great legacy. And the greatest achievement in that legacy for finally kicking the infidels from Allah's kingdom would soon be achieved in the blinding purification of nuclear white.

Almost all of the Muslim world's political leadership, from Libya to Syria, to Afghanistan to Indonesia, had agreed with this proposition—unspoken though it now largely was. That was, until Needham had started to gain traction with her new proposal of a two-state solution to the Palestinian issue. She already had several key leaders of Arab nations signed up to support the proposal's discussion at an upcoming peace summit, and more were starting to come out in favor of it.

This was unacceptable. It was a blasphemous compromise that would continue to seep into the nations around it until Allah took his favor from these lands and wrought his holy vengeance upon his people. Ayatollah Naghinejad, President Hosseini, and Parmaei all saw the folly in these actions, but many Muslims, it seemed, had grown soft and were willing to allow half-measures and deals with the enemy to supplant truth and justice. Even many in this country had fallen for the peace-loving, moral relativism that the West was exporting through its corrupt media and culture. But that was why Allah, in his wisdom, had given power to Naghinejad and Hosseini, men strong enough to fight the current of blasphemy sweeping through the Muslim world. Iran would not stand with any of the morally weak regimes that supported a compromise in Palestine. Iran would do what was necessary to perform Allah's will, even if others let cowardice and laziness lull them into complacency.

So Needham being taken out of the picture should have been a fantastic development for their cause. Only he hadn't heard anything about it beforehand. And, being Iran's liaison for their sister groups in Hezbollah and Hamas, he should have known about it long before his source in Dubai had heard the news.

He should have been the one planning the op in the first place. What a coup her kidnapping would have been for their cause. Of course, whichever militia—or terrorist group, as the US and her allies loved to refer to Hezbollah and their ilk—was responsible would receive all the credit, and rightly so. The further removed Iran's government was from the official story, the better. As the old Arab proverb went: "Beware the enemy you do not see."

But now, it was Parmaei who was left in the dark. His commanders in the field disavowed knowledge of the operation but praised Allah for its happening. Yes, praise Allah indeed, but even Allah couldn't save Parmaei from Hosseini's wrath—not to mention that of Ayatollah Naghinejad—should he lose control of Iran's subversive assets in the Levant.

He reached the massive bronze doors of the presidential office, hesitated, and knocked.

"Come in," boomed the voice behind the door.

Parmaei pulled the door open and stepped into the stately room. A stuffed falcon—in life, Hosseini's favorite of the five he'd once owned—was displayed on a perch to the side of a massive, cedar desk. The president himself—dressed in the same suit and tie ensemble he wore when making faux overtures to the United Nations—stood behind the desk, looking out the window at the panorama of Tehran beyond the treetops surrounding the palace.

Parmaei swallowed at the lump that had formed in his throat, but to no avail. He bowed his head to his president, took a deep breath, and put his neck on the chopping block.

"Your Excellency. Ambassador Needham . . . was that Hezbollah?"

Hosseini fixed him with a curious look, studying him for a moment before speaking.

"You mean you don't know?"

Parmaei shook his head, almost mournfully. "If they were behind it, they weren't answering to me when they did it. I only just found out she had been abducted."

Hosseini opened his eyes wide, brow furrowed. "Well then, if *you* didn't order the ambassador's kidnapping, who did?"

That, Parmaei reflected, was the ten-trillion dollar question.

CHAPTER 13

DUBAI, UNITED ARAB EMIRATES

Christine had lost all sense of time. Her cinderblock prison was cut off from all external light and sound, and the guards had pretty much left her to rot, save to open the door once to toss her the occasional piece of stale *naan* or bowl of cloudy tap water. It was sustaining her body, but her mind was quickly descending into insanity.

Why had no one come for her? What was her captors' purpose? Why had they killed Ben? Were Dan and Rick also dead? Where was she? How was she going to get out of here? Why had no one come to rescue her yet? The United Arab Emirates was an American ally, and Sheikh Khalid had expressed interest in attending her peace summit. So what was the hold-up? Where was the cavalry?

So many questions, so few answers. The stench of her waste filled the airless room, clogging her nostrils with acrid fumes that made every breath an effort not to vomit up the little nourishment she'd had.

She felt panic teetering at the edge of her consciousness. Her daughter, Bailey, would be nineteen next month. They hadn't spoken in nearly a year, since the divorce. Christine had left on bad terms with her ex, Ryan. Irreconcilable differences, the paperwork had said, but, in truth, he just couldn't handle his wife's career making a bigger splash than his middle-management position at a Silicon Valley tech firm. It all seemed so trivial now. Perhaps she had become so invested in her career, so focused on the mythical greater good, that she'd neglected the good that was right there in her home. And now, she'd lost it all, given up twenty years of marriage and a relationship with her own daughter for a job that had landed her in a stagnant dungeon seven thousand miles from home.

It wasn't just the job, though. She had chosen to come to Dubai of her own volition, skirting proper channels and trying to do things her way. And look where it had gotten her. Perhaps this was karma come to bite her in the butt: because of the duplicitous nature of her trip, the State Department simply didn't know about her plight, thus leaving her to suffer alone by simple virtue of having kept them out of the loop. The irony was overwhelming. And yet, if the State Department didn't even realize where she was, how had her captors managed to intercept her at the airport? A target of opportunity? Dumb luck? Or something else?

The man who had spoken to her when she'd first woken up, the clean-cut one with the British accent, seemed to be the leader of this band of terrorists. Though her Arabic was rusty at best, she had heard some of the guards outside her room refer to him as Walid. He hadn't returned since that first meeting, but the fact that Walid had allowed her to see his face did not bode well for her chances of survival.

That was it, wasn't it? she realized with horror. Her life was forfeit. The only reason they had kidnapped her instead of killing her at the airport was that her death would be more useful to them in another time and place. Likely in front of a video camera, next to a big man with a machete. She had seen far too many senseless beheadings of western soldiers, contractors, journalists, and tourists snatched from Iraq, Yemen, Afghanistan, and other hot spots in the region. Their gruesome deaths gained neither side anything, but only served to infuriate Western governments and companies while emboldening the terrorists.

She had learned early on that shouting for help in this concrete dungeon would only serve to grate her vocal cords and amuse the guards. She heard nothing from the outside world and, it seemed, neither could anyone hear her. If they were still in the city and not further out in the desert—or somewhere else entirely—her captors had constructed a virtually soundproof prison for her.

Which meant there was little to no chance of someone finding her.

She pulled herself into a sitting position, still in her "sleeping corner," as Walid had called it. At the movement, she felt a sharp pain beneath her left breast. And then she remembered.

Christine lifted herself up on her knees, studying the vent above the door where light trickled in from the outside hallway. She sat quietly for a moment, straining her ears for any indication that someone might be approaching. All she could hear was her own breathing, and what she believed was the breathing of the guard posted outside. No footsteps. No voices. But there was no telling how long that would last.

She unbuttoned the top two buttons on her blouse and reached inside her left bra cup. The tiny SD card was still where she had hidden it in the early moments of the attack at the airport. The evidence was safe. For now.

She slid the card between the fabric and the underwire at the base of her bra cup. This was no longer about her life. It was no longer about the peace summit. She had to get out of here now. If Rick and Dan had met with the same fate as Ben—and she saw no reason to think otherwise—Christine was the only thing standing between the terrorists and the deaths of untold millions.

Her only saving grace was the fact that they apparently didn't realize she had the SD card. Because if they did, they wouldn't be waiting for a carefully choreographed video execution. They never would have let her leave the plane alive.

CHAPTER 14

Dubai Healthcare City, Dubai, United Arab Emirates

Rick Weiland looked like a truck had run over him. Twice.

The ambassador's bodyguard was lying in a state-of-the-art hospital bed when Wayne and Suarez entered the room. A pair of remotes lay on a table next to the bed. One was a standard TV remote for the wall-mounted Toshiba currently tuned to BBC2. The other controlled the bed, allowing it to adjust to nearly any combination of angles the patient desired.

Everything in the Al Maktoum Hospital, from the sparkling white marble of the lobby to the futuristic-looking, fiber-optic lighting in the hallways illustrated the city planners' goals for Dubai Healthcare City. Like everything else in the desert metropolis, it was designed to be the best of the best. And while Suarez couldn't speak on behalf of the quality of care offered on site, it certainly was one of the more luxurious hospitals he had ever seen. Yet despite the shiny image of success the architects and interior designers had clearly endeavored to project, it was still a hospital. The rooms smelled faintly of antiseptic, and Suarez had passed at least one crying family on his way in. Apply as many fresh coats of paint as you want, but in the end this building was still a place where families came to make their final plays against the inevitable hand of death. And no amount of shine would ever take that sting away.

"Mr. Weiland," Wayne said. Before arriving at the hospital, they had agreed to keep this interrogation as brief as possible. Their phony IDs and cover stories had fooled the pair of low-level private security grunts posted outside Weiland's room, but if word got around that a plane with covert CIA connections had landed barely a day after the attack, Suarez had no doubt that this room would be locked up tight and their access to the ambassador's bodyguard cut off. Time was of the essence.

Wayne moved to Weiland's side and tapped him on the shoulder. Suarez stood sentinel by the door, keeping his eyes and ears peeled for company while also keeping one eye on Wayne's interrogation.

Weiland stirred, slowly opening his eyes and blinking to clear his vision.

"Mr. Weiland, we'd like to ask you some questions," the team's leader said in a soothing voice. According to the nurse on rounds, Weiland hadn't spoken a word since the attack, and his vitals were irregular at best. With Rick the only living eyewitness to the attack, Wayne didn't want to make him resistant to answering—or worse, send him back into a coma.

Weiland made a groaning noise that may or may not have been an attempt at speech.

"Rick . . . Can I call you Rick?" Suarez recognized the technique, trying to establish an informal rapport with the man and set him at ease. "My name is Tom," he said, giving him the name on his cover ID, though deciding to forsake the phony insurance adjuster angle that had gotten them in the door. The man needed to know the truth of what they were confronting if he was going to give accurate and comprehensive answers.

Weiland lifted his top lip from his teeth in what looked like a weak and humorless smile.

"You're in a hospital right now, in Dubai. Doctors say you're going to be fine, but some of your friends are still missing. We need your help to find them."

Another grunt.

"Do you remember what happened at the airport? Anything you can remember would be helpful."

Weiland opened his mouth slightly and rasped empty, syllable-less air.

"Is this yours?" Suarez asked, pointing at a Blackberry on the side table before lifting it in the air for Weiland to see.

Weiland swallowed hard, and then blinked his eyes hard. Once for yes.

"How about this one?" he asked, picking up an iPhone that had been lying next to the Blackberry. The iPhone's screen was a splintered mosaic of shattered glass.

Weiland squinted for a moment, and then turned his head to the side in what looked like a pain-truncated shake of the head. Suarez nodded once before slipping the phone into his pocket. Evidence.

"What do you remember about the attack, Mr. Weiland?" Wayne urged, retaking the floor from Suarez. "Ambassador Needham and Dan Krumholtz are still missing. Anything you can remember would greatly help us."

"Christine . . ."

"Yes, what about Christine?"

"Take . . . card . . ."

"Card? What card?"

"Evi . . . dence . . . plan . . . Israel . . ."

Weiland swallowed. His throat was parched from the blood loss and the effort of speaking. Wayne opened a bottle of Masafi filtered water from the side table and tilted it to Weiland's lips. The bodyguard drank eagerly, some of the water spilling from his mouth and trickling down his hospital gown. Wayne capped the bottle and returned it to the table while Weiland took a deep breath.

"Iran . . ."

"Iran's behind the attack?" Suarez asked, his hands balling into fists. "Of course they would be. They've just been buying time to . . ."

Wayne spun around and glared at him. Suarez took the hint and shut up. He had to remember that this was a different world compared to many of his previous ops. Too many unknowns; and even the known factors didn't necessarily add up to the normal conclusions. Even if Iran was behind Needham's kidnapping—through a proxy such as Hezbollah or something even further removed from Tehran's power center, no doubt—his outburst did nothing to serve the mission's primary objective: find and secure the ambassador.

"Evi . . . den . . . Iran . . . Christine . . . bomb . . ." Weiland gasped for air, the exertion clearly getting to him. Yet despite the toll it was taking on his beleaguered body, Rick Weiland seemed eager to share this information with someone who could do something with it. “Iran . . . lies . . . nuke . . . bomb . . . Israel . . . soon . . . Find Christine . . . evidence . . . proof . . . stop nuke . . .”

With every word, Suarez felt the room growing colder. Iran already had a nuke? Since the election of the more moderate President Hosseini, relations with Iran were better than they had been since the Islamic Revolution in 1978, though the fractious nature of the government and Ayatollah Naghinejad’s unfettered hatred of the United States certainly complicated any chance of restoring diplomatic relations. But Hosseini had pledged not to build nuclear weapons, and though that was a pledge that Israel’s leadership had warned the world not to believe, Iran had seemingly followed through on its promises of transparency.

The transparency act had helped to seduce the Western world into believing their nuclear ambitions were indeed purely peaceful. But the International Atomic Energy Agency that had been doing the regular inspections could only supervise activity at sites they knew about. If Iran had been using a secret base to build nuclear bombs, and if one of those was already complete and headed for Israel . . .

Suarez was yanked out of his thoughts by a high-pitched drone. Rick Weiland was flatlining.

CHAPTER 15

Beirut, Lebanon

Faheem Ramdallah felt every blasted bump on this godforsaken back road on the outskirts of Beirut. He rode shotgun in the van that carried three of his men, plus the driver, Maktoum. Maktoum had gotten turned around trying to find this largely abandoned part of the city, and the delay had put them behind schedule. Faheem could not afford to be behind schedule. None of them could.

Maktoum was attempting to make up the time by driving as quickly as he could to the warehouse, but the deeply pocked road sucked the van's tires into every hole, jostling the men in the back and thoroughly annoying Faheem. They would have to find a different route back, he recognized. Once they had left the warehouse with their prize in store, it would be ill-advised to subject their newfound cargo to too much physical trauma. One bad bump, and his hometown would be vaporized. He was aiming to vaporize someone else's hometown.

The wars with Israel, their despised neighbor to the south, had taken a devastating toll on his once-beautiful hometown. Beirut had once been called the Venice of the Middle East, with rich culture, layers of history, and top-notch infrastructure interweaving to form a city unlike any other in the region. And then, with an unstoppable barrage of bombing campaigns, mortar strikes, and armed incursions into the historically multicultural nation, Israel scarred the face of Lebanon forever. Even today, three decades after the first war, once-majestic mansions sat abandoned among the hills surrounding the city, their red, clay-tiled roofs punctured by artillery. Like the palatial mansions once owned by the rich and powerful from Europe and America, as well as elsewhere in the region, Lebanon had been gutted and exposed to the elements, left to rot while her destroyers enjoyed unearned gifts and unflinching support from the West.

He had been just a boy when the Israelis had launched their war with Lebanon in the 1980s. When the Zionists attacked again in 2006, he had taken up arms against the threat. And though Lebanon's greatest success in that conflict was that they hadn't suffered *more* deaths than they actually had, the conflict had given the storied nation one truly great asset.

Him.

Ever since the Israelis had finally ceased their 2006 offensive against their northern neighbor, Faheem had searched for ways to strike a mortal blow to the enemies of Allah. He had joined with Hezbollah forces in the early days of the conflict, but it wasn't until after the mortar fire had died down that he began to separate himself from the rank and file of the anti-Israel jihadists.

Ramdallah had graduated from the University of Beirut with a degree in electrical engineering just weeks before the 2006 skirmish. He was convinced that Allah had chosen him for this time to use his newfound knowledge to do something bigger, stronger, and final. The top leadership in Hezbollah, including its paymasters in Iran, had taken notice of his keen intellect and fervent drive to rid his homeland of the Israeli presence. He had quickly risen through the ranks, eventually taking leadership positions on cross-border, quick-strike attacks.

Three months ago, he had received a visit from a high-ranking commander in the Hezbollah hierarchy. The commander had told Faheem he had been chosen to lead a mission into the heart of Israel, one that would effectively destroy the infidel state for good. The jihadist had expressed a clear interest and, from that point on, he had been consumed with his task. He had studied maps of the target city to maximize the attack's physical and psychological devastation. He plotted out routes and alternate routes for his team to deliver their cargo across two countries while avoiding border patrols. And he had hand-chosen his team from the best men he had ever commanded. In any other circumstances, the prospect of taking Hezbollah's best on a suicide mission would have been ultimately detrimental to their long-term cause. But this mission would be the final mission of Hezbollah's long and hard journey, so taking the best men made sense, even if they would not live to see the fruits of their hard-fought efforts.

Maktoum turned off the cracked asphalt and steered the van up a winding dirt road that traced the edge of a massive hill. Halfway up the hill, they pulled into an unmarked driveway, navigated along the edge of a cliff overlooking the city, and finally arrived at a weathered warehouse that had fallen into disrepair since being abandoned some years before.

At the sound of the van's engine, a young man sporting a scowl and a Kalashnikov appeared at the side door of the warehouse. He yelled something to his fellow fighters inside the warehouse, keeping his eyes fixed on the van as he did so. Ten seconds later, three other men exited the warehouse through the same door. Two held matching Kalashnikovs, while the third—their leader—wore a .45 Magnum in a shoulder holster.

Faheem opened his door and began to walk toward the men. His team followed behind him.

"*Al-hamdulillah*, it's you, my brother," said the leader as he walked past his underlings and embraced Ramdallah.

"It has been too long, Nabil," said Faheem. "I am glad to have seen you one last time."

"You do great things for Lebanon, Faheem. And greater things still for Allah. May God bless you on your mission. We shall hold a feast in your honor when it is done and the enemy is vanquished." Nabil motioned to his men, and two of them retreated into the warehouse briefly before returning with a rolling suitcase. The suitcase was designed to be invisible. Navy blue, generic western brand, standard size for fitting in overhead compartments on planes around the world. There were millions of suitcases across the globe that looked identical to the one being presented to Faheem now. But despite its commonplace appearance, it was, in fact, one of a kind.

It held a nuclear bomb.

Nabil showed him how to activate the bomb, explained its electronic and nuclear inner workings as one scientist to another. Faheem nodded, the full realization of the great task before him finally coming into view as he stared at the device that would deliver the decisive blow that his people had sought for nearly seventy years. And Allah had chosen him to be his messenger.

Faheem stood and addressed Nabil's men.

"Thank you, my brothers, for your sacrifices. This weapon shall strike a mortal blow to the black heart of the enemies of Islam. May Allah bless you and your families for your work here today."

He turned to his team.

"And you, my dearest of brothers; together we will be the hand of Allah that delivers the killing blow to the infidels. Through this purging fire, we shall raze the enemies of God from this holy land and restore what is rightfully ours. Our families, our nations, indeed, the entire world shall sing our praises for the sacrifice we are about to make. *Allahu akbar!*"

Shouts of "*Allahu akbar*" rose up around him in return. These men were ready. Ready to fight. Ready to kill. Ready to die. And in all his years of jihad, Faheem had never seen a more worthy mission by which to enter the pantheon of martyrs.

Faheem beamed with pride. For nearly a decade, he had proven himself on the frontlines of a shadow war fought at the boundaries of the isolated nation. Now he would lead his men into the heart of a new battle. A battle of finality, striking a mortal blow to the very heart of the Jewish state.

By this time tomorrow, Israel would be wiped from the face of the earth. And her American protectors would soon follow.

CHAPTER 16

DUBAI, UNITED ARAB EMIRATES

Christine was jolted awake as the door to her cell was unceremoniously kicked in. She hadn't even realized she had nodded off. How long had she been asleep? How much time had she lost in useless slumber?

"Strip," said the wiry young man who walked in. A keffiyeh covered his face, incongruous with the undisguised features of Walid. Perhaps he felt it fit the persona of a jihadist better, the idealized warrior of Islam he might have seen in his hometown or on propaganda videos since his youth.

She stared back at him, uncomprehending.

"Now," he said, his heavily accented voice louder this time. "Strip. Now."

"Why?" she asked, fearing she already knew the answer to that question. The power trip experienced by jihadists—and kidnappers of many different stripes—could often lead to rape and other sexual abuse against their hostages, regardless of the purported religious piety of the perpetrator.

"You have something for I have need." He kicked the air between them. "Now."

I know exactly what you need, she silently seethed. *A bullet between the eyes.*

She slowly rose to her feet, eyeing the open door behind him. She could take him. One fluid motion. Close the five feet between them, slam the heel of her palm into his nose.

"Now!" the terrorist repeated, a leering look entering his eyes.

Christine planted her back foot, made as though to unbutton her blouse, and darted forward.

The terrorist yelped in surprise and fumbled with the Soviet-era Kalashnikov strapped to his back. He was too slow. Within seconds, the ambassador had closed the gap and connected with his nose—or where she assumed his nose should be beneath the concealing cloth of the *keffiyeh*. He squelched a cry of pain as his expression changed from lust to shock to fury.

Christine now saw her mistake. He may have looked wiry, but he had enough muscle mass to deliver a severe beatdown, and she had now given him exactly the incentive to use it: bruised pride. His jihadist brethren would expect nothing less than swift and violent retribution for the injury she had just dealt him. Anything less, and he would be forever emasculated in their eyes.

Forgoing his gun entirely now for the more visceral brutality of flesh and bone, the man swung his right fist into her jaw. She tried to turn away from the blow, but she wasn't fast enough. Realizing how much more dire her situation had just become, she twisted her knee toward his groin. She missed her target, but connecting with the sensitive nerves of his inner thigh elicited another yelp that gave her some small measure of satisfaction.

The next blow came even faster. A shot to the kidney, left exposed by her awkward counterattack. She doubled over as pain shot through her torso and down her legs. Stars sparked behind her eyelids as the room tilted to and fro. This was it. This was how it ended.

"Tariq!" shouted a familiar and strangely welcome voice. "Enough!"

With a growl of frustration at being unable to finish regaining his honor, the jihadist named Tariq stepped away from her. Taking advantage of the reprieve the newcomer had bought her, Christine slumped to the floor.

"That's no way to treat our guest," the voice reprimanded Tariq. Then its source grew nearer, a shadow moving behind Christine's clenched eyes.

His footsteps stopped less than a yard away. She could smell his cologne. The same as before. Walid.

Eventually, she willed her eyes to open. As expected, Walid, her momentary savior, stood above her. Tariq seethed behind him, hovering near the door as though unsure whether to take

Walid's reprimand as a dismissal when every bone in his body burned with the desire for retribution upon Christine for the slight to his manhood.

"Although my colleague's manners leave much to be desired, I'm afraid the main thrust of his request remains necessary to our purposes. It has come to our attention that you were the recipient of a parcel shortly before your departure from Cairo. The contents of that parcel were stolen from an associate of ours, and we will require them from you before we proceed any further with your eventual release."

So they know about the SD card, Christine realized with a jolt. She tried to keep her face as impassive as possible, but inwardly she reeled from the consequences. Her kidnapping suddenly took on a whole new perspective. It reached much further than a terrorist faction's desire to use her captivity and murder as a propaganda weapon against the United States and her allies. The associate to whom Walid so vaguely referred must have been the man implicated in the audiologs and documents recorded on the card. This was about cleaning up loose ends before unleashing hell upon the world. Or rather, before manipulating its governments to unleash hell upon themselves.

She had to protect the evidence at all costs. Without it, peace in the Middle East wouldn't be the issue. Peace—and survival—across the entire globe would be.

"I did receive a parcel," she said. "I'm afraid I must have left it on the plane, though. I wasn't able to gather all my luggage before your *colleagues* murdered *my* associates and kidnapped me."

Walid nodded somberly, his expression inscrutable.

"That's as may be, Madam Ambassador. However, I'm afraid my request stands. We have to make sure we're thorough. I'm sure you understand."

"I understand that you and your pervert buddy over there want to leer at a middle-aged American woman for some reason. What would your prophet, peace be upon him, say to that?"

"I assure you, lust for the flesh is the last thing on my mind at this moment. I merely need to verify that you are not hiding anything on your person. Now, will you willingly comply, or should I allow Tariq to remove your clothing for you?"

Christine shivered at the thought of the younger man's crazed, lustful glare, of his hands groping her, violating her as he sought his sick revenge for bum-rushing him moments earlier.

"Fine. On one condition."

"I don't see that you're in a position to negotiate right now, but I'll listen to your request."

She jabbed a finger at Tariq's leering form behind him. "I want him out of the room. And I never want to see him for the rest of my stay."

Walid lifted his eyes as though considering her plea. "Very well. Tariq, you may leave the room. You are not to interfere with our guest for the remainder of her stay. Is that clear?"

"But, Walid, what have I done?"

"Nothing yet that I cannot forgive, but I fear that your lingering will only increase your temptation into a place where neither my mercy nor that of Allah can reach you. Leave us now."

During this exchange, Walid's eyes never left Christine's nor did his tone ever rise above the calm, cool demeanor she had seen him exercise throughout their admittedly limited exchanges thus far. Despite his even tone, Walid's voice exuded a chillingly persuasive power that sent Tariq from the room without further protestation.

The door closed once Tariq left, and Christine heard a bolt slide home. Walid took a step back and motioned with a pistol he had apparently been holding the whole time.

"Just so you know, a repeat performance of *The Great Escape* would be unwise on your part." He flashed a cold smile, a token grin that did not touch his mirthless eyes, before nodding to her. "The sooner you start, the sooner we can be done with this unpleasant business."

She gulped down the rising tide of bile that threatened to overpower her senses. Offering up a quick prayer for courage and for the safety of both herself and the secreted Micro SD card, she began to unbutton her blouse.

Once blouse and pants were removed, she made eye contact with Walid, trying to telepathically plead with him to stop this insanity. Of course, any psychic connection that might have been made failed to abort this twisted striptease, but the studious expression on his face sent shivers down her spine. There was no trace of lust in his eyes. She considered whether he might be homosexual but quickly dismissed the possibility. What she saw in his countenance was neither lust nor appreciation nor revulsion nor anything most human beings experienced when gazing upon the naked form of another. He cared nothing for her firm breasts and taut stomach, still fit from her religious dedication to the gym. Nor did the skin that had begun to sag from her thighs or arms have an impact on him. He was there for one purpose, one cold, sterile, sociopathic purpose. To find the evidence she so desperately wanted to keep hidden.

A few terrified moments later, she was naked, covering her private areas with her hands. She wished she could melt through the floor and escape Walid's studious gaze, but once again the laws of physics refused to bend to her will.

"Kick your clothing over to me."

She did as instructed, praying fervently that the SD card would remain hidden inside her bra clasp.

"Thank you. Now please turn and face the wall while I go through your clothes to ensure you haven't tried to hide anything from me."

Slowly, fearfully, she pivoted away from him, catching a glimpse of him crouching down to finger and prod his way through her blouse.

She had never felt so vulnerable in her life. Naked, locked in a cell a million miles from home, with no one knowing where she was. She had offered a bald-faced lie to the terrorist leader crouching just a few feet behind her, and his fingers were mere inches from discovering the truth. Perhaps it was best that she wasn't watching his search, as an ill-timed holding of her breath could clue him in on her hiding place. But that offered little solace as her fate—and that of the world—was being prodded for in secret behind her.

Though it seemed like hours, it had likely only been a minute or two when Walid finally spoke again.

"It seems as though you may have been telling the truth," he said. "You may turn around and dress yourself."

"Of course I'm telling the truth," she said as she slid on her underwear, happy to have some sort of covering. "I'm sorry, but I don't have time to drop everything I'm doing for every random parcel that comes across my desk."

"It would seem your busyness, though it is no longer a factor for you, has proven a boon for both of us."

She slipped on her bra, feeling the slightly larger-than-usual lump in the clasp that represented the Micro SD's hiding place. It was a tiny distinction, one that only she—and others who regularly wore that style of bra—would notice even if they were looking for it. Walid didn't seem the cross-dressing type. Her secret was safe for now.

His business concluded for the moment, Walid knocked three times on the door.

"What was in the parcel anyway?" she asked, deciding that, to keep up her character and prevent another, perhaps more thorough search, she would naturally be curious about why she had had to suffer through this newest indignity. "Plans for another terrorist attack on America? Another 9/11?"

The bolt on the other side slid out of its slot, and the door swung open a crack. Walid, however, paused at the threshold.

"Another 9/11?" He smiled to himself, a softer grin that seemed genuine, though its source made the expression seem far more terrifying than any harlequin's painted grimace. "No, not like that at all."

As Walid closed the door behind him, Christine realized how true his statement was.

9/11 was child's play compared to what Walid and his associates had planned.

CHAPTER 17

DUBAI, UNITED ARAB EMIRATES

Sonorous calls to prayer from muezzins at mosques across the city filled the late afternoon sky as Wayne led his team from the hospital. The cool, air-conditioned interior gave way to the arid desert heat.

"I can't believe it," Suarez said to no one in particular. "I mean, I can, but I can't."

"I know," Wayne said. The western world had long feared what a nuclear-armed Iran could do to the region—and beyond—but recent events had largely assuaged many leaders' fears, even if they didn't fully trust the promises and intentions of the Islamic nation. But to hear that Iran now had a bomb, and they intended to use it on Israel—who else, of course—was staggering. The only other nuclear power in the Middle East was assumed to be Israel, even though the Jewish state had never officially confirmed or denied the near-universally believed rumor. If Iran used nuclear weapons against Israel, all bets were off. Israel would strike back with nuclear weapons, prompting nuclear-armed Russia and China to enter the fray on Iran's behalf, and the United States and Britain to rally behind Israel. If a second wave of allied nations joined the first—Pakistan, India, France, Germany, and beyond—the conflict would almost certainly be unstoppable. It would be every Cold War American's greatest fear multiplied a hundred-fold, with no way out until the bombs ran out. A nuclear-fueled World War III that would send the entire planet back to the Dark Ages on the wings of five billion irradiated corpses.

Wayne put a hand out to stop Suarez beside him.

"Cops," he said, nodding at the police cars that were trolling through the parking lot.

"Oh good, I was hoping for a challenge," Suarez said dryly. "Rescuing an ambassador from terrorists and preventing a nuclear-armed Iran from starting World War III wasn't quite tough enough on its own." He scanned the parking lot. "Our equipment is in the car," Suarez said. "We've got to get to it so we can tell the president what we know."

"What we think we know," Wayne said, reflecting that the shocking revelation they were grappling with was, at present, based on nothing more than a few pieced-together word fragments from a dying man. Whatever "proof" Rick Weiland asserted the ambassador possessed made her safe and quick recovery all the more paramount. And yet, conjecture or not, they certainly had a responsibility to report in to Washington.

"They're probably looking for us together, so let's split up and meet back at the car. Stay low, keep your head down, and use the cars as barriers," he said. "Slow and steady, we'll make our way across. On my go."

Wayne sighted their vehicle—one of several Land Rovers in the lot—and watched the police car cruising by in the distance.

"Now," he said. He merged with a group of three Western men walking from the hospital toward the parking lot, hoping to disguise his approach from the cops until he was deeper into the maze of cars. Suarez followed Wayne's lead and adopted his own group of expatriates for cover.

Wayne's group veered off to the right, away from the Land Rover. The nearest police car was two rows away, heading toward the opposite end of the lot. Were they here for him and his team? It seemed logical. Perhaps this hospital visit had been all they had been waiting for to confirm their theory: that the three Americans were not businessmen but agents of a foreign government, agents who had been specifically prohibited from Dubai soil by the Emirati government. He was all but sure that physical descriptions of him and his team had been dispatched to every police officer in the area.

Though he hadn't wanted to voice it, Suarez had hit the nail on the head with his sentiment: recovering the ambassador from terrorists in quasi-hostile territory was hard enough; throw in preventing a nuclear war to the mix, along with a side of Washington's bureaucratic incompetence blowing their cover, and their chances were looking slimmer all the time. Wayne would need to have a talk with the president before the team's next mission. *If* there was another mission. He didn't like to think of what his—and his newfound teammates'—fate would be should they fail to retrieve the ambassador before some bloody and likely televised end befell her.

He crouched between two cars as a cop car rounded the bend at the end of the row. As the car's engine approached, he inched himself around the front of the car, staying below the window-line. In the distance, the expatriates' banter grew quieter. He hadn't drawn undue attention to himself, which could have been devastating had one of them decided to call out Wayne's admittedly suspicious behavior.

"Almost there," came a voice at his ear. Suarez. Wayne still had two rows between his position and the Land Rover, and the police cruiser was still cruising down his lane. If Wayne made a break for it, the cop could glance in his rearview mirror and . . .

"Can I help you?"

Wayne looked up to see a middle-aged Indian man staring at him, key ring in hand.

"I'm sorry?" Wayne asked, kicking himself for paying too much attention to the known variables while apparently failing to keep an eye on his six.

"You enjoy rubbing your back against my car? I would hate for you to fall and hurt yourself once I back out and leave." The man's delivery was deadpan, but his eyes glinted with a hint of wry humor.

"Oh, I apologize, sir," Wayne said, checking to see that the police car had rounded the curve at the end of the aisle and then standing up. "A green Land Rover like this one clipped my wife's car a few days ago. Hit and run. I was checking the license plate to see if I'd found the offending vehicle."

"And?"

"Alas, the search continues. My apologies for touching your car in the process. That a fiftieth anniversary edition of the 911 Turbo S Cabriolet?"

"You know your Porsches, sir. Of course, in this city, there are more luxury cars than not."

"True enough. I'm sorry to keep you waiting, but I must be going."

Wayne turned and crossed the next two rows to the Land Rover, watching the patrolling police car turn a corner and head toward the hospital again.

"Making friends?" Suarez, already in the car, said as Wayne opened the driver's side door.

"Easier than having him calling for help at the indignity of his car being violated by a well-dressed fugitive." Wayne climbed inside and keyed up the ignition, glancing around for police before backing out of the space.

"Of course, it's not like an Indian's word would carry much weight around these parts."

"There is that," Wayne responded solemnly. It was sad but true that there was a definite racial hierarchy in Dubai, as in most of the Middle East.

At the top were the locals, Emirati citizens whose family names were plastered on buildings and corporations, who were guaranteed their own home, car, and cushy bureaucratic job—at minimum. Beneath them were other ethnic Arabs, particularly Muslims, though in a relatively open society such as Dubai, Christian Arabs from the Levant and elsewhere were begrudgingly accepted as well. Muslims in general were viewed more favorably than their non-Muslim counterparts, though ethnically, Westerners tended to come in next on the Dubai status totem pole, largely because American, British, European, and Canadian business investors had helped Dubai become the international city it was today. If Westerners were in Dubai, they were usually doing good things for the economy, either working at one of the branches of the myriad Western companies setting up shop in the city—Microsoft, Cisco, General Electric, Boeing—or overseeing one of the companies' many construction projects. In a city that once boasted more than a third of the world's active construction cranes, where new five-star hotels and flashy shopping plazas were still opening on a regular basis to draw in even more tourism dirhams, Western investments, connections, and know-how were a prize, despite how much the Islamic hardliners despised the government's catering to—and embracing of—the extravagant materialism of the "Great White Satan" showcased in the glittering desert metropolis.

Asians, particularly the Filipinos who manned the stores of the malls, came next in line, recognized as necessary to the day-to-day activities of the city, but generally viewed as inferior nonetheless. Blacks, generally from sub-Saharan Africa, were relatively rare in the city, but their racial niche was less than favorable, unless, of course, one's standing in the Muslim community superseded the lack of favor due to ethnicity.

At the bottom of the unofficial caste system were those from the Indian subcontinent. Many Pakistanis were employed as cab drivers or in other blue-collar service jobs, but Indians and Bangladeshis were largely seen as day laborers. The often inhumane working conditions of those Indians, the inhospitable labor camps, and the questionable practice of taking away workers' passports, had made this unseen element of the city's success the centerpiece of a *60 Minutes* exposé. Though the city played host to many Indian doctors, businessmen, and teachers, the entrenched stigma remained.

Regardless, Wayne reflected as he drove toward the lot's exit, a shout from anyone would have made getting out of there even more complicated. He offered a silent prayer of thanks for small blessings.

A police car appeared from behind a hulking SUV at the end of a row, flipped on its emergency lights, and peeled across the lot toward the exit Wayne had just steered his Land Rover through.

"They made us," Wayne said.

Wayne spun his wheel to the left as he floored the accelerator, leaving a smear of black rubber on the asphalt. The cruiser tried to follow, but was blocked by a van trying to turn into the parking lot from the other direction. Honking and shouting ensued while the officer tried to extricate his vehicle from the dustup.

Free of his tail for the moment, Wayne executed another high-speed turn, eliciting honks from motorists on the cross street, and then turned toward an on-ramp that would take them back toward Sheikh Zayed.

He glanced to his right to see Suarez fiddling with something. It was the iPhone he had taken from the hospital room, connected by a white cord to the stereo system's USB port.

"Any luck?"

"Not with what I've got to work with here. Screen's busted, and the phone won't hold a charge."

"This keeps getting better and better," Wayne said as he weaved around traffic on a circuitous route toward the airport. "We need to do a status update anyway. Call Ibrahim. Put it on speaker."

Ibrahim picked up on the second ring.

"You found the ambassador yet?"

"Don't I wish," Wayne said. "Actually, our main lead just died on us, right after informing us that Iran's about to nuke Israel."

"That—that's impossible. The IAEA's been all over them for months."

"Yeah, I've heard the stump speeches too. But I don't have to see a mushroom cloud over Jerusalem to believe they'd pull a fast one on us to get what they want. It's a big country, and IAEA's only searching declared nuclear sites. Who says they couldn't have a few extra sites hidden in the mountains somewhere?"

"Enriching nuclear material is a big, costly affair, one you can't really do without a certain modicum of specially designed infrastructure."

"North Korea snuck one by us with their nuclear program, and we've had tens of thousands of American soldiers patrolling their border for the better part of a century. Who's to say Iran couldn't do the same. Or they could have bought the uranium or plutonium already enriched from North Korea, Pakistan, Russia . . ."

Stunned silence came from the other end of the line as Ibrahim grappled with the plausibility of Wayne's argument and its horrific implications for their mission should it prove true.

"I'm just the messenger here, and we don't have any proof yet, though Weiland seemed to think that the ambassador could provide something to that effect."

"Which makes your mission all the more important now."

Wayne smirked. "Yeah, we figured that one out already."

"I'll let Pierce know right away."

"Do that. While I've got you on the line, though, we did recover a cell phone from the ambassador's entourage. Screen's blown to crap, and we can't get anything from it. Is there any way we can bypass the UI to extract the data within?"

"Probably. How extensive is the damage?"

"Somewhere between *The Warriors* and *Black Hawk Down*."

"That bad, huh? The data might be corrupted too, then, but I'll try to fill in the holes as best I can. What kind of phone?"

Suarez looked at the phone's connection ports. "iPhone. iPhone 5."

"Hey, Suarez, didn't realize you were there. Okay, in your pack of tech goodies, you should have a multi-connection tool. It'll look like a spider with way too many legs."

Suarez rummaged around in his pack for a moment before pulling out the tool. "Found it."

"Find and plug in the connectors for the iPhone's data port and the one at the base of your phone, then push in the corresponding tabs on the tool to complete the circuit."

"Done. Next?"

"Hang on a second." Ibrahim could be heard typing. "Okay, your screen should have a flashing red emblem at the top right."

"Remote server access?" Suarez asked.

"That's the one. Tap it."

Suarez tapped the icon.

"Okay, it's downloading now," Ibrahim said. "Should just take a few seconds."

"Any new intel on your side?" Wayne asked to fill the void.

"Nothing. Whoever these guys are, they're locked up good in the chatter department. Normally a coup like abducting the American ambassador would light up the typical channels, but they've been extraordinarily silent on the matter."

"Which means we're dealing with somebody more professional than your typical terrorists," Suarez said.

"That or the ambassador is part of a larger plan," Ibrahim said.

"Or both," Wayne said.

"Download complete on my end. I'll analyze this and get back to you as soon as I have something. After I notify the president of Weiland's allegations, of course."

"Of course," Wayne said. "Thanks. Wilkins out."

"Chances are, the phone belongs to someone who was on that plane," Suarez said. "Fingers crossed it's the ambassador, but regardless, we can't do anything with it until Ibrahim finishes her recovery.

"Which leaves us with one lead to follow up on now," Wilkins said, pulling onto the ramp for Sheikh Zayed Road, northbound.

"The airport tunnels?" Suarez asked.

"That's it. The scene of the crime. If these guys are as good as Ibrahim thinks, we may not find much of anything, but it's the best angle we've got on the ground right now."

"One question," Suarez said. "If the president didn't even know that the ambassador was coming to Dubai, how on earth did her kidnappers know?"

Wayne had no idea. It was a question he had asked himself several times in the last few hours. And regardless of the answer, he was pretty sure he wouldn't like where it took them.

CHAPTER 18

DUBAI, UNITED ARAB EMIRATES

They were here. The Americans had come to Dubai, just as Walid had predicted. Despite the sheikh's insistence to the contrary, President Talquin had decided to take matters into his own hands.

The Americans introduced an additional hiccup into what would otherwise be a smooth plan from here on out, but Walid chose to view it as a challenge. He could see the entire chessboard, all the moves yet to be made. For his American adversaries, this was all about a bunch of terrorists kidnapping Ambassador Needham. Walid knew it was about much, much more.

This was his city. His homeland. And though the pernicious influence of Western decadence had eroded the values and culture of his people in Dubai, land and family were still worth fighting for. Indeed, the region had been fighting over both for centuries.

Both figured into his decision to enter the world of jihad. While he was away at university in London, his parents and two younger sisters were killed by a drunk driver on Sheikh Zayed Road here in Dubai. An American tourist, drawn in by the lustful glitz and glamour of the soulless metropolis into which the city's leaders had transformed his hometown.

Despite undertaking dozens of operations across the Middle East, Europe, Central Asia, and North Africa since that fateful car crash, he had never conducted a mission back here, where it all started. He had been planning for this mission all his adult life. And though the stakes of the mission itself were sky-high, the personal stakes were huge for him.

It was time to settle a few old scores.

Here, in Dubai, he owned the chessboard, and the Americans were playing blind. But he still needed to take his new adversaries seriously. That was why he led his scouting team of four jihadists toward the tunnels beneath the airport. The Americans would look there before long. And Walid would make sure they received a proper welcome.

The five men were chauffeured by a sixth who drove the nondescript, white, full-size van down the D-60, weaving through the dense traffic wherever possible. If you didn't drive aggressively in this city, you would be waiting for hours for an opening to naturally materialize. Darwin's laws reigned supreme in this city, even in the traffic streams, but Walid and his team were used to taking the initiative and doing what it took to get the job done. Walid ignored the incessant drone of car horns as they cut off frustrated drivers left and right. Traffic stops were not an issue here, unlike in the police-prone West, and he and his men had a glorious get out of free card. Every man had his price. The price of the deputy chief of the Dubai police was one million dollars in gold—pocket change to Walid's paymaster. Of course, getting the payment in gold helped mitigate the loss from what would soon be a devastating crash of Western currencies. A crash that would have Walid's fingerprints all over it.

It was time to send a message, both to the city planners who had paved over his family's history and to the foolhardy Americans whose cowboy dreams deluded them into thinking themselves the heroic cavalry needed in every conflict. The attacks of 9/11 had provided a brief wake-up call. The attack that was coming, and the war it would spark, would devastate the United States, the Zionist regime in Palestine, and their allies around the globe for generations to come.

The van descended into the main traffic tunnel beneath Dubai International Airport. Walid felt the weight of his backpack on his lap as the sky disappeared above him, replaced by harsh fluorescent lighting and desert-themed mosaics that stretched for hundreds of meters along the tunnel's walls. How long would it take to replace all those tiles, he wondered. Or, after they were done with their work here, would anyone even bother to repair the damage?

The van pulled to the side of the road, and the men got out, each carrying his backpack. The driver already knew to wait in a nearby lot and listen for Walid's pickup call when the job was done, so no words were exchanged as the team exited the vehicle and pushed through a chain-link gate in the tunnel. The gate was still bent where Walid had broken a particularly stubborn padlock holding it shut a few days before. Through a maintenance door and up a ladder lay the subterranean passageway through which they had made their escape from the airport with their prisoners in tow. The American investigators, if they were worth anything, would follow the trail into these tunnels. And here their pursuit would end.

Walid led the team through the door, up the ladder, and into the tunnels beyond. They traced the route they had traveled to the attack on the ambassador's plane, the same route the Americans would undoubtedly take to arrive at the access grate closest to the attack site. When they arrived at the grate, Walid was unsurprised to find it freshly secured with not one but two sets of industrial-grade locks. This didn't faze him, however. Everything he needed today was on this side of the grate.

With two men posted as lookout, the other two began to prepare the trap as Walid looked on. One withdrew blocks of semtex from his bag and handed it to his partner, who stood halfway up the ladder to the access grate. The man on the ladder, in turn, affixed the plastic explosives to the side of the dark aperture above his head, being careful as he inserted the detonators not to jostle the apparatus too much. Once finished placing that bomb, the two-man team would move to another strategic point and set the next device, until the contents of all five backpacks were exhausted.

Each man carried enough semtex in their respective backpacks to—if properly applied—destroy a city block. Or implode a runway in one of the busiest airports in the world, with the only clues pointing to a team of Americans who had traveled into the country on a CIA plane under false identities, and who for some reason were trespassing underneath the airport at the very epicenter of the explosion. Win-win.

"Sahib." One of the men standing guard addressed Walid without turning his attention from the tunnels he surveyed. "Why are we doing this? Exposing ourselves in the middle of our operation, I mean."

"Do you know better than I what is best for this operation, Faisal?" Walid said to the foot soldier, his tone biting. "Do you know all the variables better than I, who have orchestrated this operation?"

"No, of course not," Faisal said, fear entering his voice as he maintained his focus on the tunnel ahead. "I do not wish to question your judgment. I only wondered why we would leave the compound to confront these Americans."

"You are right in your concern for our mission," Walid said. "But it is not our leaving the compound that would threaten it. These Americans are here for one purpose: to thwart our God-given destiny and what we will accomplish in the next two days."

Walid stepped to the guard's side and brought his lips close to the man's ear.

"Have you ever seen a rat pursuing a meal, Faisal? Relentless. It will climb fences, chew through walls, go to untold ends in pursuit of its prize. Western scientists put the rats in mazes to watch the vermin pursue and attain their most base goals.

"These Americans are rats, and the ambassador is their slice of cheese. Hiding the ambassador may work for a little while, but they will be relentless in their pursuit unless we take decisive action first."

"A rat trap," Faisal said, turning toward Walid for the briefest moment.

"Exactly." Walid's mouth twisted into a grin. "We bait them with what they think is a nibble of cheese. And then we spring the trap. The bomb will go off, killing the Americans while seeming to implicate them in the explosion. They're not supposed to be in the country, much less burrowing around underneath the airport. It will drive another wedge between the United States and the UAE, not to mention the Arab world as a whole. The Middle East's trust in America is just about drained already, but come tomorrow, when the US will need Arab support more than ever, none will be found. And everything we've prepared for will come to fruition at last."

CHAPTER 19

TEHRAN, IRAN

Arsalan Hosseini, president of Iran, knew the difference between seeing and believing. Right now, for example, he had a problem seeing the series of images his assistant had just forwarded to his computer screen. No matter how he tried, he couldn't fully wrap his mind around what it meant.

In the first few images, the screen was largely obscured by a geyser of black smoke, but later images grew in clarity as the prevailing winds shifted the obscuring plume out of the camera's path. A luxury private jet, ablaze and riddled with bullets. Black SUVs surrounded the plane, with at least a dozen men wielding machine guns of some sort, dragging a white female passenger off the plane.

Terrorism had been a constant in his part of the world as long as he could remember, though it had certainly ramped up in recent years. But this image wasn't taken in Kabul or Baghdad or Mogadishu or Sana'a or Damascus. It was taken in what, until the day this image had been taken, many had believed to be perhaps the safest city in the Middle East. And yet, as this shocking set of images clearly illustrated, terrorism had now made its mark on the global metropolis of Dubai.

What disturbed Hosseini even more was the fact that this wasn't just an attack designed for maximum casualties or visibility. In fact, as the normal goals of terrorism went, a charter plane on the tarmac at the airport was fairly low key, considering all the high-profile resorts and skyscrapers in Dubai. This attack was targeted at something even more specific: a single person who had already made an impressive impact on the Middle East.

Though he would never admit it aloud, particularly here in the presidential Sa'adabad Palace, Hosseini felt that Needham had some good ideas, for a woman. A Western woman at that. But, unlike many of her ilk from the United States or their allies in Europe, she knew a thing or two about the realities of the Middle East. Americans in particular tended to oversimplify peoples who weren't like them, a problem that dated back to white man's earliest days in the so-called New World, where dozens of culturally and linguistically distinct native Indian nations comprised of hundreds of individual tribes were lumped into a neat category called "savages." Needham, however, understood the myriad distinctions between the religious, cultural, ethnic, linguistic, and social traditions that had emerged in the thousands of years since Allah had first breathed life into man.

Most Americans didn't understand that millions of Christians still dwelt in their holy land and elsewhere in the Middle East. They didn't understand that Islam was hardly a singular group but rather a messy conglomerate of Sunnis and Shiites, of jihadists and Wahhabists and Sufi mystics and modern moderates, fractured by centuries of doctrinal conflicts, political divisions, and power struggles. More Muslims had died at the hands of Islamic terrorists than had any other religious adherents. Wars had raged for centuries between Islamic groups.

Further, most Americans were happy to lump the latest brown people living "over there" into a singular category of "Arabs." Needham understood the difference between Syrians and Lebanese, between Bedouins and Persians, between Arabs and Palestinians. Perhaps not as well as a true Middle Easterner, but better than most in Washington. And she knew her history, understanding that the lines on the modern-day map of the region were drawn a hundred years ago by men who had little understanding of the cultural and social nuances of the peoples who lived there, slicing up the former Ottoman Empire in the wake of the First World War for convenience of colonial rule, without an eye toward the true divisions. Needham, however, understood these distinctions very well, and had been approaching not only the nominal leaders of the countries of the region, but also leaders of ethnic and religious minorities within those countries. Though he didn't put nearly as much stake in her abilities as the Western press, several top news organizations had called her the best chance for a lasting peace in the Middle East.

And now she was gone.

Worse still, an enhanced version of one of the images showed a man he recognized, a Hezbollah operative whose face he'd seen in a briefing during his previous position as director of *Bonyad Shahid va Omur-e Janbazan*, or the Foundation of Martyrs and Veteran Affairs. Though the man's name escaped him, he did remember two key elements about the man. First, the man, like all those mentioned in that particular briefing, was a Hezbollah operative, helping to enforce Iran's vision of a Shiite-dominated, Israel-free world in Lebanon and beyond. Second, the man, as with most who crossed his desk in that particular program, was supposed to be dead.

The man in the image was clearly not dead. And kidnapping a high-profile American official in a nation that had designated Hezbollah a terrorist organization was certainly not an operation he had signed off on.

Somebody was keeping secrets from him. Someone in his own government, most likely. And he had a good idea who it might be.

He stared at the phone on his desk for a moment. One phone call could clear this up. A miscommunication, a rogue operation, some simple explanation for the unthinkable attack that had apparently just occurred. But it wouldn't be simple. And it could very well be his undoing.

He hit a few keys to lock his computer, and then stood and left his office. After telling his secretary he'd be out for an hour, maybe two, he left the palace and gave his driver instructions. Hosseini knew who would have the answers he was looking for. But he was equally sure he wouldn't like where they took him.

CHAPTER 20

DUBAI, UNITED ARAB EMIRATES

Abushakra!

Christine had heard the patronymic surname used through her cell door. Referring to her new friend Walid, no less. And it made even more pieces fall into place.

While consulting with the Senate Foreign Intelligence Committee shortly before her appointment by the Talquin administration as special ambassador to the Middle East, Christine had run across the name in a briefing. The intelligence on the man's recent activities was relatively scant, but it was the nature of what he was doing that intrigued her at the time.

Jihad for hire. Islamist mercenaries. Blackwater for the bad guys.

It was revolutionary, and a few other outfits were starting to crop up to seize their own piece of the pie, but Walid Abushakra's *Uhmar Haidar* was the first and—by all accounts—the best at their extremely specialized niche.

Usually knowing more about your enemy was a tactical advantage, but right now Walid's reputation terrified her more than anything.

Everything fit with what she knew. The London accent. The cultured appearance. Even her recollection of the photographs she'd seen of him—taken years earlier while he was still a student in the UK—seemed to match up with her captor. Including the profile of the man and his work.

A freelance jihadist group like *Uhmar Haidar* would be perfect for a mission like this. Professional. Loyal. Untraceable. And Christine had no doubt that the mastermind behind all of this would spare no expense to ensure its success. *Uhmar Haidar* was the best at what they did, as attested by the countless bodies left in their wake across nearly a dozen countries over the past few years. And as equally attested by how—to date—not one of the principals had been captured or killed; and none of the grunts had ever allowed himself to be taken alive. It was an organization that thrived more on the cold professionalism of KGB-era spycraft—cyanide pills and all—than the anger-fueled, mistake-prone youth that filled the ranks of most jihadist organizations. And that, of course, was the point.

From her understanding, there were two principals in the organization: Walid Abushakra and a Syrian named Omar Sawaf. Sawaf was a player in the early days of the Syrian Civil War, a former junior officer who defected from the military to fight against Bashar Assad's regime. He was a dedicated strategist who led his own troops into battle with dozens of confirmed kills to his name. Then one of his fellow officers had decided he had chosen the losing side, betraying Sawaf and his men's plans to the opposition on the eve of a strategic battle. After losing nearly half his men in the grisly firefight that followed, Sawaf withdrew to reevaluate. Enter Walid.

The Syrian uprising was the first playing field in which Walid Abushakra tested out his new mercenary experiment. Still reeling from his former compatriot's betrayal and desperately needing a morale-boosting victory for his men, Sawaf contracted *Uhmar Haidar* for an attack against the very base where the twice-traitor had taken refuge after leaving the rebel cause.

The attack was a resounding success, from both strategic and symbolic standpoints. The traitorous lieutenant was killed in the night assault along with three other officers and four dozen soldiers. Five fighter jets were also destroyed, thanks to bombs built and planted by Omar himself during the operation.

The mission shifted Sawaf's perspective on modern warfare. Just as the United States' war in Vietnam and the Soviets' incursion into Afghanistan had laid bare the problems with fighting a conventional war against guerilla opponents, the newest horizon in the warscape was a reinvention of one of its oldest tropes: mercenaries. Professional, talented, with a dedicated focus on the mission at hand.

In the fractious landscape of the modern Middle East, fragmented and arbitrarily shuffled around by the ghosts of colonialism, personal allegiances were often complex webs with a dozen shifting attributes. Islam, even the militant version, was hardly the monolithic entity many in the West believed it to be. Even beyond the main split of Sunnis and Shiites, there were myriad factions within each of those. And although two people or groups might believe in or worship Allah the same way, there could be enmity between the two because of ethnic strife, cultural rifts, or an unforgiven injury dealt a thousand years ago. *Uhmar Haidar* changed all that.

Walid's group pushed everything else to the side and made dedication to the group itself—and to its current mission—the principal allegiance. It didn't matter the shade of your skin, what your grandfather's name was, or which blend of cultural and religious beliefs you claimed as your own. All that mattered was unfettered loyalty and consummate professionalism at their very specific set of skills. And for that, members of *Uhmar Haidar* were very well rewarded.

After their first joint mission, Omar and Walid decided to form a partnership, each bringing their expertise to the nascent group to build it into something the world had never seen. It wasn't as easy to recruit for *Uhmar Haidar* as it was for a simpler cause—like fighting against foreign incursions, corrupt regimes, or religious infidelity—but those who did pass the rigorous vetting process stuck around much longer and were on the whole far more valuable than the impressionable cannon fodder that represented much of the rank and file of their more traditional competitors.

Over the intervening years, Walid and Omar's partnership grew into an underground legend, attracting the attention of foreign powers across the globe who feared what this mercenary organization could become. As their infamy grew, so did their pricing scheme, with unofficial estimates of the group's total assets topping eight figures in US dollars. *Uhmar Haidar* was very selective about what missions they took, but those they took were completed with an aplomb largely unseen in the jihadist world.

And now, they had been tasked with her capture and eventual execution. Which, coupled with their apparent ties to the memory card she had still managed to conceal, showed just how important this whole operation was. And how important *she* was to their plans.

Though her naked confessions of ignorance may have convinced Walid that, at the very least, she did not currently have any material evidence implicating their employer, she had little confidence that his vague reference to releasing her would ever come to fruition. *Uhmar Haidar* and the masterminds behind it were too smart to leave loose ends. Their loyalty was not to their consciences or the human condition; it was to the mission and the mission alone.

So they wanted to kill her. At a time and place of their careful choosing. So she was integral to their plans somehow. And following through on their plans was always paramount.

Christine steeled herself and stared at her cell door, thinking. It was time to mess up *Uhmar Haidar*'s flawless track record.

CHAPTER 21

DUBAI, UNITED ARAB EMIRATES

Wayne and Suarez met up with Nasef at the western edge of the airport perimeter after parking the Land Rover in a nearby lot. The sun hung low in the sky, casting long shadows across the arid cityscape and promising night's reprieve from the sun's brutal heat.

"A nuke?" Nasef said after Wayne had filled him in on what they had learned at the hospital. "I can't believe it."

"Tell me about it," Wayne said. He motioned with his head toward the airport. "What've we got here?"

"There seem to be three entrances," Nasef said, pointing to a digital satellite image of the area displayed on his PDA. "Here, here, and here. I've had to rotate between them, but I haven't seen any activity yet."

"Which one is closest to where the attack took place?"

"They're all at least half a klick away, but this one here seems to have the most direct path out. Problem is, it's also the hardest to get to from this end. See, these two have above-ground access through grates just outside the perimeter fence. This one, however, comes out in another tunnel beneath the airport. One with cars."

"These cameras here?" Wayne asked, pointing to black boxes mounted on poles near the first two entrances.

"Looks that way."

"It's the third one. The other two are too open, too exposed. Cameras, daylight, open field of view from the tarmac where they just attacked the plane. They'd have a getaway van or something to pick them up in the tunnels and drive them to safety."

"That actually makes sense," Nasef said thoughtfully.

"Don't sound so surprised," Wayne said. "There may be nothing for us to find down there, but I'd bet good money that's where they escaped from the tunnels."

They left their vehicles in the parking lot and headed toward the third tunnel entrance on foot. Cars would be confined to the flow of traffic once in the airport tunnel section of the D-60—known to residents simply as "the airport tunnel." The road was a nightmare at rush hour and, with no vehicular exits or entrances once inside, it would be a rotten place to get trapped. The team wouldn't be investigating the maintenance tunnels from the front seats of their SUVs, so it made sense to ditch them now rather than obstruct traffic by leaving them on the side of the road in the underground bottleneck and drawing unwanted attention to themselves.

Technically, there wasn't a pedestrian section of the congested airport tunnel, but Wayne wouldn't let technicalities get in the way of a mission. Technically, murder was illegal in all sixteen countries in which he'd operated as a splinter-cell assassin for the CIA, but he still went through with his hits. Technically, they were in Dubai on forged passports as foreign agents acting on behalf of another nation's government and, technically, resisting arrest, causing and fleeing the scene of an accident, and speeding were all illegal here as well. Before this mission was over, they were surely going to break another few dozen laws, likely including trespassing, assault, murder, and other standards of the trade, so introducing a foot traffic element to the tunnel's congestion seemed a minor transgression. The trick, of course, was to infiltrate the tunnel on foot without drawing attention to themselves.

They took turns changing clothes in the back of the Land Rovers, switching from their business attire into generic maintenance uniforms. The team also used the opportunity to assemble their pistols from components Support had hidden in otherwise fully functional camera and electronic equipment. The uniforms provided them with large, specially constructed pockets to easily conceal the weapons, along with their PDAs, a coil each of clothesline, and a few other tricks of the trade. Each man tested his comm unit and made sure it was secure in his ear. If things got hairy down there, either from the cops or the terrorists themselves, none of them wanted to be out of touch with the rest of the team should they get separated.

Once prepared to move out, they left their vehicles in the lot and sauntered to the road that led into the tunnel. Casual but purposeful, so they wouldn't draw too much attention. A thin, concrete ledge, a tiny excuse for a sidewalk just barely wider than a standard curb intended for official business only, traced the edge of the road as it descended beneath the runways above.

Wayne and his team walked single-file along the ledge and into the subterranean maw beneath the airport. Twin mosaics of blue and white tiles flanked the road as it dipped into the earth. Sailboats, seagulls, the Burj al Arab hotel, and other iconic symbols of Dubai stood out against a sand-stained sky, as an endless stream of taxi cabs and luxury vehicles honked their way through the tunnel. Though Wayne avoided making direct eye contact with any of the drivers and thus drawing attention to himself, he didn't think any of them took particular notice of the three non-Arab, non-Indian maintenance men walking alongside. Business as usual in Dubai. Unfortunately, this was the one exit from the airport's maintenance tunnels that Nasef hadn't been able to easily recon before Wayne and Suarez had arrived, and he wasn't happy going in largely blind. The onslaught of drivers and passengers would likely work to their benefit, since Ambassador Needham's kidnappers—were they still hanging around the scene of the crime, perhaps keeping her in a forgotten maintenance room inside—would be less prone to mount another attack with so many potential witnesses about. At least, that was what logic seemed to dictate, but already Wayne had found too many aspects of this mission to be suspect at best. And *that* was business as usual in Wayne Wilkins's world.

"We're coming up on it," Suarez said from behind Wayne. He was palming his PDA, the map screen tracking their movements with the subterranean schematics superimposed over the top. "About fifty feet ahead on the left."

"I see it," Wayne said, eyeing a chain-link break in the tiled wall that, according to the schematics, created a barrier between the highway and a small antechamber that held the entrance to the maintenance tunnel.

When they reached the tunnel, Wayne could see they were on the right track. The gate was bent on one side, and scrape marks, likely from an attempt to break through a now-missing lock, marred the metal frame. He pushed through the gate, leading the team into an alcove with a locked circuit-breaker box to one side of a previously locked door. The door had been jimmied, its lock bored out with some sort of drilling device. A scattering of metal shavings dusted the floor. Though the attack was only a day old, he was surprised that airport security hadn't fixed the door yet. Perhaps no one had discovered the door as the terrorists' point of entry yet, or perhaps bureaucracy between the airport and the transportation administration had caused a repair-hindering territory dispute. Regardless, Wayne was grateful for the already cleared egress, not wanting to have to break through the door while a constant stream of witnesses drove by on the street a few yards behind them.

Wayne pulled open the door, surprised to come face-to-face almost immediately with a short ladder set into the concrete wall, ascending to another level about eight feet above. He climbed up and waited at the top for the rest of his team to join him.

He gestured to Suarez, who pulled his PDA from his pocket and held it out. The schematic was still on the screen, and Wayne tapped an icon to shift the overlay to their current level within the tunnels. He looked at his men and used his finger to trace the route to the access hatch likely used in the attack. Suarez and Nasef each nodded in turn.

Wayne pulled out his sidearm, and the others followed suit. There would be no bluffing their way out of this if they were caught down here. No cover story Pierce and company could concoct would explain away their skulking around beneath the airport. They had reached the point of no return; everything they did from here on out would be denied and disavowed by the US government.

The route was fairly straightforward, approximately five-hundred meters as the crow flies. Their problem, however, would be to ensure that their journey to the access grate was both thorough and conflict-free. If the terrorists left any trace of themselves behind—and in a hasty retreat while transporting two unwilling or unconscious prisoners, there likely was some sort of clue—the team had to find it. At the same time, being discovered by security or even by a legitimate maintenance worker could prove fatal to their investigation and their mission.

The distant roar of jet engines on the tarmac overhead merged with the drones of fans, motors, and other machinery below to fill the tunnel with a muted cacophony of industrial sounds. The noise would help obscure their footsteps, but it would make those of others down here difficult to distinguish as well. Overhead, fluorescent lights buzzed softly in their plastic casings, illuminating the gray concrete of the walls and floor with a harsh, slightly flickering glow. Other than the occasional words or sector identification code stenciled in red or green paint on the walls, the tunnels were free from adornment, a far cry from the luxurious entryway that greeted air passengers to the city thirty feet above their heads. Another chain-link gate, similar to the one outside, blocked access to what a sign warned were tanks of jet fuel. As Wayne wasn't authorized personnel, he decided not to press his luck, checking the schematic again and navigating around the barrier to resume their course on the other side.

A few steps along, he stopped abruptly, holding up a fist to the men behind him. The others stopped and listened for a few seconds. Voices, or so it seemed over the din of airliners and subterranean machinery. He couldn't make out any words, but they were male and seemed to be speaking Arabic.

Wayne looked at the schematic and surveyed the route ahead. He pointed to Suarez and Nasef, and then traced his finger along a direct route to their destination, from which the voices seemed to be coming.

The voices grew louder as the men walked down another concrete passageway. Wayne gave a hold signal as they reached an intersection. A left turn here would, according to the schematic, take them directly to the access grate nearest the attack site. It was also the direction from which the voices were coming. Were they local authorities, investigating the site of the crime? Or perhaps the terrorists, returning for round two?

Though he spoke some Arabic, Wayne could only catch snatches of the men's hushed conversation, a mélange of accented tones echoing off walls and commingling with the thrum of machinery. *Y'allah*, roughly translated as "hurry," was repeated several times, and if time wasn't on the men's side, perhaps that was an indication that, like Wayne and his team, they had no official cover if they were discovered down here. But it was too risky to just open fire on the men. If they were cops, killing them would only serve to bring a world of hurt down on the team's heads and essentially doom the mission.

The passageway between Wayne and the Arabic men was dimmed by the loss of several overhead lights that had burnt out and not yet been replaced. As in many places around the world, the shiny, presentable exterior of the city didn't extend to the parts the target audience—tourists, businessmen, and investors—would never see. This lackadaisical attitude toward proper workplace lighting might have warranted a visit from OSHA stateside, but here, the slight darkness would aid their advance. A pair of shallow alcoves about halfway down the stretch would provide better vantage points from which Wayne and another team member could see the Arabic men.

Wayne used his PDA to silently key out instructions to his team, showing them the screen. He and Nasef would slink forward into the alcoves while Suarez made his way around to another passage that led to that intersection, holding at the entrance until Wayne's signal. If the Arabic-speaking men were investigating at the behest of the Dubai or UAE government, they would all double back to this point, exit the tunnels, and come back in a few hours. If they were a tunnel's length away from the terrorists, though, Wayne didn't want all three of them shooting down the same narrow stretch, increasing the chances of both friendly fire and of being flanked by an enemy only guarded on one side.

Suarez split off, heading further down the hallway before turning left to make his way around to a flanking position. Wayne counted to thirty after he disappeared around the corner. Then he nodded to Nasef and began their advance. What looked like a sentry at the end of the hall was talking with another man, somewhat distracted from his duties by the conversation.

When the sentry turned his attention to the other man again, Wayne scurried down the hall, keeping his head down and hugging the wall to prevent a tall, backlit silhouette from alerting the guard. Though he had to maintain speed so as to be in cover once the sentinel resumed his vigil, he plodded carefully, making sure his footfalls didn't rise above the mechanical thrum that permeated the subterranean corridors. A few interminable seconds of exposed darting later, Wayne ducked into the alcove, followed a moment later by Nasef in the alcove opposite.

Just as he reached cover, though, Wayne caught sight of a rectangular bundle one man was handing to another. It was a bundle he recognized, for he had used it many times in his career, both in the Army and in the CIA.

Plastic explosives. Which confirmed two things: these men weren't cops, and they were even more heavy duty than he was anticipating.

And then the gunfire began.

CHAPTER 22

WASHINGTON, D.C.

President James Talquin continued to rub his temples with his thumbs, resting his elbows on the Resolute desk in the otherwise unoccupied Oval Office. He had sent Logan Pierce away after he delivered the unthinkable news from his team in the field by way of Janan Ibrahim.

Iran had the bomb!

Talquin had been in seemingly impossible situations before. In fact, his track record of navigating the most harrowing minefields of life and death was one of the reasons he was in the White House today. As a fighter pilot in the first Gulf War, he had shot down fourteen enemy aircraft and led three successful air-to-ground attacks on key Iraqi installations. Despite his well-heeled background as son of Walter Talquin, the late construction magnate and six-term senator from New Hampshire, the future president had volunteered for duty after seeing graphic photographs of the horrendous results of Saddam's gassing of Kurdish citizens in his own country. He had served for a decade as the CEO of a multinational technology firm, requiring snapshot decisions on cutthroat deals with billions of dollars and thousands of jobs on the line. And, of course, he had run for president with little political experience other than growing up under the shadow of "Ol' Walt" Talquin, the politicos and pundits trying to tear him a new one while he offered the voters his Washington outsider approach that won him a narrow primary victory and an even narrower general election—both through pluralities. But now, just a few months into his young presidency, his flagship foreign policy achievement was blowing up in his face.

First Christine going off the reservation, then her abduction in Dubai, and now reports that Iran may already have the nuclear bomb the West had feared for the better part of a decade. Though the more moderate President Hosseini may have taken over the public reins of the country, Talquin knew full well that the Ayatollah Khomani Mahoud Naghinejad was the real head of state, the supreme leader, and anything but moderate.

Naghinejad was an apocalyptic Twelver who believed the return of the twelfth imam, also known as the Mahdi—a messianic figure that this branch of Shia Islam believed would return in the last days to usher in their version of Armageddon—to be imminent. Most worrisome, though, was that some of Talquin's advisors were of the belief that the ayatollah ascribed to that most extreme version of the Twelver camp—that the Mahdi would only be prompted to return by certain events coming to pass, among them the complete destruction of Israel and the reestablishment of a caliphate spanning from Spain to Libya to Egypt through the holy Arabian Peninsula to the Holy Land, Turkey, the former Ottoman Empire, the Baltic States, Central Asia, India, Afghanistan, and, of course, modern-day Persia itself, Iran.

The prospect of a nuclear-armed Iran was unacceptable, and recent years had seen the US and her allies attempting to engage the Islamic republic to dial down its uranium-enriching activities and open its facilities to UN inspectors, in return for the retraction of crippling economic sanctions. The negotiations had met with mixed success, with many detractors alleging that the West's stance was only giving Iran extra time to fulfill its ultimate goal of becoming a nuclear power, the first such confirmed state in the Middle East. Israel was largely suspected of having nuclear weapons—though even Talquin didn't know for sure—but the Jewish nation had never confirmed or denied the widely held belief. What was certain was that a nuclear strike on Israel by Iran—or a pre-emptive strike by Israel anticipating such a move by a nuclear-armed Iran—would be devastating for the region, and the world. But it wouldn't stop there. China and Russia would have Iran's back, while the US and Britain would step up on Israel's behalf. All four were major nuclear powers. Once the nuclear genie was out of its bottle, Pakistan and India—geopolitical foes since the Muslim nation had broken away from its largely Hindu neighbor decades ago—would likely launch their own atomic war. It was the World War III the world had feared since Nagasaki. And it was the end-times scenario Naghinejad and his ilk would delight in, anticipating the Mahdi's imminent return in the wake of such apocalyptic devastation.

In 1945, the United States had opened an atomic Pandora's Box by launching the first—and only—nuclear attacks the world had yet seen. Throughout the Cold War, the post-Soviet destabilization of the Baltic states and myriad former communist republics across Eastern Europe and Central Asia, the Wars on and for Terror that had followed the attacks of 9/11, the horrors of nuclear war and the fears of mutually assured destruction had served as a solid deterrent to another atomic act of war. Even the reclusive and antagonistic North Korea, who shocked the world in 2006 with its revelation of its successful nuclear weapon program, wasn't about to launch an attack on its enemies, of whom there were many. Simply being a nuclear power gave a nation a certain respect and a better place at the bargaining table, realizing that the nation could wreak untold havoc upon your country if it so desired. Mutually assured destruction had kept nuclear-armed world powers from launching full-scale wars against one another. The greatest weapon the world had ever seen had ironically become a promoter of peace, for what a given nation stood to lose from attacking her enemies far outweighed what it could gain.

The rules that had kept the globe nuclear-war-free for the past seven decades meant nothing when the aggressor felt there was nothing to lose. Who cared if tens of millions of your citizens died, your cities were leveled, your country wiped off the map, if your messiah would fix everything once the deed was done. With the balance tipped in favor of having far more to gain from destroying her enemies in atomic fire, Naghinejad-led Iran would not be swayed by warnings of its own assured destruction.

If Iran did in fact already have the bomb, and if they were already planning an attack on Israel, the only winning scenario here was to stop Naghinejad's forces before they could orchestrate the attack. Unfortunately, Israel would also have to be kept out of the loop, for if they got word that their longtime enemy now had a nuke with their name on it, the nation would not hesitate to launch a pre-emptive attack—possibly even a nuclear one—on Iran.

Considering how Wilkins's team had uncovered the intel about the nuke, Talquin prayed that they would be able to follow that thread to something more concrete, some way to intercept Naghinejad's plans or even the bomb itself and use that proof to rally the international community to pressure Iran to scrap its nuclear program altogether and fully open up its borders to IAEA inspectors under pain of devastating sanctions that would undoubtedly lead to open revolution against the ayatollah's regime. But while Wilkins and company scoured Dubai for the missing ambassador and Naghinejad's plans, Talquin had to devise a contingency plan.

His predecessor's approach in the Middle East—hands off at times, while at others supporting the wrong leader—had left many countries destabilized and had alienated several former US allies. Thankfully, the peace summit outreach project Christine had been working on had served to rebuild some bridges for his administration, and there were at least a few key friends in the region he could count on. At least, that's what he hoped.

He took a deep breath, picked up the phone, and began to dial.

CHAPTER 23

DUBAI, UNITED ARAB EMIRATES

Suarez had thought he had a clear shot, but the bomb-maker had dropped from the ladder at the exact moment he fired. His bullet flew wild, but clued the terrorists to the fact that they were not alone. Within moments, his tiny tunnel was filled with flying lead and a cacophony of gunfire. Squeezing off a few more rounds, at least one of which was met with a satisfying grunt of pain, Suarez ducked back around the corner. His advantage now lost, he had to reevaluate. And pray that his teammates could help put out this fire he'd started.

«»

The gunfire wasn't directed down Wayne and Nasef's passageway, so Suarez had either gotten trigger-happy or had been spotted. Either way, there was no going back now.

Wayne found a discarded safety helmet resting on a wooden pallet in his alcove, hung it from the muzzle of his pistol and eased it into the hallway. A burst of automatic fire perforated the helmet, knocking it loose from the barrel and into a tailspin on the floor. Wayne and Nasef exchanged a knowing look, and then each pulled a flash-bang grenade disguised as a tape measure, pressed a button to start the charge countdown, and tossed them down the hall, Wayne's a second before his teammate's.

Wayne covered his ears and closed his eyes as the nonlethal devices exploded, disorienting their opponents. Gripping his weapon tight, he pushed himself out from the safety of the alcove and ran toward the ladder at the end of the hall. From here he could see three, no, four men, the sentry and his companion firing blindly down the corridor to Wayne's right, fighting through the effects of the grenade's detonation. The man who was ostensibly wiring the semtex had fallen from his perch, but was now attempting to climb back up the ladder, while the one who had been assisting him was crouched, rubbing his eyes and looking around, trying to regain his senses.

Another man backed into the intersection, shooting down the right hallway toward where Suarez must have been returning fire. He then fell back, grabbing his chest in a futile attempt to stem the flow of blood now escaping from his bullet-pierced breast. Another cry of pain from the man on the ladder as a plume of crimson mist sprayed from his ankle, the victim of another hail of Suarez's bullets.

Fully exposed and no longer concerned about the sound of their footsteps now that the percussive dance of gunfire filled the concrete tunnel, Wayne and Nasef ran to close the gap to the intersection as quickly as possible. Suarez fired three shots at the sentry, catching the terrorist in the arm and ribs. With a pained look of fury, the man turned toward them, aiming his weapon down the hall. Wayne slowed his run just enough to aim, firing off two shots that both found their mark, one in the neck, one in the right eye socket. The terrorist collapsed, his AK-47 clattering to the floor.

His companion, who now seemed to be the leader, looked at the body, then at Wayne and Nasef bearing down on him. He yelled something in Arabic to his companions, dropping to the ground as Wayne's bullets flew overhead. He brought his rifle to bear and swept the hall with hot lead. The Americans hit the floor just in time, the bullets flying past harmlessly. Wayne aimed at the leader before he could adjust his own weapon downward.

It was a standoff neither could win. Wayne had proven himself an ace shot in his killing of the man's companion, and there would be no doubt that he could deliver a killing shot before the terrorist could kill him. They needed to take this man alive, though, since, as the leader, he would know all the security and safeguards protecting the ambassador from rescue. A maiming shot would help to lessen the threat the man posed—both before and after his capture—but firing any kind of nonlethal shot would surely lead to another, better-aimed burst of gunfire from which Wayne would have no escape.

The leader, his gaze venom-filled as he stared down Wayne, yelled something else and darted to the left, through a service door to safety. The terrorist who had been helping the bomb technician up the ladder regained his senses and followed, pushing through the door right before it shut. Wayne shoved himself off the ground and immediately pursued, but found the door locked.

Nasef ran down their hallway to the intersection, meeting Wayne in a subterranean plaza of bloodied corpses and spent cartridges. Two dead terrorists lay at their feet, with one more trying to climb the ladder to relative safety, but unable to put much weight on the leg pierced by an American bullet. Nasef grabbed the man's good ankle and yanked him down, gripping his wrists and securing them with a plastic flex tie.

"Where does that door go?" Wayne asked, still catching his breath.

"Not on the map," Nasef said, after a brief consultation with the schematic on his PDA.

A moment later, Suarez—who had apparently looped around in a failed attempt to intercept the terrorists' escape—came running back down the hall. "They're gone. No sign of them."

"Fantastic," Wayne said, fighting the irrational urge to kick one of the dead terrorists at his feet in frustration.

"Watch him," Nasef said, shoving the bomb-maker toward Suarez. He then climbed the ladder to look at the terrorist's handiwork. Ripping the detonator prongs from the plastic explosive and peeling the semtex from the ceiling, he tossed the inert components to the floor and descended in two bounding steps. "Safe as is. Could be useful as evidence; trace it to their supplier."

"Good point," Wayne said, though he doubted it would yield anything truly helpful. "Bag it, then check the bodies for ID. Suarez, take a couple of mug shots for Ibrahim to run."

Even underneath a noisy runway, there was no way the gunfight had gone completely unheard by everyone above and below the tarmac. They had to make their escape now, before the authorities showed up, and before the escaped terrorists could get too much of a head start.

He gestured to the backpacks on the floor. "Everybody grab a pack or two. Strap one on our new friend here. He's coming with us."

Several tense minutes later, the trio and their newfound companion made it to the entrance of the tunnel system and back on Tunnel Road. In an effort to prevent their prisoner from throwing himself in front of a car while they made their way single-file back up the narrow shoulder and back into daylight, Wayne decided that Suarez would watch the man while Wayne and Nasef fetched the cars. Five minutes later, Wayne honked his Land Rover twice at the chain-link gate, and Suarez shoved the captured terrorist into the back seat, forcing his head below the level of the tinted windows.

"Where now?" Nasef asked over comms once they were on their way again, nearby cars' horns subsiding then growing anew as he pulled into traffic behind them.

"Somewhere I can think and we can talk to our new friend here. You sent those headshots to Ibrahim yet?"

"Yes, sir. No reply yet, but those facial recognition programs aren't exactly as efficient as they are in the movies."

"You get anything out of our friend yet?" Wayne asked.

"Other than a few Arabic invectives against us infidels, not much. I think he just needs a little persuasion."

A plan was forming in Wayne's mind. He didn't like all that it entailed, but it seemed the best course of action. And he had seen a certain tool in Ibrahim's pack of goodies that would serve him well in its execution. This was one of his least favorite parts of the job. Diving down the same rabbit hole had eventually driven him to leave the military. It was times like these that made him doubt who he was and what his job was molding him into. But, distasteful as it was to him, it had to be done. Millions of lives more innocent than their blood-stained captive's depended on it.

"Find us someplace isolated," he said to Suarez, who pulled up the GPS map function on his PDA. "Somewhere we won't attract unwarranted attention. Somewhere no one will hear our new friend's screams."

CHAPTER 24

DUBAI, UNITED ARAB EMIRATES

Walid was tempted to shoot his companion in the face, but that wouldn't solve anything. Their driver—summoned by an irate call for a pickup a good thirty minutes before anticipated—was focused on swerving through traffic and getting back to their base as soon as possible, attempting to ignore the furious diatribe that was being launched at their leader in the van's cabin behind him.

"What was that for?" Samir yelled, sitting opposite Walid in a facing bench seat. "What possible purpose did that serve? We exposed ourselves, we lost Faisal, Tamer, and Karim, and now they know who we are. Does that mean nothing to you, Walid?"

Walid slapped the man, leaving a deep red mark across the man's stubbled cheek. "Of course it means something to me, you fool. It all means something to me. Perhaps if Faisal had been a better shot, perhaps if you hadn't just given up like a woman . . ."

"Don't you dare speak of my brother like that." Samir's face contorted into a twisted portrait of fathomless rage and sorrow. "Don't you dare."

In truth, Walid was just as furious as Samir with the turn things had taken—and his foresight-addled role in bringing them to pass. Yes, he had now identified the enemy, but he had lost three men and, as far as he knew at least, hadn't so much as wounded the Americans. The rats had stolen the cheese and now had at least an inkling of what the hunter smelled like. If he was in Samir's shoes, he would be tempted to let loose with a similar tsunami of vitriol, but the fact remained that he was the boss. This mission and its successful completion were his responsibility, and his men—his employees—knew the risks before signing up. But the risks involved with the high-stakes missions they received were only part of the reason Walid and his team was paid so well. The other part was that they were the best at what they did. Their performance in the tunnels, being surprised, outflanked and outgunned by the very men for whom they were laying their own surprise was unacceptable. Privately, he took that blame upon himself. To his men, though, there would be no mea culpa. This defeat could be used to strengthen the rest of the men's resolve, tapping into the litany of reasons they had joined his cause, from nationalism to Islamic fundamentalism to anti-imperialism; from pride to youthful aggression to pure, simple greed. Revenge for their fallen comrades was always an effective rallying cry. He could use this embarrassing failure to his advantage, but only if he played it right.

"Faisal knew the risks. He is in paradise now, and you, left behind, must finish his work. If you want to quit now, let me know." He paused, allowing Samir—mouth still set as though needing to spit out something distasteful but unable to do so—to nod his continued support of the mission. "The men who killed your brother are still looking for us. You must bring justice to his spirit by spilling the blood of his murderers. Only then will there be time for mourning."

In lieu of a reply, Samir leaned back against the seat and closed his eyes, his arms crossed against his chest as he shrank back inside himself, allowing grief to fuel his rage at the American invaders. Walid had seen fighters who had lost loved ones to enemy attacks assume this position before, and when the battle-scarred men came out of their dark shell, they often proved far more ferocious fighters than they had been before. Though pure rage could be an asset or a liability in a firefight, the fact that Samir's fury was no longer focused on Walid but on their mutual enemy was an immediate boon.

With Samir's grief temporarily sated, Walid dialed a preprogrammed number in his phone. After a few electronic whirs and clicks as signals were scrambled and decoded and the line became fully secure, he heard Omar Sawaf's gruff voice pick up.

"And now we wait?" he said.

"If only," Walid answered. "Their visit at the hospital wasn't nearly as long as we had anticipated. And Dahhan yet again failed to contain them."

"They showed up in the tunnels while you were still there?"

"Killed Tamer and Faisal. Samir and I got away. Karim took a bullet or two, but I think he escaped through the hatch."

"And the bomb?"

"Karim failed to finish rigging it."

"Did you kill any of the Americans?"

"No."

Distantly, as though he had set the phone down, Sawaf's dic-tion-less roar of frustration echoed through the phone, followed by a percussive tumult that was likely furniture being kicked.

"I told you this was a fool's errand," Sawaf said when returning to the receiver. "You're so eager for your own personal vengeance that you've endangered the mission."

"I've done no such thing. As always, Omar, the mission is everything. You should know that better than anyone."

"I do, but this is different. Being here, your hometown, you've changed somehow."

"You're mistaken. Right now, though, the mission needs a different tack."

Omar grunted. "Plan B?"

"Plan B," Walid said, looking out the window at the sun vanishing behind the jagged Dubai skyline. "Make the necessary preparations."

PART TWO

Target Locked

"What is wrong with the Iranians in addition to the nuclear bomb? This is the only country on Earth in the 21st century that has renewed imperialistic ambitions. They really want to become the hegemon of the Middle East in an age that gave up imperialism."
– Shimon Peres

"The two biggest threats to international security are Iran getting a nuclear weapon, and Iran being bombed to stop it getting a nuclear weapon. Both would precipitate a long and dangerous conflict in an already unstable Middle East. Both would be a disaster."
– David Miliband

"The officials of the Zionist regime (Israel) threaten to launch a military invasion, but they themselves know that if they make the slightest mistake the Islamic Republic will raze Tel Aviv and Haifa to the ground."
– Ayatollah Ali Khomenei

CHAPTER 25

DUBAI, UNITED ARAB EMIRATES

"You sure this will work?" Nasef asked. "I'm not sure how comfortable I am with this."

The three team members were huddled at the far end of the expansive room. It was a half-finished home in the middle of an upcoming housing development at the edge of the Mirdif residential area, on the outskirts of the city. The faded sign at the community's entrance promised it would be opening in Spring 2013, and the multiple layers of graffiti marring the concrete walls indicated that this building and those around it were not a priority for the builders or the authorities. Like the boom towns of the Old American West, Dubai had been subject to fluxes of investment. When the financial return looked to be in a different part of the city, or with a different focus for construction projects, half-completed projects were often abandoned. Available land, particularly out here at the edge of the city's current scope, was everywhere, so when the money train went elsewhere, there was no reason to reclaim this partial investment for the time being. Which was exactly what Wayne had been counting on.

"It'll work," Wayne promised, though Nasef suspected he was hedging his bets against the rest of the terrorists activating a contingency plan. "Just follow my lead."

Nasef followed Wayne back across the open house to their captive, stepping between studs in which interior walls would have been constructed. The terrorist was tied to a pipe in an unfinished bathroom, the bare metal tube embedded in concrete on one end and affixed to a stud by a series of brackets on the other.

"What's your name?" Wayne asked the man.

"America will burn, and Allah will be victorious," came the thickly accented, defiant reply. It was the same phrase he had repeated in reply since his capture, the only words he had spoken outside of some rapid-fire cursing in Arabic. Nasef figured it to be a safety phrase, similar to the name, branch, and rank that the military taught their soldiers to repeat ad infinitum in response to a captor's requests for intel. The terrorist's safety phrase would have been created to give him something he could hold on to if captured, intended to give him confidence and instil fear in his captors.

"Take his shoe off," Wayne instructed Suarez, who pulled the man's blood-soaked right boot from his foot. Nasef had wrapped the man's leg wound in gauze, a stopgap bandage that stemmed the bleeding without providing too much comfort to the wounded.

"How's your leg doing?" Wayne asked. "You feeling good? Bullets hurt, don't they? Bet it hurts a lot more than they told you up at jihadist summer camp, huh? There's a lot they lied to you about. Like the seventy-two virgins in heaven. Or like kidnapping the ambassador will stop the peace plan from coming to pass."

The terrorist spit at his interrogator, a glob of expectorate landing on the thigh of Wayne's maintenance uniform.

"You want to disrupt peace, but you fail to realize it will be your families, your homes, your mothers and sisters and children who die when the bombs start falling, not mine. You're playing with the tail of a lion, son. Let me help you."

"America will burn, and Allah will be victorious," his captive repeated.

"Look, I'm trying to make this as painless for you as possible. My colleague over here thinks he's got a more effective way to make you talk, but that ends with us still getting the answers we want, and you with more of your blood on this nice concrete here. Last chance to get out of this thing mostly intact."

The man spat again. Nasef could see in the terrorist's eyes a curious dance of hate-fueled mania and well-masked fear. As much as this whole scenario was distasteful to Nasef, the man would give them what they needed. Wayne's plan would work.

It had to.

"Fine." Wayne stepped back, allowing Suarez to take over.

Playing the part to a T, Suarez grinned wickedly as he approached the bound captive. "You should've taken his offer," he said, overemphasizing his Latin accent in a bad impersonation of Tony Montana. "You're not going to like mine nearly as much."

He flipped open a multitool and crouched beside the man's foot.

"I really like this knife," he said, watching his captive's eyes widen slightly as the tip of the blade touched his exposed big toe. "You see, it's got so many different options. Got this blade for slicing, this one for stabbing, this one for digging, and this one for sawing. Even got this *pico* guy here for screwing into stuff. Like wine bottles . . . No, you don't like wine, do you, Señor Towelhead. Well, maybe I can figure something else I can use it for . . ."

The terrorist glared at Suarez with fiery vehemence. "America will burn—"

Suarez chortled deeply, continuing with his sadistic Mexican-torturer persona. "Hold on, hold on, don't tell me. 'And Allah will be victorious?'" He grinned wickedly at the bound captive. "No, no. Wrong answer, *amigo*." With a flick of his wrist, Suarez sliced the blade across the arch of the man's foot, just deep enough to draw some blood and—more importantly—activate the millions of tightly packed pain receptors crowded in the region.

The man screamed, and then shouted a plea for help in Arabic, locking eyes with Nasef while doing so. In a different world, the man and Nasef might have been comrades, both lured in by the darker side of Islamic teachings and fighting tooth and nail against any and all perceived enemies. Nasef thanked God that he had been given the opportunities he had, raised in a land of plenty with parents and a community that taught him the value of his fellow man, regardless of how he worships or even if he worships at all. Many terrorists like the man before him had been raised from the cradle on a steady diet of fanaticism and hatred. With poor job prospects in the turbulent and corrupt lands from which he likely hailed, jihad seemed like the best option for a young and angry man to make a difference in the world, even if that difference was achieved through the blood of the innocents.

"He's not going to help you," Suarez said, moving the blade in between the terrorist and Nasef in an attempt to recapture the man's attention. "No one can hear you out here. Not even Allah. It's just you, me, and the truth. The only thing left is to figure out how much pain you want to endure along the way to giving me what I want."

He flicked the knife again, this time nicking the underside of his little toe. Wayne looked on with a pained expression that he was struggling to hide. Nasef knew the feeling.

"I can do this all night, buddy. It would be my pleasure to cut you into a thousand pieces *and* get the information I want. My friends back there, they're not into this torture stuff really, but they want results, and boy does this get results."

Suarez pressed the heel of his palm against the man's gauze-wrapped wound. The terrorist let out a noise, starting as a groan and passing into growl territory before bursting through as a scream. The man cursed again, this time in English, before launching into a rapid-fire repudiation of his captors.

"You will get nothing from me. By this time tomorrow, the Zionist oppressors will be turned to ash and Allah will blow you from the land of our fathers. America is finished. Your children will be wiped from the earth and the stain of the Great White Satan will be blotted from the earth."

"Tomorrow?" Nasef asked, forgetting the overarching interrogation plan in light of this revelation. "What's happening tomorrow?"

The terrorist just laughed, seemingly finding some joy in the fact that, despite his circumstances, his knowledge gave him some measure of power over his captors.

Nasef's PDA buzzed. He glanced at it.

"Hey," Nasef said, holding his phone up for Wayne to see. "Mother Hen is calling."

«»

When had they given Ibrahim that call sign? Wayne pondered as he saw the screen. He looked at Suarez. "Keep him company. We'll be right back."

Wayne and Nasef walked across the room, through another wall, and to the far end of the adjacent room.

"Yeah," he answered by way of greeting when he thought he was far enough out of earshot.

"Wilkins?" Ibrahim asked.

"Yeah. What've you got?"

"Database came back with hits on two of your guys. One of your dead ones is Tamer al-Maliki, Hezbollah, field-level commander. Did a number on an Israeli convoy back in 2006. Responsible for the kidnapping of a couple of IDF soldiers a few years later. Nothing on the other dead guy, but your live one also scored a hit: Karim Ismail. Syrian Special Forces; supposedly died in clashes with anti-Assad militants in 2012."

"So what's a Hezbollah commander and a dead Syrian commando doing kidnapping an American ambassador in Dubai?"

"It would fit with the Iran narrative. Syria's an ally, and Hezbollah gets a huge chunk of its funding from the Persian regime."

"It would, but why so diverse? Why not just Hezbollah? Why a faked death? And the Hezbollah commander was taking orders from another guy, one of those who escaped."

"What are you thinking?"

Wayne shook his head. "I don't know. But I don't think this is just Hezbollah working on behalf of Iran. Hezbollah wouldn't waste this much plastic explosive blowing up an Arabic airport. They would save that for attacking Israel directly."

"Next to a nuke, a truck full of plastique would be a hiccup."

"Still, something doesn't sit right. How is the ambassador connected to the nuke plot? Do the terrorists know she has intel about the bomb, or did these two parts of their plot just happen to coincide? Needham is a pretty big player in the Middle East for those who actually want a lasting peace." Wayne paused, realizing he was thinking out loud more than anything, but maybe something he said would spark an idea for Ibrahim as she sorted and analyzed the intel. "Anything on the phone from the hospital yet?"

"The registry is all screwed up. I'm rebuilding the kernel to try to access it from another channel. It's a beast, but if I can get something from it, you'll be the first to know."

"Copy. Thanks, and let us know if you get anything new."

"Of course."

Wayne disconnected and handed the phone back to Nasef.

"What am I, your secretary?" the Arabic agent asked.

"Not with that attitude, you're not." Wayne winked. "I'm assuming she just hit redial or whatever, considering how it was your PDA that sent the mug shots. Keep it close. Remember, it was your unit that transmitted the data from the mystery phone from the hospital."

"Good point. So what did Ibrahim have on our boy over there."

"Nothing that means good things for us." Wayne gave him a brief rundown of her side of the conversation.

"Syria, Iran, and Hezbollah, operating in Dubai to nuke Israel and kill an American diplomat?"

"We don't know that they're only here in Dubai, but yeah, it feels too broad, too disconnected. There's a piece we're missing, a thread that ties everything together."

"I've got to say, for the record, I'm not comfortable with what we're doing to our captive."

Wayne made a face and nodded knowingly. "It doesn't exactly give me warm fuzzies either, but he's our only lead. We have to make it look real, otherwise this won't work."

"Fine." Nasef's expression said it was far from fine, but if he was willing to drop it, so was Wayne. Nasef shot a thumb toward Suarez and the terrorist. "Should we go join them, then?"

Wayne nodded and led the way back across the house. Karim was writhing on the floor, grinding his teeth as the pain from a fresh nick, this one on the palm of his hand, brought tears to his eyes.

"Zorro," Wayne said, realizing like Nasef had that neither real names nor cover identities could be vocalized now. "Take five. I want to talk to our friend here myself."

Suarez swapped places with Wayne, who saw a combination of relief, rage, and fear flash across the Syrian's face. In the delicate dance of power Karim was sharing with his captors, the scales had tipped even further in their favor.

"Karim, Karim, Karim," Wayne tutted. "You should have told me what I wanted the first time. Now it's going to get really interesting. I'll give you one more chance, though. Where's the ambassador? Tell me the truth, and we can forget all about this"—he waved his hand as though searching for the right word—"little mix-up."

Karim squinted up at Wayne, jaw set. "America will burn, and Allah will be victorious."

"So we're back to that again. Fair enough. You're making me do this. Just remember that." He turned to Nasef. "Prepare ten mils of liquid torture, please."

Nasef used a syringe to extract an amber-colored fluid from a vial.

"My friend there isn't a medical doctor, of course. They took his license away years ago. That fun little toy he's got there is filled with a special concoction he likes to call 'liquid torture.' It's a bit of a misnomer, to be honest, as the pain doesn't start right away. You'll still have time to do the right thing. If you do, my colleague here will give you another injection to counteract this one, saving you from an agony few have ever known. And that's the brilliance of his special recipe, the secret ingredient: sodium pentothal. Maybe they mentioned it at jihadist camp, but it's more common name is 'truth serum.' Soon you'll be telling us everything, from the ambassador's location to the nasty things you used to do to your neighbor's goat. It'll kick in about a minute after injection, which means you'll have about four minutes to spill your heart out before the pain begins.

Wayne drew close to the captive, lowering his voice conspiratorially. "And oh, the pain. When it does start, it'll feel like a slow burn pulsing up your muscles, like after a really good workout. Then the heat will flare up and you'll feel like someone poured acid into your veins, which isn't too far from the truth. Then your skin will feel like it's being devoured by ants, and after that . . . Well, let's save that one for a surprise, shall we? Suffice to say, after thirty seconds of that, you'll be begging us to put a bullet in your head. But we won't be able to understand your screams, since your tongue will be swelling up, cracked and bleeding. You'll be drowning in your own blood. And we've got enough of this fun juice to last all night. As long as it takes, in fact."

"You can't do that," Karim protested. "It's against Geneva."

"That's cute," Wayne laughed. "You hold up the Geneva Convention when you're the one in the hot seat, but are happy to tear it to shreds when you're the ones torturing and beheading your captives."

"But you're Americans! Your government has to follow Geneva!"

"I imagine so. But who ever said we worked for the government?"

Karim remained silent, glaring up at his captor, but a faint tremor had entered the man's legs. A vein on the side of his neck pulsed visibly. The threat was getting to him. He would play right into Wayne's hands.

"Last chance, big guy. No?" Wayne nodded at Nasef, who took Karim's left elbow in his hand. The terrorist struggled against his grip, eyeing the syringe with now-evident fear in his gaze.

Wayne held up his hand. "One word of advice here, Karim. Don't struggle. If he misses, he'll puncture a vein. It won't kill you, but it will hurt like crazy, possibly causing permanent circulation damage. And we all know what that means." Wayne nodded at Karim's crotch. "Plus, if he slips and injects this directly into your muscle, the pain will start immediately, and it'll be much, much worse. So don't make this harder on yourself than you need to. Take it like a man, Mr. Baby Killer. Your countdown to redemption begins . . . now." He glanced at his watch while Nasef injected the fluid into Karim's vein. For his part, the terrorist grunted and bit his lip, but otherwise, he said nothing.

"The sodium pentothal will start to eat away at your mind's defenses in about twenty seconds," Wayne said, still looking at his watch. "Forty seconds after that, you'll tell us anything we want to hear. And you'd better talk quickly, because you'll only have a few more minutes before the pain kicks in. And Doc can't give you the counteragent while you're writhing around in agony, so once you feel the pain, we'll be just as powerless to stop it as you."

Karim's breathing became labored as the seconds ticked by. Wayne saw fear take hold as the terrorist fought to keep control of his faculties, afraid of what secrets he might betray should the injection destroy his defenses.

"Where is the ambassador?" Wayne asked, with urgency now that the clock was ticking.

"America will burn, and Allah will be victorious," Karim replied, the mantra now delivered with fear-stilted quivering.

"Who are you working with?" Nasef asked, starting a round robin of questioning intended to throw their captive for a loop.

"America will burn, and Allah—"

"Where is the ambassador?" Suarez this time.

"America will—"

"Why did you fake your death?" demanded Nasef.

"America—"

"You're running out of time, Karim," Wayne warned. "Where is the ambassador?"

"Ameri—"

"Who are you working with?"

"Amer—"

"What are Syrian operatives and Hezbollah doing in Dubai?"

"Amer—" Karim's face was starting to melt, as fear, panic, and confusion threatened to tear his secrets from him. His mantra, continually cut off by the escalating intensity of the interrogation, no longer held any hope of escape or of victory.

Wayne's voice rose in anger. "This is about to get a whole lot worse for you, pipsqueak. In about forty-five seconds, it'll be too late to give you the counteragent."

"Where is the ambassador?"

"Amer—"

"Where is the ambassador?"

"Amer—"

Suarez leapt forward and seized the Syrian's neck. "I'm not going to wait around anymore. Where's the ambassador, Karim?"

"Fifteen seconds, Karim."

"Jebel Ali!" Karim gasped, indicating a port town on the far side of the city. "Jebel Ali. 19th Street. Number 63."

"And what's there?" Wayne asked.

"A house! The ambassador is there! Please, the antidote!"

Wayne nodded at Nasef, who injected a second syringe into Karim's arm. Suarez backed off as relief washed over their prisoner.

"Dress those wounds for our guest here, Anubis," Wayne said. "Karim, you've been most helpful. I think this is the beginning of a beautiful friendship. I'm sure Gitmo will love to make your acquaintance after we finish pumping you for more information. But I think you've earned a little rest tonight. Loosen his bonds a little after you finish dressing him. Too tight, and he won't get any sleep. He'll be useless to us in the morning, and we can't have that. Let's get some sleep, and then we'll see what else our new buddy here has to tell us."

Wayne and Suarez walked back to the far side of the house, where they prepared a makeshift camp, using backpacks for pillows. When Nasef joined them a few minutes later, they doused their lights and pretended to sleep.

Wayne estimated that no more than five minutes had passed before he heard Karim finally slip his wrists out of the tight bonds and start to slink toward the moon-draped aperture where a window should have been. Suarez checked his PDA.

"Got him. Heading northwest."

"He lied to us," Nasef said.

"Of course he lied to us," Wayne countered. "He thinks he's smarter than us. He feels superior thinking that he beat our high-tech drugs and outwitted American commandos."

Suarez chuckled. "Freaking stroke of genius, Phoenix, using the 'liquid torture' cover story as an excuse to inject him with the nano-tracer serum."

Wayne smiled in the dimly lit room. "We played right into his stereotypes of the ruthless, infidel American commandos, and my description of the drug's effects led him to believe that there really was truth serum in that vial. And now, thinking he's just orchestrated the most ingenious escape since Steve McQueen, he'll lead us right to their real home base." He checked Karim's position on the PDA again. "Okay, he's got enough of a head start. Let's go."

CHAPTER 26

Dubai, United Arab Emirates

Christine had just succumbed to the irresistible call of sleep when the squeal of metal on metal jolted her awake. She shielded her eyes with one hand as she pushed herself upright with the other.

A man entered the room, though his features were hard to make out in the backlit murk. Through the door behind her guest, she could see more Arab men running past, moving equipment, pushing crate-laden dollies down a hall and out of sight.

"Get up," said the gravel-voiced man.

"What's going on?"

He extended something toward her. She moved to take it, and then her eyes, finally adjusting to the new light dynamic, recognized the object. He wasn't offering her something. He was aiming an assault rifle at her. *Probably already exhausted the limits of his English vocabulary*, she silently mused with black humor.

She stood, fearful that her moment had come. Trapped in her lightless cell, after scouring every surface for something, anything, that would help facilitate an escape attempt, she had played the scene out a dozen times in her head. The draped-wall backdrop, harshly lit for the cameras by blinding floodlights. The bearded faces masked with black scarves and *keffiyehs*. The indignant denunciation of the American policies that had wrought her death, followed by the prepared script they would try to force her to read. But most of all, she saw the oversized blade perched by her throat, ready for the sawing. She wouldn't go down without a fight. She had too much to live for to bow to their whims. She wouldn't betray all she had worked for, all she believed in—her country, her heritage, and her cause—by giving in to their demands. They could take her life, but they'd never get her to participate in their deranged propaganda piece.

This would be her only chance. It had to be now. While they moved her to the makeshift studio within the compound, she should try to make a break for it. Go for the gun if she could, but if not, run and get to cover as quickly as possible. She had to act while in transit. The studio would surely be populated with far more rifle-toting terrorists, and, once inside, she wouldn't be leaving with her head attached.

"*Y'allah*," the man yelled at her, as he backed out of her cell doorway, beckoning for her to follow him through. A slow walk through, and then a quick grab for the gun to catch the man off guard. She could do it. But as she stood and began to walk toward the door, she realized how weak she felt. Fear, adrenaline, malnutrition and sleep deprivation had ravaged her body and mind for the last . . . How long since they attacked her plane now? Two days? Three? How long had she been unconscious before awakening to the smelly Arab in her cell? How much time had passed since then? Too long for her body and mind to respond as quickly and perceptively as they needed to, to mount a successful escape.

As though to drive home the point and stave off any foolish attempts to steal the man's gun, she realized, stepping out of her cell and into the well-lit hallway, that his rifle was slung around his neck by a strap. Even Jack Bauer would be hard pressed to swipe the weapon without either party firing rounds that would be sure to bring the rest of the compound's security forces down on her head. As despair threatened to squeeze her last rays of hope out of existence, she trudged down the hall, the terrorist's gun barrel prodding her in the back every few steps.

If it had been three days since she'd landed in Dubai, she thought as her mind scrambled for a method of extricating herself from this situation, if it was, in fact, Friday night, her time was surely up. If it was two days, perhaps she still stood a chance of being rescued. But if it wasn't Friday night and they weren't offering her death as another nail in the American and Israeli coffins, where were they moving her? And why now, in the dead of night, amid so much other hustle and bustle. Surely they would have had plenty of time to set up the studio before bringing her in. But where else would they be taking her?

To her right, an open doorway beckoned. She didn't know what was inside, but she knew it wasn't where they wanted her right now. And that was good enough for a start.

She dropped to one knee as though to tie her shoes, and then swept her leg behind her, catching her guard in the ankles. Knocked off balance, he fell sideways in the tight corridor. As he fell, his head hit the concrete wall, and he slid to the ground, unconscious, a trickle of blood appearing from a wound on his temple.

Christine grabbed at the guard's gun. Still attached to the strap, and unlike many straps that were detachable via a clasp, this one had been soldered together. A terrible design in most combat situations, but here it worked in the terrorists' favor. The only way to take the gun was to maneuver the strap around the unconscious guard's body. Not an easy proposition, especially considering how the man had fallen.

She stooped and struggled with the strap. Voices sounded around the corner. She wrestled with the guard and yanked on the weapon for a moment more. The voices grew louder. In a few seconds, more terrorists would arrive, see their unconscious brother-in-arms, and recapture Christine—or worse. Even with the gun, she wasn't going to win a shootout with these men. They had numbers, firepower, and knowledge of the location and situation on their side. All she would have was a single gun, awkwardly firing from a fixed position in the middle of a coverless hallway. And that was if the unconscious guard the weapon was still tethered to didn't wake up.

Painful as it was to leave her best measure of protection behind, the decision was a no-brainer. Her goal was to escape, not to singlehandedly duke it out with the terrorists on their own turf. She had to get out of there and tell the president what she knew. She leapt to her feet and darted into the open doorway she had noticed earlier.

Immediately, she realized her mistake. The black drop cloth, the jihadist flag hung proudly, the camera tripod. In her haste to escape her captors, she had run right into her execution chamber.

And yet, something was amiss. One of the lighting assemblies was only half constructed. Had they waited until the last minute to set up the room? She had been here for days, or so it seemed. So why weren't things finished yet? Unless . . .

A shout from the doorway behind her jolted her from her suppositions. They must have discovered their comrade's body. Her escape window was rapidly closing.

She bolted across the thankfully empty studio and exited through a door on the other side. Turning right, she nearly barreled into a man holding a large, empty sack. His surprise at seeing their prisoner running loose was his downfall. Christine took advantage of his shock by slamming the heel of her palm into his nose. Feeling cartilage crunch as the man bellowed in pain, she followed up with a knee to the groin, which crumpled the terrorist to the floor. Another kick to the head as she ran past put him out of commission for the moment.

Another few quick turns and she reached another door. Deadbolted. It was warm to the touch. The heat of the desert must lie on the other side.

She cranked the dead bolt open and shoved through. Gasping her first breaths of freedom since being captured at the airport, she found herself confronted with a large privacy wall that surrounded the property. Perhaps seven feet tall, it was too high to jump. And the voices behind her were growing in number and proximity.

She ran to the left and saw a pile of wooden pallets against the corner of the perimeter fence. The pile was two, maybe three feet tall, but given a little time, she could rearrange and stack them so they were not only taller but also more stable.

The door through which she had exited burst open as a pair of angry Arab men pushed their way out of the building. Time was up.

She leapt onto the pile of crates, watching her landing so as not to make too much noise, though it likely mattered little now. It was no longer a matter of whether they could find her. All that mattered now was if she could get over the fence before they reached her.

Catching her balance, she jumped toward the top of the fence, arms extended. Her fingertips grabbed the cool, concrete surface, but slipped loose. She crashed back to the pile of pallets, which shifted beneath her weight, causing her to stumble.

Footsteps behind her now. She'd been spotted for sure. Last chance.

Taking a deep breath, she leapt once more, and, as if by some miracle, her fingers found purchase on the top of the wall. Despite the turmoil of her capture and imprisonment, she had a lifetime of regular workouts and adrenaline on her side. Flexing her arms and pressing her feet against the wall, she began to clamber toward safety.

Just a few more feet now. A neighborhood lay sleeping beyond the fence. Civilization. She was going to make it. She could feel it. She was almost home free.

A coarse hand gripped her ankle and yanked, wrenching her from the wall. She fell and landed on her back. The impact cracked several of the pallets, with one of the splintered fragments puncturing her side.

She gagged and heaved, trying to catch her breath. Her back and ribs were killing her. It felt as if she'd broken something. But worse than that, she'd failed. As the crowd of Arab faces hovering in her blurred vision grew to five, she realized how very badly she'd failed indeed.

"Hel—" Her attempt to rouse one of the neighbors from their slumber was snuffed out by a dirty rag shoved between her teeth, and then quickly tied behind the back of her head.

"Get up," said one of them, before kicking her in the ribs. Another spark of pain exploded in her torso. Something was definitely broken now.

A pair of hands grabbed her forearm and yanked her to her feet. Another man secured her wrists behind her back with zip-ties. She felt like throwing up. So close. So incredibly, horribly close. And for what?

A familiar face emerged from the periphery of her vision. Walid.

"Come, come now," he said. Christine noticed how he didn't call her "ambassador" now that, theoretically, other ears might be listening in. "We have a schedule to keep." Turning on his heel, he led the way back inside, with the others flanking the ambassador and following their leader. Five rifles were trained on her every step of the way, two on each side, one directly behind. She didn't see how she could get out of this. And yet, she couldn't give up hope. No matter how badly she just wanted to curl up and die, she was a fighter. Somehow, she'd find another window and escape.

They wound their way back through the house, past her old cell and the TV studio, which she now realized was in the process of being *de*constructed. At the far end of the building, she reached a door.

"Open it," came the voice of the man directly behind her. Walid had long since disappeared, leaving the five underlings to complete his dirty work.

"Where are we going?" she asked through the gag, cursing the quiver in her voice for betraying the fear she was trying to suppress.

The pressure of the gun barrel in her back. "Open it."

She complied, turning the handle and stepping through the inward-swinging doorway. A short flight of stairs led to a large garage or loading bay of sorts, with several doors along the wall leading back into the building. Three full-size vans were parked inside, each with several of its doors flung open. Men loaded equipment and crates into the vans, while unloading other boxes to carry back inside the building for the return trip.

She could have stolen a van. If she hadn't tried to escape earlier, maybe this would have been the ideal place to attack her then-single guard and make her getaway. But with five terrorists now focusing their attention solely on her, there was no hope.

This wasn't the studio she so dreaded, but her fears weren't completely assuaged. Though her time may not have yet come, she had never felt more in the dark.

All her professional life, Christine had prided herself on being able to read people's motivations and desires and predict how they would act. She credited this gift with her ability to make tremendous inroads toward her peace summit, getting previously antagonistic leaders to agree to come to the negotiating table and try to flesh out a bloodless solution to the world's most beleaguered region. Even in her surprise captivity, she had sussed out her captors' intentions. Between her gift, her experience, and the evidence she had plumbed on the plane here, she thought she knew everything the terrorists had planned. This garage, and her presence in it, demonstrated that she was wrong in that assumption.

"Move." The gun barrel butted her into motion again. The swarthy man to whom she had first awoken in her cell waited by the open rear doors of the first van. He grinned a wicked smile, exposing disease-ridden gums and rot-blackened teeth, and threw a burlap mesh bag over her head.

Heavy hands at her back shoved her forward into the van, but just before she disappeared into the vehicle's claustrophobic belly, she caught a glimpse of something she thought all but impossible. Hope again bloomed in her chest, though virtually everything else told her to give up.

Were it almost anyone else, she would have chalked up the sight to a hopeful hallucination, sleep- and food-deprivation combining with a desperate situation and the vision-marring screen of the bag over her head. But she wasn't just grasping at illusions. She had worked with the man for five years, and would know his face anywhere. Even here, in the loading bay of a terrorist stronghold, as another jihadist at the back of another van cinched another burlap sack around the neck of her assistant, Dan Krumholtz.

He was alive. She wasn't alone after all. And despite his being in an equally dire and hopeless situation, she drew hope from the fact that he was still alive and fighting, just as she was.

Then the loading bay disappeared as she was thrust into the van. Doors slammed shut, the din of men loading and unloading replaced by the roar of an engine and the chatter of passengers. Lying on the floor, blindfolded and bound, with sweat-stained burlap clogging her nostrils with every breath, she heard a garage door open, and the van drove away. As quickly as he had reappeared in her life, Dan was gone again. And then, so was she.

CHAPTER 27

RIYADH, SAUDI ARABIA

Prince Basim al-Attar bin Khalid heard his younger brother approaching on camelback long before he acknowledged him. He kept his eyes fixed on Iman, his prized falcon, soaring overhead through the desert skies, until Jaffar was too close to tactfully ignore.

"My brother," Jaffar said as he dismounted his camel and joined his elder sibling atop the sand dune. Though both men would usually be attended by a coterie of servants, Basim always falconed alone, something Jaffar knew all too well. Which meant his presence here was for more than just idle chit-chat.

Basim, fifth in line to the Saudi throne and Minister of Natural Resources for the world's top petroleum producer, turned to his brother and embraced him, Jaffar's *dishdasha* flapping in the breeze and threatening to slap the prince in the face.

"What brings you to me, Jaffar? Not father, I hope?" King Khalid bin Saud, ruler of Saudi Arabia and head of the royal house of Saud, was not well. The finest doctors on three continents could find nothing wrong with him beyond the wearing out expected of a man of eighty-three. But Basim suspected the problem was his heart. The king had grown weak in recent years, unwilling to stand up to the militant strains of radicalism that had swept the region in recent years, losing his resolve and instead turning inward to the luxuries of his position. Khalid had earned a respite from all the challenges he had steered the kingdom through during his three decades of rule, but his pleasure could not come at the expense of the kingdom's future.

"No, the king is well, *Al-hamdulillah*," Jaffar replied, though Basim thought he detected a note of somberness in his voice.

Was it sadness at their father's failing health, or bitterness that he wasn't yet dead so someone with more backbone could assume the reins of the kingdom? Perhaps, like Basim's own sentiments, it was a mixture of both.

"*Al-hamdulillah*," the elder prince gave the rote reply.

"He did, however, just receive a very interesting phone call from the American president, Talquin."

Basim had spent a good deal of time in the United States, serving as Saudi ambassador for several years in the nineties before assuming his current post. That was the problem with being a prince in a land of a thousand princes: there was always someone higher up. But while many of his siblings and cousins chose to fritter away their days in luxury-filled decadence, treating their birthright as their own personal trust fund, Basim felt compelled to use his station to actually make something of his life—for his country, for Allah, and for himself.

While serving as ambassador, Basim had run into Talquin's father, the senator, several times and had been impressed with his affable demeanor. He had not met the president, but he was eager to do so someday soon.

"Directly from President Talquin to the king?" Basim asked. Most communications between heads of state were funneled between intermediaries: ambassadors, secretaries of state, and other spokespeople. Direct conversation was usually limited to diplomatic visits conducted by the heads of state themselves, or emergencies.

"Directly. He wanted reassurances that Saudi Arabia would support the United States if military action had to be taken against a mutual threat in the region."

Of these there were many. The Arab Spring of 2011 had resulted in a cascade of revolutions and uprisings that had toppled governments from Tunisia to Egypt to Libya to Yemen, kicked off civil wars in Iraq and Syria, and birthed several new extremist groups, while giving fresh legs to several others. Saudi Arabia, along with a few other regional governments, had escaped the sweeping movement relatively unscathed, but it was the secondary effects, the destabilized governments and the emboldened extremists, that now threatened the kingdom.

Talquin's predecessor had been content to let the whole matter play out, as though he were a mere spectator and not the leader of the most powerful nation on earth. This hands-off approach, coupled with his support of unpopular Shiite leaders in Syria and Iraq, had helped to facilitate the rise of ISIS, the so-called Islamic State, that was now one of the most dangerous threats to the region and to Saudi control of the Arabian Peninsula. The fact that the ruthless and ruthlessly efficient group had appropriated the teachings of eighteenth century cleric Muhammad ibn Abd al-Wahhab, the very same cleric whose Wahhabist teachings had been a foundational underpinning of the Saudi kingdom since its inception more than a century ago, was no coincidence. ISIS never could be a true caliphate without the holy cities of Mecca and Medina under its control, and the House of Saud was standing squarely in the way.

But although ISIS was brutal and very quickly on the rise, a much older and far more powerful foe worried Basim even more.

"What threat?"

Jaffar frowned, his mouth disappearing into his thick beard. "He was cagey about who exactly, but all signs point to Iran."

Basim turned his eyes skyward, seeking out Iman and following her as she soared overhead in a majestic glide, searching for prey below.

"What signs?" he said, still watching the falcon above.

"At the end, he mentioned nuclear war. If nukes were used, would we still stand with the United States?"

Basim suppressed a gasp. The desert winds devoured what little escaped his lips and stole it away to parts unknown, but the concern that had surely appeared on his face would be evidence enough of his understanding. The United States would not be the first to use nukes, not after the worldwide condemnation of the horrors Hiroshima and Nagasaki had wrought. Any nation that issued a nuclear first strike would be vilified by the international community, and even the United States wouldn't risk becoming an economic hermit state, much less kicking off a worldwide nuclear conflagration from which there could be no winners. If Talquin was worried about a regional conflict devolving into atomic war, the scenario he feared was obvious.

"They have the bomb?"

His younger brother nodded slowly. "It would appear that the Americans believe that they do."

"Why don't they attack, then? Or call them before the United Nations with whatever evidence they have?"

"Perhaps they don't yet have sufficient evidence. President Talquin is trying to establish peace in the region, but launching a war without indisputable evidence would be very much counterproductive to that end."

Basim exhaled in frustration. "What did the king say? Will we attack Iran while Talquin searches for his testicles?"

Jaffar smiled wryly. "What evidence do you have to present the king with? He struggles to stand up to extremism within our own borders. Do you really see him launching a full-scale attack on a potentially nuclear Iran?"

"No. Of course not. So what will the king do?"

"For now? The same thing that you and I should do. Pray that the Americans are wrong."

CHAPTER 28

Dubai, United Arab Emirates

Wayne circled the outer perimeter of the compound in the Land Rover, Suarez riding shotgun, with Nasef trailing them in the SUV behind. The wall-encircled building was at the edge of Hor Al Anz, on the older side of the city.

The neighborhood was across Dubai Creek from the more iconic sights, the most popular nightclubs, the tourist traps of glitz, glamour, and fast money. Here, the city took on the more traditional Arab urban feel that Wayne had seen across Iraq, Jordan, and other locations he'd been sent to on official and unofficial government business. Neon didn't blaze amid sparkling glass façades and architectural superlatives. Instead, most of the low-slung buildings topped out at four stories, the ground floor playing host to a variety of local businesses, restaurants, and shops catering to the less well-heeled crowd who lived in apartments here on the forgotten outskirts of the city. As Wayne pulled up, he noticed a post office with an adjacent parking lot, desolate at this hour of the night. A lonely Arabic graffito marred an otherwise forgettable desert beige wall on one side of the lot, and a long row of darkened storefronts curved into the distance.

Karim's signal had led them here, to this walled compound at the edge of the neighborhood. Flanked on one side by an empty parking lot and with a football-field-sized expanse of desert at its back, the location seemed ideal for housing a terrorist operation and imprisoning the ambassador. With Karim's tale of escape surely shared with his comrades by now, Wayne half-expected the front gates to open and for a vengeful surge of terrorists to come pouring out, looking to exact their vengeance on the Americans camped back in Mirdif. Karim had been inside for less than ten minutes, but Wayne had a decision to make: mount an incursion now, while the men inside were still taking in Karim's story and trying to decide what to do, or wait until they left, picking them off as they exited or, perhaps, letting them pass and mounting an assault on the skeleton crew they'd leave behind to guard the ambassador.

If Iran did have a nuke and was preparing to attack Israel, a delay of mere minutes could mean the difference between their mission's success and the demise of millions. Further, the ambassador's life was still in danger, and Karim's unexpected return and purported intel on her would-be rescuers might stir the terrorists to some unforeseen action, including moving up her surely planned execution. Further, there was no guarantee the terrorists would leave the compound in pursuit of the Americans. Instead, they could be using the delay to bolster their defenses, making the team's necessary infiltration more difficult the longer they waited.

Timeliness won out. Wayne parked the Land Rover across the street, with Suarez parking nearby—strategically close enough, but not so close as to cause suspicion they had arrived together. They had changed gear now, dressed in all black, ski masks pulled down over their faces. It made the already sweltering night almost unbearable, but it was a necessary inconvenience. If some kid with a cell phone caught them on video and uploaded their faces on YouTube, their mission—and all prospects of future ones—would be shot, and Talquin's administration would be in a world of diplomatic hurt from the fallout.

Wayne led the way across the street, leading them in staggered formation. Suarez went left, while Wayne and Nasef went right, collectively circumnavigating the compound and meeting at the rear. They crouched in the shadows, listening for sentries or other indications of the activity on the other side of the wall. Nothing. They boosted each other over the wall, dropping silently to the concrete courtyard below. Wayne was grateful for the lack of overt security measures such as sentry guns, cameras, or barbed wire. The terrorists needed this house to blend in, and anything out of the ordinary would attract unwanted attention.

Safely inside the compound, the team kept low, crossing the small courtyard to the rear door. Though the building had been built as a sizable house, the back door looked more like a business's service entrance than the homey wooden or glass portal he would expect. Tan-painted steel was accented by a stationary silver knob and two separate deadbolts. Suarez and Nasef kept watch while Wayne slid a rake pick and tension wrench into the first deadbolt and began to work the lock.

"Quick, a sentry's coming," Suarez whispered as Wayne turned the first deadbolt and began to work on the second.

Wayne glanced to his left, but kept working. Two seconds later, an Arab man armed only with a radio turned the corner. Suarez stood and punched the man in the throat. While the guard choked on his own broken trachea, the American agent moved behind him to cover his mouth as he choked him out. The guard fell limp in his arms, unconscious, a split second before Wayne finished with the last deadbolt.

The team leader nodded approvingly as Suarez dragged the man's body into the shadows behind a planter. They'd dodged a bullet there, but someone would come looking for the guard before long. The clock was ticking.

Wayne opened the door into a laundry room that looked as if it hadn't been used in ages. Devoid of drying clothes, empty hangers, or any semblance of detergent, the dust-covered room only served to bottleneck their approach into the rest of the house. Wayne, now on point, put an ear to the door, listened for a moment, and then nodded. Each of the team members readied their pistols, while Wayne nudged open the door.

They were at the corner of two hallways, with corridors stretching to the right and straight ahead. When he poked his head out to assess the layout, Wayne heard a shout from his right.

They had been spotted.

Wayne tossed a flash-bang grenade in the direction of the shout, waited for it to explode, and then pursued, with Suarez right behind. Nasef headed down the hallway straight ahead, as they split up to neutralize the threats in the building and quickly locate the ambassador.

The terrorist who had spotted them clawed at his eyes, staggering from the blast as though he were drunk. He let loose a burst of blind fire from his AK, stitching a line of bullets into the wall to Wayne's left. Wayne aimed and shot the man twice in the face, reaching the room—an unfurnished living room by the look of it—just as the terrorist hit the floor.

"Clear," Wayne said, picking up the man's rifle as he entered the room.

"One more dead bad guy," Suarez said.

Suarez and Wayne checked out an adjacent den area, empty, before heading down another hallway. Also empty.

"Kind of a skeleton crew here, wouldn't you say?" Nasef asked.

"Yeah, just as wasteland over here," Suarez said. "Did they really do all of this with such a small force?"

"Satellite images of the attack showed a bigger force than this," Wayne said. "Unless they've got multiple teams."

"Still haven't seen the guys who escaped from the tunnel," Nasef said. "Nor our beacon boy who led us here." A gunshot. "Never mind, there he is."

"Non-lethal shots, wherever possible," Wayne ordered over the sounds of a brief but furious gun battle in another part of the house. "If these guys have split up, we'll need more follow-up intel."

Nasef sighed into his mike. "Too late for this one. Headshot."

Wayne cursed his lack of foresight at this possibility. Surely the actual nuke—made in Iran and destined for Israel—wouldn't be hanging out in Dubai. Another team, either prepping a rocket in Tehran or in one of Israel's neighbor states, like Lebanon, Syria, Jordan, or Palestine, would be delivering that payload. The terrorists were a multinational force from across the region, and—if Rick was to be believed—their plans were much larger than just the abduction of the ambassador.

He turned a corner and immediately ran into another terrorist, the red and white checkered *keffiyeh* of Hezbollah wrapped around his neck. The man was pointing his AK toward Nasef's part of the house rather than in Wayne's direction, a fact the American used to his advantage. Seizing upon the terrorist's brief moment of surprise, Wayne grabbed the gun and pivoted around the man, using the strap securing the rifle to choke the man from behind.

"Knife!" Suarez yelled as the terrorist's hand reached for a long bowie knife in a sheath at his beltline.

"Then get it!" Wayne shouted back, spurring Suarez into motion. The terrorist swung the knife wildly, slicing Suarez's forearm. Wayne yanked back on the strap with one hand, grabbing the man's ear with the other. In one quick motion, he pulled on the ear, ripping skin and cartilage. The terrorist screamed and dropped the knife, instinctively reaching for his wounded ear to protect it from further harm.

While Wayne continued to choke the man, Suarez grabbed the terrorist's arms and pulled them together, cinching a zip-tie around them.

"We've got our prisoner," Suarez said as Wayne shoved the terrorist forward to his knees.

"Good," came Nasef's voice. "Because the rest of this place is looking pretty empty."

"Ditto back here," Wayne said. "You find anything that looks like a command post or holding cell?"

"I did find a big garage up front," Nasef said. "Empty also. Smelled like fresh exhaust, though."

"So there *were* more of them here recently," Wayne said, almost to himself. He pressed the comm again. "Rally up on our position, Anubis. You get to play babysitter for the moment and see if our newest friend has anything useful to say. When you get here, Zorro and I are going to do one final sweep before we ask Mr. PLO here where his friends went."

"Copy. Be there soon."

A few moments later, Nasef appeared around a corner. His shoulder was soaked in blood.

"You hit?" Wayne asked.

Nasef looked at him curiously for a moment before following his eyes to his own shoulder. He shook his head. "No, not mine. Got up close and personal with a jihadist back there. He doesn't have much use for the blood now anyway."

"Suarez, how's your arm?" Wayne asked. Zorro's arm was dripping with crimson as the cut continued to ooze blood.

"Better than it looks," Suarez said, looking at his wound. "Nothing some gauze can't fix for the moment."

Nasef tossed him a roll from his pack.

"Thanks," Suarez said.

"Don't mention it," Nasef said, patting down the terrorist prone on the ground. "Happy hunting, guys."

"Hoo-ah," Wayne said as he and Suarez padded down another hallway.

The corridor was lined with doors along either wall, each of which Wayne eyed suspiciously. They double-checked each of the rooms, ensuring that terrorists hiding in one of the unchecked rooms hadn't switched to one of the previously cleared ones while the team was rallied up elsewhere. Then they got to a room they couldn't check as easily.

"Got a steel door, padlocked," Wayne said. "Could be a cell."

"Fantastic," Nasef said. "We might be almost home free after all."

"Tread carefully," Suarez cautioned. "I don't like any of this."

Wayne lifted the butt of his pilfered rifle and glanced back at Zorro, who nodded. He slammed the rifle against the lock, wincing at the loud bang that heralded his arrival. If the door weren't steel, he would fear bullets slicing through the barrier and mowing him down before he could even see his opponents. As it was, the sturdy door locked from the outside seemed to portend one very good thing. But Wayne had been burned enough in his tumultuous career to not break out the streamers just yet.

The lock held up under the second blow, but the third knocked the tumbler inside loose. The shackle dropped from the padlock's case, allowing Wayne to remove the lock and the clasp securing the door. He readied his pistol, which he trusted more than the terrorist's AK and—should there be one or more terrorists inside using the ambassador as a hostage—was far more accurate for shooting around their primary objective. He glanced back at Suarez again, and then eased the door open.

The stench of urine and vomit hit Wayne's nostrils as soon as he entered the dim room. The only light was ambient, cast from the hallway behind them. As he scanned the room, he saw a form curled in one corner. The figure was dressed in a homely garment of brown burlap, a tangle of long hair furthering the beaten and bruised image.

"Ambassador Needham," Wayne called out as he entered the room. "Guys, we found her."

"*Al-hamdulillah*," Nasef said over the comms.

"Hey now, none of that," Suarez returned. "We've got enough crazy jihadists around here without you going off on us."

"Being Muslim is not the same as being a jihadist, Zorro. You know well and good my feelings on that."

"Yeah, yeah." He remained by the door, holding it open to allow as much light as possible into the dark room. Wayne crossed to the prone form and touched her shoulder. The figure rolled back toward him in a grotesque mockery of their mission.

It was a mannequin, naked in front, with "Allahu Akbar" scrawled in Arabic across the plastic face. But it was the semtex strapped to the mannequin's chest that really drove home the terrorists' point.

We win.

"Bomb!" Wayne yelled as he jerked away from the blinking apparatus of the armed weapon. The high pitched whirring that started when he moved the mannequin told him they had mere seconds before detonation.

Suarez held the door with one hand as he readied his feet to flee.

"Just go!" Wayne ordered as he reached the door. Suarez complied, turning into the hall and running back toward where they had left Nasef and their captive. Once through, Wayne shut the door again and quickly closed the clasp. It wasn't much, but hopefully the steel door would help mitigate the blast's impact.

"Rally up front, through the garage," Wayne yelled as he turned into the hallway. "Move, mo—"

The explosion drowned out the rest of his order. Something heavy hit him from behind, knocking him to the ground. The door. He couldn't feel his right arm. His eardrums erupted in pain as the overpressure mounted. Everything was ringing. Everything was distant. The world had fallen down a well, and he was being crushed to death by the very barrier that was supposed to save them from the bomb's destructive power. He had to get up. Were his men okay? Was the captive still alive? They had to find the ambassador. They had to stop the nuke.

He pushed with his left arm, trying to free himself from the crushing weight of the door, when their worst-case scenario became impossibly worse. The subpar construction standards that came with building quickly and cheaply on a foundation of sand were no match for an explosion of that magnitude. The ceiling crumbled into a devastating hail of concrete and plaster, burying Wayne under ten tons of gray death.

CHAPTER 29

30,000 FEET ABOVE NORWAY

Arsalan Hosseini was still seething from his meeting. Though his suspicions were as strong as ever, he was no closer to confirming them than when he had left his office. Another brick wall, another slap in the face. And he, the president of the country! Though it was yet another secret thought he could never share aloud, sometimes he hated what Iran had become.

It was an important distinction. He loved everything Persian, and was ultimately faithful to his nation's current geopolitical incarnation, despite his reservations about its present direction. Modern-day Iran was many times removed from Persia's former grandeur and glory, the culture, ethnicity, language, and history that had built one of the world's most creative and influential civilizations for millennia.

After being a beacon of innovation and prosperity in antiquity, the nation played a key role in the Islamic Golden Age, nurturing myriad scholars, poets, and scientists that helped to shape the modern world, all while Europeans were crawling around in the mud and slaughtering each other in an endless series of Dark Age wars. Through a series of caliphates and dynasties, the Shiite Muslim incarnation of Iran's Medieval and Early Modern eras were shining days for which he often waxed nostalgic.

The encroaching West, of course, had been the catalyst for its downfall. From Tsarist Russia's nineteenth-century conquering of much of Iran's territories around the Caucacus Mountains to the overbearing influence of European colonialism throughout the region, Western powers had made their indelible mark on the once-great empire for more than a century before the greatest blow finally came.

Awash in the Cold War paranoia of anything that stank even remotely of communism, a joint CIA/MI6 conspiracy ousted the democratically elected president Mohammad Mossadegh in 1953. The popular socialist-leaning politician had made moves to nationalize the country's oil resources, but the Anglo-Persian Oil Company—the precursor to British Petroleum—rallied British special forces to bring him down. When their plot was discovered and Iran cut off all diplomatic ties with the UK, London got their allies across the pond to do the job for them. Once the CIA had effected the coup against Mossadegh, they installed the shah in his place. Despite the propaganda attacks against him and the eventual arrest that removed him from power, Mossadegh remained one of the most popular figures from Iranian history.

When the shah's greed and corruption eventually became too much for his subjects, the Iranian Revolution broke out in the late seventies. The CIA's role in Mossadegh's removal played a key rallying point in the anti-US sentiment that swept the nation and resulted in the storming of the American embassy and the 444-day hostage crisis that shook the world and laid bare the deepening rift between the West and the Middle East.

But though the revolution ostensibly reinstated free elections and democratic rule to the people, the most important change was that the theocratic, pro-West shah was replaced by the theocratic anti-West supreme leader. And despite the power that technically resided in Hosseini's office as president, much of the policy for the nation was, in fact, set by the current supreme leader, Ayatollah Naghinejad, a man who held tremendous executive power and was politically bulletproof.

The man behind the curtain, Naghinejad was the commander in chief of the nation's armed forces, among many other unilateral powers delegated to the high office by the nation's constitution. Hosseini suspected he would know why a dead Hezbollah operative was kidnapping an American diplomat in Dubai. But when he confronted the ayatollah after seeing the shocking images of the airport attack, Naghinejad had laid into him, questioning his devotion not only to the state, but also to Islam itself.

Hosseini hadn't meant to yell back, to defend his honor and faith so vehemently, but he had been caught so off-guard by the ayatollah's attack, with his head already spinning from the impossible images he had seen back in his office, that he had fought back.

Never a good thing to do with anyone whose job title is "supreme leader."

Naghinejad, with whom Hosseini had already had his share of heated disagreements over policy foreign and domestic, had lowered his head and waited for Hosseini to finish. Realizing that the ayatollah wasn't fighting back anymore, the president stopped short his impassioned self-defense. The wall-to-wall cedar bookcases of the supreme leader's office, filled with religious texts penned in Farsi and Arabic, seemed to crush in on him. The ayatollah just stood there, on the other side of the antique wooden desk, head down, eyes closed. Was he thinking? Praying? Relishing the power he held over one of the region's most powerful nations, with ambitions to become a major player on the world stage?

What, he wondered, did the supreme leader have up his sleeve? Would he let him in on whatever secret operation was being conducted in Dubai? Or would he send him from his presence before renouncing him to the Guardian Council, who had the power to remove him from the presidency?

"Read this," Naghinejad said after allowing a prolonged silence to rattle the president's nerves further. Hosseini took the proffered sheet of paper from the aged theocrat's vaguely tremulous hand and read the typewritten script. It wasn't a brief on the Dubai attack, nor was it a letter of resignation for him to sign. Instead, it was something more confusing and, in light of the ambassador's kidnapping, potentially far more dangerous.

"What is this?" Hosseini had asked, though in his wrenching gut he already knew.

"Your speech. For the United Nations tonight in New York. Your flight leaves in thirty minutes. A car waits outside to take you to the airport. Prove your devotion to our great nation by making our case tonight, and we'll forget about your little outburst."

"But this speech—"

The Ayatollah put up his hand to silence him. He slid open a drawer and pushed a button. A moment later, two officers of the Revolutionary Guard entered the room.

"President Hosseini requires an escort to his car," Naghinejad said. "He doesn't want to be late for the airport. See that he makes it there in time."

"What? You can't do this," Hosseini argued. "I'm the president!"

"Exactly," Naghinejad said with a sneer. "So start doing your part and do as you're told. Your country is depending on you."

Then the guardsmen had removed him from the room and helped him to the car out front, which had delivered him to the airport in time to make his non-stop flight across the Atlantic on one of the ayatollah's Gulfstreams. In a few hours, he'd land at JFK. And if his pilot was to be believed, the diplomatic retinue that waited in New York would cut an efficient path through traffic and deliver him to the United Nations Headquarters just in time to address the nations of the world.

He read through the prepared speech for the eleventh time since boarding. It made no sense. Was this the ayatollah's revenge, showing who really pulled the strings in Iran, making a marionette of his own president? He felt as if the supreme leader was the ventriloquist, and he was the dummy.

The speech was well-written, and no doubt it would have a tremendous impact on those in attendance. But he feared the backlash it could inspire, backlash that could very well lead down a dark path of no return. There was something he wasn't seeing.

He had sought out the ayatollah in search of answers. In the end, all he got were more questions.

CHAPTER 30

DUBAI, UNITED ARAB EMIRATES

Christine tasted blood as Walid's well-manicured hand slapped her cheek yet again. She had gotten under his skin. Or something had. Clearly he was upset at something that had gone wrong. Was the change in location planned, or a last-minute decision necessitated by some rescue team—American, or perhaps even Emirati—getting too close to ferreting out the terrorists' hideout?

"There still is fire in your eyes," Walid said. "You haven't given up hope yet. That's cute. So American; so brash. Too many cowboy movies, I say, always expecting to shoot your way out, waiting for the cavalry to swoop in and save the day." He chuckled derisively, mocking her hope. "Your cavalry is dead, blown to pieces in your old cell. See? You didn't have to die there after all." One corner of his mouth twitched open in a twisted smile. "This is why you hope, but let me assure you, all of your hope will soon be gone."

Christine fought the urge to try to twist away from his attacks. Doing so previously had only served to anger him further, and she had already tested her bonds before he came in. Her new cell looked to be an unfinished bathroom, a long one with rows of piping and tiles along each wall, indicating multiple toilets and sinks. Wherever she was, it wasn't residential. A skyscraper under construction? Or just another half-finished architectural dream abandoned when the economy crashed in 2008? There were scant clues available to piece together where she was. She had been knocked out with some foul-smelling liquid her captors smeared over the bag on her head shortly after being loaded into the van, and when she awoke she was here, handcuffed to a pipe at the far end of the room.

Her captors had rebuffed all questions about Dan, and she was beginning to think that the sighting in the garage was just a hallucination after all. There were still too many questions, not enough answers, and definitely too little time.

Walid smiled, pulled up a stepstool, and sat on it, facing her.

"You've wanted to transform the Middle East your entire career, Ambassador. Make it more Western, more 'civilized.' You dedicated your life to it. Threw your marriage down the toilet, failed in your duties as a wife and a mother, all for a misguided pipe dream of peace for Israel. You should know by now that the only peace Israel will know is when it is reclaimed as Palestine, with the Zionist pigs and their Western puppets eradicated from the land. With the Jews and the American occupiers gone, the people of Allah can finally purify the land and become a true caliphate for the first time in centuries."

He chuckled to himself, a laugh that made Christine's skin crawl.

"That's what you expect me to say, isn't it? Your stereotype of every Islamist in the region. But, of course, what we're doing here is much more exciting than that. Much more complex, and much more creative than that. I'm an artist, Ambassador. And believe it or not, I'm a capitalist at heart. Growing up in London taught me the value of turning a profit."

"Whatever you're planning, it will fail. They know who you are, Walid Abushakra."

His eyes widened at the realization that she knew who he was, but he quickly recovered his composure. She pressed the attack.

"My government will find you, even if you think you've succeeded. You'll always be looking over your shoulder. Stop this madness now before—"

The next slap knocked her head to the side, causing her world to spin for a few moments. A fresh wave of blood filled her mouth. One of her incisors felt loose.

"I'll be honest, I was going to let you finish, just to see what curious arguments you might come up with to try to dissuade me from my work. But calling what I am doing madness is something I will not abide; certainly not from you, Ambassador. This is a plan of sheer brilliance. Madness is continuing to prop up the Zionist state and pouring your life into the lost cause of an Israeli peace. But fear not. Though your life has been spent in pursuit of a futile and blasphemous cause, your death will serve as an exclamation point to redefine the Middle East after all. Just not in the way you've been hoping. In a much better, much purer, and actually possible way."

He stood, kicking the stool behind him across the room.

"Rest assured, the next twenty-four hours will be the most interesting of your life. History in the making, Ambassador. And you'll have a front row seat."

Walid exited the room, and Christine heard the deadbolt engaging from the other side. Twenty-four hours. So it was only Thursday night after all. Thank God. But if her captor was telling the truth about her would-be rescuers' deaths, she prayed that another team was en route now. Because as dark as things seemed now, in less than twenty-four hours, hope for peace—for Israel, the Middle East, and the world—would be lost forever.

CHAPTER 31

Dubai, United Arab Emirates

Wayne was inches from death, caught in a blackish-gray purgatory without senses or motion. He was on his back, but he could not move, could not feel, could not hear above the echoes of tinnitus, the ghostly bells' tolls dulling as he slipped back into death's cold embrace.

The bomb, he thought as pieces began to slip back into place, realizing that he hadn't yet taken that final step into the hereafter. *The mannequin, the bomb, and . . . the door, the ceiling*. It was all coming back now, one calamitous sequence of disasters culminating in his being buried alive beneath a crushing mass of concrete and steel. He tried yet again to free himself from beneath the heavy door that pinned him down, but if it was a failing effort before the ceiling came crashing down, it was surely a futile one now.

Trapped in this state between death and life, he felt his breath growing more and more shallow. The pressure of his burial compressed his ribcage, and the air that he was able to inhale was tainted with ash, dust, and other particulate matter. With one last, all-or-nothing shove, he pushed against the door with all his might. A slight budge, but not enough to dislodge the oppressive weight. As his limbs gave out and the door settled anew upon his chest, Wayne felt himself lapse into a quasi-dreamlike state, something between sleep and waking, between life and death, where all his dreams, fears, and doubts came together in one haunting confluence of semi-conscious thought.

He had long struggled with his role in today's world. After his parents' deaths in Tower Two on September 11, 2001, he had quit college and joined the army. His were some of the first boots on the ground in Afghanistan, and between that field of operations and Iraq two years later, he had been responsible for well over a hundred deaths. Most, if not all, had deserved the one-way ticket to hell he had delivered them, but Wayne wasn't immune to the ravages of being an agent of the grim reaper. For better or worse, he was a phenomenally skilled orchestrator of raw justice and, though he had already received a stark lesson in the dangers of blindly following orders against his own conscience, he could not escape the pull of the great game. The knight piece his opponent was never expecting, leaping into the fray, making his kill, and then disappearing again.

At times, he hated his role, but it was who his choices had made him, and it seemed there was no coming back from the reaper he had become. Even in his darkest times, though, he understood that those he killed would murder a hundred innocents were it not for his intervention. That made it a little better. Sometimes.

Then sometimes he hated the man he had become. He wondered what his parents would think of the life-course adjustment he had taken in order to avenge their deaths. Strong, upstanding individuals who had worked hard all their lives, sacrificing to give their only son the life they never had. And then, less than a year away from graduating with the college degree that would have made his parents beam with pride, Wayne dropped everything to kill those who murdered his parents. Only nearly everyone he had slain in the intervening years had nothing to do with the attacks on the Twin Towers. They were dangerous men, perhaps, men with blood on their hands and heads full of plans to claim more victims. But what about their families, grieving over their bodies, with sons swearing vengeance upon Wayne's kind much as the erstwhile college student had taken up arms when his parents had been swallowed in a billowing cloud of ash and hate?

The irony was not lost upon him, as part of his mind tried desperately to hang on to life and consciousness. His parents had died in a building that terrorists had brought to the ground. Now he was on the verge of joining them in the same fate, failing a mission he never would have taken had his parents' fate—and his impetuous reaction to that fate—been different.

Something shifted above him, a mild vibration radiating through the mound of detritus. A muffled voice broke through the deadened ringing in his ears. The terrorists coming back to see what had fallen into their trap? The police, ready to imprison and execute them on charges of terrorism and espionage? Or was it just another hallucination of his trauma-addled, oxygen-starved brain?

The shifting continued, but grew more faint, as though its source was moving away from Wayne's position. Should he try to signal whoever was topside? Though a sticky end likely waited—a fate with either the terrorists or the police—his chances down here on his own were nil. Better a fighting chance at a violent death than a coward's surety of this slow and painful asphyxiation. Besides, the mission was still unfinished, and no matter what else he may have become in the years since 9/11, he was no quitter. That was one thing his parents had gotten right.

He tried to shift his legs and arms, bracing them against the door to give a concerted shove upwards all at once. There was too much debris atop the steel surface to dislodge it entirely, but he hoped to create enough movement on the surface to draw attention to his position. It was an absolutely horrible tactic, considering his defenseless position and his topside opponents' obvious advantages, but he had no choice.

Shoving with all his might, he yelled as the door moved, sucking in another breath before yelling again. His legs and arms wobbled under the weight, and he yelled once more before his strength gave out. Using his weakened limbs to lower the door as gently as possible so as to prevent the full force from cracking a rib—or worse—Wayne found himself again trapped beneath the crushing weight, even more exhausted and sore than before.

From above, he heard shouting. More than one voice. He couldn't hear the language or inflection, but they were definitely yelling at each other, seemingly converging on his position. Wayne offered up a quick prayer of thanks, followed by another for the wisdom and protection to somehow escape from his erstwhile rescuers. Out of the frying pan and into the fire was very much a mantra he tried to avoid. But aside from some sort of divine intervention, he could see no way out. Both his gun and the automatic rifle he had taken off his first terrorist in the compound had gone flying when the bomb exploded, buried somewhere out of reach under the rubble. So he prayed for a miracle.

The vibrations were stronger now, the voices right overhead. They were digging. Wayne closed his eyes again. He could see virtually nothing down here anyway, and the movement above was starting to rain more dirt and debris into his tiny pocket of life beneath the door. He would already be at a stark disadvantage when they reached him, and he didn't want to add blindness to the deck stacked against him.

Scraping, something hit the other side of the door. Another shout. English? Wayne couldn't tell for sure. Wishful thinking, or another auditory hallucination? What was going on up there?

More scraping from above as, Wayne assumed, they were digging loose the edges of the door so they could lift it up. He braced himself, mind scrambling for a plan. Running and fighting would both likely be suicidal, but so would just lying there while they captured him.

Wayne sucked air as the door was lifted from his chest, slowly pivoting to the side. The night air was still hot and exhaust-tinged, but it was the most refreshing thing he'd breathed in . . . Wayne realized he had no idea how long he had been down here. What had happened to the rest of his team? Had they made it out alive? Or were they already captured, or worse, crushed to death beneath the rubble that had nearly claimed his own life?

As the weight was raised and the door was opened to the rest of the world, Wayne squinted open his dirt-dusted eyes. After so much darkness, even the ambient glow of distant streetlights seared his retinas. Figures overhead stared down as the door toppled to the ground beside him. Wayne sat up, fighting through the pain and exhaustion, ready to burst through his would-be captors and disappear into the night.

"Well, aren't you a sight for sore eyes?" said one of the figures.

"Zorro?" Wayne rasped, recognizing his voice. He couldn't believe it.

"Like a phoenix from the ashes," Suarez said. "Back from the dead. You're really living up to your namesake there, Phoenix."

"And none too soon." Nasef. "I hear sirens."

"Come on, man," Suarez said, putting his arm under Wayne's right arm as Nasef did the same with his left. "On three."

Once Wayne was finally on his feet, wobbly though his stance initially was, the team ran through the crumbling remains of the house, across the street, and into their waiting Land Rovers.

"Wait, where's the guy you captured inside?" Wayne asked.

Nasef shook his head. "I had to ditch him when the bomb went off. Stubborn fool refused to come with. He'd take his martyrdom however he could get it, I guess."

"Let's get out of here," Wayne said once he was in the passenger seat of Suarez's vehicle. "The desert, somewhere we can figure this out without drawing any more attention."

"Already on it," Suarez said. Wayne saw the flicker of flashing police lights in the side-view mirror right before the Land Rover turned the corner onto a highway.

Wayne's phone started ringing.

"Yeah," he said by way of answer.

"Got some potentially good news for you," Ibrahim said.

"Fantastic. We're fresh out over here."

"Are those sirens I hear?"

"Good ears. They're not coming for us though. Just the bombed-out shell of a house we just left."

"What?"

"Long story."

"Give me the short version."

"The terrorists set a trap for us. Our captive led us right into it. They sacrificed half a dozen of their own men just to make the trap look convincing. Still doing damage assessment for our part, but if the cops weren't on edge after we arrived in a CIA charter plane and left some dead bodies in the tunnels beneath the airport, they sure are now."

A sigh from Ibrahim's end. "You do know you guys are supposed to be invisible on this, right? None of this can be traced back to the agency or to the government."

"I'm well aware of how covert ops are supposed to work, thank you very much. Still, I usually have a little more to go on than 'our ambassador was kidnapped in a city of two million; go find her.'"

"The population of Dubai is actually—"

"Ibrahim, I don't need a geography lesson, I need intel. What is this potentially good news you promised?"

"Sorry," Ibrahim said. "It could be a lead, but I don't like what it might portend."

"What is it?"

"Dan Krumholtz, the ambassador's assistant, purchased a prepaid international phone a few weeks ago. Untraceable, had you not found it in the hospital there. Well, I finally pieced together what I could of the damaged data. He made seventeen calls to a Dubai number on Tuesday, while in the air. The first for two minutes, but the rest were not answered."

"Our consulate? Sheikh Khalid's people?"

"Neither. The number is listed as a holding corporation, Shiraz Imports, headquartered there in Dubai."

"Shiraz. As in Shiraz, Iran?"

"One would assume. Fairly new company, founded just over a year ago. Owner has an Iranian name, but I can't find any record of him. Lots of Iranians do business in Dubai, though. Lots of profits to be made, if you know the right people. Shiraz Imports is privately held, so no stockholders to impress, which is good because their cash flow is ugly. Small staff, but they seem to have been hemorrhaging money from the word *go*."

Wayne rubbed his forehead, smearing more dirt across his face. "You think it's a shell corporation."

"I do. And one of the places Shiraz was throwing its money was into a Cayman bank account registered to one Daniel Krumholtz."

"But if Krumholtz was in league with this shell corporation, and if this shell corporation might have ties to the attack . . ."

"Then that's how they knew the ambassador was coming to Dubai."

"So was he calling them to initiate the attack? Or maybe it was already planned and he was calling them off? Because of what? The intel Weiland said the ambassador had?"

"It would seem so. Embassy records in Cairo indicate that a package was hand-delivered to the ambassador as she was boarding the plane. The package originated in Iran."

Wayne clapped a hand behind his neck and let his head roll back, staring at the SUV's ceiling. "So Krumholtz was a traitor who helped facilitate the attack on the ambassador, but then had second thoughts when he saw the evidence of Iran's plans to nuke Israel?"

"That I don't know. But I can tell you that a burned and empty envelope was found amid the charred ruins of the plane, but nothing that could be construed as evidence."

"So Krumholtz, Needham, the terrorists, or the police have it now."

"If the police had it, we would have heard about it by now. Iran and the UAE aren't on the best terms with one another."

"Krumholtz, Needham, or the terrorists, then."

"Who we can assume for now are all in the same place."

Wayne nodded. "Send me the info for Shiraz Imports."

"Already did. I'll let you go so you can check it. Keep me in the loop."

"Of course," Wayne said, and hung up.

"Krumholtz was a traitor?" Suarez asked.

"Seems that way," Wayne said. He filled in the gaps for Zorro and the rest of the team via comms.

"Wonderful," Nasef said.

"It's a lead," Wayne said, looking through the intel on Shiraz Imports on his phone. "Let's go find somewhere to clean up. We've got a big day ahead of us."

CHAPTER 32

ISRAEL-LEBANON BORDER

Faheem Ramdallah's back hurt from the long drive. Driving direct, the trip from Beirut to their target would have only taken a few hours. With the decades-long conflict between Hezbollah and Israel, not to mention all the chaos spilling over from neighboring Syria, both sides of the border had plenty of military checkpoints aimed at deterring militants from visiting more destruction upon the people and infrastructure of the region. Dutifully going through each of the checkpoints would have boosted the driving time by at least another hour. But avoiding them, as was necessary considering the cargo they were transporting, increased their travel time substantially.

The tortuous journey through the Lebanon Mountains, on unmarked and unpaved roads through perilous switchbacks as the van wended its way through the range, was murder on Faheem's back. The fact that the vehicle Maktoum was driving was manufactured back in the nineties didn't help matters, but there was no reason to waste finances on a shiny new model. A newer vehicle would stand out in these impoverished hills, and the van—and its occupants—would soon be gone from this world, destroyed in a triumphant blast the faithful would proclaim across the world.

The circuitous route had paid off thus far. Many of the checkpoints in Lebanon were, in fact, run by Hezbollah, and those that weren't were known by Nabil, who had marked their locations on the map Faheem studied.

The checkpoint ahead was not on the map.

"Slow down," Faheem urged Maktoum, who eased on the brake. The group's leader eyed the men manning the checkpoint, realizing that their uniforms were not those of Lebanese or Hezbollah forces. They were Israeli.

"When did we cross over the border?" Maktoum asked, apparently also noticing the uniforms.

"I think this *is* the border," Faheem returned, glancing back and forth between the map and the checkpoint.

The van was the only vehicle on this backwoods road, and all four of the Israeli border policemen flanking the checkpoint ahead had their eyes locked on Faheem and his men.

"Get ready," Faheem said to the three men in the back of the van. Just in case.

Maktoum started to roll down his window as the van came to a stop a few feet before the yellow-and-black-striped arm barrier that stretched across the road. The barrier looked like a length of PVC pipe, with a counterweight on the other side of its pivot point to enable hand-powered raising and lowering of the gate. A small, aluminum-roofed hut stood to the side of the barrier, likely housing a restroom, snack machine, radio, and other amenities for the border police unit. It had all the hallmarks of a rural checkpoint, the kind of boring, crappy assignment handed down to IDF soldiers who had crossed the wrong officer somewhere in their careers. But that didn't mean it couldn't disrupt Faheem's plans.

A policeman moved to each side of the car, one for Maktoum's window, one for Faheem's. Each held a SAR 21, a high-end rifle that made Hezbollah's AK-47s look third-world by comparison. The policemen were making a statement—they may be stuck in this rural outpost, but they were still a serious threat to be reckoned with. Faheem just hoped they could also be reasoned with.

"Identification, please," the soldier at Maktoum's window asked in English. Somewhere along the line, border guards using Hebrew had ticked off enough Palestinians and other non-Israelis traveling into the West Bank, Gaza, or the Golan Heights, so they took the conciliatory move of changing its default language to the *lingua franca* of the modern era: English.

Faheem smiled slightly as he withdrew his forged passport, not wanting to seem too eager to be friendly, but not wanting to put these men in anything less than a good mood. The former would draw too much attention—no Arab, Palestinian, Syrian, or Lebanese was genuinely happy to encounter any Israeli in a uniform—while the latter would cause consternation that might result in the policemen demanding a full search of the vehicle just to further ruin the travelers' day. And that was not an option.

Faheem and Maktoum handed their passports to the officers standing outside their respective windows. The other three members of the terrorists' unit were in the back with the bomb, hidden behind a partition, unseen by the policemen. As long as they stayed quiet, and as long as the Israelis bought Faheem's story . . .

"Jordanian, huh?" said the man with Faheem's passport. "Why are you coming to Israel?"

"We are returning from visiting our sick mother in Duma."

"Really? And what's in the back of the van?"

Faheem drew his eyes downward in mock sorrow. "Our mother. She died in our arms. We are trying to get her to our family plot in Bethlehem before the smell is too horrible for us to bury her."

Faheem's officer made a face in disgust, but Maktoum's wasn't buying it.

"We'll just have to verify that for ourselves, Mr. Abdellatif," he said, reading the name on Maktoum's fake passport.

"Sir, please," Faheem said, leaning across the seat. Maktoum, for his part, wasn't saying or doing much of anything other than looking scared and guilty. "My mother, her hair is uncovered. Do not rob this wonderful woman of her last shred of religious dignity."

"Remove your keys and step out of the vehicle, sir," the officer told Maktoum.

As Faheem's driver reluctantly complied, the Israeli called in Hebrew to one of his compatriots still manning the gate. The man joined him and Maktoum, and they followed the driver toward the rear door of the vehicle.

Faheem prayed that Allah, who had thus far smiled upon their mission, would see fit to continue to protect their cause. Plan A had failed. Plan B could not. He held his breath, trying not to raise suspicion as the officer outside his door glanced back and forth between Faheem and the rear of the van. He was likely glad he wouldn't have to smell the rotting corpse of a Muslim woman as his partners would be, assuming Maktoum had been telling the truth. But the truth was far more deadly than any stench they dreaded.

The scratching of the key as it slid into the lock, the screech as Maktoum—or one of the officers—turned the handle, the low metallic thud as the latch broke free of the lock. Faheem prayed that his men heard the telltale signals that Plan B was now in effect. He prayed that Maktoum would drop in time, that his men's aim would prove true, that none of the Israelis would be able to return fire . . .

A barrage of percussive blasts buffeted the air. The officer by Faheem's window moved to aid his men, a fatal mistake. Faheem pulled his Glock, hopped out of the van, and shot the man in the back of the head. Swiveling back toward the checkpoint, he fired three more rounds at the final Israeli border guard, who was only now aiming his weapon at the van. The first round hit the barricade and caromed in a different direction, while the second hit the Israeli in his abdomen, an ultimately fatal shot that unfortunately wouldn't kill the man for several minutes or hours, depending on the severity of the wound. Faheem wouldn't have to wait for that, though, as the third bullet splintered a rib and blasted through the man's aorta, dropping the officer to the ground as his heart pumped its final burst of blood directly onto the cracked asphalt of the road beneath his now prone body.

Faheem ran to the back of the van to survey the damage. He was happy to see the bodies of the two other guards lying dead on the road. What grieved his heart, though, was seeing that Maktoum's body joined theirs, a bullet hole not unlike the one Faheem had delivered to the first guard piercing the back of his skull. He had known and worked with Maktoum for years, and he deserved better than this.

Regardless of the setback, they had to get going. Maktoum had given his life in service of jihad, even if not in the way he had planned. He was in paradise now, and no longer a concern of Faheem and the mission. They had to press on. The clock was ticking, now more than ever.

"Any injuries?" Faheem asked the rest of his men, still crouched in attack positions around the bomb.

"Maktoum's dead," said Abdel, a seventeen-year-old recruit whose older brother had died in the blast from an Israeli shelling in the 2006 war.

"I can see that. Are any of you hit?"

"No, Faheem," said Ashraf, a Pakistani recruit. "The bomb may have been hit, though."

Faheem climbed into the van and inspected the device. A bullet had lodged itself in the outer casing of one of the device's two main cylinders. He knew how to activate the bomb, but that was the extent of his operational knowledge. If the bullet had pierced anything integral to its detonation, or, worse, if radiation was spilling out from the device right now, he had no way to repair it. Once again, he would have to trust in Allah's will—and in the team's speed—to finish what they had started.

"Let's get these bodies out of here and get going," Faheem said. "Somebody's going to miss a radio call and come up here to check on the men. We want to be long gone when that happens."

The men hopped out and dragged the bodies behind trees and rocks at the edge of the road. Maktoum's body, however, they put in the back of the van. Faheem's story about a dead body came true after all. Ayman, a Syrian who had worked with Faheem and Maktoum before, assumed driving responsibilities as they made their way through the checkpoint and down the road ahead.

A kilometer later, the van crested a hill and Faheem caught sight of a beautiful sunrise breaking above the treeline. The next time the sun hit the opposite horizon, Faheem mused, everyone in the van would be joining Maktoum in paradise, followed by a million screaming Israelis falling into their own infidel afterlives of torment. And even that, the death of a million Jews by his hands, was just the beginning.

He smiled to think of the divine wrath that was about to be unleashed on the Zionist state and her imperialist supporters. The world was about to change forever, and he, Faheem Ramdallah, had been chosen to help push that shift into place. He felt honored and, at the same time, scared for those left behind.

What was coming was Allah's will. But it wouldn't be pretty. For anyone.

CHAPTER 33

United Nations Headquarters, Manhattan, New York

Arsalan Hosseini, president of the Islamic Republic of Iran, was feeling far less potent than his office should suggest. Embroiled in power struggles in his own government and against most of the world, caught between bravado and reality, he felt diminished to the role of a child, scolded by one parent for doing things one way, by another for doing things the opposite.

He stood in the small antechamber just outside the UN's General Assembly. In a few moments, he would address the august global body and, by extension, the world. This was the organization that had issued wave after wave of economic sanctions that had served to cripple Iran's economy and instigate the social upheaval that had led to his election over a slate of more conservative choices.

The Iranian people had voted him in on a platform of moderate rationalism, reaching out to the world and shedding its pariah status on the global stage. In truth, the people of his nation were more liberal, more favorable toward Americans and other Westerners, and more globally minded than his predecessor's regime signaled to the world. It was this vision he had every intention of fulfilling when he assumed office. And then he realized his greatest challenge would not be navigating the geopolitical minefield his predecessor had left him, but rather the more powerful elements within his own government, whose stark ideals his regime had embodied.

A red-haired aide named Liam touched his earbud and turned to Hosseini.

"They're just about ready for you, sir," Liam said, with the distinct lilt of an Irish accent.

"Fine," Hosseini said without emotion. In truth, he didn't know how to feel. His presence here was not his choice. At least, with his current script it wasn't. He had a role to play, but it wasn't the one he had been elected for. Iran's security, its prosperity, and its future were his responsibility. But his vision of that and the ayatollah's were very different indeed.

Of course Iran's nuclear program was designed to produce atomic weaponry as well as a new energy source. And of course he saw Israel as a blight upon the Middle East, though certainly not the only one. But actually following through on the posturing of his predecessor—and that of the ayatollah—was suicidal. Becoming a nuclear power was an entry into a very elite club. Knowing that you have the ability to—as his predecessor had so aptly put it in his threat to Israel—wipe an enemy nation off the face of the earth made adversaries and allies alike treat you with a certain respect. But to actually use them would be national suicide.

The last time atomic weapons were used against another state, the United States had been the only power with the technology at their disposal. A few years later, their top geopolitical foe, the Soviet Union, acquired the technology, kicking off the Cold War, when the world hung on a razor's edge over the perpetual fear of one trigger-happy despot pushing the wrong button and kicking off a chain reaction that obliterated the entire human race. Though the tension of the Cold War had dissipated after the collapse of the Soviet Union, the threat of mutually assured destruction had not. Israel was a nuclear power. Of that Hosseini was sure. So were the United States, Britain, France, and Germany, all historical allies of the Jewish state. To unilaterally launch a nuclear first strike would be to invite untold destruction upon his nation. In today's climate, no rational man would be the first to push that button.

But Ayatollah Naghinejad was not a rational man. And there was much he was hiding from Hosseini.

"All right, then," Liam said, opening the door to the General Assembly chamber. "They're ready for you."

A polite but reserved scattering of applause greeted President Hosseini as he entered the massive room and ascended the steps to the platform. His attempts at reform in his own country had met with tremendous resistance. And as much as he wanted to speak for his country, the fact was that his country was moving in a different direction, against his will and against the will of the people. Such was the nature of things, for better or worse.

"Good evening and greetings to the members of this revered body and to the nations you represent. For many years, our great nation has sparred with the United Nations over our inherent right to a nuclear program. If India can have one, if Pakistan can have one, if France, Germany, Russia, China, and the United States, among many others, can have a nuclear program, why shouldn't Iran? If even North Korea is allowed a nuclear program, why on earth not our forward-thinking and historic people?

"You send aid money to the rogue Korean nation, which openly flaunts this body and threatens its member states. You offer billions to impoverished nations, where time after time the money only serves to line the pockets of despots bent on murdering their own people. And yet Iran is penalized with continual sanctions that damage not only our great nation, but your own standing in the world. More than a dozen nations have nuclear weapons. Why aren't IAEA inspectors investigating every element of their nuclear programs, when it's clear that developing weapons is, in fact, a major purpose of that? Why do you continue to penalize the Iranian people for pursuing a far more peaceful nuclear program than even our host nation here, the United States? To what level of hypocrisy have you fallen when the permanent members of the security council and their allies—nuclear powers all—decide to stonewall the attempts of other 'lesser' nations to better themselves."

Hosseini could hear tittering in the audience. He could see that many of the representatives, particularly those from non-nuclear states, were amenable to the ideas he was advocating. His words were taking root.

"For the United Nations, which was founded on the democratic principle of every nation having an equal voice, to give some nations a free pass while keeping others down is the worst kind of colonialism. The United States has claimed for itself the role of staunch defender of democracy. Well, here's your chance, Mr. President. If you believe in democracy, stop trying to hinder the future that our people have chosen.

"That's the beautiful thing, of course. The United Nations doesn't have to *do* anything. We are not asking for billions in aid packages. We are not asking for you to go to war on our behalf. Many have asked for these things here and received them. Our request is far lighter: simply to be left alone to pursue our rightful destiny. Freedom and equality are two pillars upon which both America and the United Nations were supposedly founded. So let the Iranian people be free to pursue our own equality with the favored powers. Anything less would be a slap in the face of everything this body claims to stand for. Thank you."

Hosseini's final words were greeted with uproarious applause. The delegates from the US, Britain, Germany, and several other states remained seated, but most of the rest stood, cheering in a manner not normally seen in the more staid confines of this chamber. Preferring to let the message linger while not wearing out his own welcome, the Iranian president bowed his head in appreciation, and then walked offstage back to his antechamber.

In the hallway beyond, a coterie of reporters assaulted him with microphones and digital recorders, ambushing him with a deluge of incomprehensible questions. He gave them an affable smile but let his security personnel push through the crowd. His speech would stand on its own. Anything else he might say would take away from the impact he could still hear echoing in the chamber behind him.

The consequences of his speech, of course, had not slipped by him. Iran was much further along the road to being a nuclear power than any other nation in that room. Even without any potential shift in sanctions against Iran and other states that might pursue nuclear programs, the Islamic Republic could forge through until their work was complete. After they had already achieved their nuclear ambitions, the world would no longer bully Iran into giving up its program. It would be a part of the club, nuclear-armed and ready to be taken seriously.

But that speech could come back to haunt Iran once they were part of that elite group of nations. The club only remained elite so long as the barrier to entry was high and those in the club were few and powerful. If the floodgates opened to allow even another dozen nations to become nuclear powers, the clout diminished significantly. And, for better or worse, the status quo's traditional resistance to new atomic powers had served to keep their numbers low for the better part of a century. Not to mention the fact that, with more fingers on nuclear buttons, the chances of an apocalyptic World War III skyrocketed.

Either the ayatollah wasn't as forward-thinking as he led himself to believe, or there was something far darker going on.

What wasn't he being told?

CHAPTER 34

EMIRATES TOWERS, DUBAI, UNITED ARAB EMIRATES
FRIDAY

The telltale silhouettes of Emirates Towers stood out against the azure sky, perhaps the first time since Wayne had arrived that the sky hadn't been tinged beige with the sand particulate from the surrounding desert hovering high over the city. Suarez sat in the passenger seat, while Nasef followed in the other vehicle. After all the gunplay and double-bluff attempts at subterfuge, the team finally had a solid lead.

Shiraz Imports was on the twenty-seventh floor of the Emirates Office Tower, also known as Emirates Tower One. At 1,163 feet tall, it was the one of the tallest building in the world, yet still only the tenth tallest in the city itself. Completed in 2000, it was older than the nine skyscrapers that topped it in Dubai's cityscape, but its triangular footprint and iconic design mirrored its sister tower, the slightly shorter Jumeirah Emirates Towers Hotel, or Emirates Tower Two. Located in the financial center of the city, the illustrious Emirates Towers Plaza had been a showpiece of the first wave of Dubai's boom at the close of the twentieth century, and despite its age relative to the newer, taller, and more daring projects the city's engineers had undertaken since, the buildings retained their air of world-class elegance.

"Do you ever doubt what you're doing, Zorro?" Wayne asked, surprising even himself by actually giving voice to the question that had plagued him for years.

"What do you mean?"

"When I was down there, in the rubble, thinking I was about to die, I was just thinking about all I've done, all the people I've killed. They were bad people, for sure, but they were also sons, husbands, fathers. For years I glossed over all of that—after all, they robbed me of my family, so it was only fair that I returned the favor. But it's an endless cycle, isn't it? The death of one jihadist prompts two more to join the cause. The death of my parents caused me to enlist and become the army's most lethal covert asset, and then the CIA's. But where does it end? Are we ultimately doing more harm than good?"

The question hung in the air, unanswered. Wayne drove in silence for a few moments, regretting his emotionally charged outburst questioning their mission. He hardly knew Suarez, who was technically his subordinate in this new unit, yet here he was pouring his heart out to him and potentially undermining his confidence in both his leadership and their very purpose here.

"I'm sorry," Wayne finally said. "Forget I said anything. I probably inhaled too much asbestos when the house came down on me."

Suarez didn't reply. Instead, he pulled out his wallet, full of a convincing assortment of ID and credit cards all in the name of his alias. Wayne had one just like it, so he wasn't sure what his teammate was doing. From behind a folded 100-dirham note, Suarez pulled a photograph of a smiling boy and girl, both with a dusky complexion that may or may not have hinted at Hispanic lineage.

"Your kids?" Wayne asked.

"Nope. I have no idea whose kids they are. But they're someone's. It's a stock image, for all I know, but I keep it with me every time I'm on assignment. It's a symbol to me, a symbol of the future. You're right, some kids may grow up hating others who don't think or look or act or pray the way they do, and men like us killing terrorists may encourage them to join up. But that's their choice. The men who have already taken up the banner of jihad, or are preying on the innocent in sex trafficking or the drug trade—those who would kill, steal, and destroy for their own selfish aims have not only made their choice, they take away agency from their targets. A boy shopping with his grandmother in a market, killed by the indiscriminate blast of a car bomb. A girl snatched from her home and forced into a lifetime of dehumanizing servitude. A family forced to the brink of starvation by the exploitative threats of a greed-consumed drug kingpin. They had their choice stolen from them. What we do restores that choice, if only by increments. We fight for the human right to choose their own destiny."

A barricade loomed ahead, forcing traffic to merge around a construction zone. Wayne slowed the SUV, taking in what Suarez was saying.

"These types of men are like a cancer," Zorro continued, "feeding off their victims and growing ever more powerful and deadly if left unchecked. Broader wars are like chemo or radiation therapy, blasting away at the cancer while leaving behind innocent casualties as an unfortunate byproduct of the wider approach. We, however, are the surgeon's scalpel, a highly trained and focused approach that seeks to root out the cancer itself, sparing those around from both the destructive effects of the cancer as well as from the Plan B of the wider, more destructive approach of a full-scale military campaign."

Wayne had heard that sort of talk before, from a leader he had trusted, only to realize how very misplaced that trust was.

"Are there adverse consequences?" Suarez continued. "Absolutely. Is there collateral damage sometimes? Unfortunately, yes. But are we the good guys in the grand karmic scheme of things? These guys killed at least two United States civil servants and kidnapped a diplomat, one working toward achieving peace for tens of millions in the most tumultuous region on earth. They're apparently planning to murder millions of those very people in an unprecedented nuclear attack. And we may be the only people on earth who can stop them. So weigh that in the balance: the lives of a few dozen men who have made murder and destruction their creed, or the lives of millions of Israeli civilians. Are we the good guys here? Unequivocally."

Wayne thought for a moment, and then nodded. "I guess I'll need to get me a picture of some kids for my wallet."

"You can borrow mine if you need to," Zorro said ingenuously.

"No, that's fine. I'll just sneak a peek every once in a while if I need some inspiration."

Suarez smiled, and Wayne suddenly didn't regret opening up to his teammate.

They pulled into a parking garage adjacent to Emirates Tower One, soon joined by Nasef. The three of them, bedecked in their business professional best, walked the impossibly green-lined path to the front entrance.

It was just after 7:00 a.m. and the lobby was virtually deserted. A young Arab man, dressed in the traditional white Emirati *thawb*, sat at an information booth to one side of the main elevators. A digital directory nearby aided guests looking for their destination's location in the fifty-four-story building. Armed with the intel Ibrahim had given them, Wayne led the team directly to the elevators, skipping the information booth altogether to avoid being remembered by the young Emirati manning it.

Wayne punched the button to call the elevator, and the left-most door opened almost immediately. The three Americans stepped inside the cab and Wayne punched the button for the twenty-fifth floor, two floors beneath their intended target. He was cognizant of every discreetly hidden security camera he had seen since they entered the building, and took for granted that for every camera he saw, there were probably two more he didn't. It was Friday, the Muslim day of worship, so hopefully the building's security would be running on a skeleton crew. The human element that he did see, so far only the man in the lobby, was the first of several reasons for the floor-changing subterfuge. If the authorities were looking for them—and between the CIA plane they'd landed in, the visit to Rick Weiland, the gunfight under the airport, and the destruction of the house in Hor Al Anz, he had no doubt they would be—he didn't want to be too easy to find. Further, if Shiraz Imports was nothing but a front for terrorism, the direct approach from the elevator would be too operationally risky.

A five-hundred-foot ascent later, the elevator dinged as the doors slid open on the twenty-fifth floor. The team had studied schematics Ibrahim had uploaded to their PDAs en route. They split up, Suarez and Nasef going right, Wayne going left. There were stairwells at each end of the hallway, which in turn formed the front edge of the building's triangular footprint. Shiraz Imports was located in the triangle's other corner.

Wayne walked down the thick-carpeted corridor. The once-lush flooring had been flattened with the burden of ten thousand footsteps over the years, but the deep purple, green, and brown hues of its swirling, arabesque patterns remained vibrant. He carried a briefcase, which held some bogus paperwork and a few gadgets from Ibrahim. A shoulder holster beneath his suit jacket held his Glock, while two miniature flash-bang grenades and one frag grenade were clipped to his belt, housed in what looked like a run-of-the-mill pager.

Despite his equipment and training, Wayne felt uneasy as he padded down the hall, certain that unseen eyes were watching, preparing to pounce. Combat was combat; surveillance was surveillance. The house last night and the airport tunnels before that were combat scenarios from the word *go*. The hospital was purely information gathering. This—an information-gathering mission straight into the belly of the beast, housed in a much larger building secured by men and technology in no way related to the terrorists—was in a complex hinterland that ripped up the traditional rules of engagement. Go in too soft, and the enemy could get the drop on Wayne and his team. Go in too heavy, and the building's security would try to stop them before they even got close to the information they needed. They had to find a happy medium, and for now, that meant trying to look normal while being continually vigilant, almost to the point of paranoia. It wasn't an operational strategy Wayne would choose normally, but they didn't have much choice.

When he finally reached the stairwell, Wayne glanced down the hallway to his left without breaking stride, trying to get an idea of what their approach would look like two stories up after their final ascent. He pushed through the door, checking that its latch wasn't set to lock automatically, preventing re-entry to any floor but the bottom, like some stairwells he had encountered in the past. Assured they would be able to access the twenty-seventh floor hallways from this door's counterpart two stories above, he climbed the stairs. Pausing at the door outside their destination floor, he listened, heard nothing, and exited the stairwell into the twenty-seventh floor hallway.

For all intents and purposes, this corridor was the twin of the one he'd just traversed. Wayne made his way down the hall, still attentive to his nonchalant, professional demeanor befitting the businessman he made himself out to be. The main Dubai work-week was Sunday through Thursday, so the fact that they were visiting on a Friday—the Muslim holy day—didn't help their ruse, but they didn't have the luxury of coming back on a different day.

A minute later, he arrived at a glass door. "SHIRAZ IMPORTS, LTD." was etched in its frosted surface at eye level. Suarez and Nasef arrived a moment later. None of them spoke. They already knew what needed to be done.

Wayne tried the door. Locked. A keypad was next to the door, with an intercom system mounted directly above. He pushed the call button while Nasef said "*Salaam alaikum*" into the microphone. They waited. Nothing.

"Watch my six," Wayne said as he withdrew his lock-pick set from the briefcase. A few tense moments later, the door clicked open. Stepping into the suite, Wayne noticed a blinking alarm panel.

"Zorro, can you override that?"

"I can try."

"There is no try. Just make it happen. If that calls in the troops, we're gonna find ourselves in a very tight spot. All right, Nasef, let's see what we can find out."

The suite was small, just a front reception area and two locked offices. Wayne cracked both locks in a matter of seconds, and then he and Nasef each took an office.

Wayne flipped through the tabs in a standup filing cabinet to the side of his small office. He didn't know exactly what he was looking for, but what he had found thus far was entirely innocuous. In fact, there wasn't very much here at all. No personal effects, no nameplates on the doors or desks, not the slightest hint that this was anything other than a halfhearted setup to hide what was really going on behind the scenes. The files were scant, but one labeled "Assets" piqued his curiosity. The folder held a single sheet of paper. It wasn't a financial record as he'd expected, but a list of properties throughout the city. One he recognized as the house from last night. Another was a 4500-square-foot McMansion on a prime piece of real estate on the Palm Jumeirah. The sheet cut off halfway through the mansion's listing, perhaps portending more properties on the missing sheets, but there was enough on the mansion to warrant another look.

"I've got nothing," Nasef shouted from the other office. "Either these guys don't keep records of their illicit activities, or they don't keep them here."

"Zorro, how's that alarm coming?" Wayne asked.

"Almost got it . . . Just a few more seconds . . ."

The piercing wail of the alarm rang out, turning the tiny suite into an echo chamber of banshee cries. Their time was up. Their window for escape was officially closing.

"Stuff whatever you can in your briefcases, then let's go," Wayne yelled over the sirens. "Ten seconds, and we're gone."

But as Wayne shoved the "Assets" folder and a few other files into his own briefcase, he feared that they probably couldn't even afford those ten seconds.

CHAPTER 35

DUBAI, UNITED ARAB EMIRATES

As the morning sun ascended toward its celestial apex, Walid paced at the edge of his new headquarters, gritting his teeth as his client chewed him out.

"And the Americans are still alive?" came the irritated voice from the earpiece of his encrypted sat phone. "What am I paying you for?"

"You are paying me, sir, to execute a specific series of tasks. Those tasks are successfully continuing as planned. Dealing with these Americans was not part of the plan. As it is, all of our efforts thus far to stop the Americans have been *pro bono*, as it were. If you'd like us to make that an additional priority, we can discuss a readjustment of my fee. I've already lost several of my men because of this contingency."

"I'm already paying you far more than your services are apparently worth. I don't care if the Americans live or die, but if anyone or anything interferes with my plans, I will hold you personally responsible. I don't like loose ends, Abushakra. And if this falls apart because your men couldn't handle three little infidels, there is nowhere on this earth you will be safe from my wrath."

"Do not threaten me." Walid realized his boldness was risky, but he had worked too hard building *Uhmar Haidar* into what it was today to let a client—even one as powerful as this one—to treat him so disrespectfully.

"Then finish the job. No loose ends. None."

The caller disconnected and Walid clenched the dead phone in his fist until his knuckles turned white. He wanted to scream into the desert, to summon Allah's wrath to fall upon the

Americans and his pride-filled patron, but he had to maintain his cool. That was the bad thing about being the boss, sometimes, particularly in a role such as his. His men looked to him for guidance, direction and confidence, as well as a paycheck. Yes, they were all paid well, far better than they would have been working directly for any of the organizations or leaders who contracted *Uhmar Haidar*'s services, but they were also putting their lives on the line. If Walid showed anything less than complete resolve in the face of whatever odds the task at hand dealt them, their own resolve would falter. And that was when men died, missions went belly up, and everything he had worked for would crumble like a house of cards.

His men were better trained and skilled than 99.9% of those working for ISIS, al-Qaeda, Hezbollah, or anyone else flying the flag of jihad these days. Due to his high client fees, his men were better equipped than their counterparts as well. And, if he did say so himself, as a strategist he was smarter than all the terrorism plotters in the caves of Afghanistan and the cells of Guantanamo combined. But one element remained necessary that no amount of training or funding could replace: faith. And, if he was honest with himself, sometimes Walid lost that himself, even if he couldn't show that face to his men.

The voice of one of those men stirred him from his thoughts. "Walid, *sahib*."

Walid turned to see his second in command, Omar Sawaf, walking up the sand-swept path toward him. Sawaf had been with him since the beginning, and had earned his trust many times over.

When Walid and Omar met, the terrorist leader was on the cusp of launching *Uhmar Haidar*, and he realized the fearless Syrian would be a perfect addition to his project. Excited about the high-profile operations such an outfit could undertake, and about the massive impact it could make on behalf of the holy struggle, Sawaf quickly signed on. It was a decision neither man had regretted.

Sawaf's one flaw, theoretically speaking, was that he was more dedicated to jihad itself than to preserving and protecting Islam's presence in the world. It was a conversation Omar and Walid had shared twice in their friendship. Twice was enough.

Though plenty of jihadists worshiped the burning anger that propelled their violent struggle far more than they did Allah himself, Sawaf was the first Walid had met who was honest about it. It was a secret they kept from their men, since many of them were, in fact, true believers. Or at least they had convinced themselves that they were.

It wasn't Walid's place to judge, after all. He had more than his share of struggles and, when he was honest with himself, he realized that his personal vendettas against the West got in the way of the holy struggle in the purest since of the word. But if their impure motives led them to righteous ends, who could blame them? Allah's work was being done. And very, very effectively.

Only then did he notice that his hand hurt, still subconsciously squeezing the phone in a death grip. He relaxed his hand and slipped the phone into a pocket as Sawaf approached.

"We have a problem, Walid," Sawaf said when he reached the crest where Walid stood. "One of the laptops was damaged in transit. The launch software is corrupted."

"Please tell me this is your idea of a sick joke."

"No, Walid, this would not be the time for joking."

"Of course it's not. It's a colloquialism. Get the sand out of your ears, Omar."

Sawaf clenched his jaw, swallowing a retort before continuing.

"Ahmad is working to see if he can repair the code, but if not, we'll need to reinstall it from the backup disk."

"Then what's the problem? Reinstall it already."

"The disk is at the Palm estate."

Walid rolled his eyes in disgust. He hated being proven wrong, but his irate paymaster seemed more on the money about *Uhmar Haidar*'s incompetence with every word Sawaf spoke.

"So if Ahmad can't fix it, Phase Two is a bust without the disk?"

"I'm afraid so."

"So who have you sent to retrieve the disk?"

"Being short staffed as we already are, getting set up here, especially after losing so many men in the airport tunnels and in the trap we set for the Americans"—missions Walid had either spearheaded or planned—"I wanted to double check with you on our asset reallocation to retrieve the disk."

Walid's phone rang before he could respond. He checked the caller ID and held up a hand to Sawaf as he answered.

"By Allah, are the Americans dead yet?"

"Not quite, no," came the voice of Deputy Chief of Police Saeed Dahhan.

"What on earth am I paying you for, then?" He realized he was echoing his own client, but unlike Walid's mission parameters, Dahhan's sole responsibility was to watch out for and eliminate any potential contingencies that third parties—like the Americans—might present. In fact, if anyone deserved the wrath of his powerful paymaster, it was Dahhan, not Walid. So he felt no qualms about laying into him. That is, until the deputy chief shared the reason for his call.

"I thought you might be interested to know that the burglar alarm just went off at Shiraz Imports," Dahhan said, irritation creeping into his voice. The shell corporation belonged to his client, and though Walid had never been to its Emirates Towers office, it was on his radar.

"Get them. Find them, stop them, shoot to kill. These men are enemies of the state, so technically, apprehending them would be in your best interest even if I weren't paying you so handsomely."

"We've got two units entering the building now. They won't escape."

"See that they don't. Call me when it's done."

Walid disconnected, thought for a moment, and then turned back to Sawaf.

"The Americans seem to have found out about Shiraz Imports. They just set off the burglar alarm in the Emirates Towers office."

"Really? And our faithful Chief Dahhan is on the job, I assume?"

"Of course, assuming he doesn't cock this one up, too." He paused for a moment more, thinking. "The Palm Jumeirah mansion, that's owned by Shiraz, isn't it?"

"I believe so, yes."

Walid nodded, physically confirming what he had been mulling over. "I'm going to the mansion to retrieve the disk. I'm bringing Sultan, Aswan, Mohamed, and Usama with me. Tell Ahmad to work hard on fixing the program, just in case."

"Why you?" Sawaf asked. "Why not just send Sultan and the rest on their own?"

"You can handle the preparations on your own. If the Americans somehow slip through the police's grasp, they'll likely be coming to Shiraz's property on the Palm next. So my trip would kill two birds with one stone, as it were."

"Fair enough, but why you? Couldn't an extra couple of men help Sultan and the rest to finish off the Americans?"

"Yeah, they could, but it's no longer just about scratching them off our radar," Walid said, thinking about the embarrassment he had suffered, the men he had lost, the damage that had been done to person, property, and reputation because of these three American agents.

"Then what?"

Walid looked back toward the cityscape, growing bright as the glassy surfaces of audacious skyscrapers cast reflections of the rising sun.

"Payback."

CHAPTER 36

EMIRATES TOWERS, DUBAI, UNITED ARAB EMIRATES

The high-pitched chirp of Shiraz Imports' security alarm was a sonic blade through Wayne's skull, every blast of sound an assault on his eardrums and faculties. Briefcase in one hand, pistol in the other, Wayne led the team out of the office and down the hall to the stairwell he had taken from the twenty-fifth floor just minutes earlier.

The alarm's blare lessened as they put distance between themselves and the breached office, indicating that the alarm was local only, instead of triggering sirens across the floor—or worse, throughout the building. An obvious choice, so one company's secretary punching in the wrong code after a bad night's sleep wouldn't completely disrupt business for the building's other tenants.

Of course, that didn't mean the local alarm hadn't triggered an alert for the building's security. In fact, Wayne was all but sure it had done just that.

Despite the fact that he and his men were five-hundred feet above the building's ground-level exit, Wayne knew the elevators weren't an option. If the building's security was worth its salt, they would shut down the elevators after a breach, particularly if the suspects in question were seen on CCTV boarding the elevator. There was, of course, the off chance that the security forces were asleep at the wheel or would be so paralyzed by lack of real-world experience in an actual breach that they would fail to close off that automated means of egress, but Wayne wasn't willing to risk the mission or his team's lives on a losing bet. And even if that best-case scenario did come to pass, the only real downside to their taking the stairs meant that they'd be a little more tired by the time they reached the lobby.

No matter the method of descent they took, Wayne didn't anticipate getting out of there with the same cover of self-assured business professionalism that had granted them entry initially. Their luck had already run out on that count.

The team reached the stairwell without encountering anyone or anything to impede their way, save for the now-distant chirping siren Wayne was glad to be rid of. Today being Friday meant that many of the office tower's tenant businesses were closed or only playing host to a handful of dedicated weekend workers, ergo fewer witnesses to the Americans' breaking and entering scheme. The flip side of that was that, with less chance that innocent, rent-paying tenants might get caught in the crossfire, the building's security forces—or worse, the police who were already out for the team's heads—would have fewer reservations about using deadly force.

Wayne pushed open the stairwell door and listened. It was hard to hear for sure with the alarm still sounding down the hall, but he didn't think he heard anyone else in the stairwell below them. There were no guarantees that would last, but he was happy to take whatever small blessings he could at this point.

The team emptied into the stairwell and began their long descent, Wayne leading the pack with Nasef and Suarez close on his heels. They moved as swiftly and silently as they could, keeping their weight on the balls of their feet, their backs at a slight angle toward the outer wall.

Twelve spiral flights down, just after passing a door with "15" marked on it in both Western and Arabic numerals, Wayne held up a fist, prompting his men to stop in their tracks and listen. The voices of at least two men speaking Arabic drifted down to them, followed by the sound of a door slamming.

"You're sure it was this stairwell?"

"That's what base said. Call them again if you like."

"Can't. No reception in here. Too much concrete. You go up, I'll go down."

"Why on earth would they go up?"

"They're criminals. Who knows? We should check to be safe. Besides, the police should be arriving any time now. I just want to make sure we're thorough."

"Fine."

Footsteps sounded as the two men split up, one heading upstairs toward the roof, the other heading down toward Wayne and company.

Wayne signaled for the team to follow him downward with renewed haste, hoping that the security officer's own footsteps would mask theirs. They reached the fourteenth floor, then the thirteenth. Wayne thought he heard the security officer's footfalls growing louder and closer with each passing floor, but he was pretty sure that was just in his head. Assuming the two officers had started on the twenty-seventh floor, where he and the team had disappeared into the stairwell and away from the cameras' view, the American agents had a solid head start. What waited below, however, remained a concern.

Wayne had just cleared the ninth-floor landing when a door burst open below, followed by several men shouting over one another in Arabic. Their voices commingled in the concrete echo chamber of the stairwell, making it impossible for Wayne to make out more than a few disjointed words. The voices were more confident, more forceful than the security officers searching the landings above. The police were here, and this wasn't their first rodeo.

Nine floors to go. So close, and yet so far.

Listening intently to the cadence of the men's voices and footsteps, he took a chance and snuck a look over the railing. There were at least four policemen eight floors below, hugging the center of the stairwell as they ascended. If they hurried, Wayne's team could squeeze out another few flights before needing to find a different way down.

As Wayne reached the landing between the seventh and eighth floors, a door slammed open above them, no more than two or three stories away. More police stomped into the stairwell, and at least some of their footsteps seemed to be coming downward. The Americans were caught in a pincer attack between two police units which—considering the rap sheet of espionage, breaking and entering, theft, trespassing, murder, and terrorism the Dubai authorities were likely ready to pin on Wayne and his team—were undoubtedly authorized to use deadly force. These guys weren't the enemy, though, even though they definitely were an obstacle. Wayne thought back to his conversation in the car with Suarez. These men hadn't chosen a path of unmitigated evil like those they had killed beneath the airport or in the Hor Al Anz house. If it came down to him or them, the lives of millions depended on his being the truer shot, but if there was a way that didn't end up with the blood of innocent policemen on his conscience, he'd take that path. And considering how ricochet-prone this stairwell was, with no cover and cops closing in from both sides, direct confrontation seemed the least likely path to success, crisis of conscience or not.

At the sixth-floor landing, Wayne pulled open the door and led the team into the hallway. Even if the police band radios had as poor reception as those of building security, once the men met in the middle, they'd realize they'd been given the slip, and one step into a hallway—any hallway—would give them the information they needed from the CCTV cameras on which the American agents had just again appeared.

Wayne spied a fire ax and hose hidden behind a pane of emergency glass, set into the wall to the left of the stairwell's entrance. Using the butt of his pistol, he smashed a hole in the glass, clearing away enough shards to reach the ax within.

"Go," he urged his men as he hoisted the ax. He had no idea if this would work. At best, it would buy them a few precious moments in which to escape. At worst, it would cost them their lives and their mission. If his men could get a head start, there might be some hope for the ambassador and for preventing Iran's attack on Israel, even if this last-ditch attempt to slow down their pursuers blew up in his face.

Angling his swing with what he hoped was a perfect balance between accuracy and force, Wayne slammed the ax into the door, carving a thin hole in the steel as the blade embedded itself deep in the metal. He had swung the tool sideways, with the handle now protruding two feet across the jamb, effectively barring the inward-swinging door. Unfortunately, the ax hitting the door had likely sounded like cannon fire inside the stairwell, drawing the cops to the sixth-floor landing like moths to a flame. He picked up his briefcase and pistol and ran after his men, hoping against hope that his makeshift barricade would hold long enough for him and his team to make it to safety.

He had reached the hallway's halfway point, just a few paces behind the rest of the team, when he heard the ax handle smack against the door jamb. The gig was up. The cops had not only reached the sixth floor, but were now surely all but certain the American interlopers were on that floor as well. Wayne prayed that the ax would hold, though he knew that eventually the narrow hole in the steel or the ax handle itself would give way, providing the cops with a long-distance shooting gallery if he and his men weren't in the other stairwell by then.

Two more slams, followed by a persistent, percussive shaking as the police tried to jar the ax loose. Wayne continued running and praying, now making pace alongside Nasef.

When they were twenty feet from the door to the opposite stairwell, Wayne heard a bang from behind as the ax burst free and clattered to the floor. He risked a glance back, seeing two policemen leading the way into the hallway. One shouted "Stop" in Arabic, and then in English, neither of which Wayne had any intention of obeying.

Ten feet from the door now. The unmistakable report of the first bullet, then the second, rang out. One shot embedded itself to the left of the door, while the second found Nasef's back, the impact pitching him forward from his normal running gait.

Suarez was the first to reach the door, shoving it open as the team poured into its relative safety. A third bullet flew by Wayne's ear and hit the wall beyond, while the fourth lodged itself in the steel door just as Nasef kicked it shut.

"Anubis, you hurt?" Wayne asked as they began to descend the stairs anew.

"I'm fine," Nasef said with a grunt. "Let's just get out of here."

Six stories to go, Wayne mouthed to himself as he ran. *Six floors to freedom.*

Then there were only five floors left. Then four.

On the third floor landing, the door burst open as a security officer entered the stairwell. Without breaking stride, Wayne kicked the half-open door. The impact swung the door inward, knocking the officer against the wall. With an *oomph*, he fell to the ground, sliding down several steps before crumpling unconscious on the mid-floor landing.

If security and the police were looking for them throughout the building, the lobby would be a deathtrap. Surely the security tapes were being scrutinized at this very moment. Their route in was undoubtedly covered. The lobby wasn't an option anymore. Their cars in the parking garage—and all the tools, clothes, and weapons therein—were now forfeit. They had to find another way out.

Wayne flashed back to the schematics he had studied before arriving. The lobby was on the ground floor, but there was a basement which housed a showroom for BMW—which kept its regional headquarters in the Emirates Office Tower—and a loading bay for deliveries. The loading bay would be their way out. It had to be.

Passing the ground floor, they arrived at the basement level and the bottom of the stairwell. The team exited and found themselves in the BMW showroom, with dozens of luxury cars, both new and classic, residing on low platforms dotted across the room. Overhead spotlights that during business hours would have made the shiny paint and chrome gleam for dramatic effect were doused, leaving a dim labyrinth of six-figure Beemers for Wayne and the team to navigate. The loading dock was located on the far side of the building, through the maze of cars.

When they finally reached the loading dock, Wayne was disappointed to find that the door was locked. The push-button panel that activated the massive loading bay doors, however, still had juice. Suarez pushed the "UP" button, and the door began to slide open. Wayne slipped under the door and dropped down to the concrete room below. Another panel sat to one side, this one controlling the outer doors. He pushed the "UP" button for that one, and the room was filled with the stereophonic sounds of whirring as both doors' motors drew the barriers into the ceiling.

Over the whirring, when the doors were just over halfway raised, Wayne heard two unpleasant sounds at once. The first was the sound of police sirens in the courtyard around the corner of the building. They wouldn't be able to evade the police outside on foot. Not for long anyway. And with their cars trapped in the parking garage on the other side of the lobby and central plaza—which were by now overrun by police and security personnel—they couldn't rely on their old wheels to get them to safety.

The second sound was even more unpleasant. Across the showroom, the stairwell door through which the team had entered opened, with more Arabic voices following. Wayne and his team were stuck in another pincer attack, but this one didn't have a convenient detour through a different floor.

Then a most welcome sound, one he hadn't expected, greeted Wayne's ears: the revving of an engine. Then a second engine joined the first. Both were BMW engines.

"Phoenix, get up here!" Suarez shouted from the showroom.

Wayne hoisted himself up to where the two closest luxury cars were running. Nasef sat behind the wheel of a black M6, while Zorro had commandeered a red Z4. Wayne slid into the Z4's passenger seat, buckling up just as Suarez hit the gas.

A bullet pinged off the loading dock door overhead as the Z4 accelerated through the aperture. The car hit fifty kilometers per hour before the wheels left the concrete, falling down six feet into the empty loading dock and scraping the bottom of the chassis before the spinning tires found purchase again and sped through the second set of doors and into daylight. Nasef's M6 seconded the *Dukes of Hazzard* routine, its newer shocks taking the landing more in stride before following Suarez and Wayne out of the building and back toward the highway.

"That was way too close," Wayne said, silently offering another prayer of thanks for another bullet dodged—literally and figuratively.

"Thank goodness it's Friday," Suarez said. "That could have gotten a lot messier if there were a bunch of other people around."

"Anubis, how's that bullet wound?" Wayne asked over comms.

"I hurt like a mother, but I'll live. The vest took the brunt of it."

"Thank God. Glad you're okay, brother."

"You and me both, Phoenix. Let's hope our luck holds."

"Where to now, boss?" Suarez asked as they approached the on-ramp for Sheikh Zayed Road.

Wayne remembered the "Assets" folder he had procured from Shiraz Imports. He pulled the file from his briefcase and scanned the papers briefly before he found what he was looking for.

"Head for the Palm Jumeirah. I've got a feeling that's where we'll find the next piece of the puzzle."

"Fantastic. I was hoping we could get a tan while we were in town."

"If only," Wayne said. "Even if I'm right, this will be anything but a walk on the beach."

They lapsed into silence for a moment as Suarez navigated the on ramp to Sheikh Zayed.

"Oh wow," Suarez said. "Today's Good Friday."

Wayne smiled with one side of his mouth, somewhat pleased to have that element of tradition, normalcy, and the impending celebration of Easter brought to mind in this chaotic time. And then he realized the more sinister implication of the holiday for their purposes.

"Passover," Wayne said. "One of the most important Jewish holidays. One of the most important holidays in Israel. Good Friday and Passover align this year, as they did 2000 years ago during Jesus' trial and crucifixion. Passover starts at sunset tonight."

"*Dios mio*."

"Yeah. The ambassador's kidnapping, the intel on an Iranian nuke. If I were a betting man, I'd say they're planning to attack Israel at sunset tonight." Wayne punched in some figures on his PDA. "That's at 7:00 Israel time, 8:00 p.m. here. We've got nine hours."

Suarez set his jaw, staring at the road ahead as he stepped on the gas by way of response. He didn't say it, but Wayne knew exactly what he was thinking.

Time was running out.

CHAPTER 37

LANGLEY, VIRGINIA

Janan Ibrahim was running on fumes, powered by adrenaline, Red Bull, and bad coffee. Since the team had landed in Dubai, she had managed to snag a grand total of four hours of sleep, all at her desk, all while keeping one ear open for an urgent call for help. Still, it was more sleep than Wilkins, Suarez, and Nasef had managed, and their work was far more taxing, no matter what Ibrahim was juggling back here from the safety of her office.

That was one nice perk of this assignment—due to the small, closed circle of people who knew about the mission, she wasn't working out of her regular cubicle but, rather, from a secure office used for coordinating missions in the field. She had been given the name of two other CIA analysts she could enlist to help if the situation warranted, but Pierce's instructions were to only broaden the circle of secrecy if absolutely necessary. The wider the circle, the greater the chance of a leak. And this was one mission where a leak—before or after the fact—would be fatal.

Ibrahim was primarily in listening mode right now, hearing the men's conversations over the radio while busying herself with researching Shiraz Imports' connections on one screen, watching police car GPS trackers on an aerial view of Dubai on another, running a biometric screening program on a third, and preparing schematics and pertinent information about the Palm Jumeirah mansion on the fourth.

Wilkins's observation about Passover jarred her, but it fit. To her knowledge, there hadn't been any chatter on the usual channels about a Passover attack, but then, there was an unusual dearth of usable intel on the Iranians' plans at all. That either meant the intel they did have—which was largely circumstantial and owed much to the dying gasps of a severely injured bodyguard—was either wrong or the sole leak in an otherwise tightly controlled campaign.

It was no secret that the CIA, the NSA, and the rest of the Beltway's alphabet soup of agencies had cast a very wide net for intercepting electronic communications about potential terrorist attacks. When it had come out that the NSA was spying on the phones of the prime ministers of some of the United States' closest allies, it was a wake-up call to would-be terrorists—stay offline. If good, old-fashioned, in-person communication and physical letters had been good enough to coordinate the vast majority of wars, attacks, and conspiracies for most of human history, it could work for a close-knit terrorist group seeking to fly under the radar until they roared above the surface with explosive intensity.

Still, the lack of concrete evidence was troubling. Hopefully Wayne's team would find both the ambassador and the smoking gun for the planned attack before the bomb went off, but it was also disturbing that the world's foremost data-mining facility hadn't managed to uncover more than a few bread crumbs indicating an attack. If Iran had already developed a nuke, why not make it public? Even among those who contended that the Islamic republic was using its nuclear energy program as a cover to develop atomic weapons—a group that included most of the intelligence community—the most logical scenario would be for the country to announce its breakthrough, flexing its muscle by proclaiming itself to be an ascendant superpower to be taken seriously.

But it hadn't.

And though the timing certainly would fit if they were planning an imminent attack on Israel—a move that would surely be decried by the vast majority of the world—their silence on their breakthrough indicated they might not want credit for the attack to fall on them after all. When al-Qaeda claimed credit for the attacks of 9/11, it painted a big target on the organization and all who sought to aid them. Iran's leadership surely wanted to avoid the same fate.

Still, that didn't completely eliminate the issue of developing the nuke itself. Despite the Iranian government's resistance and recalcitrance when it came to complying with the IAEA's inspection demands, UN personnel had been all over the country's nuclear facilities. None of them were fully prepared to develop the enriched fissile material necessary to create a nuclear bomb. And without some sort of smoking gun, that was the exact conclusion the UN would reach after the bomb leveled an Israeli city.

A pop-up box appeared on her primary screen. Flashing red text indicated a Level 1 Alert. Something big was going down. She had only seen this sort of alert in training. The attack on the Benghazi embassy had only wrought a Level 2 Alert, something that, in retrospect, should clearly have been a Level 1, but that was the closest Ibrahim had gotten in her tenure with the agency.

She clicked the box and read the intelligence brief with stunned horror.

> *IAEA DISCOVER PREVIOUSLY UNKNOWN NUKE FACILITY NEAR RASHT TODAY 1130 LOCAL. FACILITY WAS DISGUISED AS GRANARY, NOW DESTROYED. SCIENTISTS DEAD. RADIATION PRESENT. FISSILE MATERIAL MISSING. NO STATEMENT YET FROM TEHRAN. UN SECURITY COUNCIL TO HOLD EMERGENCY MEETING TODAY.*

"Allah save us all," Ibrahim gasped as she finished reading the brief.

She called Deputy Director Pierce, who said he had received the alert as well and would speak with the president about what action the US would be taking next.

"How are our boys doing in Dubai right now?" Pierce asked.

"They're following up a lead now, sir."

"I don't need to emphasize how much more important all of this just became. This is an international nightmare as it is, but if they kill the ambassador and if that bomb goes off . . ."

"No, sir, you don't need to emphasize it. I'm well aware of this new development's implications and the importance of the mission."

"Good to hear. I'll come by later today to help out. I know the president wants some concrete results here."

"We're all working hard to ensure he has them soon," Ibrahim said, trying to disguise the frustration in her voice.

"Great. I'll see you soon."

Ibrahim hung up and called Wayne from a different line. She relayed the information from the intelligence brief, which Wayne received with measures of both shock and determination. After a brief exchange of intel about the mansion the team was driving to, Ibrahim offered a closing sentiment that would become the mantra for the day.

Hurry.

CHAPTER 38

DUBAI, UNITED ARAB EMIRATES

Passover. Christine Needham's grandmother had been ethnically and religiously Jewish. Though her marriage to a nominally Protestant man had drained her ancestral faith's importance in her life, Granny Miriam still imparted nuggets of Judaic wisdom to her granddaughter.

One of those had been the importance of Passover, the festival that celebrated God's sparing of the faithful Jews during the tenth and final plague in Egypt, prompting Pharaoh to finally release the enslaved Jewish populace as Moses led them toward the Promised Land. The tenth plague, as recounted in the book of Exodus, was the slaying of the eldest child in every family by the Angel of Death. God instructed the Jews to slay a lamb and paint the doorposts with the blood of that lamb, and the angel would pass over those households. That night, after the angel had fulfilled its gruesome purpose, the wails of Egyptian parents mourning their lost children filled the air, including those of Pharaoh himself, whose eldest son and heir had died as prophesied. The Jewish firstborn, however, had been spared.

In a twisted inversion of this tale, forces tied to her captors now sought to turn the Jewish celebration of Yahweh's mercy on the faithful into a slaughter to symbolize the wrath of Allah upon the infidel. The Promised Land the Jews had settled in after escaping Egypt became ancient Israel. This new attack sought to remove that promise and destroy modern Israel. The symbolism, something most terrorists and world leaders understood was instrumental in cementing a point, was striking. But Christine feared that, if she died, or even if she was rescued after the bomb went off, the world the sun rose upon on Saturday would be forever changed for the worse, and not just for Israel, the Jews, and the Middle East. The world was a lot smaller than that now, and the fuse that was now burning toward a sunset explosion would quickly embroil most of the planet in an all-consuming war from which none could truly escape.

The door to her cell opened and she leapt to her feet, handcuffs sliding up along the pipe to which they were secured. She began desperately hoping, praying, for an opportunity to facilitate a successful escape. If she was being realistic, the chances of getting out of there on her own accord were virtually nil, but if she gave up all hope, there would be nothing left for her.

A young, bearded man in his early twenties stepped inside, glancing back into the hallway once more before shutting the door behind him. She blinked twice before she recognized him.

It was Tariq, the one who had tried to get her to strip earlier. The one whose pride she had badly damaged.

He locked the door with a small key, dropping it in his pocket. Turning back toward Christine, he held up another key, one she recognized as the same sort used to unlock her handcuffs. He was mocking her, demonstrating how much power he held over her, how very much their positions had changed since their last encounter. As he pocketed the handcuff key, a salacious grin crawled across his face. Several of his teeth were blackened with rot, but the leer in his eyes was what she found most disgusting.

No, she thought. *Not this*. After the pain and indignation she had been forced to endure over the past few days, this was just too much. And yet, the keys the vengeful Arab had dropped into his pocket could just be the ticket she needed to get out of there.

Tariq moved toward her, hands raised for groping. She took a few steps away from him, pivoting along the handcuff's reach, until her back hit the wall. Sliding along the wall to the right, she tried to anticipate his moves. If she could get her hands on the keys, knee him in the groin, and reach the door before he recovered, she might stand a chance after all. She'd be running blind once she left the room, but it was something. She still hoped that a rescue team was inbound, but she—and the fate of the Middle East—couldn't depend on it. All her life she had been an active participant, and she wasn't about to be relegated to damsel-in-distress status in the most crucial hour of her career, even if her situation severely limited her options for action.

She let him reach her a few feet from the corner of the room, allowing some maneuvering space for running around him to the door once she made her move. Almost instantly she regretted that decision. The man grabbed her by the throat with one hand, yanking at her blouse with the other. Buttons popped off and clicked on the tiled floor as she fought to keep from vomiting at the man's hot, rancid breath. Her shirt was now open, exposing her bra and naked stomach to the terrorist. His breathing grew heavier, his eyes bulging as his lust fed off her nearly naked form. Still gripping her neck to keep her subdued, he began to grope her breasts, one at a time.

She struggled against his grip, trying unsuccessfully to reach his pocket, and then testing the reach of her knees. Neither was an option from her current position while he held her neck against the wall. She had to break free somehow.

A flash of realization brought her a renewed urgency. As horrible as the prospect of being defiled by this beast was, there were even wider-ranging national security implications at stake. The man's groping was taking his hands perilously close to where she had hidden the Micro SD card bearing the evidence of the bomb. Without the card, the bomb would go off, millions would die, and the United States would be swept into an all-consuming World War III from which the human race might never truly recover.

She slapped Tariq's face, trying to deflect his attention from her breasts. He lifted his eyes to hers, burning with indignation at her gall for interfering with his taking that to which he felt he had a rightful claim. She was expecting his return punch, but that didn't stop it from hurting like crazy. She chose to let the adrenaline propel her through, ignoring the ringing in her ears and the dizzying swing of the room as she jerked her knee into the man's groin.

Tariq howled in pain, doubled over while Christine tried to reach into his pocket to claim the key. He caught her hand with his, holding on while he tried to regain his focus. She heard a click a split second before seeing the flash of a switchblade in his other hand. She wrenched her hand away just as he managed to stand up, his leering stare replaced by one of fury and vengeance. He would have his fun, and then he would kill her.

A squeaking sound came from the door behind him, but he paid it no heed. He should have. The door swung open to reveal Omar Sawaf, Walid's second in command.

"Tariq!" Sawaf yelled at the man. Tariq made no move to acknowledge Sawaf, focused instead on his plans for Christine.

Sawaf pulled a pistol and shot Tariq in the back of the head, splattering blood and gray matter across Christine's face and chest. So much shock, relief, and fear was coursing through her veins that instead of screaming, she simply remained silent, save for her labored breathing.

A black blanket of sackcloth flew at her face. She caught it, but the billowing edges draped over her head.

"Cover yourself, harlot," Sawaf said, plucking the knife from Tariq's grasp and grabbing the door key that had fallen from his pocket. "I will return in a moment. If you insist on exposing your idolatrous body again, I will kill you myself."

He closed the door, locking it behind him. Suppressing her disgust and extracting the handcuff key from Tariq's pocket, she removed her shackles and rubbed at her reddened wrists. Without the door key, though, she still had no chance of escape.

Fearing she had no real choice at the moment and happy to have some way of covering up her nakedness and the memory card's hiding place, she slipped on the heavy burqa. Heavy, large, and heat-absorbent black. In the desert. For more than a millennium. *How on earth had these women not staged a massive rebellion by now?* Christine wondered.

The door opened again. Sawaf entered, dragging another man behind him, but she couldn't see what he looked like through the mesh eye-slit of the burqa.

"If you were lonely, you should have just asked, woman," Sawaf jeered. He gestured to the man he'd just brought in. "I figure he's more your style anyway."

He left, closing and locking the door again, but not before Christine heard him say to someone in the hall outside, "This should be interesting."

Stepping away from Tariq's body, she adjusted the burqa so she could better see the new man who was now on hands and knees, trying to stand up. And then she recognized him.

Casting off the burqa, she drew her shirt around herself as best as she could, then threw her arms around her long-lost assistant, Dan Krumholtz.

"Ow, careful," he said, wincing in pain. He had several large bruises on his arms and face, and his shirt was bloodied and torn. A black eye and two missing front teeth completed the package. With Ben and Rick dead and Dan looking like this, she had been the lucky one, despite her dire circumstances.

Never give up hope, she reminded herself.

"Oh, Dan, are you okay?"

"I've been better, but I'm not dead yet."

"I'm so sorry to have gotten us into this. We never should have come to Dubai without official clearance."

He looked at her, an odd expression on his face. She didn't know what to make of it until he spoke again, and then the pieces began to slide into place, forming another side of the horrible picture she wished she'd never seen.

"No, Christine, *I'm* sorry," Dan said. A tear formed at the rim of one eye, yet refused to break free of its ocular bounds. But his guilty expression gave away the truth even before he spoke. "This isn't how it was supposed to happen."

PART THREE

The Screaming Descent

"This is the reality of nuclear weapons: they may trigger a world war; a war which, unlike previous ones, destroys all of civilization."
–Joseph Rotblat

"To me, the thing that is worse than death is betrayal. You see, I could conceive death, but I could not conceive betrayal."
– Malcolm X

CHAPTER 39

PALM JUMEIRAH, DUBAI, UNITED ARAB EMIRATES

"Two minutes," Wayne said into his comm as Suarez turned their stolen Mercedes down a side street. "Get ready for anything."

"Copy," came Nasef's reply.

The American team had lost the cops in a traffic snarl near Business Bay, and apparently the authorities hadn't yet picked up their scent thereafter. Still, Wayne wasn't taking any chances. Regardless of whether the property they'd discovered on Shiraz Imports' asset listing yielded a tangible lead, they would need to ditch their vehicles and pick up new wheels very soon.

Palm Jumeirah was the first completed of one of Dubai's most ambitious projects—creating artificial, beachfront real estate just off the coast of downtown and selling lots to the world's richest. Comprised largely of sand dredged from the Gulf's floor, the palm-frond-shaped complex attached to the mainland via a bridge. Eight slender peninsulas branched off each side of the main road, providing every house with a backdoor beach and access to the channel for yachts and other aquatic pleasure vehicles. A ring-shaped island barrier encircled the palm, providing protection from erosion, as the lapping waves sought to reclaim, grain by grain, the sand stolen from its floor. Broken only at the entrance to the palm and once on each side to allow boats access to the Gulf beyond, the barrier island's crown jewel was the Atlantis resort complex, an architectural mirror to its progenitor in the Bahamas, complete with a water park, aquarium, and all the ridiculously luxurious amenities Dubai's top hotels had made their claim to fame.

It would be nice to relax like that, Wayne thought, after losing sight of the hotel behind the endless string of mansions and palm trees that lined this side street. Sometime, some day, maybe he'd come back and do Dubai the way it was meant to be done—wining, dining, and getting some extreme R&R. If they made it through today, that was. There were a lot of ifs still standing between Wayne and vacation.

"Just drive past," Wayne said. "See if you see anyone." Suarez, and Nasef in the car behind, did as instructed. The property, a small, walled complex with an iron gate providing a glimpse of the modest mansion beyond, betrayed no obvious signs of current habitation. The driveway was empty, the blinds were lowered over darkened windows, and no one was visible inside or out. That didn't preclude the presence of a car in the garage, or terrorists guarding Ambassador Needham behind the blinds or in another part of the house entirely, but it was something. And, considering how there *should* be men guarding the ambassador, part of Wayne was disappointed at the lack of clear security. And yet, after the bruising he and his team had taken over the past twenty-four hours, he didn't mind the reprieve that much. He only hoped that, whatever purpose this house served for Shiraz Imports and perhaps the terrorists, their lead wouldn't dry up here.

They parked the cars on the street a few houses down, each hidden from the route they had traveled by a hulking SUV. It wasn't much protection against discovery, particularly if the demo sports cars had been outfitted with GPS trackers, but Wayne would take every advantage they could get, however slight.

Wayne instructed the team to do a quick inventory of what they had escaped with. It wasn't pretty. Each man still had his sidearm and a few spare clips, but the bulk of their equipment had been left in their rentals in Emirates Towers garage. Thankfully, they hadn't left anything behind to lead probing Dubai investigators to uncover their identities or mission, but they were crippled regardless.

"If we have to engage, choose your shots carefully," Wayne said as the three men approached the property.

"Can we call in for more equipment?" Nasef asked. "The firepower these guys are packing . . . I don't want to be outmanned and outgunned in the next fight. We might've already used up our share of good luck for the day, getting out of the tower alive."

"I hope not," Suarez said with a grin. "I think we'll need a bit more luck on our side before this is all over and done."

Wayne shook his head. "Mother Hen said backup's a no-go. The whole point of our covert presence here is to fly under the radar. With the UAE's gun laws such as they are, we'd be risking the mission, the ambassador's life, and a key regional ally if we tried to get more equipment from Ibrahim. And with today being the likely day of Iran's terror attack on Israel, we don't have the luxury of time to wait for care packages from Washington."

"Fair enough," Nasef said, resigned. "But I still don't like it."

Wayne grunted. "You don't have to like it. But those are our orders. And a whole lot is riding on our ability to execute those orders, regardless of how much the odds might turn against us."

"Yes, sir," Nasef returned.

Wayne thought his fellow agent's tone sounded slightly mocking, but now was not the time to press the issue. He signaled for the team to stop at the edge of the wall. He peeked around the corner, taking the house and its rough layout into consideration. A flat, gray box was set into the stucco on their side of the gate. Keypad.

"Zorro, let's see some of your digital magic."

Suarez moved up, crossed in front of the gate, and hooked up his PDA to override terminals hidden beneath the keypad.

"Try not to set off the alarm this time, Mr. Wizard," ribbed Nasef in a stage whisper.

Suarez yanked the wires from the terminal and continued to tap away on his device as the gate's motors whirred to life and the iron barrier swung inward. "I hacked the office's entry code in less than five seconds. It had a failsafe on it that I couldn't bypass. It would only accept the code if entered by a registered thumbprint. One of three, which I was able to hack internally, but not in time to reroute it to the code entry setup."

"You got thumbprints of the people who run Shiraz Imports?" Wayne asked. "Why is this the first I'm hearing of it?"

"My system just finished rebuilding them. Raw image files, no accompanying personnel info, though I'm sure whatever was there would have been fake."

"That's a great lead, Zorro," Nasef said.

"Could be," Wayne agreed, careful not to get his hopes too high. "Send it over to Ibrahim and see what she can come up with."

"Just did," Suarez said, pocketing the PDA.

"Fingers crossed," Wayne said.

"Mine haven't been uncrossed since we got here," Nasef said.

"So *that* explains your shooting," Suarez said.

Wayne put a finger to his lips. "Silence from here on out, you guys. The ambassador might be here, after all."

"I kind of hope not," Nasef said. "Considering how empty it all looks, if she's here, she's probably already dead."

Wayne tried not to think about that as he led the team through the gate and into the small front yard. The two-story edifice was blocky and tiered, in a quasi-modernist approach to Middle Eastern luxury. Dual garages sat to the left of the front entrance, doors closed and the accompanying carport spaces empty. Narrow stretches of pebble-lined ground traced a path to the rear of the building, but a fence blocked easy passage between front yard and back. Wayne could hear the light waves lapping at the shoreline on the other side, but not much else. Out here in the middle of the Gulf, even the constant din of Dubai's construction and traffic was muted. Which, depending on how this went down, could be a boon or yet another threat.

The entry was locked and dead-bolted, but Wayne's lock-picking skills made quick work of the domestic defenses. They were in.

"Watch your corners," Wayne ordered as he swung the door open. "Zorro, at the ready on the alarm."

Suarez nodded and was the first inside, quickly followed by the rest of the team, sweeping the entry hall with their eyes and weapons in case a terrorist welcoming committee decided to offer stiffer resistance than they had encountered outside. The hallway, at least, was clear.

"The alarm's already off," Suarez said.

Wayne looked at the tech wizard. "What? You sure?"

"Positive. Says 'Unarmed' right there on the panel."

It wasn't that he doubted Suarez, but he had to be sure for the mission's sake. Looking at the panel, he saw that Zorro was right.

"That's good, right?" Nasef asked.

Wayne shushed them. He and Suarez started clearing the east wing and then the west. Nasef stood guard in the open foyer to watch the entrance and to make sure no terrorists doubled back around the Americans' sweep.

Half of the furniture was sheathed in dust covers and clear plastic, but the other half looked recently used. Fine, residual sand had gathered against walls, making Wayne think this place had been purchased as a vacation home of some sort, to be seasonally used. But the tidying job was half-baked, as though whoever had recently used it couldn't be bothered to clean up after themselves. Were they still in the building? Was the ambassador?

Once satisfied that no one was on this floor, Wayne and Suarez rallied up with Nasef. With cautious haste, they ascended to the second floor. Now that only one floor was in question, Wayne had Nasef scout a wing as well. Time was running out, and they'd need to squeeze every second they could.

Wayne and Suarez came up empty with their wing. Nasef had better luck.

"Phoenix, Zorro, get in here!" Nasef shouted as Wayne and Suarez made their way back toward the stairs. They headed toward Nasef's voice and found him in a hallway just outside an office.

"What?" Wayne asked.

Nasef was already turning back into the room. "Intel jackpot."

The office was spacious and airy, with a huge bay window that looked out on the back deck, pool, strip of private beach, and the water. A conference table with six rolling office chairs was the centerpiece of the room, with a three-drawer filing cabinet sitting to one side. Suarez jimmied the filing cabinet's lock and rifled through the files.

"The alarm was off, right? So why isn't anybody here?" Nasef asked.

"Forgetfulness?" Wayne said. "Or, more likely, it could be they just don't want an alarm alerting the cops in case the terrorists screw up the code. The Dubai authorities may be after us for our B&E back there, and probably for tearing up the airport tunnels and Hor Al Anz, but they're not exactly keen on terrorists operating in the city and screwing up its pristine image."

"You sure about that?" Suarez said.

Wayne crossed to the filing cabinet. "What are you talking about?"

Suarez showed him a computer printout with a detailed bio of the deputy chief of police. Clipped to it was a handwritten note.

Intel, protection, immunity. One million dollars.

"So they did buy off the cops?" Wayne asked.

"Or at least one of them; but this one's high enough up the food chain to redirect inquiries, set priorities, issue BOLOs. He can cause us a whole lot of pain."

"Let me see that." Wayne took the printout and squinted at the photograph accompanying the bio. The printing wasn't very high quality, but it was good enough for him to recognize the official.

"You've got to be kidding me."

"What?" Nasef asked.

"That's the guy who pulled Zorro and me over right after we landed. The freaking deputy chief of police? Who also happens to be on the terrorist's payroll? That's bigger than the wrong tail number on a plane. That would have been called down long before we were in Emirati airspace."

"What are you saying?"

"I'm saying we've got a leak. An ugly one from the sound of it."

Suarez looked as though he had a mouth full of bile. "Ibrahim."

"Why, because she's a Muslim, Suarez?" Nasef countered. "I swear, it's that sort of bias and hatred that drove me to the agency in the first place, but I can't believe I'm stuck on this op with such a racist, prejudiced—"

"Let's look at the facts, *Anubis*. Her parents are from Iran. She probably still has family and contacts there. And she's our gatekeeper for all the intel in this op. Everything we need, and everything we discover, it all goes through her. And everywhere we've gone, the terrorists—and the cops in their pocket—have been two steps ahead of us. The police stop us right after we arrived. The bomb in the airport tunnels. The trap in the Hor Al Anz house."

"Then why did she give us Shiraz Imports? That was a solid lead, that has now led to another very solid lead."

"Maybe Pierce was standing over her at the time, so she couldn't set up another ambush. Of course, remember, you said yourself that the alarm couldn't have been bypassed by us, so perhaps it was a trap after all."

"An alarm is hardly an ambush. There were no terrorists on scene, and the only one of us who actually got shot is the last Muslim you suspected of being a secret traitor. Me."

Suarez shrugged, unwilling to concede any ground. "She probably realized she had to give us at least some solid intel, otherwise we'd figure out her scheme and blow the lid on her betrayals."

"Enough!" Wayne bellowed. "We're not doing this again. Certainly not right now. Yes, something is definitely wrong here, but we've got enough enemies gunning for us right now without turning on each other. This leak is a serious issue, but it's not coming from this circle right here. Let's see what else we can find in the files. Maybe we can find out what's going on and where the leak might be coming from."

A moment of tense silence moved in. Suarez swallowed, and then spoke. "There's a lot here, but I don't know what it all means yet. Wire transfer records, blueprints, wiring schematics, maps—"

"What kind of maps?"

Suarez started pulling some out, handing them to Wayne as he did. "All sorts. World maps, regional, ones of Israel, Iran, Dubai . . ."

Wayne looked over the first one, a world map with hand-drawn circles around Washington, Moscow, Tel Aviv, Tehran, London, Paris, Berlin, and Beijing. The capitals of Iran, Israel, and the six nations behind the UN's negotiations to prevent a nuclear-armed Tehran. What was weird were the lines drawn between the cities. Tel Aviv to Tehran, Washington to Tehran, Moscow to Tel Aviv, Moscow to Washington, London to Moscow, Beijing to London and Washington, Berlin and Washington to Beijing. It looked like a map of airline routes, but Wayne knew in his gut that the payloads being sent between the world capitals in this nightmare scenario would be far more deadly.

"They're trying to start a war," Wayne muttered in disbelief. "A global nuclear war." He handed the map to Nasef behind him.

The next map Suarez handed him was of the eastern Mediterranean, with points indicated in Beirut, Haifa, Tel Aviv, and off the coast of Cyprus. One line connected Beirut and Haifa, while another connected Cyprus and Tel Aviv. The routes of operatives? A dual attack on two of Israel's most important cities?

His sat phone began ringing. Ibrahim. Wayne answered it.

"Got a hit on one of those thumbprints. Walid Abushakra, picked up for his role in a riot in London right before the Iraq invasion in 2003."

"That's all we've got on him?" Wayne asked.

"Hardly, that's why we have his ten-card on file. I'll send you a headshot in a minute. He's local, an Emirati citizen, born and raised in Dubai, got his degree in business from the University of London. We think he was radicalized in the UK, but he's never conformed to the traditional militant role from what we can tell."

"What do you mean?"

Ibrahim sighed. "You know Blackwater, right?"

"Yeah. Private security contractors brought in to help the military stabilize Iraq and Afghanistan after the invasions. Mercenaries."

"Controversial as all get out, yeah, and expensive, but effective. Well, Abushakra decided that he wanted to get in on the action. Formed his own mercenary operation."

"So we've been fighting against jihadists-for-hire all this time?"

"If Abushakra's connection is what it seems to be, then essentially, yes. Don't misunderstand; his men are dedicated, true believers for the most part. They're just good enough to take things to the next level and get paid for it. Handsomely."

Wayne bit his lip. "Expensive, but effective."

"Exactly."

"We're on site at the Palm Jumeirah property listed on Shiraz Imports' real estate holdings list. It's empty, but seems to be a treasure trove of intel. There's some wire transfer records in here, so maybe the age-old trope will pan out after all."

"What trope is that?"

"Follow the money. We'll digitize it and get it to you ASAP." Wayne nodded at Suarez, who immediately began taking pictures of the records with his PDA.

"We also found some maps." Wayne told Ibrahim about the markings, the cities, the lines traced between metropolises which, in the minds of its architects, were now targets full of millions of expendables. "I think they're planning to start World War III."

"By killing the ambassador?"

"By nuking Israel *and* killing the ambassador. Russia and Iran are tied together militarily. China has Iran's back to an extent as well."

"And Germany, France, and the UK would rally behind a US-led attack on Iran if they nuke Israel while lying to our faces about the purpose of their nuclear program."

"Exactly. Assuming Iran now has the bomb, all eight nations are nuclear-armed. The worst Cold War scenarios just got a whole lot more terrifying."

"One question, though. Tehran's listed as a target. Why would they plan for their own capital to get nuked?"

Wayne thought a moment. That was a very good question. "Perhaps they see Tehran as collateral damage. There's enough internal strife in the Iranian government that the moderates could blame the attacks on the hardliners, or vice versa. We all know the ayatollah and the president don't see eye to eye over there."

"Maybe. Maybe not. I'll see what I can turn up with the rest of the intel. I'll get back to you as soon as I have something."

"Sounds good. Over and out."

Wayne turned to the team, who were looking at him expectantly.

"It looks like we're dealing with jihadist mercenaries."

"What?" Suarez asked. "Doesn't that kind of mess up the whole 'fighting for the purity of Islam' thing?"

"Not in their minds. They're good at what they do, and they get paid well for it. These wire transfers might hold some clue as to who hired them, and for exactly what purpose."

Suarez held up the sheets detailing the wire transfers. "A total of more than a hundred million dollars sent to multiple recipients over the past few months. Account numbers are just that—numbers."

"But Ibrahim is running them down to put some names behind the numbers," Wayne assured them. "In other news, we've got a probable ID on the cell's leader. Walid Abushakra, radicalized in London, but a local boy from right here in Dubai."

"So he knows the city," Nasef said. "Probably has connections."

"Even if he had to pay a million bucks for them," Suarez added.

Wayne looked back at the world map Suarez had discovered. Tehran shouldn't have been on there, not with lines of fire pointed at it. Accepting counterattacks on Iran as potential collateral damage was one thing, but actually making it a base-level part of their plan was a wholly different animal.

"Crazy idea, but hear me out real quick."

Wayne's men looked at him expectantly. *Down the rabbit hole we go.*

"What if Tehran's not behind this at all? What if someone's trying to frame Iran, knocking out Israel and Iran in one fell swoop?"

"A false flag operation?" Suarez asked.

"Exactly, just on a very big scale. A secret nuclear facility just happens to be discovered in Iran, just hours before the planned attack on Israel. Terrorists kidnap the most powerful voice for peace in the region and shoot up one of the safest, most outwardly western cities in the Middle East. The shell corporation tied to all of this is ostensibly owned by an Iranian citizen, of whom there's no public record, and is named 'Shiraz Imports.' They may as well have put up a big neon sign over Iran saying *attack here.*"

"Whoa," Suarez said. "You might be right. But who would do that?"

"Saudi Arabia," Nasef said with conviction.

Suarez raised his eyebrows. "Go on."

"You know the difference between Sunni and Shia Islam, right?"

"Sort of."

"Oh, Allah help me. This is why you're so prejudiced against Muslims and Middle Easterners. All right, so after the Prophet Muhammad, peace be upon him, died, there was a big crisis over who would be his successor. The Prophet fulfilled a dual role for Islam. He was the final and greatest prophet of Islam and gave us the Holy Qu'ran, but he was also the leader of the religion for its first several decades. He was instrumental in spreading Islam across the land and, by the time of his death, he wielded a tremendous amount of power, both religious and secular. But for all his conquests and foresight, he did not leave a clear successor who would lead the movement once he died.

"With that much power up for grabs, it was only natural that a succession crisis would erupt. The two major camps that came from the controversy were the Sunni—who believed that the caliphs, starting with Abu Bakr, were the rightful heirs of the Prophet's religious and political empire—and the Shia—who believed that Islam's future should be wielded by Ali, the prophet's cousin and son-in-law. Obviously, plenty of doctrinal differences grew from this schism over the years, and nowadays most of the terror attacks in the Middle East aren't on Jews or Westerners, but, rather, Sunni on Shiite or vice versa.

"Like post-Reformation Europe," Wayne said, "with Protestants and Catholics waging countless wars over whether the Pope held God's final say on earth or not."

"Exactly. Muslims all worship the same god, but those small differences in doctrine and power can make all the difference in the world, especially to jihadists."

"And both the Twelver stylings of Shia Iran and the Wahhabist extremism of Sunni Saudi Arabia seek to establish a caliphate in preparation for the imminent end of the world."

"But they disagree on exactly what kind of caliphate," Suarez said. "Sunni or Shia?"

"Exactly. Extremists in either camp are no friend to Israel or the West, but ever since the US withdrawal from Iraq, the civil war in Syria, and the surge of ISIS, the power dynamic in the Middle East has shifted."

The pieces started to come together for Wayne as he picked up the conspiracy ball and ran with it. "Saudi Arabia has long been an ally of the United States, and it has leveraged this alliance, its oil reserves, and its status as the home of Islam's two holiest cities to become a major regional player over the past century. Until recently, it was the closest the Middle East had to a superpower. But then Iran started pursuing nuclear weaponry. And al-Qaeda and ISIS started making bad press for Sunni Islam and for the Saudi state. Meanwhile, the Saudi-allied government in Yemen is toppled by extremists, Iraq is a power vacuum filled with the most terrifying rogue force in a century, and Iran is making inroads with Saudi Arabia's closest superpower ally."

"Iran is an enemy of Israel and the United States, except when we need them to help quell the Sunni-led threat of ISIS," Suarez said. "So we buddy up to them, quid pro quo, removing sanctions while Iran continues to build its nuclear program. And Saudi Arabia starts feeling the heat."

"Saudi Arabia is losing influence in the region and in the West," Nasef said. "The rise of alternate fuel sources and an oil glut are crashing their bread and butter. And their greatest regional rival is not only expanding its influence into Iraq, the Levant, and Washington, but they've also got a fully functional nuclear program that neither crippling UN sanctions nor threats of military aggression can do anything to stop."

And there it was, Wayne realized. The perfect false-flag operation.

"So Saudi Arabia builds their own nuke, leaves a trail of bread crumbs to implicate Iran, and wipes Israel off the face of the earth," he said. "The Israel-Palestine question is no longer an issue, since no one wants to live on the irradiated land anymore. The international community destroys Iran, and Saudi Arabia goes back to being the most powerful player in the region for the foreseeable future."

"Plus, oil futures skyrocket because of instability in the region and Iran's nullified output after the rest of the world bombs them back to the Stone Age," Nasef said. "Saudi Arabia's back in the black, big time."

"But wouldn't Saudi Arabia get caught in the crossfire? If Israel, Iran, Russia, China, the UK, and America are all lobbing nukes at each other, what would protect the Holy Peninsula from being polluted by fallout, or even direct attacks?"

"Perhaps they're planning on being everybody's go-to supplier of oil," Suarez suggested. "Playing both sides against the middle, and raking it in while the world's superpowers use Saudi fuel to power their war machines. They're not going to bite the hand that feeds, even if the Saudis are also supplying their enemies."

"Even more than that, the Wahhabi school of Sunnism that the Saudis ascribe to has its own strain of apocalyptic goals," Nasef offered. "Perhaps they simply don't care. To some, protecting the Holy Peninsula from Shiite influence would supersede all other considerations, even if it meant the deaths of millions of their own people. To that sort of person, nothing else matters. Nothing."

"But that all sounds like a conspiracy theory without any concrete proof," Suarez said. "Nobody's going to believe this convoluted false-flag plot when all the evidence points in the opposite direction."

"Especially when the evidence on hand confirms what millions have suspected all along about Iran and its nuclear intentions," Wayne said.

"Playing devil's advocate here, but what about Weiland?" Nasef asked. "He seemed pretty sure Iran had the bomb and was planning to attack Israel."

"He was dying," Wayne said. "He gasped out some words that we strung together to fit our own preconceived context. Just like the rest of the world is going to do if a nuke goes off in Israel this evening."

"So our interpretation of Weiland's dying words just added to the heap of potentially false evidence that could lead to World War III."

"Exactly. Which means we're all the more responsible for getting to the bottom of this and making sure that the truth comes out. Whatever it is."

Suarez nodded. "One thing that seemed clear from Weiland. Ambassador Needham has crucial evidence about who's really behind this. We find her, we find out who's really behind all this."

"Assuming it's not already too late," Nasef said sullenly.

Wayne's PDA buzzed. The image that filled the screen was one he recognized, and immediately he was filled with anger and regret.

"Walid," he said under his breath. After a moment, he showed the photo to the rest of the team.

Nasef's eyes narrowed, and then widened. "The guy from underneath the airport? The one who escaped through that door?"

"It would seem so. He's not content to play Osama bin Laden and hide out in caves while sending his men to martyr themselves. Walid gets his hands dirty with the rest of them. Less bin Laden and more Saladin."

"Saladin?" Suarez asked.

"Egyptian sultan in the late twelfth century," Nasef said. "Personally led the Muslim armies that defeated the Crusaders in the Battle of Hattin, the turning point in beginning to wrest Jerusalem and Palestine from Western control. Revered as a warrior and leader in the Muslim world, yet respected by many in the West, even in those days."

"Gold star to you, sir," Wayne said. "But I don't think Walid will be winning anyone in the West's respect any time soon."

Over Nasef's shoulder, through the bay window overlooking the water, Wayne saw a yacht cruising in from the gulf. As the boat turned their way, Wayne noticed five men on the foredeck, one hefting something long and thick onto his shoulder.

"RPG!" he yelled. His men turned toward the window and registered what was going on. The tube was now pointed in their direction. Smoke billowed from the rear of the weapon. Then the rocket-propelled grenade flew from the shoulder-mounted weapon outside, blasted through the window, and fulfilled the singular purpose for which it was created.

The doorway back into the hall was only a few feet away, but that offered little solace to Wayne and his men when the room erupted in a percussive fireball. Wayne shielded himself from shrapnel and shattering glass as he dropped to the floor. Papers and maps that had been set on the table were now curling black in the flames. Suarez leapt up to retrieve what he could, and then jerked away.

"Another incoming!" Wayne yelled, and bolted for the door, the other two men right behind him. Suarez was the last into the hall, just as the blast hit the wall where the filing cabinet stood.

This was a cleanup mission, Wayne realized. His team had thrown a monkey wrench into Walid's plans, and so they were erasing their tracks. The Americans' getting here first necessitated a more bombastic approach than throwing the paper trail into a fire barrel, so the terrorists whipped out the big guns. And doing it from the safety of the yacht, though more likely to draw attention, precluded the chance that the terrorists would lose more of their men to the American agents, as they had in the airport tunnels and at the first safe house.

Or so they thought.

"Back door," Wayne yelled over the roar of fire and cracking mortar. "We're taking these guys down now."

He led the way down the stairs, dodging glass from falling pictures knocked from their hangers by the percussive blows of the assault. Another blast shook the building as they reached the bottom.

"Look out!" Nasef said as he grabbed Wayne and dragged him across the atrium. A split second later, the elaborate chandelier—loosed from its ceiling fixture by the blasts—crashed to the floor and shattered in a crystalline explosion of glass and silver.

"Thanks," Wayne huffed as he regained his balance and crunched his way through the devastation, his men right behind. As he burst through the rear doors and into daylight, he saw the man with the RPG had lowered his weapon and was walking back toward the main cabin. Engines revved. The yacht was making a wide turn back toward the Palm's barrier ring, and the Gulf beyond.

"Come *on*!" Suarez fumed. "They are *not* getting away again."

Wayne ran to the water's edge. The yacht had completed its turn and was cruising back toward safety. Its occupants were seemingly content with the thought that the Americans couldn't have survived the blasts, and if, by some chance, they had, the Dubai authorities would have enough questions to tie the agents up until after Walid's plan had been accomplished. But they were wrong.

Wayne spied the answer in the yard next to theirs, accessible via the beach itself. He grabbed one of three Jet Skis that had been parked a few feet above the high-tide line and dragged it down to the water. Seeing the key in the ignition, and the fuel level just under half a tank, Wayne mounted the vehicle and cranked it up. He cast a glance behind him and saw that his men were mounting their own Jet Skis.

"No, Zorro," he said, though no one could hear him over the revving engines. "They're not getting away this time."

CHAPTER 40

THE GULF, DUBAI, UNITED ARAB EMIRATES

The yacht cut a wide trough in the water as Wayne and his teammates sped after it. Salt spray stung Wayne's eyes. He blinked it away, trying to clear his vision. The goal was to reach the boat unseen and board her. Perhaps the ambassador was on board, though shooting RPGs from the bow of the ship holding the most-sought-after woman in the country seemed overly conspicuous. And if Ibrahim's intel on Walid Abushakra was correct, the terrorist leader would have taken his chances on shore against the Americans rather than risk the entire operation for a little payback. But this boat was now an active lead and, ambassador or not, Wayne meant to board her.

The speeding quartet threaded the passage out of the barrier island and into the Gulf proper. The terrorists turned right, heading up the island's coast toward the Atlantis resort at the tip of the Palm. Or, Wayne thought with a chill, toward the nation that lay less than a hundred miles to the north: Iran. The yacht certainly had the range to make the trip to the Islamic Republic, but the Jet Skis would run out of gas long before they neared land. Which made boarding the boat—and soon—the Americans' only option.

Wayne goosed the throttle, closing the distance between him and the yacht to two hundred feet, then one hundred fifty. The pleasure vessel was easily fifty feet long, and he'd seen five men on the deck before the hail of shoulder-fired artillery had made the intel-gathering exercise secondary to his immediate survival. There could easily be two or three times that many on board. The terrorists had the high ground and, if the RPG was any indication, were very well armed. Hence the need for stealth.

Suarez came alongside him, with Nasef following a few yards behind. They knew the drill.

As they gained on the yacht, the wake trough became deeper, with more and more water kicked up by the boat's massive twin propellers spinning just beneath the water line. Thus far, the thrum of the larger boat's engines had masked the sound of their own crafts, but as they drew closer, the threat of being heard also grew.

Fifty feet. The churning whitewater immediately behind the vessel made boarding from the stern impossible. Wayne thought he had noticed something on the side of the boat, though, a set of rungs bolted to the yacht's starboard hull. Perhaps they were set there by someone who was tired of lowering and raising the ladder every time they wanted to go for a swim, or who had felt the hopeless fear of being lost at sea after tumbling overboard. The terrorists hadn't taken the time to remove the makeshift ladder from the boat. Their oversight would be Wayne's advantage.

Now less than twenty feet away, Wayne eased the Jet Ski to the right, preparing to come alongside the yacht and board her. But just as his craft moved past the stern, the larger boat turned right as well. Wayne eased off the throttle, letting his Jet Ski slip back out of the path of the yacht's hull. Had he been spotted? Why the sudden turn? He braced for the inevitable hail of gunfire.

Glancing to his right, he saw the massive pastel façade of Atlantis looming nearby as the barrier island curved away. The yacht was turning. The terrorists were heading up Dubai's coast, not to Iran. Wayne smiled. He hadn't been spotted. And with sunset just a few hours away, he was grateful not to have to go to Iran itself to recover the ambassador and whatever intel she held about the impending attack on Israel.

They were still in the hunt.

On the second try, Wayne pulled alongside the yacht and grabbed hold of a rung. Checking behind him quickly, he leapt off the Jet Ski and began to climb. His craft stopped immediately, floating abandoned and adrift in the Gulf. His men, seeing what he was about to do, had maneuvered out of the Jet Ski's path then come quickly back into formation.

Hand over hand, one slippery rung after another, Wayne ascended the hull. His hands clenching the top rung, he slowly raised himself until his eyes were just over the gunwale. No one. Here on the transom at least, the lowest part of the deck, astern of the rest of the boat, he was alone. He climbed aboard, staying low, while signaling his men to follow.

A few moments later, Suarez's face appeared over the gunwale. Wayne peeked above the transom just in time to see a terrorist at the other end of the boat lean overboard and shout a warning in Arabic. More voices joined the first, and a spray of automatic gunfire filled the air.

So much for stealth.

Wayne shot the first man from cover, the late sentinel who had shouted the warning. Still clutching the Kalashnikov he had been firing over the side, the terrorist tumbled off the boat and into the sea. Wayne ducked back down and crossed to the other side of the transom, Suarez following closely on his heels.

One down.

A black plume of smoke drifted past, drawing Wayne's eye. It was Nasef's Jet Ski, a hail of iron rain having penetrated its engine and killing it, dead in the water. Nasef slammed his fists against the crossbar in frustration, but there was nothing Wayne could do for him. Anubis was out of the hunt for moment. It was up to Phoenix and Zorro now.

Wayne exchanged a wordless look with Suarez. Using the wheelhouse as cover, they stood as one, firing at a pair of machine-gun-wielding terrorists. The one on the left—Wayne's side—was crouched behind a low ledge, in the midst of changing magazines. A pair of rounds from Phoenix's pistol pierced the back of his skull, toppling the terrorist forward, crimson staining the polished wooden deck.

The terrorist on Suarez's side fired off a pair of three-shot bursts as soon as the Americans rose from cover. The bullets flew wild, ricocheting off metal and blasting through fiberglass. None of them hit Zorro, but he grunted as a shard of hardened fiberglass sliced across his cheek.

The terrorist ducked below cover and shouted something in Arabic. Between the roar of the boat's engine and Wayne's rustiness with the man's dialect, he only caught one word for certain: *y'allah. Hurry*. To where? And why?

Wayne moved out from cover, trying to get a better angle on the shooter while keeping an eye out for his cohorts. The entrance to the cabins was behind the terrorist's position, but the wheelhouse was almost directly above the Americans. At least one man would be at the controls, possibly more. Wresting control of the boat would give them some power over the terrorists aboard, as would the high ground the wheelhouse represented.

He pointed upward, toward the stairs that sloped to the wheelhouse. Suarez nodded and moved to where he could cover Wayne's approach.

Crouching, his gun pointed toward the wheelhouse door, Wayne crept to the base of the stairs and began to ascend. Halfway up, a three-bullet burst of gunfire erupted beneath him. He froze and looked toward the stern, to see another terrorist fall to the deck, his *dishdasha* turning from white to crimson. *Suarez*, Wayne thought as he climbed the final few stairs.

One man was visible through the window next to the door, and his attention was fixed on his newly fallen comrade at the front of the boat. Gun drawn, Wayne whipped open the door and shot the man through the neck. The helmsman fell forward onto the controls, his body knocking the throttle to full.

Wayne stumbled, trying to regain his balance as the boat lurched forward. Another terrorist leapt into view from the rear of the room, his weapon aimed at the American's head. Wayne dove across the room while firing, two of his bullets finding the man's skull. The terrorist managed to get off three shots before Wayne's bullet exploded through his brain, but none hit their mark.

They hit the console instead. Sparks flew from the punctured surface, exposing severed wires and leaking hydraulics.

Keeping a wary eye out for any other surprises, Wayne stood. From this vantage, he could see the rest of the wheelhouse, including the hidden nook where the second man had been. He was alone now.

He shoved the helmsman's body from the console and pulled back the throttle. It moved, but the boat's engines remained at full thrust. Not good.

The ship's wheel was equally unresponsive. He spun it to the left as hard as he could, but the boat retained its heading.

Directly toward the Dubai Creek Marina.

Movement at the front of the boat as two more terrorists briefly stuck their heads out of the cabin, and then retreated.

Not wanting to cede the high ground just yet, Wayne touched his earbud to activate comms.

"Zorro, good news, bad news time."

"Good news first."

"The terrorists are no longer in control of the boat."

"Excellent. What's the bad news?"

Wayne stared at the sloops, boats, and very solid shore now looming less than one hundred meters ahead.

"Neither am I."

CHAPTER 41

DUBAI, UNITED ARAB EMIRATES

"I'm so sorry, Christine."

She didn't know if she believed him. Christine Needham wasn't sure of anything anymore. Sure, the world was crashing down around her, but this betrayal was too much.

"What did you do, Dan? You sold me out to these terrorists?"

Dan Krumholtz, once her most trusted advisor, frowned. "I didn't sell anyone out. I tried to get you to see reason. These people don't want peace. Arabs, Palestinians, Iranians, Syrians, and the whole motley crew have been slaughtering each other since before Moses was a gleam in his father's eye. It's always been that way, and it always will be. Forcing Israel to cede more land and power to people who want to see Jews erased from history is just inviting another Holocaust."

"So you thought a first-hand experience with terror might change my mind?" Christine asked, her voice dripping with scorn and indignation.

"This was never my idea. Honest. I was approached a few months back. It just happened to work out for Passover."

"Just happened to work out? How is any of this 'working out' for us, Dan? And do you still think the timing is just coincidence? You've seen and heard what's on the chip. This was all part of the plan from the beginning. And you bought right into it."

"I didn't know, okay? Our foreign policy has been so pro-Arab, pro-Islam, pro-Iran, pro-Palestine, that we forget everything America has ever stood for. We're supposedly Israel's staunchest ally, yet we ostracize their leaders and advocate for terrorist organizations like Hamas and the PLO. Iran has threatened to wipe Israel off the map, and we remove the sanctions keeping them from developing the very nuclear bombs that will help them do just that. We neglect our few true regional allies in deference to 'the people' rising up and installing new, more radical terrorists to power. Have we so quickly forgotten the lessons of 9/11? We send billions of dollars we don't have to regimes that hate us, and then we chastise our allies for defending themselves when terrorists attack them with American-bought weaponry."

"Don't presume to lecture me," Christine said, furious. She had heard this argument before, but she never imagined her longtime associate and friend would go to such traitorous lengths to make his point. "I'm well acquainted with our recent foreign policy missteps, but you forget who you are talking to. I'm not going to sell out the Jewish people or Israel's sovereignty. Any peace deal we establish would be ironclad and mutually beneficial. Israel's ability to defend herself from aggression will never be ceded by any peace agreement I ever put my hand to. And I'm shocked that you believe otherwise."

"Despite all this, you still want to press ahead with a peace conference?"

Christine slapped him. "This is *your* doing, Dan. *You* are the reason I'm in a cell in the middle of the desert, instead of being out there actively working for peace. And you're the reason the intel on that chip isn't in the president's hands, being used to stop today's attacks. You wanted to save Israel, but if we don't get out of here really soon, you'll be the reason millions of Israelis die today."

"I had no way of knowing. No one was supposed to die. They promised."

"You trusted the word of a terrorist, Dan. You gift-wrapped them the highest-profile kidnapping since the War on Terror began. They'd say anything to get me."

"I tried to call it off as soon as I heard the recordings and saw the documents on the chip. I swear. The number I had used before was disconnected, but I tried."

"Once they knew where I was and what was going on, they had no further need for your intel. And you were too much of a coward to fess up so we could turn the plane around and avoid this whole debacle."

"I tried! I told you I was feeling sick and that we needed to land somewhere else, but you didn't listen."

"Because your reason was bull!" Christine fought to keep her voice down and her emotions in check, but it was all too much. "We were already on approach to Dubai, and we were already risking a lot just by coming here. To abandon it because your tummy hurt would never work. Now, if you'd been honest about why we needed to stay away from Dubai, then yeah, we would have rerouted. But you didn't have the balls to admit what you'd done. And now Rick, Ben, and who knows how many others are dead because of your cowardice and treason. And millions more are at death's door."

Dan looked as if he was about to cry. Her words had hurt. She'd meant for them to. But they were also the truth.

He stood abruptly and crossed the room.

"Hey!" he yelled, banging on the steel door. "Take me instead! Let her go and take me instead!"

"Dan, what are you doing?"

He turned and lowered his voice. "Getting you out of here. I'll distract the guards. You escape. I can't change what I've done, but I can try to put some of it to rights."

"They'll kill you. Probably me too."

Footsteps approached the other side of the door.

"I deserve to die. And I'd rather do it helping you than at the whim of these pigs."

The door swung open with such force that it knocked Dan off his feet. A big man, one Christine had learned was the second in command, Omar Sawaf, stepped into the room.

"Who are you calling pig, Jew-rat?" he boomed.

"Your mother, you goat-loving son of a whore," Dan said. He scrambled to his feet and began to back toward one corner of the room. He was trying to bait Sawaf into leaving the door unattended so that Christine could escape. It wasn't working.

Omar's expression became very flat, overly controlled, masking the rage that Dan's comments had surely enflamed. "You're right, you know. You do deserve to die. I can help you with that."

He lunged at Dan and grabbed a fistful of his shirt. Christine didn't want to abandon her former advisor, but with the lives of millions in the balance, there really wasn't much choice. She made a dash for the door, trying to use what might be the last opportunity for escape.

Pain shot through her scalp as Sawaf yanked her backwards by her hair. He kicked the door closed, and Christine watched her last hope of escape slam shut.

"Allah does not abide blasphemers or infidels," Sawaf said, turning Christine's head to face him. "As I am his solider, neither do I."

He palmed the back of Dan's head and smashed his face into the cinder-block wall. Blood sprayed from her friend's broken nose and forehead. A broken tooth fell to the floor.

"Stop!" Christine cried. Sawaf ignored her.

"You are a traitor, even to your own kind," he said to Dan. "After today, the Jew plague will be erased from Palestine. This very evening, the true Islam of Wahhabi shall wipe the earth clean with the blood of the infidel. The ambassador's death will serve as the critical element to tip the world over the edge. Your treachery helped make that happen. Proof that Allah can use even a Jew for his purposes."

Sawaf smashed Dan's face into the wall again, and again, and again. Each time, more blood painted the whitewashed surface, and more teeth were spit onto the ground. Christine's cries had devolved into a helpless whimper, but Sawaf would not let up.

After eight impacts with the wall, Dan's face was swollen, broken, bloodied, and unrecognizable. After ten hits, his body had lost all tension. After twelve, his legs gave out entirely.

Sawaf slammed Dan's face into the wall twice more, and then dropped his lifeless body to the floor. Christine crawled over to him, trying to hold her composure together and failing miserably.

"Don't shed too many tears, Ambassador. You'll be joining him in a few hours. But first, you'll get to witness the deaths of millions of the Zionists you wasted your life trying to save."

He kicked her in the stomach, sending a fresh wave of pain through her core. She curled up on the floor, gasping for breath.

Sawaf walked to the door, paused, and looked back at her with a wicked sneer.

"I am serious. Too much crying and you'll mess up your pretty face. Your execution will be televised, after all."

He chuckled, a sound that made Christine's skin crawl.

"You always wanted to make a difference, Ambassador. Now, finally, you will. Your death will help launch World War III."

CHAPTER 42

Riyadh, Saudi Arabia

The priceless porcelain vase shattered against the wall, the noise startling the man who had thrown it almost as much as the man whose head it had nearly missed. Prince Basim al-Attar felt the blood rushing to his face, but he didn't care. He never had tolerated insolence, and he wasn't about to start now. *Especially* not now.

"You think this is good news, you fool?" the prince bellowed.

Rafa Alowais, his chief of staff, cowered before his boss, putting his hands up in surrender and supplication. "Of course not, Your Highness. But it could mean higher oil prices in the short and long term."

Now that *was* good news. News that, Alowais should have known, had occurred to the prince long before his assistant had waltzed into his office purporting to be the bearer of an unforeseen upside to current events. But his report that the ambassador's kidnapping was making international headlines was not the kind of news he wanted taking up newsprint. There wasn't a true leader in the Arab world who had shed a tear at the woman's abduction. She was a manipulative, deceitful little half-Jew who was trying to play powerbroker on behalf of the American empire. He found it hard to believe that any leaders in the region—with the possible exception of some of the war-weary Palestinian leaders—would see a two-state solution as an end goal. The Zionists had to be removed from Palestine in their entirety. Any compromise would only open the door to more compromise, eventually eroding away everything al-Attar's ancestors had stood for. Fought for. Died for.

And yet, the ambassador was merely a player in a much larger game. One in which Basim controlled all the pieces.

"Perhaps you're right," al-Attar said, softening his tone. "What has been the Americans' response?"

"They've demanded her safe return by the UAE government. Both Abu Dhabi and Dubai have rebuffed Washington's request to help out with the investigation. But, of course, that doesn't mean that Talquin will do as he's told."

"No, indeed," the prince said. "Though considering his concerns about Iran acquiring a bomb, he had best take care not to alienate any more of his allies."

The Arab world had been in violent tumult for years. The revolutions of the so-called "Arab Spring" and the continuing civil wars in Egypt, Syria, and Yemen were the most easily noticed. Washington's wars in Iraq and Afghanistan had created new strongholds for terrorists and millions of displaced refugees. But most irksome of all was Israel, whose constant conflicts with its neighbors and its abusive treatment of Palestinian refugees—all backed by American dollars and bullets, of course—were the single greatest element that had long seeded strife within the region.

The Americans' thirst for oil had helped make his family incredibly rich. If all his assets were disclosed, al-Attar himself would be in the top twenty of the world's richest billionaires. But that wealth had come at a great price to his homeland. The Saudi king was the Custodian of the Two Holy Mosques, a priceless honor and responsibility to Allah and his prophet. But the land of Mecca and Medina, of the holy prophet Muhammad where he revealed the true path of Islam to the world, had become tainted. American troops had made the Saudi frontier their base camp when preparing for Desert Storm. Arabs in Dubai and other me-too oil metropolises on this sacred peninsula had opened their arms to Western money and ideals. And, most tragic of all, the Saudi government—protector of the land of Islam—was considering a peace treaty with the impostor state of Israel.

It was no coincidence that al-Qaeda had launched the most devastating and iconic terror attack in history on September 11. That date not only drew on the American connection of 911 with emergencies, but also came on the anniversary of the end of the growth of the last caliphate, when, in 1683, the Holy Roman Empire turned back the advance of Islam's armies, beginning three centuries of continued Western dominance of the world. It also evoked memories of the more recent 1978 Camp David negotiations between Israel and Egypt, the result of which was the first treaty between Israel and an Arab nation. Jordan followed with their own US-brokered peace treaty with the Zionist state in 1994; but, thankfully, no other nation had capitulated. Until now.

Ambassador Needham threatened to bring down everything his family had worked for. The Saudi royals had brought order to a land of desert lawlessness, riches to a land of desiccation, peace to the land of Muhammad. The royal family—like many across the peninsula in countries like the United Arab Emirates and Oman—had, *al-hamdulillah*, been spared the Islamist upheaval that swept the Middle East in 2011 and destroyed regimes in places like Libya, Egypt, and Syria. Egypt was more a mess than ever, but Allah's favor had left them once they signed their deal with the enemy. Jordan's day of reckoning would surely come as well, though thus far the Hashemite kingdom was still intact.

But Needham's peace-summit proposal—and the response it was getting from rulers throughout the region—was an explosive game of dominoes. Any regime that made peace with Israel—even with the notable compromise of moving back to their pre-1967-war borders and granting the Palestinians a physical homeland—would be immediately invalidated by both Islamists within their borders and by Allah himself. Even in pre-Arab Spring, peace-mongering Egypt, whose citizens had to share a border with the Zionists, more than ninety percent of the populace viewed Israel as an enemy state. And then, when the tide began to shift and populist and Islamist movements—well-organized by social media and other technological communications—finally said *no more*, Egypt collapsed like the hollow house of cards it had become. Some feared that Saudi Arabia's own collapse might not be far behind.

The Middle East's instability had allowed enemy powers like Iran and Russia to make inroads in the region, fueling insurrections and propping up puppet governments to promote the Shiite-friendly policies in what were once Saudi strongholds. From the Syrian civil war to the revolution in Yemen, from Hezbollah and Hamas's increasing boldness to the unmitigated victory scored in the much-maligned nuclear deal, Iran was becoming an increasingly dangerous foe. Many pundits were broadcasting that Saudi Arabia's hegemony in the region was coming to a close and that the Persians would soon supplant them as the chief power in the region. A century of dominance by the House of Saud as keepers of the Holy Peninsula, all gone because of Iranian aggression, Zionist infiltration, and Western cowardice.

It was unthinkable. Al-Attar would not let that happen.

So the ambassador's kidnapping was certainly a step in the right direction.

But it was only the tip of the iceberg compared to what was to come.

CHAPTER 43

DUBAI, UNITED ARAB EMIRATES

"We've got to jump!" Suarez yelled.

Wayne was already leaping over the railing of the wheelhouse stairway. He landed hard, rolling into a ball to absorb some of the momentum, but a lancing pain shot from his ankle up to his knee. But with the yacht seconds from impact, he had bigger issues to contend with.

At the marina ahead, tourists were running away from the boat's looming hull. The yacht crashed through a small dhow ferrying Indian workers across the creek, sending the men flying into the water. The wharf was a scene of panic as the massive yacht careened ever closer to shore, until finally . . .

Wayne and Suarez jumped over the side of the boat and into the water just as the bow smashed into the concrete dock. The reinforced fiberglass hull caved with the impact, pushing the yacht's full-throttle trajectory to the left.

Directly toward of a massive refueling tank.

Wayne ducked beneath the water a second before the yacht erupted into a fiery geyser of diesel and splintered wood. When he surfaced, the boat was awash in flame. No one aboard could have survived.

He and Suarez swam to a nearby dock. As inconspicuously as possible, they climbed a ladder to join the throngs gawking at the flaming wreckage. His wet clothes clung to his body, likely revealing the outline of his sidearm to anyone with a trained eye. He tugged at his shirt in front and in back to separate cloth from skin, disguising his purpose once again.

Their sidearms and PDAs were waterproof up to 100 feet, so they should still work. The question now was whether the mission itself had just gone up in smoke with the rest of the yacht.

Nasef was still stuck halfway down the coast with his disabled Jet Ski. Their cover had just been blown sky high with a massive explosion in the heart of Dubai. And their only active lead was burning to ash while a forest of iPhones recorded every detail for viral consumption.

In less than two hours, a nuclear bomb would kill millions of Israelis, the first domino in an apocalyptic endgame poised to set the world on fire with an all-consuming World War III. Without the proof the ambassador held, the United States and her allies would be manipulated into a globe-spanning conflict from which there would be no escape. By the war's end, the death toll could number in the billions, and those who survived would wake up to a completely unrecognizable world.

And now, there was nothing Wayne could do to prevent it in time. Even though Walid and his men surely died in the blast, they had ultimately won.

Suarez tapped Wayne's arm. "Phoenix, is that . . ."

He didn't need to finish. Wayne saw who he was pointing at.

Walid. Bruised from his own leap from the boat, apparently off the opposite railing, but alive nonetheless.

Wayne had never been so happy to see that a mass-murdering terrorist hadn't bit the big one. They were still in this. They still had a chance.

The jihadist leader was only thirty feet away, but dozens of shocked onlookers separated him from the American agents. With tourists' smartphones turning the area into a cover-blowing nightmare for Walid and the agents alike, Wayne anticipated their common need to get away and started to move inland, away from the horde.

The crowd started to thin out as the wharf gave way to an open-air marketplace. Merchants hawked fresh fish, designer clothes knockoffs, and cheaply made jewelry from their stalls. Walid ducked down one row of shops, followed closely by the two men Wayne had seen poke their heads out from belowdecks on the yacht shortly before the crash.

So it was three versus two.

Wayne and Suarez followed Walid and his men down the row. All five men walked in a hurry, but not so fast as to draw suspicion. Just fast enough to make a getaway so no one would know they were ever there. Unfortunately for Walid and company, they'd already been spotted.

The CIA agents slowly closed the gap between themselves and the terrorists, trying to get in range for a takedown in which they could capture and interrogate Walid about the ambassador's whereabouts. He would be hard to break, but if he was in the jihadist game for the money, he wasn't such a die-hard true believer as some men Wayne had forced to give up their secrets. He just hoped Walid would spill his secrets before the nuke exploded.

The jihadists disappeared around the side of a building at the edge of the marketplace. Their pursuers used the opportunity to close the distance, escalating their pace to a jog. Wayne was three feet from the corner of the building when he saw something that made him hit the brakes.

A shadow, cast long and low by the late afternoon sun, outlined a human form waiting just around the blind corner. An ambush.

Wayne darted to the corner and dropped to a crouch an instant before the terrorist came into view. The Arab's expression went from shock to anguish as Wayne punched him in the balls. No reason to waste their few remaining bullets on this clown, he reasoned, collecting the terrorist's SIG Sauer P220 as it clattered to the pavement. His prize lay ahead.

Walid had broken into a run with the other terrorist. The gap was now forty feet and widening. The jihadist leader turned back to see if Wayne and Suarez were dead, but instead was greeted with the sight of his pursuers dogging his steps anew.

He dashed into the street, where three motorcyclists waited at a stop light. Walid yelled something at one of them and punched the rider off his bike, commandeering it for himself. His remaining terrorist colleague stole a second motorcycle, and the pair drove up onto the shoulder to escape the traffic snarl.

As Wayne entered the street a few seconds later, the third motorcyclist had dismounted and was checking his fallen friends. The CIA agent donned a spare helmet and climbed aboard the last remaining motorcycle.

"*Aasif*," Wayne said by way of apology. The man didn't look particularly Arabic, but there was no reason to broadcast that his bike was being stolen by an American. As he crested the sidewalk, following the same illegal egress as Walid, Wayne glanced back at Suarez.

Go, Suarez mouthed, nodding in agreement that splitting up here was the only way to catch Walid before the bomb went off.

Feeling better that he had his one remaining team member's support, he squeezed the throttle. It had been years since he'd ridden a motorcycle, but the feeling came back within moments. Just like riding a bicycle. A two-hundred-horsepower, quarter-ton bicycle.

Walid and his companion had widened the gap to four hundred feet, racing southwest toward the skyscrapers, tourist traps, and glittering luxury of new Dubai. Wayne followed, trying to narrow the gap, but failing to gain much ground. All three vehicles were at close to maximum speed, weaving around cars and dodging traffic barriers.

Suddenly, they were free of the crush of traffic and cruising down the eight-lane highway that was Sheikh Zayed Road. A glass pyramid loomed on the right, marking the posh, Egyptian-themed Wafi City mall complex and its accompanying Raffles Dubai hotel. A little further along, the twin wedges of Emirates Towers loomed in the sky, lengthening shadows crawling along as the sun sank deeper toward dusk. Wayne wondered if the police were still looking for the stolen BMWs, now several vehicle changes ago. High-rise apartments, hotels, and office buildings soared on either side, creating a wide canyon of commercialism and excess in the middle of the desert.

Walid took a sharp right onto an exit ramp, cutting across two lanes of traffic and drawing the horns and ire of several vehicles. Wayne was suddenly grateful for the gap he'd been unable to close, as it gave him just enough time to react to the sudden turn and cross to the exit in pursuit.

A quick glance at the sign overhead told Wayne where they were headed: Dubai Mall. The largest mall in the world, Dubai

Mall counted among its attractions an amusement park, an Olympic-size ice rink, a three-story food court, and a record-setting aquarium. The city was home to a dozen malls that would stand out in any city in the world. The Dubai Mall made them all look like peanuts by comparison.

As the ramp curved over Sheik Zayed Road and headed toward the mall complex, Walid stole a look behind him. His eyes locked with Wayne's, a fierce determination burning beneath. His prey now knew he was being hunted. Another advantage lost.

The jihadist yelled something to his subordinate, and both motorcycles pulled into Parking Garage B, a massive, four-story garage built to house three thousand vehicles. Wayne followed.

The garage's entry level was nearly full, but several SUVs circled, looking for parking spots. Walid drove straight toward one such vehicle, playing a game of chicken that his motorcycle would surely lose. The Emirati behind the wheel of the SUV panicked, though, and jerked his wheel to the right, smashing into a parked Ferrari. Walid dodged the wreck and executed a quick fake out on the Lexus behind, causing another crash.

Is Walid trying to cause as much destruction to his hometown as possible? Or is he just trying to put more obstacles between himself and me? Wayne wondered as he skirted the first wreck and slalomed around the second. Did the terrorist have a plan in coming here? Or was he just as desperate to get away as Wayne was to stop the bomb? Were they both just winging it now?

Another Land Rover turned the corner at the end of the row. Walid dodged it at the last minute, but his companion wasn't so lucky. The motorcycle hit the grill, and sent the terrorist flying through the SUV's windshield. His employer looked at the scene for a brief moment but continued racing ahead.

Walid whipped around another corner and up a ramp to the second level, Wayne hot on his heels. On the next floor, Walid pulled out a compact MPK5 machine pistol and gunned the engine. Wayne reached for his sidearm as he struggled to maintain control of the motorcycle.

A shootout was the last thing he wanted here. Way too much attention. And if either of them died, so did the ambassador. And untold millions more.

Walid aimed the MPK5, but not at Wayne. Straight ahead. At the glass doors of the mall itself.

A three-shot burst rang out, still audible over the roar of Wayne's motorcycle. Glass shattered and fell to the floor, opening a motorcycle-sized hole in the mall entrance. And just like that, Walid was racing his motorcycle through the mall. Three seconds later, so was Wayne.

Shoppers dove back into stores and cowered against walls as the roar of engines filled the echo-chamber hall. Wayne kept his head low despite his helmet's disguising properties. This was about as public as you could get. Pierce would not be pleased.

Ahead, Walid was holstering his MPK5, pulling something else from his pocket. Why wasn't he shooting at Wayne? He seemed desperate to get away, shooting out a door and driving through the mall like this. One well-placed bullet could end the chase for him. What was his game?

The row of shops opened up into one of several open plazas, this one showcasing the aquarium. Home to one of the world's only whale sharks in captivity, among many other fascinating aquatic creatures, the facility was on a par with some of the greatest aquariums in the world. This plaza offered a view of the main tank—said to hold ninety-five million gallons of water—through the largest acrylic panel in the world. Even at this high velocity, it was a sight to behold, a fact attested to by the array of tourists snapping selfies in front of the tank.

Walid made a sharp left directly in front of the aquarium, sending tourists scrambling out of his way. As he turned, the jihadist tossed something toward the tank, which stuck about halfway up. He raced off, and Wayne realized, with horror, what was now stuck to the acrylic.

A so-called sticky bomb, plastic explosive coated with a strong adhesive, designed for taking out the sides of tanks and other heavy artillery.

Or a massive, acrylic window with the pressure of millions of gallons of water on the other side.

Wayne hit the plaza and started to make the turn just as the bomb exploded. The blast took out an initial hole, and then the water did the rest, cracking and crumbling the building-sized sheet of acrylic.

Walid was just ahead. If he could just . . .

Wayne's thoughts were cut short as he was caught from behind by a tsunami of salt water, fish, sharks, and drowning shoppers.

CHAPTER 44

WASHINGTON, D.C.

Logan Pierce steepled his fingers as President Talquin read through the latest briefing on the UN's discovery of a half-destroyed, secret nuclear facility outside of Rasht, Iran. The Oval Office was silent as everyone present, including Secretary of State Lyle Molina and Secretary of Defense Ted Brinson, waited for the president to digest the latest piece of bad news.

"They're denying everything, of course," Talquin said, his eyes still on the papers. "President Hosseini is being called before a special session of the UN Security Council, but he's claiming it's a conspiracy orchestrated by, and I quote, 'Zionist aggressors and their Western imperialist allies.'"

The president took off his glasses and rubbed his eyes with the thumb and forefinger of one hand. "Even with the evidence staring them in the face, these fundamentalist fools still have the gall to deny that they've been secretly developing nukes."

"What else can they do?" Pierce said. "They're caught red-handed developing weapons of mass destruction in clear violation of every resolution the international community has hammered out over the past decade. The sanctions we had in place when we just suspected they were developing the bomb nearly crippled Iran's economy. They've just reaped the ire of the entire world for so brazenly lying for all these years and wasting our time, energy, manpower, and goodwill. They're about to be destroyed economically, and that's just for starters. Of course they're screaming conspiracy."

Brinson nodded somberly. "It seems the conservative punditry was right after all. They got the sanctions relief they wanted, then went and broke the deal behind our backs. But the fervent denial is intriguing. After Hosseini's speech before the UN, it's surprising they didn't just throw it back in our faces and say, 'Ha! We're a nuclear power now! Respect us!'"

"That hasn't worked out so well for North Korea," Molina said. "And they're facing crippling sanctions for the foreseeable future if this secret Rasht facility pans out. I agree with Pierce on this one."

"There's one other element we're not taking into consideration," Talquin said. "The timing of the denial. If a nuke goes off in Israel today, the international community would have first suspected a non-state actor: ISIS, al-Qaeda, and so forth. Possibly with the aid of a nuclear power, but then, as far as we knew before now, Iran wasn't even in that elite club. And they destroyed the facility so no one would realize they ever had these nukes in the first place. Now that the facility's existence has been exposed, Iran has to deny its role in developing nuclear weapons at a site clearly designed to subvert the agreed-upon IAEA supervision."

"Any word on whether this might delay or stop the attack?" Molina asked.

"None as yet," Talquin said. "Passover begins at sunset, so there's a definite symbolic choice to the date, snuffing out Israel on the anniversary of the Jews' exodus from slavery in Egypt en route to the Promised Land."

"So we proceed as planned?" Brinson asked.

Talquin took a heavy breath, held it for a moment, and then exhaled.

"I'm afraid so. I hope to God this exposure changes their plans and they pull the plug, but if not, we may be at war with Iran by morning, gentlemen. Ted, escalate all air, sea, and land forces in the Gulf region and within 500 miles of Tehran to battle-ready status."

"What about our nuclear launch tubes in Turkey and Bulgaria?"

Talquin swallowed, looking as though the weight of the world had come crashing down on his shoulders in the past few days. "As an absolute last resort, yes, have them ready. But God help us all if we need to cross that line."

He turned to his secretary of state. “Lyle, talk to our allies and get their feel for a broad military coalition against Iran if they should attack Israel.”

Pierce felt the president’s eyes on him next, burning with an intensity that had cowed political opponents and intractable foreign leaders.

“And Pierce, help your men find the ambassador and get whatever intel she holds by whatever means possible. If faced with that as proof of their complicity, Iran might call off the attack for good.”

“And if they don’t?” Molina asked.

Talquin grimaced, repressed panic dancing behind his expression. “Then we’re all in trouble. Every last person on the planet.”

CHAPTER 45

DUBAI, UNITED ARAB EMIRATES

The makeshift tsunami propelled Wayne off his motorcycle and down the massive, tiled mall promenade. Lifted by the wall of water, he fought to remain upright and facing the direction Walid had driven after planting the bomb on the aquarium's glass. Doggy-paddling to stay afloat, he floundered his way forward, trying to avoid debris, shoppers, and sea life caught in the crushing wave.

The *whoop-whoop* of an emergency alarm filled the air as the mall's vibrant and conscientiously designed lighting was supplemented by intermittent red flashes. Whether automatically triggered by the bomb or initiated by a guard somewhere, the mall's security staff was officially in full, antiterrorism mode. And the only two people Wayne was particularly concerned about right now—himself and Walid—would be at the top of their hit list.

After traveling about twenty meters, the water level lowered to the point where his feet could touch the ground. He wasn't sure if this was a good thing, though, as the tidal wave continued to sluice past and through him, threatening to knock him to the floor under five feet of fast-moving water and debris. He struggled to keep moving forward, using the momentum of the surging flood to regain whatever lost ground he could in his pursuit of the terrorist leader.

Then he saw him, perhaps fifty meters ahead, struggling to right his fallen motorcycle in the thigh-high current that had caught up to its orchestrator.

Wayne wasn't out of this chase yet.

Walid glanced behind him and saw his pursuer, still alive with his head above the waves. He scowled at Wayne, popped off two rounds from his MPK5, and started running down the promenade, abandoning the motorcycle to the rushing torrent.

Wayne pushed through the shoulder-high waves, taking leaping steps as the current helped him gain some ground on the fleeing Walid. Then the tide hit a bend in the hall and some of the water rebounded, catching Wayne and impeding his progress. Walid looked over his shoulder and sneered at his pursuer just before he rounded the corner, leaving Wayne with a face full of water as the opposing waves splashed higher.

Phoenix ducked beneath the surface and began to swim. Walid was out of sight, steadily gaining a lead. Wayne's window of opportunity was rapidly closing, and trying to run against the current wasn't getting him anywhere.

The slimy-feeling underbelly of a stingray slid across his face, triggering an instinctive shiver to crawl down his spine. He gently pushed the creature aside so as not to incur its barb-fueled wrath, and continued his freestyle stroke.

A few seconds later, he surfaced to draw a quick breath and assess his progress. It was working. He had passed the Abercrombie store that was to his left shortly before submerging, and the bend around which Walid had disappeared was only a few dozen meters ahead.

Just as he ducked below again, his knees hit something, a planter, or a bench—something affixed to the floor. He didn't open his eyes beneath the water for fear of burning them with salt and fish poop, but whatever the barrier below was, it was a good sign.

Wayne stood again and found that the water had dropped to just below his knees. Bad news for the store owners whose shops were now flooded with the surge that had spilled out from the main promenade. Good news for Wayne's pursuit, which, in the grand scheme of things, outweighed pretty much everything else going on in the mall today. Everything except the deaths of the shoppers behind him, who had died in the bomb blast or the subsequent tsunami.

Wayne shoved those thoughts to the side and focused on picking up the pace. He prayed that Walid would still be visible when he finally rounded the bend. If the terrorist leader had ducked into one of the shops, moved to another of the mall's four main floors, or managed to escape the mall altogether before Wayne caught sight of him, it would be near-impossible to find him in time. He sloshed through the still-ebbing tide, dodging leopard sharks and giant groupers that jostled to explore their surprising new environment.

And then he saw him: Walid, looking over his shoulder as he pushed through the exterior door and into the bright Dubai sunshine. Wayne offered a quick prayer of thanks as he redoubled his efforts, raising his knees high with each leaping step. The water dissipated to ankle depth, and within a matter of seconds he was bursting through the door and onto the plaza.

Wayne expected Walid to double back toward the road, a parking lot, somewhere to commandeer another vehicle and escape his dogged pursuer once and for all. But, instead, he was running toward the other centerpiece of the Dubai Mall complex.

Craning his neck upward, Wayne recognized the building ahead as the Burj Khalifa, the world's tallest building, dwarfing America's tallest—New York's Freedom Tower—by nearly 1000 feet, and more than 600 feet taller than the world's second-place skyscraper. With all the sand particulate in the air from the ambient desert winds, Wayne could barely make out the top of the skyscraper. He had been inside and around plenty of massive buildings across the world during his time as a field agent, but awe was the only word to properly describe his reaction to the soaring spire stabbing defiantly into the sand-stained heavens. In a city full of skyscrapers, the Burj Khalifa gave the word a definition all its own.

Racing across the plaza, he tapped the comm unit still nestled in his ear. "Zorro, Anubis, come in."

"Zorro here," came the crackled reply. "I've picked up Anubis. What's your status?"

"Chasing the target at the Dubai Mall complex," Wayne huffed between breaths. "It looks like he's headed for Burj Khalifa."

"Really? Why? Does he know you're on his tail?"

"He does. No real escape from there, unless he's going out the back entrance, or he's planning to *Mission Impossible* his way into a helicopter nearby."

"You think he's making a last stand? Gone suicidal?"

"God, I hope not. He doesn't seem the type. Maybe he's got a weapons stash up there, or some final play he hopes will save his hide."

"We're on our way." Suarez's voice sounded genuinely concerned. "Be careful, and good luck."

Wayne reached the front doors to the skyscraper mere seconds after Walid had disappeared through them. Once his eyes had adjusted to the dimmer light of the interior, he saw a pair of security guards writhing on the ground, each sporting a chest wound oozing blood. There was no coming back from this for Walid, Wayne realized. Whatever he was trying to do in the Burj, he was playing for keeps.

Walid was running for the elevator bank ahead. He dove inside an open one and hit the "Door Close" button. Wayne was almost there. Just a few more steps . . .

The doors shut just as he reached the elevator. Wayne slammed a fist into the chrome-plated doors. He'd lost him. And yet . . .

He hit the "Up" button to call a new car, watching as the floor numbers above the door Walid had disappeared into ticked over, the digits flying by courtesy of one of the world's fastest elevators. They stopped on floor seventy-six, the highest floor this bank went to. According to a placard next to the door, transfer was available from there to the remaining eighty-plus floors via an adjacent elevator bank.

The doors of a new elevator opened as an Emirati man and two hijab-covered women stepped out. Wayne darted inside and hit the button for floor seventy-six, then "Door Close." A pair of Asian businessmen started to follow him inside, eyeing his soaked apparel and wild demeanor with a mixture of apprehension and disdain.

Wayne met them at the door with his pistol raised. "This one's taken."

The men stepped back and started to chatter excitedly among themselves in Malay as the doors closed. They would likely report him to building security or even the police, but Wayne didn't care. Both were already after him. And his confrontation with Walid and whatever the terrorist was planning high above the city would likely be over long before either could make a difference.

Sixty seconds and nearly a thousand feet later, Wayne stepped out of the elevator just in time to see Walid's form disappear behind the closing doors of the elevator bank opposite. The digital display above stopped at 143. Was he using the same tactic that Wayne had employed at Emirates Towers? Taking the elevator to a decoy floor before ascending or descending to his true destination? Wayne decided it didn't matter right now. His next step was obvious.

When the next elevator arrived, Wayne climbed aboard and hit the button for floor 143. After another brisk-yet-smooth ascent, the doors opened upon a scene of carnage.

Two blonde women lay dead on the ground, twin puddles of crimson staining their collection of shopping bags from high-end boutiques in the mall. A white-lace teddy had spilled from one bag, never to be worn, never to be appreciated by her new husband-cum-widower.

Walid was here. And he was getting more desperate and dangerous by the minute.

The hall split in three, with each passage leading to a different section of the lotus-footprint building. Walid was nowhere to be seen. He could be holed up behind any door in any of the three corridors. Or he could have moved to a different floor entirely after murdering the two shoppers in cold blood.

Wayne looked at the ground surrounding the women. Walid had made a mistake. It was faint, but Phoenix could see blood-stained footprints—just the left shoe—leading away from the grisly scene and down the right-most hallway. His Glock at the ready, he followed the blood trail until it stopped at an unmarked steel door. Moving his body against the wall, he tried the handle. It was unlocked. He eased the door open, leading with his pistol.

The office suite was engineered to be spacious, but a litany of file cabinets, cupboards, tables, desks, and other office furniture filled the room like an IKEA-centric episode of *Hoarders*. A small pile of BASE-jumping parachutes and AK-47s sat in one corner. Binders, folders, and loose-leaf papers were strewn about without any obvious system of organization. The place was a real mess.

A handful of maps adorned a corkboard at the far end of the room. Two were regional maps, along with a city map and an aerial surveillance photo of an abandoned amusement park project to the south of the city in the ambitious Dubailand complex. What looked to be schedules and shipping routes written in Arabic sat in a stack on a nearby table. Clearly some sort of planning had gone on in this room at some point, but no one in their right mind would use this as an office in its current state. There was just too much furniture crammed in here.

Something was very wrong here.

Walid popped out from behind a partition and fired a pair of shots. Wayne ducked instinctively, taking cover behind a man-sized aluminum cabinet. Depending what kind of ammo the terrorist was using, it wouldn't necessarily stop the bullets, but it was the best Wayne could do at the moment.

"It's over, American," Walid sneered. "Give it up. You've lost. You were always destined to lose."

"Come on, Walid, there's no way out of here. Let me help you."

"Oh, now that's not fair is it? You know my name, but you haven't introduced yourself."

Wayne took a breath. "I'm Phoenix."

"Cute. Are Goose and Maverick out there waiting for me to come quietly?"

"The police are on their way. You're trapped, and you know it. I'm your only hope now. Let's work this out together. Tell me where the ambassador is, and we can find a way to fix all of this."

Walid scoffed. "Oh, that's not exactly true is it? Do you really think I haven't watched my share of American spy movies and cop shows in my time? I know all your ruses. Hear that language I'm speaking? My hatred of Western culture isn't just some blind, distant disdain whipped into a fury by fundamentalist imams preying on impressionable young men. I've lived in the infidel culture, seen the natural outcomes of your relentless pursuits of every vice mankind has ever devised. It stole everything I ever loved. My city, my family, my purpose.

"You were always destined to fall like Rome. I'm just helping to rid the world of your pernicious influence sooner rather than later."

Wayne clenched his jaw, trying to find words that might hit his soft spot. "How much did *you* get paid to kidnap the ambassador? You're not doing this for Allah. You're just as profit-hungry as the Western culture you claim to hate. All that blood on your hands, all for the almighty dollar."

Two more bullets flew overhead. He'd hit a nerve with that one. "Work with me here, Walid! The only way out of here is through me. Give me what I want, and I'll help you get out of here."

Walid started laughing, a throaty, malevolent laugh that chilled Wayne's marrow. "I already have what I want, *Phoenix*. And you're the one who needs help getting out of here."

Something buzzed near the entry door, and Wayne saw an electronically controlled deadbolt slide home. He traced the wires along the wall, back toward where Walid was hiding. Some branched off, diving under desks and into cabinets. With a tremulous hand, Wayne eased open the cabinet he was relying upon for cover.

It was filled with dozens of blocks of C-4, all with detonators in place. Suddenly, all the excess furniture made sense. Hidden within their innocuous exteriors, each housed enough plastic explosive to make a very lasting mark on Dubai's skyline, and an even more permanent mark on Wayne.

Walid's final play had been for keeps after all. The entire place was wired to blow. And Wayne had walked right into his trap.

CHAPTER 46

DUBAI, UNITED ARAB EMIRATES

For the first time in recent memory, Walid Abushakra was scared.

He couldn't believe he'd allowed himself to become cornered, but after the American had not only survived the aquarium blast but also nearly caught up to him in the plaza outside, he realized there was really no other option.

This room had been used for planning parts of the operation, contingencies and such. Presentations to their sponsor had been held here, and the man's elite stature in the Middle East ensured that the room itself was kept from the prying eyes of overly diligent security guards over the intervening months. It was this high-end brand of secrecy and discretion which allowed Walid to smuggle in more than a ton of explosives, along with the extensive collection of furniture.

He was their benefactor's second choice for the ambassador's kidnapping. The first team—amateurs in whom Walid never would have put his trust—had failed miserably in Cairo a few days before. Originally, *Uhmar Haidar*'s Dubai operation had been prepped for the UK ambassador, who was scheduled to land the day after Needham's surprise visit had changed the target. When her assistant had called to tell him of the American representative's covert trip to DXB, it was almost too perfect. She was a far more high-profile target, due to the nature of her work on the planned peace conference. Logistically speaking, it was a coup, as her desire to keep the trip off the grid ensured she was flying with a minimal protection force and that no security force or Emirati delegates met the plane before Walid could make his move.

The fact that she, the embodiment of the American imperialism he hated most in the world, was coming to his city had to be a sign from Allah. The representative of the culture that had destroyed and perverted the heritage of his homeland and murdered his family just blocks from his home was coming to the scene of the crime.

Walid would have done this one for free.

Instead, his paymaster shelled out $100 million in oil futures—one of the only currencies that would be worth anything after the coming war turned Iran into glass and America into a nuclear wasteland. With an added $10 million due to the last-minute change in plans. Clearly, Allah had blessed their plans.

And then the Americans had shown up, despite clear warnings not to by the Emirati government. An unfortunate wrinkle, but Walid chose to view it as another opportunity to embarrass the United States and expose its relentless policy of doing whatever it felt like around the world, regardless of the express wishes and sovereignty of their so-called allies. The arrest by the Dubai authorities of three armed American agents would be the final straw for Emirati-American relations, with other regional allies likely to follow suit. But despite the massive bribe Walid had paid Deputy Chief of Police Dahhan, the American spies continued to be a thorn in his side.

He had prepared a contingency for Dahhan. Evidence to implicate him not only in the airport bombing but also in the Akers affair, all of which would be easily uncovered if anyone dug in the right spots. And if Dahhan, greedy and useless as he largely was, tried to tell anyone what he knew—which was far less than he thought he did—he would end up in an Emirati jail or at the perforated end of a firing squad faster than you could say "treason."

Unlike in some of the operations *Uhmar Haidar* had undertaken over the past five years across Syria, Yemen, Iraq, Afghanistan, Libya, and Jordan, Walid wasn't content to limit his involvement to the planning and supervision of the operation. He wanted to be in the thick of it. His family's blood was on the Americans' hands, and he needed to be the one to exact vengeance. This was his city, his mission, and nothing could take that away from him.

But the Americans dogged him every step of the way. Especially this "Phoenix," who had killed his men in the airport tunnels, survived the blast in the Hor Al Anz hideout, infiltrated Shiraz Imports, escaped the Jumeirah mansion, boarded his yacht, and chased him across the city into Burj Khalifa. The man simply would not die. Phoenix indeed. But no one lives forever.

He looked at the small black pad he held in his quivering hand. The safety guard was raised, the switch pointing to "ARMED." All that remained was to push the button.

The American would die, hopefully implicated in the blast and tied back to the United States' policies of not playing well with others. Dubai would be deprived of its most impressive landmark, for there was enough explosive in this room to destabilize and topple the upper three-hundred meters or so of the building, even if the remainder of the colossal eyesore remained, a truncated, smoldering reminder of the folly of chasing a corrupt Western ideal. Westerners would be scared away from the city that had long prided itself on being distinctly different from the violent, terrorism-plagued highlight reel that primetime news and Hollywood showcased as the Middle East. And, in light of the coming war and the absolute destruction of America and her destructive influence, perhaps Dubai's leaders would step back from the precipice of bowing down to the deep pockets of the Great Satan and return to the ideals that had once made Islam the greatest empire in the world.

This had been the plan from the beginning. Phoenix's death and possible implication was just a bonus. But there was one rather large snag.

Walid was supposed to be far, far away from here when the Burj fell. The trigger could also be operated wirelessly and, in fact, was designed to be used as such. He would have to manually arm the detonator sequence on-site, so as to ensure that any freak electrical signals during the months-long build-up to the actual event didn't cause a premature explosion. But when actually sending the code to trigger the bomb, he would have been safely across the creek, miles away, where he could watch

Dubai's pride fall back to the earth in a flaming heap of avarice and screams.

But he wasn't safely across the creek, out of harm's way. He was in the middle of it all, out of bullets, out of options, with his unexpected nemesis blocking the way to freedom.

He didn't want to die. He had 110 million new reasons to live now, not to mention the vengeful glee he'd experience when he watched America fall prey to its own insatiable bloodlust.

The fourth Sura of the Qu'ran expressly forbade suicide, despite the justifications offered by some imams and other fundamentalist leaders for the effective yet misguided practice of suicide bombings for jihad. And yet, regardless of what "Phoenix" said, there wasn't any other way out. He hadn't strapped on a vest and walked into a crowded marketplace to become a living bomb. He had been chased here, trying to finish the work he was sure Allah had tasked him with. And now he was out of options. So, no, he reasoned, this wasn't suicide. This was simply his only option.

He gripped the trigger pad, sweat-slick in his palm. It wasn't all loss. He would die knowing that his actions had helped restore Dubai's focus on what truly mattered. And though he would be gone, within two hours, his team would have set in motion a chain of events that would ultimately result in the death of the Great Satan. When the smoke cleared, it would be the Arab world that once again became the pillar of human civilization, free at last from the toxic influence of imperialist infidels. And, most importantly, he would soon join his family in paradise.

Slowly, purposefully, he stood, his body still hidden from the American by the partition. He turned toward his assailant's position, noticing with a measure of satisfaction that the hand gripping the trigger had stopped shaking. This was the path Allah had ordained. And he had no choice but to walk it.

He smiled inwardly and then stepped out, a look of defiance on his face as he glared towards where Phoenix was hiding.

"*Allahu Akbar!*" Walid shouted, with a newfound conviction deep within. And then he pushed the button.

CHAPTER 47

DUBAI, UNITED ARAB EMIRATES

Wayne's mind threatened to seize with panic. There had to be enough C-4 in the room to blow a crater ten stories high in the side of the building. If the building was standing at all afterward.

The door was locked, and whatever electronic controls Walid had dead-bolted it with would not allow circumvention through brute force. At any second, the terrorist mastermind could hit the button and blow himself, Wayne, and the Burj Khalifa sky high, along with any hope of recovering the ambassador or the intel she held before a nuke exploded in Israel and the world was irrevocably swept into an all-consuming World War III. Wayne had to escape.

But how?

Inching away from the explosive-filled cabinet he had been using as cover, he remembered the pile of supplies he had glimpsed during his quick survey of the room moments earlier. AK-47s. And BASE-jumping parachutes.

He lunged out of cover, grabbing a parachute and strapping it on as he bounded around and over the clutter of excess furniture now filled with plastic explosives. A massive, plate-glass window—mirrored from the outside for privacy and protection against the desert sun's merciless rays—loomed ahead.

To Wayne's left, Walid stepped into view from behind a partition, holding something that looked dangerously like a remote detonator in one hand. This was it. Wayne hadn't pegged him as being suicidal, but perhaps the rules had changed for his final play. This was his desperate swan song to preserve his deadly secret and make a massive mark on the city he had once called home.

There was no time to check the chute, to check the fall, to check any of the variables he normally would have verified before attempting a jump. It was literally now or never.

"*Allahu akbar!*" shouted Walid.

Wayne picked up a chair and threw it at the window, splitting the pane into a spiderweb of fissures. Lowering his shoulder and averting his face, he plowed into the center of the web, the glass resisting for a split second before giving way.

A quick flurry of beeps sounded behind him. Now suspended in the harsh desert air and surrounded by a storm of glass shards, he looked down at the desert floor looming two-thousand feet below.

Time seemed to slow as a panorama of the city sprawl spread out before him, from the skyline of Sheikh Zayed to the resorts and beaches of Jumeirah to the old city of Deira near the creek. But despite all the development over the past few decades, much of the region visible from this great height was still untouched, the same desert wasteland that Bedouins, Arabs, and nomads had called home for millennia, eking out a living from the arid sands that seemed devoid of life. One area that stood in stark contrast to this natural desert was the Dubai Mall complex. Specifically, the expansive stone plaza at the foot of the Burj Khalifa, of which Wayne was presently ten seconds of free-fall away from becoming a permanent fixture.

The skyscraper shuddered behind him as the 143rd floor was racked by Walid's room full of explosions. Flames roared from the side of the building, and Wayne could feel the heat several stories below the blast. Windows shattered floor-by-floor as the detonation reverberated through the tower's core.

Wayne had fallen five stories now and was picking up speed. The wind was murder up here, with sand particulate lashing his face. He needed to deploy the parachute soon to avoid breaking his legs—or worse—on impact. This close to the Burj, however, the wind could catch the parachute and slam him back against the building. Furthermore, the further from the ground he deployed, the more time he gave the terrorists or the police to shoot him down or intercept him when he landed. There was little room for error, and Wayne wasn't even sure he knew the exact right time. He prayed he'd instinctively know when to deploy. A moment too soon or too late and he was a dead man.

And then he saw another problem, one that was hurtling toward him almost faster than his mind could process. Because of the terraced nature of the tower's design, large, curved swathes of deck protruded from the side of the building at varying intervals, each heralding another stage in the base's growth. Wayne's initial leap through the window had provided him with a degree of forward momentum, but the further he fell, the more that dissipated. Without a major change in course, he wouldn't have to worry about hitting the plaza. One of the decks on the building itself would do him in.

The first such terrace loomed just a few floors below. The 124th floor of the Burj Khalifa housed the famous observation deck that allowed visitors a spectacular, panoramic view of the city from its highest publicly available vantage point. To prevent guests from tumbling over the side—either by accident or on purpose—a Plexiglas wall had been erected around the platform's edge. And Wayne's freefall was putting him perilously close to being sliced in half by this very safety barrier.

He could see the tourists now. Cowering and screaming as shattered glass and flaming debris continued to spout from the floors above. Pointing at the man who was falling from the blaze straight toward them.

It was going to be close. Falling headfirst, Wayne tried to push against the air, to move that fraction of an inch he needed to clear the Plexiglas and continue his descent. Time slowed to a crawl as he neared then reached the top of the barrier. With a hair's breadth to spare, he made it. An array of shocked and curious faces stared back at him as he passed on the other side of the clear divider. He hoped they'd soon forget his face, but whatever was left of his cover after the past thirty-six hours of break-ins, explosions, shootouts, and crashes was secondary to his current plight.

By the 117th floor, Wayne had separated from the wall by several inches, but he could see the next terrace looming some ways below. Only moving outward an inch or two per floor now, and continuing to gain speed as he approached terminal velocity, his current path could only end in blood.

He took a deep breath. In one coordinated motion, he pushed against the 116th floor window with his palms and feet, propelling himself away from the building. Three, now four feet of clearance. And growing.

Wayne fought now to right himself. After struggling to swivel his body in freefall, he managed to gain a horizontal position and survey the plaza below. A dozen black-clad tactical police officers had taken positions in and around the square, though the explosion two-thousand feet overhead had likely shaken whatever plans they originally came there with. The plaza offered the most obvious landing site—flat, open, and easily accessible. But the police presence would destroy his chances of escape or of rescuing the ambassador.

"Phoenix, we've got you on scope," buzzed Suarez's voice in his earpiece.

Wayne's face lit up with hope. "Zorro? Where are you?"

"Light-blue utility van coming off the Sheikh Zayed ramp now. Land at the ramp's base. We'll pick you up."

Wayne pulled his rip cord, releasing his parachute in an arc above him. He used the toggles to angle his path toward the ramp. Some of the police in the plaza began to move, following his new path. His chute rippled as he fought the wind, guiding his descent toward the designated target.

He was two hundred feet up now, steadily descending toward the van that had just stopped at the base of the ramp.

One hundred feet. Police sirens sounded from somewhere.

Fifty feet. The rear door of the van slid open, and Suarez's face appeared in the portal.

Ten feet. Wayne could see the smile on his new friend's face, and the large knife he held in his hand.

Despite the parachute's drag, touchdown was more painful than Wayne had hoped. He landed a few feet from the van, knees buckling from the impact. Suarez bounded from the van, brandishing the knife. When he reached his leader, he cut the ropes on Wayne's back, setting loose the parachute to fly free once again in the desert winds.

"Good to have you back, boss," Suarez said, helping Wayne into the back of the van. Once both were aboard and the door shut, Nasef hit the gas, making a U-turn and heading back onto the thoroughfare of Sheikh Zayed.

"Get out of the city," Wayne ordered Nasef. "Head south."

"Please tell me he told you something before . . ." Suarez nodded toward the Burj, its top stories haloed in flame and wreathed in plumes of black smoke. Wayne couldn't help but stare, flashing back to another set of towers burning in another city. The attacks on that horrible day had stolen his parents from him. Today, he had barely escaped a similar fate.

"Yes and no," Wayne replied. "Walid was defiant to the end, but I think I know where they're keeping the ambassador."

He borrowed Suarez's PDA and called Ibrahim, who picked up on the first ring.

"You didn't have anything to do with this explosion at the Burj just coming across the channels, did you?"

"Walid blew himself up, but believe it or not, that's not why I'm calling right now."

"You were involved in destroying something more noteworthy than the tallest building in the world?"

"The Burj is still standing, Ibrahim, and I'm calling about the mission, not collateral damage."

"I wonder if the sheikh would see his crowning achievement as 'collateral damage.'"

Wayne gritted his teeth. "I think I know where they're keeping the ambassador."

"You do? Where?"

"Pull up satellite and thermal imaging on the Arabian Nights amusement complex in Dubailand."

Wayne could hear keys tapping in Langley before Ibrahim spoke again. "Running scans now. Quick intel on the site: funding ran out after the financial crisis in 2008, and the place is purportedly abandoned at present."

"Not anymore."

"I'll have that data to you in ten minutes. One thing you guys should know from here, though."

"What's that?"

"Talquin's preparing for war. He's got bombers in the air over Turkey and three carriers heading for the Gulf. If the nuke goes off, we'll have passed the point of no return."

"Good Lord. How long do we have?"

"Intel still says sunset, Israel time."

Wayne gulped, thanked Ibrahim, and disconnected.

"Dubailand?" Nasef said.

"I sure hope so," Wayne replied. "I'm all out of other options now."

He looked at his watch, did some mental calculations, and frowned.

They had sixty-eight minutes to save the world.

CHAPTER 48

LANGLEY, VIRGINIA

Logan Pierce was ready for today to be over with. Between the ambassador's kidnapping and his team's blundering efforts to rescue her, blowing up half of Dubai, too much had already gone wrong.

He walked through the halls of CIA headquarters, receiving deferential looks from virtually everyone he passed. Despite the disadvantage fate had thrust upon him by stealing his leg and his commission, he still commanded the respect of hundreds of the most highly qualified operatives and technicians in the world. Long ago, his father had taught him that a man makes his own fate. He didn't believe that when he'd been sent home from Desert Storm with one less limb. But despite everything that had gone wrong, he believed it today.

President Talquin was preparing for war, and more than a dozen allies had voiced their military support if Iran mounted a nuclear attack on Israel. Of course, Pierce considered himself a true friend to Israel, so he wouldn't allow the attack to go through. But an eleventh-hour rescue, especially after the discovery of the Rasht facility, showed the world how untrustworthy Iran had been, and would seal the Islamic Republic's fate even in absence of a body count. Pierce would make sure of it.

An anonymous benefactor had come to him with the intel a few months ago, along with a proposition—allow the attack to get to the final stages, then stop it at the last minute. The damage to Iran's reputation would be irrevocable, and Israel would ultimately be more secure for it. Iran, not Israel, would be wiped off the map, and its massive network of sponsored terrorist organizations along with it. Win-win.

To reward Pierce's insight and bravery in going outside the box to do the ultimately right thing, the benefactor paid him the tidy sum of one million dollars. A very nice addition to his retirement package, if ever the allure of the power he wielded grew dim enough for him to consider retiring.

The ambassador's kidnapping had to have been a fluke, Murphy's Law gumming up the works. She wasn't even supposed to be in Dubai, and yet her kidnapping seemed to tie in somehow with the impending attack on Israel. And, as proved by the sight of the Burj Khalifa burning in the desert sky that now dominated news media alongside Iran's denials about the Rasht facility, the terrorists who kidnapped her were anything but small time. Walid Abushakra's outfit had been high on the agency's most wanted list for several years now, but this was the closest they'd ever been to routing their leadership in direct combat. If only so much else weren't riding in the balance at the same time.

Janan Ibrahim had called him moments earlier, reporting that the Dubai team had apparently discovered the ambassador's location and were en route. It was coming down to the wire now. Ideally, the team would rescue the ambassador and recover the intel she apparently held implicating Iran in the attack. But if, worst case scenario, the team was unsuccessful, her kidnapping and death would serve as more fuel to stoke the flames of war. One way or another, the terrorist-sponsoring, anti-Western, holocaust-denying fundamentalist regime in Iran would fall. And even if Pierce's role in making that happen would never grace the pages of history, he would know that, once again, he had made the necessary sacrifices to preserve and protect America and her allies from foreign aggressors.

When he reached the office they'd designated for Ibrahim's work on this mission, he knocked twice and entered without waiting for a reply. The technician's eyes remained glued to her screen, her face assuming an otherworldly pallor in the monitor's glow. He closed the door behind him and cleared his throat.

Ibrahim looked up at her supervisor, startled. She offered a conciliatory nod before returning to her work. She must have been assuming that if her boss had something he needed to ask her, he would. He admired her work ethic. It was crunch time, and she didn't stop what she was doing to brown nose. In a politically charged atmosphere like the CIA, he appreciated those traditional, professional values.

"What's the latest, Ibrahim?"

"I just sent the surveillance photos and thermal-imaging scans of the target area to the team," she said, finally meeting his eyes. "There's nearly a dozen separate mobile heat sources on site, so it looks like they've got the right place."

"Excellent. How close are they now?"

"ETA five minutes. They've switched vehicles since leaving the Dubai Mall area and have apparently lost the local authorities."

She looked back at the screen, which had lit up with a pop-up window. Her eyes narrowed as she began reading the new report. Pierce stepped closer.

"What is it?" he asked.

"The bank accounts we traced from the intel the team found at Shiraz Imports. One hundred ten million dollars in oil futures to Ishmael Enterprises, a holding company that fronts for Walid Abushakra's *Uhmar Haidar*. One million dollars to a Moishe Ben-Ezra in Israel. And . . ."

Alarm bells had begun sounding in Pierce's head at the mention of Ben-Ezra's name. Ibrahim's abrupt pause all but confirmed his worst fears.

She turned around to face him. "One million dollars to you, sir."

Pierce chuckled uncomfortably. She hadn't tried to hide her discovery, to call security to take care of it for her. She was confronting him directly.

"Very funny," he said. "Seriously though, where else is the money going?"

"What's going on here, Mr. Pierce? Why are you taking money from terrorists?"

She had gall, and she wasn't backing down. Denials weren't going to work with her. The proof was right there, and now that the first stone had been turned over, the slightest amount of digging would provide corroborating evidence that would end his time at the agency for good.

"It's all part of an elaborate sting operation, strictly need-to-know," he said, sighing. "But since you're apparently already in the loop now, I'll show you."

He pointed to the monitor. "Pull up a new window for secure server A7."

With caution still showing in her eyes, she turned back to the screen and began to open the window. As soon as she was facing away from him, he gripped both sides of her head and twisted. He heard her vertebrae break, crushing her trachea and killing her almost instantly. Two fingers to her carotid artery confirmed the lack of a pulse.

After locking the door, he rolled her chair to a corner and dumped her body on the floor, partially hidden behind a side table. Then he sat down in the chair and returned to her workstation, deleting any incriminating evidence he could find, both on the computer and on the server.

Nervously glancing at the corner, he felt her lifeless eyes on him, cold and accusing. Several strands of black hair had fallen from her headscarf as a result of his violence upon her. One Muslim scholar he had once heard taught that for every hair an immodest woman displayed to an unrelated man, she would receive that many burning flames of punishment in the afterlife. Yet now that some of Janan Ibrahim's hair was revealed for the first time to him, he couldn't escape the feeling that it was he dangling over the maw of hell.

He powered down the computer and removed the hard drive, pocketing it. Had he remembered everything? The dead body of his employee kept him from focusing entirely, but then there was the other matter on his mind as well. Both he and Moishe had been paid by Shiraz Imports, who had also paid *Uhmar Haidar* to kidnap Ambassador Needham. Suddenly, the coup he'd been expecting for Israel and the Western world in its battle against the virulent strain of Islamic extremism coming out of Iran took on a much darker and foreboding tone.

All this time, he thought he was the game master, watching Iran move its pieces along the board while he stayed three moves ahead. Now he wondered if he and Moishe were nothing more than pawns, given a false illusion of power, but not even knowing the rules of the game.

In one fell swoop, everything he thought he had been working for had come crashing down. Colluding with terrorists, endangering America's allies, murdering a CIA analyst, and about fourteen different breeds of treason were just the start of his new crimes. Within less than an hour, all his efforts to protect America, Israel, and Western civilization may have backfired. After all his sacrifices, he might ultimately be the unwitting architect of Israel's downfall.

He crossed the room to the door, unlocked it, and switched off the lights. Stepping through the door, he shut it behind him and used his keycard to lock it and reprogram the pass code for entry.

The evidence of his latest misdeed now locked away for the moment, Logan Pierce did the only thing he could think to do.

He ran.

CHAPTER 49

RIYADH, SAUDI ARABIA

Prince Basim al-Attar stood inside the luxuriant living room, one of six in his palace, transfixed by the surreal scene playing out on the screen. On the 108" LED television, the events playing out were illustrated in ultra high-definition, but they still seemed blurry in his mind.

For the rest of the day, he owned Dubai. Walid had assured him of that, from his complete control of the operation to his buying off the deputy chief of police. Yet for some reason, the Saudi prince was staring at a city in flames. A crashed yacht, multiple bombed houses, a mall in ruins, and the tallest building in the world looking like a bad rerun of New York's Twin Towers on 9/11.

How had it all gone so terribly, terribly wrong?

He punched in a number in his phone, a secondary phone he only used for communications such as this. Conversations that would hang him before the International Court of Justice if ever exposed.

The first number he dialed didn't even ring. It just clicked off as soon as the connection was made. Unless Walid was being extremely careless about charging his phone, it seemed all but certain that the terrorist leader had somehow fallen victim to one of the Americans.

Which was why Basim had a backup contact. For contingencies, even those as unlikely as the scenario unfolding before him.

"*Salaam alaikum*," the voice on the other end said. Omar Sawaf, with whom he'd only spoken twice to date.

"What is going on down there?" Basim asked, forgoing the traditional response of *wa alaikum as salaam*.

"Walid ran into some trouble with a group of American commandos. The ambassador is still secure at an uncompromised site, and the attacks are still on schedule."

"I'm glad to hear the last bit, considering the amount of money I'm paying you. Am I to assume Walid is no longer running the operation, since he's not responding to my calls?"

A stilted pause. Basim thought he might have heard the ruthless terrorist's voice crack a bit, but it could have just been a bad connection.

"Unless Allah wills it otherwise, I believe Walid may have martyred himself to destroy the commandos."

"Well, good for him. So am I to understand that, barring his miraculous reappearance, you are now in charge of the operation as his second in command?"

"That's correct, yes."

"Have you found any evidence that the nuclear scientist was in contact with the ambassador?" Basim asked, still concerned about one potential flaw in his plan, the bomb maker with a conscience. The intel that Omid Khosh had assembled on the flash drive and tried to mail to the ambassador from the sealed and irradiated bunker could not only absolutely destroy Basim, but also unravel every part of his plan. The scientist must have fancied himself a spy of some sort, considering the listening devices he had installed around the lab, the camera footage. The Saudi prince was tied irrevocably to the Rasht facility and, if the world's spy agencies started looking hard enough at him, the rest of his frame-up would come undone as well. His false trails all pointed to elements within Iran's own government, and the Islamic Republic's own rhetoric and policies would paint a clear enough picture for the world to lay responsibility for today's attacks at the Shiite adversary's doorstep. If anyone ever started to doubt the scenario he'd concocted, it would come far too late to stop the destruction of both Israel and Iran. That was the beauty of his plan—the attacks would be so horrific and the blame so clear that action would be swift and merciless.

Unless Omid Khosh had given his evidence to someone else. Someone like the ambassador.

"Nothing. You're in the clear."

"Good. Gag her for the execution, just in case."

"I will see that it is so."

"Don't fail me, Omar. And don't fail Allah. This mess has already attracted far too much of the wrong kind of attention. The aftermath of your playtime with the Americans is stealing airwaves from the ambassador's execution and the eradication of Israel. Finish this right, or you'll wish you had martyred yourself with your partner."

"I understand, Your Highness"

"Don't call me that. Not over the phone at least."

"I thought it was a secure connection."

"It is," Basim said. But he still had every reason to be at least somewhat paranoid. Too much had already gone pear-shaped, and none of his goals had yet been realized.

Soon, though. Very soon.

Still staring at the destruction on his massive television screen, Basim asked, "These American commandos, why isn't the news reporting them?"

"Probably censored. You know Western media."

"I'm watching Al-Jazeera, you idiot. Why aren't they reporting about them?"

Omar chuckled nervously. "I'm guessing they managed to stay off the radar before getting themselves blown up."

"Stay off the radar? With that much destruction? How is that even possible? A dozen men or more, wreaking that kind of havoc."

"We think it was three men, your . . . sir."

Basim raised his eyebrows, though no one could see his surprised expression. "Three? Three commandos almost completely destroyed my operation? I thought you were professionals. Had men on the inside, sites set up in the city months in advance, dozens of trained operatives under your command. And three guys just fly in and wreck everything I've worked so hard for?"

"The threat has passed. They're dead, and the fruit of your labors and your investment will be here by nightfall, *inshallah*."

"No *inshallah*, Omar. Allah does will it. If he didn't, I wouldn't have gone to all this trouble. And if you derail his plans, know that the gates of paradise will forever be closed to you. Finish this."

"It will be done."

Basim disconnected the call and slumped down on the overstuffed sofa in front of the TV. The world had the most sensational news story it had seen in years. Terror on this scale, particularly in a place like Dubai, was unprecedented. And yet it was all ancillary to the big show.

The ambassador—and the Omid Khosh evidence—were no longer any threat to him. It was too late. No one could connect him to the attacks. Khosh had waited too long to play his hand, and his secret would go with him to the grave. The scientist's work, however, would soon be on display for the world to see.

The prince checked his watch, a Patek Philippe custom piece with platinum filigree and diamonds lining the hands and bezel. As the second hand sparkled its way across the face, Basim took a measure of comfort in how close the moment was. He had been preparing his entire life for this moment, though he didn't realize how it would manifest until a few years ago. Allah had given him a vision of a holy land free from blemish or spot. No Shiite infidels, no Jewish pigs, no Christian puppets of the West, no "moderate" Muslim apostasy would stain the original land of Allah's people.

Only the cleansing fire of a nuclear blast could fully purge the land of its unholy filth. So that would be a start. No more talk. Just action. Wiping Israel off the face of the earth, once and for all.

And then, Iran would fall, destroying its insidious plans for Shiite hegemony of the region. After that, who knew? Maybe America would implode, taking Europe down with it and erasing the stink of their colonial memories and imperialistic ambitions from the region. Maybe China and Russia would go down in the crossfire, leaving Saudi as the foremost superpower among the new world order that would emerge from the wreckage. And with nuclear power now haunted by the ghosts of millions of the freshly dead, oil would once again be at a premium. The world would need Saudi oil more than ever before, and Basim would be only too happy to supply it.

He glanced at the TV, and then back at his watch. The sweep of the hands gave him a thrill. A mundane motion normally, but Basim realized the significance of what he saw on its face.

By the time the minute hand traced its path back once more to where it was now, the world would have changed forever.

In less than an hour, he would have his war.

CHAPTER 50

Dubai, United Arab Emirates

The sun hung low and red in the sky as the team approached Dubailand. Originally conceived as the largest theme park complex in the world—more than twice as large as Walt Disney World's forty-seven square miles—Dubailand was a shadow of its promised self. A decade ago, deals had been brokered with top theme park brand and entertainment partners around the world, from Six Flags and Legoland to DreamWorks and Marvel. When the global recession hit, investment dipped significantly. When the subsequent Dubai financial crisis hit, construction on Dubailand ground to a halt. Even now, nearly a decade later, the vast majority of the projects were still in the planning stages.

One project that had gotten off the ground before the money dried up completely was the Arabian Nights theme park. Unfortunately for its owners, the financing had stalled in late 2008 and never recovered, leaving an array of half-finished buildings, rusting amusement rides, and sandblasted fantasy settings scattered across the desert landscape.

What was left of *Uhmar Haidar* was holding the ambassador—and the future of the free world—somewhere inside the complex.

Wayne opened the passenger door of the Audi they had swapped the van for a few miles back and stepped into the raging heat. Moments later, he was joined by Nasef and Suarez.

They had studied the satellite images and the thermal overlays multiple times en route. Eight to ten men, roughly half of whom were walking routes around and through the epicenter. Two heat signatures hadn't moved at all during the period in question. The larger of the two, Wayne assumed to be some sort of generator, though why they needed that much power—especially when the exhaust could betray their position to locals—was a mystery. The smaller of the stationary heat sources, however, was far more interesting. It had to be the ambassador.

It had to be.

Wayne and his team left the safety of the car and ducked through a hole torn in the barb-wire-topped fence. The sand piled around their feet, snaking into their boots as they crossed the unpaved expanse to the cluster of buildings and attractions ahead.

A Ferris wheel creaked back and forth in the wind. Its paint had been eaten away by years of heat and sand-filled wind, steel beams shining bright in the sunlight.

Wayne held up his fist and dropped to the ground. His men followed suit. Through the long-distance rifle scope Nasef handed him, Wayne confirmed his suspicions. A sniper perched in one of the wheel's buckets, maintaining watch over the terrorist base below. The team was only three hundred feet from the base of the wheel, but the sniper was facing the opposite direction at present and hadn't yet seen their approach.

"Wind reading?" Wayne asked.

Despite the growing tempest around them, Nasef gave his best estimate. Wayne aimed, adjusted for gravity and wind, and squeezed the trigger. Miraculously, the bullet found its mark, the sniper slumping over the bucket's side, dead. His rifle, however, fell from his grasp and clanged against the massive spokes beneath him on its way down. Two more terrorists appeared from the cluster of buildings to investigate the disturbance. With his next two bullets, Wayne felled them as well.

"Nice shot, Phoenix," Suarez said.

"With this wind, luck has as much to do with it as skill. Let's just hope our luck holds."

They stood, and Wayne led a quick but stealthy march across the remaining desertscape to the closest building. From the corner furthest from the Ferris wheel came another guard, walking his route. He was too far away to grab and force intel from, so Nasef shot him with a suppressed pistol round. The report was mostly drowned out by the howling desert wind, which seemed to increase in ferocity with each passing moment.

Rounding the building, Wayne entered a large, square plaza. At its center, an aerial carousel ride promised would-be visitors journeys on one of twelve "magic carpets" that revolved around a giant lamp that had once been painted gold. A sign advertising the attraction as "Aladdin and His Magic Lamp," in a flashy arabesque script, was missing several letters, and those that remained looked weathered and worn. The boarded-up façade of a gift shop stood to the right, across from which was an empty video arcade. The building that now stood behind the Americans had been designed as a restroom facility, though a broken hole in one wall revealed that most of the fixtures had long since been stolen.

Across the plaza, the centerpiece of the abortive park looked at once regal and dilapidated. Scheherazade's Palace was a massive, three-story complex that, judging by the absence of a ride-loading area out front, either held its queue inside or was a walkthrough attraction. According to Ibrahim's scans, the ambassador was inside the palace. Unfortunately, so were most of the remaining terrorists.

Keeping low, Wayne, flanked by Nasef on the left and Suarez on the right, stalked his way to the Aladdin ride, each man keeping his eyes peeled for more sentries. When they reached the central attraction, Wayne indicated that they would cross to the gift shop and sneak behind it to continue their approach to the palace. Suarez nodded, but Nasef's attention was elsewhere. Wayne followed his eyes to an angry wall of roiling silicate, heading straight for them.

A sandstorm. Bigger than any Wayne had seen in his years in Iraq. A lot bigger.

Two men appeared from the entrance to Scheherazade's Palace, each toting an AK-47. One pointed at Wayne and yelled something that was lost in the coming maelstrom.

"Forget the gift shop!" Wayne yelled over the wind. "Beeline to the palace! Protect your eyes and your lungs!"

He wrapped the lower half of his face with a red paisley handkerchief he'd kept in his pack, à la a Spaghetti Western bandit, prompting Nasef and Suarez to do likewise. Wayne fired two rounds at one of the terrorists, Nasef and Suarez firing at the other. One man went down, the other was just winged, holding his arm and slipping back into the relative safety of the palace.

Past the Aladdin ride and only thirty feet now from the entrance to the palace, Wayne ran full tilt across the plaza.

And then, with the ferocity of a hurricane laced with sand-paper, the storm came down in full force, and everything went yellow.

CHAPTER 51

DUBAI, UNITED ARAB EMIRATES

Christine was at her wit's end. It had to be almost sunset in Israel by now. She hadn't heard any cheering from elsewhere in the complex, so she could only assume that the horrible moment had not yet come. But judging by the angle of the sun filtering through the tiny window at one end of the room, she knew it wouldn't be much longer.

She was in possession of the most explosive intel in modern history, and she was absolutely powerless to do anything with it. Millions of people were about to be murdered in blazing white nuclear fire. Tens of millions more would die in the devastating war that the United States would launch in retaliation. Washington, Jerusalem, London, New York. All gone. Forever wiped from the face of the earth. Only she had the power to stop the imminent maelstrom. Except she couldn't.

"Let me out!" she screamed for the fifth time in as many minutes. Her hands were raw and bloody from tearing at the too-small vent and trying to pick the lock with an array of nails she'd found abandoned in the dust against the walls. Just as every time before, her screams went unanswered. And yet, she couldn't give up.

"Tariq sold you out to the Americans!" she yelled this time, trying a different tack. "We know everything! Your plan has already failed!"

She heard movement on the other side of the door. Footsteps. A key in the lock.

Stepping back behind the door, she held her breath. The man who entered the room looked immediately toward the pipe where he thought she was still handcuffed. When he didn't see her, he stepped further into the room, likely assuming that she was hiding behind Tariq's or Dan's body, both of which were clustered by the pipe.

Christine stepped out from behind the door and tried to slip out, but the man turned and grabbed her wrist.

"Not so smart, American," he said in rudimentary, accented English, his eyes flashing with hate-filled victory.

Using the nail concealed in her other hand, she stabbed the terrorist in the throat, puncturing his trachea. He released his grip on her wrist and grasped at his neck, unable to stem the flow of blood and oxygen escaping through the wound. And, more importantly, unable to scream for help. He collapsed to the floor, one leg preventing the door from closing.

"Smarter than you," she said as she stepped over his lifeless body. Just a few days ago, she would have been appalled at what she'd just done, relegated to dry heaving in the corner and scrubbing at her crimson-stained hands like Lady Macbeth. And maybe when all this was over, she'd have to confront a whole new set of demons for what she'd just done. But now, she was singular of focus, her sense of purpose overriding all other considerations.

The roaring sandstorm outside would have drowned out their brief scuffle from the ears of the dead man's fellow jihadists, but it also prevented her from hearing whether or not someone else might be on their way to check on him or her. Still, she recalled the problem of being defenseless the last time she tried to escape. It was worth the extra few seconds to steal the man's rifle.

Wresting the Kalashnikov and a set of keys from the dead terrorist, she bid silent farewell to Dan's battered form, shoved the jihadist's body into the cell, and locked the door.

She might be outnumbered and outgunned, with time working very much against her, but she now had a fighting chance, and she was going to use that for all it was worth.

A few steps into the darkened corridor, she heard a noise that made her heart stop.

Gunfire.

She was too late. They were celebrating the nuking of Israel and the fruition of their insidious conspiracy to ignite the world in apocalyptic flames. She cursed her luck, asking God how on earth she could have come so close only for it all to be for naught.

The gunfire continued, and she realized she might have been reading it wrong. The cadence was off. It wasn't a unilateral celebration. It was a battle.

She gripped her rifle and strode toward the door that beckoned at the end of the hall. She wasn't alone. And for the first time since she'd been taken captive, she felt that her hope might not be entirely misplaced. Maybe it wasn't too late after all.

CHAPTER 52

HAIFA, ISRAEL

The Mediterranean was ablaze with the reddening light of evening as Faheem Ramdallah and his team arrived in Haifa. The Jewish feast of Passover began at sunset, but the residents of this populous city would have little to celebrate this year.

Once they arrived at the coordinates predetermined for maximum damage and fallout, the bomb would explode, sending enough radioactive material into the populace and atmosphere to kill and sicken more than a million Israelis, including those who relied on this historic port for their dietary and other essential needs. Though some nearby Palestinians would die, they were necessary casualties in this war, and if they were any sort of proper Muslim, they would gladly offer their own deaths as a sacrifice to the cause. Any Palestinian who felt otherwise didn't deserve to live in this holy land in the first place. The attack would be the greatest blow against the Zionist occupiers since the British had handed over the land to the Jews decades before, as though it was theirs to dole out in the first place.

After the border crossing, Ramdallah and his team encountered no more troubles, bluffing their way through one checkpoint and circumnavigating three more thanks to their map. After an incredibly long and arduous journey over rutted back roads and spine-jarringly rough mountain passes, they were finally here. Death awaited them, but theirs would be a flash, a momentary gateway to paradise. The Zionists who died by his hand, however, would endure a most painful death. As befitted their long overdue punishment for befouling this land.

Ramdallah was now in the driver's seat, the third and final shift change the team had made during the non-stop journey. As he neared their destination, a series of Israeli flags fluttered in the wind, the blue Star of David standing boldly against a field of white. He allowed himself a smile. Ironic, he thought, that these symbols of the Zionists' pride should spell their very downfall. For the strength and direction of the wind demonstrated by the flags' behavior showed how very favorably Allah was smiling upon them.

The initial explosion would destroy the immediate area and contaminate it for decades to come. The wind would do the rest, sweeping invisible devastation upon the sprawl of ancient cities and villages to the southeast. Those who survived to see the sunrise would wish they had perished in the night.

The attack would dominate the news in Europe and the United States for the remainder of the day, with fear and horror spreading like a plague across those bastions of iniquity. Never before had something so audacious been attempted. And Ramdallah was about to make it a terrifying reality.

Turning the next corner, just a few blocks from their destination, he immediately realized that something was wrong. It was still half an hour before sunset, but the street was deserted. He knew Jews retired to their homes to share a Sabbath meal with their families and celebrate their Passover feast, but not all Israeli Jews were faithful in this regard. In fact, he had seen statistics reporting that a startlingly large percentage did not observe the religious rites through which they had forged their perpetually persecuted identity. Though the proximity to Passover and the Sabbath would surely indicate that many of the more faithful would have ceased work and returned to their families for the evening, there still should have been some pedestrians, street vendors, or cars on this street.

There were none.

"Hold on," he said as he turned right down an alley, only to find it blocked by a dumpster dragged diagonally across the passage. He backed up, performing a three-point turn to head back the way he had come, only to find the very thing he had feared. A trio of Shin Bet assault team vans blocking the road.

It was a trap.

"What do we do, Faheem?" asked Ayman from the passenger seat.

Ramdallah didn't answer. His mind had frozen with shock. How had they known? Was there a leak in Hezbollah? In his own team? The irony, after acquiring this incredible weapon, after the arduous overnight journey, to be stopped mere blocks from the target area.

And yet, they were only blocks away. Better a slightly reduced death toll than to surrender the whole attack.

"Prep the bomb. Now."

"Now?" asked Ashraf from the back.

"There is no time! Now! Before all is lost."

A fusillade of bullets tore through the passenger's side window, shredding Ayman's face and shoulders in a shower of blood and teeth. Ramdallah felt a searing pain in his right shoulder as one of the bullets lodged itself in his bone. Two Shin Bet men opened Ayman's door and tossed the body to the pavement.

Ramdallah reached for his Kalashnikov, hidden between the seats, but the bullet in his shoulder made him cry out in pain with the movement. He fought through it, staring down the Israeli officer who continued to train his weapon on him.

Stop was shouted in Hebrew, Arabic, and English, but Ramdallah didn't care. He came here to die. Now that his moment had come, he wasn't going to back down.

There was a blaze of light as the van's back door was yanked open, exposing the men in back to more carefully aimed gunfire. Shin Bet would be sure not to hit the bomb for fear of releasing the nuclear plague on their own city, but Ramdallah prayed that irony would strike these infidels as harshly as it had his own team.

Another flash of light, this one smaller but brighter, was accompanied by what felt like a red-hot poker being shoved through his chest. He put his hand to the wound and stared dumbly at the scarlet streams that pumped through his fingers.

Blow it up, he urged his men silently, somehow forgetting the muscles needed for speech. *Send us all up together, my brothers.*

The world was becoming wobbly, as when a former friend of his had slipped something in his tea as a practical joke years back. Ramdallah had given the man eight stitches and two broken ribs to show him just how funny he thought the joke was. But this time, it seemed even less humorous.

A breeze hit him from the left, followed by a pair of rough hands that grabbed his shoulders and yanked him from his seat. Manhandled facedown onto the pavement with a boot pressing between his shoulder blades, he felt the world slipping away. Had they really failed? Was Allah really that displeased with their work that he would deny them this victory over the enemy after coming so close?

He prayed and prayed, trying to convince his god of his piety and worthiness, for his brothers in the van to successfully detonate the bomb before it was too late.

The next bullet struck him across the top of his skull, puncturing bone and tearing a groove through his scalp before embedding itself in the asphalt. And then, it grew quiet.

No more gunfire. No more shouting. Had they done it? Had the men succeeded in repelling their attackers? Would the next sound he heard be the beautiful, fiery completion of their deadly mission?

"Hey, it's Moishe," said a voice standing over him, apparently taking for granted that the last bullet had killed him. Ramdallah slowly twisted his head to see a balding man wearing the uniform of a top Shin Bet commander with a mobile phone to his ear. He was standing a few steps away from Ramdallah. "We got it. The device is secure, and all the terrorists are dead. The intel was right after all." A pause, and then, "I don't know what the connection is with the ambassador, but at least this panned out. Israel's safe, and these guys are definitely Hezbollah. I recognize the driver from our file photos. If the material in the bomb traces back to Iran's secret nuke facility, it's a done deal."

Someone had told Shin Bet about the attack? Who had betrayed them? The circle of those who knew about their plan was incredibly small, and yet someone had decided to side with the Zionists. Unthinkable.

"She got my name too? Crap. All right, I'll work out another contingency on my end, too. Good luck with getting out of there. I thought you'd like to know that you hadn't doomed Israel after all. *Shalom* and goodbye, old friend."

Everything was starting to slip away now. His face was sticky with the blood trickling from his head wound. It was late spring, and yet the world was getting so very cold.

Ramdallah didn't know what all of the Shin Bet officer's conversation meant, but he did know two important facts that chilled his bones as he slipped toward unconsciousness for the very last time.

They had been betrayed. And they had failed.

«»

Two-hundred miles to the northwest, in international waters off the southern coast of Cyprus, a refurbished industrial tanker was anchored alone in steady seas. Upon its deck, a fully-functional replica of a RQ-170 Sentinel stealth drone rolled down a makeshift runway and took off into the evening sky. The original RQ-170 Sentinel was an American unmanned aerial-reconnaissance vehicle, the same model that Iran infamously claimed to have reverse-engineered and built from one they had shot down in 2011. The drone that now streaked eastward above the dusk-tinged waters of the Mediterranean was an exact replica of Iran's copy, with one key exception.

Soldered to the bottom of the drone was a missile launcher, housing a single, high-yield nuclear warhead. In twenty-four minutes, it would arrive in Tel Aviv to set the world on fire.

CHAPTER 53

DUBAI, UNITED ARAB EMIRATES

Thousands of tiny wasps stung the exposed parts of Wayne's face and arms, the wind buffeting his body as the sandstorm raged. He was only a few yards from the entrance to Scheherazade's Palace, but it might as well have been a thousand. He pressed through, pushing against the wind and sand, hoping and praying that he was still going the right direction, and that his men weren't far behind.

Breathing through the handkerchief was difficult but necessary to keep from inhaling a lungful of sand. Gale and gust sucked the air past in such a hurry it was a battle to draw in what little oxygen he could.

He was so close now. They couldn't give up.

Something solid struck him in the face, causing him to stumble backward. Regaining his footing, he reached out and touched a wall. He had just walked into the side of the building. Not his proudest moment, but he had made it nonetheless.

Tracing the wall to the right, he found the entrance through which he had seen the injured terrorist disappear before the sandstorm had come down in full force. Keeping his gun at the ready, he slipped inside and finally opened his eyes. The wind and sand still blew through the open door, but its fury was much diminished inside. A gold and purple counter, draped in now-tattered velvet, spanned the length of the wall directly ahead, while the queue to the ride continued through a door on the left.

A head popped up from behind the counter, and then immediately ducked back down. The wounded terrorist who had retreated inside right before the sandstorm descended upon the plaza. Over the resounding howl of wind from outside, Wayne was still able to hear the unmistakable sound of a pin sliding out of a grenade. A second later, he rolled out of the path of what looked like an M61 frag grenade, arcing toward his previous position.

Taking refuge behind a stack of unused props in the corner, he waited until the grenade had detonated, and then peeked out. The terrorist was doing the same, looking for what remained of his target and clearly confused by the absence of any sort of mangled corpse. Wayne solved the mystery for him by shooting him in the temple, killing him instantly.

Leaving cover, Wayne crossed the room toward the open door. Something thumped behind him, and he spun around to see Suarez pulling himself off the ground.

"Who leaves a body on the front step?" Suarez said, dusting himself off. "No wonder this park never took off."

Wayne patted him on the shoulder. "Good to have you back."

Nasef stumbled in next, literally coughing up a storm. He doubled over for a moment while he fought to regain his breath.

"You all right?" Suarez asked.

Nasef nodded between coughs, holding up his hand. Finally, he stood upright.

"Wind whacked me with a plastic palm frond. Knocked my handkerchief loose halfway through the storm."

"Glad you're still with us, Anubis," Wayne said. "The ambassador's got to be somewhere in here."

Suarez checked his watch, still working despite the onslaught of airborne abrasives it had just survived. "She'd better be. Less than twenty minutes to sunset, Israel time."

Wayne led the way through the open door to the left, the trio checking corners and covering each other as they advanced. The next room was largely barren. Holes were cut in grid-like intervals for queue area stanchions. A groove in the floor along one side had been designed to house the ride track that was never installed. The planned track led through a purple curtain that had faded to a dusty lavender.

Pushing through the curtain, the team maneuvered through a series of rooms depicting various stories from the classic *One Thousand and One Nights*. The voyages of Sinbad, the fisherman and the jinni, the tale of the three apples, and another iteration of Aladdin and his magic lamp made appearances, though some of the scenes remained half-finished. Construction area floodlights had been set up in each room, casting each scene in bright illumination and stark shadows. The men they'd encountered outside must have left the lights on after they'd passed through. Food wrappers and other detritus littered the floors; unpainted decorations and discarded hardware were scattered about, seemingly owing to the hurried abandoning of the project. The Sinbad room even held a pair of cots that looked as though they had been slept in recently, along with several empty water bottles. Despite these signs of former human habitation, the team encountered no resistance as they made their slow, curving ascent through the room's scenes.

The final story chamber was larger than its predecessors. Ali Baba's forty thieves lined the track pathway, with Ali Baba himself with his hands on hips, standing above a rock wall dead ahead. "Open Sesame" had been written in lights with arabesque flourishes in an arch above two sections of rock that were designed to open and allow entrance into the next chamber. As the team approached, Wayne saw that one of the rock doors had been left slightly ajar. Peering through the gap just large enough for one man to squeeze through, he glimpsed a sniper perched on a steel-framed cloud, his rifle pointing lazily in their direction. Swapping his pistol for an MP5, Wayne shot the man in the chest before he'd even realized his long-awaited enemy was finally in sight.

Wayne squeezed through the gap and took cover behind a faux-marble balustrade. Nasef and Suarez took the cue and raced through after him, splitting up, each rushing for his own piece of cover.

Wayne quickly surveyed the new room. A grand, palatial throne room, the three-story hall stretched toward a star-filled, painted sky on the ceiling above. More banks of floodlights placed throughout the room offered glimpses of a sultan's menagerie: animatronic elephants and tigers with tattered fake fur and exposed steel skeletons. Four spiral staircases at the corners of the room offered access to the stories above, though the weaving track that wended its way through the hall seemed designed to carry tourists only along the bottom floor.

At the far end, where the sultan's throne would have been, black tarps and sheets covered the walls and floor. The flag of the Iranian Revolutionary Guard hung from the backsplash, and a solitary metal folding chair sat empty in the center of the display.

The ambassador's execution chamber. The fact that the chair was still present and not stained with her blood buoyed Wayne with the hope that they were in the right place, and they weren't too late.

A spray of bullets fired from somewhere above chipped away at Wayne's cover, forcing him back behind the barrier. They were pinned down. Six, maybe seven targets left, plus the ambassador. The Americans were woefully outgunned and out-positioned, and time was not on their side.

Wayne needed a miracle.

CHAPTER 54

DUBAI, UNITED ARAB EMIRATES

Five minutes before the shooting began outside, Omar Sawaf was making his final preparations. He was in charge now, and he had two key objectives to achieve within the next half hour. Three, if any of the American agents had survived, and if they had somehow found out about their Dubailand hideout.

Sawaf had seen the explosion that claimed the top quarter of the Burj Khalifa, the smoke billowing against the unforgiving yellow sky. He knew all too well that his boss, associate, and, yes, friend, was the source of its destruction. Walid would not have blown up the skyscraper at this pivotal moment unless it was absolutely necessary. Which meant he had been cornered, likely by the American agents, and now he was dead. It wasn't a pleasant thought, but it was what it was. There would be time for mourning their dead later. Now was a time for action.

There were four of them here on the upper level, while more men guarded the entrance and their prisoner down below. From an effects booth on the balcony, to the left of the execution chamber, Hassim was working the controls for the drone flying over the Mediterranean toward the Zionist capital of Tel Aviv. Suleiman and Issa stood guard at the railing, ready in the unlikely chance that the Americans might find their way here. Their AK-47 automatic rifles would ensure that any attempted infiltration would be a short one.

From here, the plan was simple, something Sawaf had gone over many times with Walid. In roughly fifteen minutes, the nuclear-armed drone Hassim was remotely piloting would turn Tel Aviv into an irradiated wasteland. The American ambassador would be shown the first shocked news footage of the attack, and then she would be executed for the cameras. Her look of abject terror, not only for herself but for the plight of the world, would be forever emblazoned in the minds of the public, who would enjoy the footage in the next news cycle. This one-two punch against Israel and America would be the greatest act of jihad ever accomplished. And that was just the beginning.

Enraged by the attacks and made certain of Iran's hand in both of them, nuclear-armed Israel and America would strike back at the growing Persian empire, destroying Tehran in an eye-for-an-eye retaliation that would, ultimately, seal their own fate. Russia and China, both of whom had allied with Iran in an effort to help decrease the West's market share of international influence, would respond with their own nuclear attacks on Washington and whatever was left of Israel.

Zion and the Great White Satan destroyed in one masterful manipulation. The Shia aggressors in Iran would be reduced to rubble. And the world would be forever rid of its most dangerous puppet masters, tricked by one of their greatest allies in the region.

That sort of betrayal, the shock and awe of everything they believed in crumbling like sandcastles in a monsoon, was the icing on the cake for Sawaf. His role would never be revealed, but he would know. Allah would know. And the world would be a better place for his actions today.

Sawaf's ears perked up. Gunfire? He strained to hear over the distant thrum of the generator that powered the floodlights and the drone control hookup.

There it was again. Distant, but closer this time. Then more gunfire, some close, some further away.

The men outside. The guards walking the perimeter of the site were engaged in a firefight with someone.

"They're here," he muttered to himself fatalistically. Then, louder, "They're here! Get ready!"

He ran across the balcony to the back room.

"How soon?" he asked Hassim.

"Ten, twelve minutes," Hassim responded, without taking his eyes from the screen.

"It will be getting loud out here soon. Be sure to concentrate. Everything depends on your completing your task."

"I understand, Omar."

Sawaf left the room and moved to a metal crate he was hoping he wouldn't have to open. If he was forced to open it, it meant something had gone wrong. And yet, he couldn't think of a more fitting ending for whatever intruders were spoiling his moment of jihadist rapture, the glorious culmination of a life dedicated to the artful destruction of those he despised.

Removing the clasps that held it shut, Sawaf opened the crate and stared briefly at his prize. An M72 rocket-propelled grenade launcher.

It was beautiful.

As he lifted the weapon from the molded-foam cushion, he heard the beginnings of an unearthly howl from outside. *Sirocco*, the violent desert wind, was sweeping the land. The exterior wall shuddered with the gale-force winds that pounded the world beyond. It seemed nature herself didn't want the Americans to succeed.

Still, he knew better than to leave something this important to the fickle forces of weather. If the sandstorm devoured the agents outside, so be it. But if they made it inside, he'd be ready.

Joining Suleiman and Issa at the balcony railing, Omar Sawaf shouldered the now-loaded grenade launcher and waited.

CHAPTER 55

Dubai, United Arab Emirates

Wayne's back was to the wall, literally, as he tried to think of a solution. The shoulder-high balustrade offered a modicum of cover from the shooters above, but they held the high ground as well as the upper hand in weaponry. His back to the shooters for the moment, he spoke softly into his comms.

"You guys all right over there?"

"For the moment, yeah," came Nasef's voice.

"I saw three tangos on the balcony across the way," Suarez said. "At least one more across the room on our level."

Wayne hadn't noticed the terrorist on their level, but it gave him an idea of what they might have been up to. Keeping his head out of sight from the shooters above, he leaned away from the balustrade, angling so he could see the main hall of the throne room.

"Two tangos heading this way," he reported, leaning back into cover. "In the middle of the room, looking like they're about to try to flank us."

"*Try* being the operative word," Suarez said.

"Stay down, but slide over several feet from where you were when the shooters up top lost sight of you. On three, we'll pop up and take the tangos on our level."

"Copy," Nasef responded. "On your count."

Wayne shuffled to the other side of the balustrade, waited a beat for his men to get in position, and then began counting aloud. On three, he leaned out of cover and fired two of his precious remaining rounds at the nearest terrorist, who had already split from his compatriot in their flanking attempt. A spray of crimson fountained from the target's chest, and he dropped to the ground, unmoving.

As he retreated back into cover, Wayne heard Nasef's voice. "Got the other one."

An explosion cracked the room, followed quickly by another. The second one rocked the floor beneath Wayne, sending a searing wave of heat from near Nasef and Suarez's position.

"Report, report!" Wayne said, trying to hear over the percussive echo in his ears.

"Near miss." Nasef's voice. "Got hit with some splash damage. Surface burns. We'll fight through . . ."

Automatic rifle fire from above cut him off. A scream, not over comms, but from his men's position.

"Nasef's been hit." Suarez's voice in his earbud. "Leg wound. Bleeding pretty bad."

The explosion had been a diversion, intended to flush them out of hiding so the riflemen could pick them off. Thankfully, his men were still alive, but Nasef's leg wound might well take him out of the fight. And, if they didn't get his injury patched up soon, blood loss might take him out of every fight from here out. That was, if the next round of attacks didn't finish them off first.

The men trying to flank them from their floor might be dead, but they were still no closer to taking out the terrorists ruling the roost and raining fire from on high. Something had to shake up the current order, or the agents' mission—and their lives—would be over.

Changing his position, Wayne slid a few feet to the side again, and stole a look at the men on the balcony. Two men holding AKs, one reloading a rocket launcher.

Crouching back down before they could play *Duck Hunt* with his skull, Wayne started to piece together a plan. It was a long shot, but then he owed most of his professional career—including much of this current mission—to his ability to recognize and execute long-shot plans. He hoped he still had one more miracle left in him.

Above the terrorists' position, an elaborate, stone ceiling frieze, carved with typical arabesque swirls and flourishes, offered a grand if unfinished view of the designers' plans for this climactic scene for tourists riding through Scheherazade's Palace. Timing would be everything. Off by a split-second one way or the other, and it was all over.

He strained to hear the telltale sounds of the rocket launcher's loading over the ringing in his ears. Wind and sand beat at the exterior walls. From somewhere nearby, a generator rumbled along, oblivious to the bloody drama unfolding in this half-finished throne room. And, though he acknowledged it could be an overabundance of desperate hope on his part, he thought he heard the muffled shouts of a woman from the far end of the hall.

There. He heard the sliding home of the rocket, the bolt engaging the firing mechanism, the shifting of cloth as the man lifted the launcher to his shoulder.

Rising, running sideways to ensure a moving target, Wayne aimed at center mass on the rocket-launcher-wielding terrorist, and fired twice.

The man's face contorted and he stumbled backward. His fingers, already tense from his preparations to fire, spasmed with the pain. The newly loaded rocket exploded from its tube, which was now aimed at the heavy ceiling.

A split second later, as the riflemen flanking their comrade swung their weapons toward Wayne, the frieze overhead exploded in a calamitous cascade of stone and plaster. The trio lifted their hands in vain, to prevent the crushing collapse from taking them, but within moments, they had been buried under the rubble.

After double checking to ensure that the threat had ended, Wayne dashed over to where Suarez and Nasef were holed up. The Arab agent was lucid, though in obvious pain. He had already torn a strip from his shirt and was attempting to stem the bleeding with a makeshift bandage.

"You've been watching too many *Die Hard* flicks, man," Suarez said to Wayne.

"Did you see any other solutions?"

"No. But still."

"They don't call me Phoenix for nothing, *hombre*. How are you holding up, Anubis?"

"I think I'll be sitting out the next D.C. marathon, but I'll live."

"Just hang tight here, then. I think that's the last of the bad guys. And I think I heard the ambassador's voice down the way."

"Don't forget me on your way out," Nasef said with a weak smile.

Wayne and Suarez ran the length of the room, hopping over the vehicle-track groove that wended its way through the hall. At the end, just to the left of the black-draped execution chamber, a door opened. Wayne aimed, his finger on the trigger, but stayed his hand.

"Ambassador Needham?" Wayne said. "Are you okay?"

Her face lit up. "Almost. We have to contact President Talquin. And Prime Minister Shihmanter. A nuke's about to go off in Israel."

"He knows. They both do. Iranian-made, allegedly. Though we're told you received some concrete evidence about who's actually behind this."

"How would you—"

"Rick Weiland."

"He's alive?"

"He was when he told us the little he was able to, though he was in bad shape." Wayne thought it prudent to leave out the matter of Rick's flatlining for the time being.

"The nuke's a setup. My God, I hope we're not too late." She undid the first few buttons on her blouse, prompting Wayne to instinctively avert his gaze. Reaching into her bra, she withdrew a small object which she held toward her rescuer.

"A Micro SD card, sent by an Iranian nuclear scientist. Recordings, schematics, communiqués. Did they find the secret facility in Rasht?"

"They did. Just this morning, in fact."

"It's all a lie. Basim al-Attar, a Saudi prince, is behind it all. It's a false-flag operation to trick us into attacking and destroying Iran."

"And there's proof of that on here?" he asked, taking the tiny memory card from her.

"Enough to bury him for a thousand lifetimes. I don't doubt the Iranians are trying to circumvent their nuclear agreement again, but this attack, at least, is nothing but pure manipulation."

Wayne slid the card into his PDA, which had miraculously survived the sandstorm and firefight intact. With a few taps of the screen, the contents were uploaded to Ibrahim's server at Langley.

Once the transfer was complete, he called Ibrahim's secure line. It rang twelve times before Wayne hung up to check that he had dialed the correct preprogrammed number. He had. Strange. She shouldn't be away from her phone, especially this close to zero hour.

He tried calling again. In between the eighth and ninth ring, a pair of gunshots rang out on the floor above. Wayne instinctively faced the door, placing himself between the danger and his newly rescued charge. Was there another terrorist they had missed? He looked around, peeking out the door back into the great hall. Where was Suarez?

"Good news, bad news," came Suarez's voice over comms.

"Where are you, Zorro?"

"Good news first. Found our last bad guy. He's dead now."

"Are you on the balcony?"

"Upstairs, some sort of control room just above your position."

Wayne gestured to Needham. "We're coming to you now."

"Please do. You're going to want to see the bad news for yourself."

CHAPTER 56

DUBAI, UNITED ARAB EMIRATES

This was not paradise.

Omar Sawaf felt the weight of a thousand worlds crushing down upon him. If he was dead, this was far from the beautiful gardens tended by dozens of lovely virgins he had expected. Perhaps he wasn't as faithful to the traditional tenets of Islam as he should have been, but his devotion to jihad was unparalleled. And if he was dead, surely his death would have counted as martyrdom.

Something clearly wasn't right.

Had his failure to finish the job, to destroy the American interlopers and execute the ambassador for the world's viewing pleasure, condemned him to this dreary fate? One mistake in a lifetime devoted to killing the enemies of Islam, and this was how he was repaid?

He heard voices. Far off. Below. Below? The ambassador's voice?

Then it clicked. Omar Sawaf wasn't in paradise because he wasn't dead. The American's bullets had hit the grenade launcher, sparing Sawaf from the reaper's kiss. Omar had been given another chance to finish what he'd come here to do. One last shot at redemption.

Buried under the ponderous weight of shattered ceiling décor and slabs of carved stone, Sawaf tried to move his arms. His left arm was pinned by a large hunk of rock, but his right was unencumbered. Pivoting his body as much as he could, he lifted and shoved the stone from his arm. Now free from direct pressure, he pushed aside the heavy debris, as though swimming from the bottom of a rock-filled pond.

The first breach of illumination from the world beyond this rock pile lanced his eyes, filling him with further determination and pushing him to redouble his efforts. After another few desperate seconds of clawing and kicking at the rubble, he was free.

He surveyed the fallen landscape before him. His men were down. The ceiling was in ruins. And from the sound of it, the ambassador was not only free from her cell, she was talking in the control room where Hassim should have been piloting the nuclear-armed drone. If Hassim had been in danger, he would have locked the drone on autopilot, which would get the nuke close enough to the heart of Tel Aviv to make their point and set in motion the domino chain that would soon consume Israel, America, Iran, and the world. But autopilot wasn't good enough, not when the Americans still had several minutes to deactivate the setting and abort the mission.

Then he heard more voices from the room. Male, American. Two of them. He couldn't make out the words, but their very presence meant that everything had gone so very wrong.

It was time for Sawaf to set things back on track. Even if all his men were now dead. Even if he was the last thing standing between the plan's success and failure. He had devoted his entire life to jihad. No matter how the tables may have turned against him, in this, his finest hour, he would not fail.

As though in confirmation of his newfound determination, Sawaf sighted the drab green of his rocket launcher, half-buried beneath a light dusting of debris. Digging it out, he discovered to his delight that the weapon was undamaged. And two feet away was the final rocket.

Sawaf stood, the rubble beneath his feet the tomb of his fallen brethren. He would not be so easily beaten. It was time for him to rise up and take his place in the halls of legendary jihadists.

Grabbing the rocket and the launcher, Sawaf took a step toward the enemy-held control room. The Americans were celebrating what they thought was their victory. But within seconds, the control room would be their grave.

CHAPTER 57

DUBAI, UNITED ARAB EMIRATES

Wayne wanted to punch something. To be so close, and yet to be powerless to stop the impending disaster.

Now in the control room, where Suarez had found the last terrorist, a cinematic countdown of doom played out on a workstation monitor. From the bubble camera mounted beneath a remotely controlled drone, the glimmering waters of the Mediterranean flew past. A GPS map in the lower right corner of the monitor showed its position less than fifty miles from the Tel Aviv coast. At its current speed, mere minutes separated a million Israelis from the nuclear attack they had long feared.

"It's locked on autopilot," Suarez said, frantically trying to get the controls to respond. "Password protected."

"Can't you crack it?" Wayne asked. "That's your forte, right?"

"What do you think I'm trying to do?" Suarez retorted, frustration thick in his voice.

On the other side of the small room, Ambassador Needham was talking on Wayne's PDA, trying to avert the other side of this crisis.

When he had tried to reach Ibrahim again and failed, Wayne called Director Pierce himself. That effort was also fruitless, as Pierce's direct line went straight to voicemail three times in a row. A call to his secretary revealed that she hadn't seen her boss in several hours, though he had offered no word about where he was going and when he might return.

What was going on in Langley?

Wayne had only one other possible point of contact. With Ibrahim and Pierce both unreachable, the only other person he was sure knew of this operation was the man who hosted that initial meeting back at the White House.

President James Talquin.

Needham offered to call Talquin, since her diplomatic and personal channels might offer easier access to the commander in chief, and since she didn't have to conceal her identity from those outside the loop of the mission parameters. Emphasizing the emergency nature of her call, she had the president on the line within minutes, and quickly proceeded to bring him up to speed.

"Thirty-five miles to D-Day," Wayne said as the screen continued to count down the distance to its preprogrammed target.

"That's not helping," Suarez snapped, continuing to tap away at the keyboard.

"The president wants to talk to you," the ambassador said, holding the phone out toward Wayne. He walked across the room and took it from her.

"Mr. President?"

"Christine just told me there's a drone-mounted nuke heading for Tel Aviv right now. Please tell me her time in captivity has given her a really sick sense of humor."

"It's locked on autopilot, flying over the Mediterranean. Suarez is trying to disengage it before it hits the city."

"Lord God in heaven. Can he deactivate it in time?"

"I certainly hope so, sir. Unfortunately, it's a closed system, so no one from Langley or NSA can jump in to help."

The president sighed heavily into the phone. "God help us all. Ambassador Needham also told me about the intel sourced from the package she received before the attack on her plane. Does Prince Basim al-Attar's being behind this as a false-flag attack to lure us into open nuclear war with Iran square with what you've seen over there?"

"Based on what I've seen at present, yes, sir, it does. It seems like it was gift-wrapped a little too neatly. And the ambassador's intel seems to back that up."

"Insanity. One of our closest allies is trying to manipulate us into starting World War III? Even if we stop this attack... How do we come back from this?"

"I know the feeling, sir. We haven't been able to get into contact with Ibrahim or Director Pierce since rescuing the ambassador. Do you have any idea why they might be incommunicado?"

A pause, the silence weighted with loss. "Agent Ibrahim was found dead in her office fifteen minutes ago. Her computer's hard drive had been stolen, and the room's door locked to prevent discovery. Director Pierce is MIA."

Wayne felt as if he might vomit. Another betrayal? Pierce, the decorated war veteran and staunch patriot, a traitor?

"One bright spot: Shin Bet stopped a Hezbollah cell from detonating a bomb filled with uranium from the Rasht site. In Haifa, a little over an hour ago."

A second attack? Terrorist groups from al-Qaeda to ISIS loved to coordinate multiple attacks for maximum shock value. But a mushroom cloud over the Israeli capital was about as shocking as it could be. A dirty bomb in a lesser city wouldn't have near the impact of a full-blown nuke. Unless the Haifa attack was a diversion, meant to siphon off any nuclear-related chatter for the day into an ancillary attack in order to ensure that the main attack was successful. Unless, the ambassador's evidence aside, this was al-Attar's endgame all along.

"Twenty miles!" Christine shouted from near the monitor.

"Not helping!" Suarez yelled back, typing frantically.

A noise from the great hall caught Wayne's attention. Was Nasef trying to climb the stairs to get to them? He handed the phone back to Needham and walked to the doorway to see why his compatriot was risking further injury by moving around so much.

Twenty feet away, at the base of the massive pile of rubble that had buried him just minutes before, the rocket-launching terrorist stood grinning. His weapon once again loaded and shouldered, he closed one eye, aiming.

"Death to America!" he shouted.

Wayne heard an explosion. And the world tilted on its axis forever.

CHAPTER 58

Dubai, United Arab Emirates

Wayne flinched at the explosion, but he did not feel the pain, heat, or abject nothingness he expected in the split second his mind had to process the resurrected terrorist.

Instead, the jihadist's head exploded, a bullet cracking through his skull and catapulting a fragment of his frontal bone through his forehead. Blood and gray matter spurted from the wound before the falling body altered the fountain's trajectory into a pool beneath its lifeless face.

The rocket launcher fell free of the terrorist's grasp, hitting the floor beside the body in an impact that made Wayne hold his breath. But the weapon didn't fire, the missile remaining dormant in its tube.

Nasef.

Wayne ran to the balcony and looked down at the lower level. Propped up against the cover where they'd left him, Nasef smiled weakly and let his rifle fall to the ground.

"Anubis, you hang in there!" Wayne shouted to the man who had just saved all their lives.

There were too many pieces up in the air at once. Nasef was bleeding to death. The drone was seconds from destroying the Israeli capital. And Wayne felt powerless to do a thing about either of them.

«»

These were the moments that defined a man, Suarez realized. The stakes were higher than for most, but the principle remained. All his training, all his experience, everything led to this moment. As his *abuela* would have said, now was the moment he had to see what everything he had done with the life he had been given added up to. Would the sum of his choices and experience be enough?

He had hacked into the back end of the controlling software. His fingers flew across the keys, but morphing algorithms designed to combat exactly this sort of backdoor intrusion fought him at every turn.

Focusing on the coding window he'd opened, he tried his best to ignore the video of the Mediterranean screaming by and the numbers steadily counting down the miles to doomsday. He tried one command string after another, but every step forward was rebuffed, forcing him two steps back. All the coding notations were in Arabic or Farsi, which made him the absolutely least qualified person to read them, though whatever the translation was would likely have made little sense to those unversed in the nuances and linguistics of programming.

Then he noticed something. A set of markings on the underside of the drone, something he hadn't noticed in light of the seemingly far more important waters below.

This was an RQ-170 Sentinel drone. Or, at least, it had begun as one. Which meant the base code was American-made. The Iranians—or Saudis or whatever party had compiled and executed and programmed this particular version of the code—would not have rebuilt the whole system from scratch when they had a perfectly functioning version already available. Which meant he was working with a hybrid system. And the underlying code was something in which he was very well versed.

Flashing back to his time in the marines, he remembered meeting one of the key programmers on the RQ-170 project. Both he and Suarez were huge *Star Wars* nerds, and the programmer couldn't help but share a clever little in-joke he had built into the system's rarely used autopilot function. For locking in coordinates via autopilot, he had created a batch file titled "/UseTheForceLuke.bat." And for getting out of autopilot mode, he had co-opted Admiral Ackbar's famous warning from *Return of the Jedi.*

Even though the terrorists had added extra code on top of the original American version, the function should still work. At least, he desperately prayed it would.

Help me, nerdy Star Wars *programmer guy. You're my only hope.*

Suarez keyed "EXECUTE Root/Functions/Autopilot/ItsA-Trap.bat" into the command window and hit return.

In the corner of the screen, the red "Autopilot Lock" display that had mocked him since he discovered the control room blinked out.

"Got it!"

Wayne ran back inside the control room. Suarez continued to squint at the monitor, one hand on the joystick to the left of the keyboard.

"You broke through the autopilot?" Wayne asked.

"And none too soon," Suarez said, nodding at the screen. "Nine miles."

"Can you steer her to an airfield? One of ours?"

"Afraid not. She's almost out of fuel."

Wayne grunted. "And whenever she runs out of gas, she drops like a rock."

"Boom."

"Is the nuke already armed?"

"It's set to arm itself when it's within two miles of the target. So, basically, when it crosses the Israeli coastline."

Wayne was silent for a moment, thinking through the same conundrum Suarez had been contemplating. They couldn't land the drone somewhere safe, and as soon as it was over land, it would be too late.

"Sink her," Wayne said.

Suarez stole a look at his team leader. "Sink the drone?"

"Before it hits land. Before it can arm the nuke. Drown her in the Mediterranean."

Nodding slowly as the last-ditch plan became clear, Suarez agreed. "Down she goes."

He tilted the joystick forward. The nose of the drone pitched forward, the water growing nearer, nearer. Avoiding a trio of freighters just a few miles out of port, Suarez navigated the UAV toward the darkening surface of the deep, now just fifty meters away.

He offered another silent prayer. Another desperate plan balanced on a razor's edge.

Just a few feet above the water now. Then, with an explosive intensity belied by the single-view lens of the bubble camera, the drone crashed into the waves, the digital image on the monitor rent apart by the forces of water, gravity, its own engines exploding, or—*please God no*—a nuclear fireball.

«»

Receiving no answers from the now black monitors, Wayne turned to Ambassador Needham, who was providing live updates to the president on the drone's progress. He crossed the room and took the phone from her.

"Mr. President, the drone has crashed into the Mediterranean, a few miles off the Israeli coast. Is there *any* indication of a nuclear explosion?"

"Give me a minute, son," Talquin said, his voice heavy.

During the pause, Wayne looked at Needham. When they had rescued her minutes earlier, her face had been fixed with defiant purpose, despite all she had endured the past few days. Now, trapped in the interminable space between the last gasp and the plunge, her face was fraught with worry.

Suarez still sat at the workstation, but he had pushed the keyboard and joystick to the side. His elbows were now perched on the desktop, and his hands were folded in fervent prayer.

"You did it," Talquin said, his voice considerably lighter, though still tinged with sobriety. "The drone apparently broke apart in the water. Not even a fuel explosion. I'm ordering salvage operations to recover the nuke."

"Thank God," Wayne exhaled, realizing he had been holding his breath.

"Yes. Thank God. And thank you. Your country, and indeed the whole world, owes you a deep debt of gratitude."

"Thank you, sir. Ambassador Needham and Agent Nasef will need medical attention. Seeing as you're our last remaining contact for this mission, can you arrange exfil for us?"

"Already on it. I'll send the details to your PDA."

Wayne hung up and patted Suarez on the back. "You did it, man."

"What are you talking about? *We* did it."

Finally releasing all the tension that had wracked his body from the constant mission pressure of the past thirty-six hours since landing in Dubai, Wayne started laughing. Christine smiled, the realization that they had come to the brink and survived, that they were finally about to go home, filling the room. She threw her arms around Wayne, then Suarez.

"Thank you both."

"It's our pleasure, Ambassador," Wayne said.

"Heck of a thing, saving the world," Suarez said, a big grin on his face.

Wayne smiled back. "It sure is."

EPILOGUE
Fallout

"For the Lord watches over the way of the righteous, but the way of the wicked leads to destruction."
– Psalm 1:6

LAKE CONSTANCE, SWITZERLAND
SIX DAYS LATER

After the sand-scarred desert heat of Dubai, Wayne was happy to be in a more temperate climate. Lake Constance, a massive inland body of water bordered by Germany, Austria and Switzerland, provided a beautiful and placid respite from the oppressively hot climate and skyscraper-clogged cityscape from which he and his new partners had recently departed.

It had been nearly a week since they had rescued the ambassador and averted the specter of nuclear war, but Wayne was still struggling to process it all.

Logan Pierce's body had been pulled from the crumpled remains of his Lexus. Though some details remained spotty, it appeared that, after his murder of Janan Ibrahim at CIA headquarters, he sped out of the city. Within a matter of seconds after finishing a cell call with a Shin Bet agent he had worked with on a joint op years back, Pierce was broadsided by a semi with the right of way. Since Pierce had run the red light, no charges were filed against the truck driver, a fortuitous happenstance that allowed the reason for his flight to remain unprobed by any official investigation. The data on Ibrahim's stolen hard drive, recovered from the floorboard of the wrecked car, provided a plausible motive for Pierce's desperate act, though why he had been involved with the terrorist plot at all remained a mystery.

Meanwhile, the press had gone nuts over the apparent near misses that Israel had experienced. Running with the Passover angle the terrorists had looked to subvert, the media continued to refer to the event as "The Passover Miracle," claiming that, like their ancestors in Egypt thousands of years before, the Angel of Death had again spared God's chosen people.

The violence and explosions in Dubai, especially the destruction of a good chunk of the Burj Khalifa, had been laid on the doorstep of Walid Abushakra and *Ummar Haidar*. A falling out within the ranks, coupled with Walid's personal hatred against what his hometown had become, provided the necessary motive for the destruction they had wreaked. Wayne didn't know if any sort of backroom negotiations between the Emirate's leaders and Washington smoothed the way for this more simplistic approach, but he figured the embarrassment of allowing the ambassador to be kidnapped by terrorists helped offset the covert insertion of three Americans who may or may not have actually been working at the behest of the US government. In the official story, it was Emirati forces that liberated the ambassador, allowing the Arab nation to redeem its image somewhat, as well as offering a warning to other would-be terrorists who sought to operate within their borders. Political theater at its finest.

The drone and its nuclear payload had been recovered by a joint US-Israeli salvage team, a fact their respective governments managed to keep out of the press. Analysis showed the fissile material in the drone's bomb, as well as the Hafia dirty bomb, matched that recovered from the Rasht site. This was the bargaining chip they had been looking for. Though both Israel and the US knew the whole plot had been a lie, they were not above using the averted attacks and the appearance of Iran's role behind them to force the Islamic Republic back to the negotiating table to dial back their nuclear program to a level far more acceptable to America and her regional allies.

As the world ran wild with speculation, attempting to make sense of recent events, Wayne, Suarez, and Nasef had kept busy as well.

After a debriefing conducted by President Talquin and the interim director of the National Clandestine Service, the trio had received a week's paid vacation, along with orders to rest up. That order had been suspended when they had been called back to Langley for a new briefing.

Which brought them to Switzerland.

After a quick convalescence, Nasef walked with a limp and was supposed to use a crutch, but he said his leg didn't really hurt anymore, a lie Wayne and Suarez let slide, knowing they would have held fast to the same claim in his situation. Injury or not, they wouldn't deprive Nasef of the opportunity to help them finish what they had started together.

The cool night air soughed through the trees as it rolled across the surface of the Obersee, the largest part of the lake. More than twenty kilometers from the nearest town of Kreuzlingen, the only visible lights were those twinkling in the chalet's windows, save for the crescent moon and a dusting of stars in the black sky above.

The house overlooked the water. Security was lighter than Wayne had expected, even in such serene settings. Their target was overconfident, sure that, even though both attacks against Israel had failed and the ambassador was still alive, and even though Iran and America were not currently locked in an all-out war, he was safe. Beyond suspicion.

He was wrong.

Basim al-Attar, Saudi prince and longtime ally and friend of the past six US presidential administrations, had betrayed that friendship. He had led the world to the very edge of annihilation, using deceit, kidnapping, and terrorism to manipulate America into its own self-destruction. And for that, he had to pay.

Lying on a hilltop overlooking the chalet, Nasef provided watch over the house's entrances and exits, covered by the scope of his long-range rifle. Meanwhile, Wayne and Suarez approached the house from the shoreline, the waves lapping at the rocky beach concealing their footsteps.

"Hold," came Nasef's voice over the new earbuds they each wore.

Wayne and Suarez froze.

"One guard, circling toward you from the back of the house."

A deck surrounded the chalet on three sides, the ground beneath sloping gently away toward the shoreline. Standing still, holding his breath, Wayne could hear the guard's steps on the wooden planks above. He and Suarez dropped to a crouch.

Within seconds, the guard's head came into view over the railing. Wayne aimed, felt Suarez nod beside him, and fired. The guard's cheek burst with the impact before he fell from view.

Despite the sound suppressor screwed onto the barrel of his Glock, the report was merely muffled, not the sleek *pew* that secret agents' "silenced weapons" emitted in the movies. Whatever security the prince did have, they would have heard the shot and realized that the chalet was under attack.

Stealth was no longer their preferred option.

The front door burst open as Wayne began to strafe up the bank. Another well-placed headshot dropped the guard who emerged. A man wearing a similar uniform appeared in the front left window, but Suarez fired two bullets into that guard.

"Let's go," Wayne said, making a break for the entrance.

The house was dimly lit. Thick, wooden beams crossed the open-plan living room, while a staircase to the second floor sat to the left of the entryway. A massive stone fireplace, set into the right-hand wall, provided the centerpiece of the room, the embers from the night's fire flickering as they cooled. The rented house seemed small considering the palaces the prince was used to inhabiting, but it had a rustic charm that Riyadh and Jeddah could only dream about.

"Upstairs," Wayne said. Suarez nodded, conceding that the only place down here al-Attar could be hiding would be behind a couch or inside the pantry, neither of which offered much in the way of long-term survival. As Suarez started up the stairs and Wayne moved to check the kitchen, the throttling of an engine cranked, once, twice.

Wayne recognized the sound. An outboard motor.

He ran through the living room and out the back door to the deck overlooking the lake. Below, the engine finally caught and the motor roared to life.

Al-Attar was trying to escape.

As the jon boat appeared from beneath the house, the moonlit form of the rogue prince manning the motor, Wayne climbed atop the railing and leapt.

Landing hard after the ten-foot drop, his legs buckled, but held. Al-Attar, just a few feet away at the back of the boat, pulled something from the folds of his robe. A Glock 19, the same model that Wayne and Suarez carried.

Before the prince could aim it, Wayne kicked his hand, knocking the weapon overboard and into the deep.

"What do you want?" al-Attar asked, rubbing his hand.

"Justice."

"Justice? Who are you?"

"Just a concerned citizen. I'm curious, what did you hope to accomplish by attacking Israel and framing Iran. I mean, besides the obvious."

The prince's eyes widened with the recognition that someone had connected him to the plot after all. He quickly regained his composure, concealing his shock, and narrowed his eyes at Wayne.

"Iran's been meddling in the Middle East for too long. Their proxy terrorist organizations are wreaking havoc and unseating stable governments from Lebanon to Palestine to Yemen to Iraq. They've got their eyes set on the Arabian Peninsula, wanting to subvert Saudi rule and take the holy cities for themselves. Imagine, great cities of Islam, the Kaaba itself, in Shia hands."

"So your solution was to nuke Israel and get the US to do your dirty work for you?"

"Iran hasn't risen to power overnight. The United States is just as complicit in all of this as anyone. You turned a deaf ear to the plight of all those persecuted by the Persian usurpers, a blind eye to their funding of terrorism across the region. You supported them in their fight to help stem the advance of ISIS, conveniently ignoring their own power grabs along the way. You've ignored the pleas of your own allies, while bending over backwards to appease Iran; while they, in turn, lie and break their agreements every chance they get.

"I tried reasoning with your last two presidents," the prince continued, "but you are so blinded by your desire to land a foreign policy achievement by restoring relations with Iran that you don't care what you have to sacrifice in order to get there."

"And you think the lives of millions of Israelis, and millions more Iranian civilians, and who knows how many Americans, Russians, Chinese, Europeans, Arabs, and beyond, are worth sacrificing?"

"If it means preserving the sanctity of the holy peninsula and the continued protectorate of the Saudi kingdom, yes, absolutely."

Wayne scoffed. "You've got your priorities seriously out of whack."

He aimed his Glock at the prince's face.

"Wait!" al-Attar shouted. "I can pay you. I can give you more money than you've ever dreamed of."

Wayne chuckled. "What good is it for a man to gain the whole world, yet forfeit his soul?"

"What's that supposed to mean?"

"It means, where you're going, money will be the least of your problems."

Without warning, al-Attar jerked the motor to the right, spinning the boat and knocking Wayne's feet from under him. The American agent fell to his knees. His arm hit the side of the boat, the impact knocking his own pistol free, tumbling into the depths below.

As Wayne struggled to his feet, the prince jerked the motor in the other direction. This time, Wayne maintained his balance. He leapt toward al-Attar, grabbing his hair and slamming his head into the metal rim of the boat. A bloody tear opened across the prince's forehead, his eyes rolling back as he slipped into unconsciousness.

This was better. An accident. A disagreement between the guards caused al-Attar to try to slip away in the boat, but he hit his head and drowned during his escape. Nothing for the Swiss to find. Nothing for the Saudis to find.

Wrapping the anchor line around the prince's leg so it looked as though he'd tripped on the rope before hitting his head, Wayne slipped his body overboard. With the motor still running, the further the boat traveled, the further the rope played out.

Eventually, the line ran out and the weight of al-Attar's body pulled the anchor overboard. Within seconds, anchor, rope, and prince had all disappeared beneath the surface.

Staging the crime scene elicited a twinge of guilt-laden familiarity, of a darker time in his life when he almost took that final step into the shadowy side of the soul. But he had broken free, and though concealing the nature of his lethal actions tonight definitely bore some similarities to his brief employment by the Division, he knew at its core it was very different.

Wanting the boat to eventually hit land where it would be discovered without Wayne's footprints nearby, he hopped out of the boat and swam back toward the chalet. By the end of his ten-minute swim, his arms were burning, but his spirits were buoyed by the company that received him on the shore.

"Is it done?" Nasef asked.

"It's done. An unfortunate accident."

"Such a shame," Suarez said.

The trio walked up the shoreline toward their exfil point. Despite the call of the idyllic surroundings, they all knew they couldn't stay in Switzerland right now, even if they had successfully staged everything to look like an open and shut case, with all the perpetrators dead.

"As ye sow, so shall ye reap," Suarez quoted.

Wayne smiled as something finally clicked into place. "There it is."

"What?"

"What we were talking about back in Dubai. My dilemma about killing, even if they are terrorists."

"Ah," Suarez said.

The pale moonlight illumined the three Americans retreating back to the cover of the woods, another successful mission under their belts, another enemy of freedom sent to meet his maker.

"For better or worse, that's what the world needs us to be, and that's who we are," Wayne said. "We're the reapers."

ACKNOWLEDGMENTS

This book was a long time in the making, and I am immensely grateful to a number of people who helped it see the light of day.

Thanks first to my incredible wife, Meredith, for your love, encouragement, patience, and support. I couldn't have done this without you by my side.

Lou Aronica, for your keen editorial eye and faith in my storytelling abilities.

Aaron Brown, for another great cover.

The team at The Story Plant and The Fiction Studio, for helping make this book what it is today.

My Dubai friends and my former colleagues and students at UAS, for making my unofficial two-year research trip that much more rewarding.

And to everyone who bought, downloaded, read, and otherwise supported my first book, especially those who took the time to tell a friend about it or talk to me on social media or email. Thank you so much for your investment in my stories and for your helping my books reach more people. You are the ones who make this real, and I hope to one day get to thank each of you in person. For now, this will have to suffice. It's been a long while since *From the Ashes* first hit shelves, and I thank you for your incredible patience and unflagging excitement for my next books. I especially hope you enjoyed this book and, rest assured, the wait for the next book won't be nearly as long.

Finally, thank you, dear reader, whether you've read my debut or not. None of this would be possible without your support. I'd love to hear from you via my website (www.authorjeremyburns.com), one of my social media channels, or in person at a signing.

Until the next adventure...

ABOUT THE AUTHOR

Jeremy Burns lived and worked in Dubai for two years, conducting first-hand research in many of the locations featured in *The Dubai Betrayal* and immersing himself in a variety of Middle Eastern cultures. His first book, *From the Ashes*, introduced Wayne Wilkins and is a two-time #1 category bestseller on Amazon, with more than 95,000 total ebook copies downloaded to date. A seasoned traveler who has explored more than twenty countries across four continents, he lives in Florida with his wife and two dogs, where he is working on his next book. Visit him online at AuthorJeremyBurns.com and on social media (@ JeremyBurnsBooks on Facebook, @authorjburns on Twitter, and @AuthorJeremyBurns on Instagram).